OCTOBER SCREAMS

KANGAS KAHN
PUBLISHING

www.kkpublish.com

OCTOBER SCREAMS

A HALLOWEEN ANTHOLOGY

EDITED BY
KENNETH W. CAIN

Dedicated to my parents who, though they probably regret it now, gifted me the love of Halloween…the gateway to horror for a child.

TABLE OF CONTENTS

"SWEETMEAT"
  BY CLAY MCLEOD CHAPMAN 11
"THE MAGIC TRICK"
  BY GREGORY L. NORRIS 29
"THE TREAT-OR-TRICKER"
  BY EVANS LIGHT 45
"TUTTI I MORTI"
  BY STEVE RASNIC TEM 51
"THE LAST HALLOWEEN"
  BY LARRY HINKLE 61
"KATRINA'S HALLOWEEN CANDY JOURNAL (2023)"
  BY PATRICK FLANAGAN 71
"THE WIND"
  BY BRENNAN FREDRICKS 83
"FREE CANDY AND TELESCOPE VIEWS"
  BY RED LAGOE 95
"THE HALLOWEEN LOST"
  BY FRANK ORETO 111
"TATE"
  BY RONALD MALFI 119
"A PERFECT NIGHT FOR A PERFECT MURDER"
  BY JEREMY BATES 137
"ELEVEN ONE"
  BY PHILIP FRACASSI 147
"IN THE NIGHT, A WHISPER"
  BY ROBERT STAHL 173
"THE HOOPER STREET HALLOWEEN DECORATION COMMITTEE"
  BY GEMMA AMOR 181

"Sown"
    by TJ Cimfel 201

"The Iron Maiden"
    by Rebecca Rowland 209

"Spiders Under My Skin"
    by Larry Hodges 225

"November Eve"
    by Bridgett Nelson 231

"Let the Dark Do the Rest"
    by Kealan Patrick Burke 251

"Twin Flames"
    by Gwendolyn Kiste 265

"The Collecting"
    by Cassandra Daucus 277

"The Puppeteer of Samhain"
    by Todd Keisling 285

"Any Other Wednesday in a Bar"
    by Cat Voleur 301

"No Such Thing"
    by Jacqueline West 309

"Masks"
    by Brian Keene & Richard Chizmar 323

"Doll"
    by Ryan Van Ells 339

"Scattergoods"
    by Kevin Kangas 349

Afterword & Acknowledgments 385

About the Authors 389

About the Editor 419

OCTOBER
SCREAMS

SWEETMEAT

by Clay McLeod Chapman

Melts in your mouth. That's what they always say, isn't it? Here I was, drowning in a high-fructose flood guttered between my cheeks, and I never wanted to come up for air again.

I couldn't tell you what the hell that candy was. If it even *was* candy, for Christ's sake. Whether it was taffy or marshmallow or some other spongey kind of confection, the second that sweet settled over my tongue and my saliva seeped in, those enzymes started working their magic. Dissolved it down as fast as flesh in a fucking acid bath. Its sugar eased into my bloodstream—straight for the mainline—and I was just…*just gone*. Obliterated before I could even swallow. I had never tasted anything like it in my entire life. I didn't know if I ever would again.

That was why I needed to find it. Taste it just one more time.

That goddamn sweetmeat.

So, this was the first year Jasper asked if he could go trick-or-treating without me, which I'll admit…*ouch*. Stung. He only had a year before he was too old for all this. Once he was in the sixth grade—seventh, tops—he'd have to call it quits. No more ringing doorbells, demanding candy. His pals wanted to hit up the houses without any adult supervision. Without me. Ol' fuddy duddy here.

Look, I get it. A parent-free Halloween. Total rite of passage. You need at least one year where you don't have your dad breathing down your neck. You want to be free with your friends. Roam the streets. I definitely wreaked a little Halloween havoc when I was their age.

"Promise you won't toilet roll the neighborhood?"

"Promise."

"No egging anybody's houses."

"*Daaad…*"

At least Jasper still put in the effort to dress up. His friends didn't even wear costumes anymore. They just rubbed some fake blood over their faces, looking like drooling lunatics. As if that was enough to qualify as a costume. If they came to my door, I wouldn't give them any candy.

Not that I knew exactly what Jasper's costume was. He told me its name, but I promptly forgot. *Peek-a-chewy* or *Yugi-yo-yo* or something like that. I can't remember now. He looked like some mascot for an extraterrestrial basketball team, Space Jamming as far as I could tell.

"Just come home by nine, got it? Not nine-oh-one now."

"Okay."

"And don't eat anything until I've had a chance to check!"

"Okay, okay…"

"Have fun, pal," I called after him. "Bring home something good!"

He didn't say anything back.

It had to be hard, letting go of the holiday. This was Jasper's final

Halloween. One last hurrah around the 'hood before hanging up the ol' candy sack. I really felt for the kid. Growing up can be hard.

That went for both of us.

I felt like we were running out of rituals here, Jasper and me. We carved our jack-o'-lanterns earlier that evening, like always, leaving a slimy mess spread all over the countertop. The knife was still out, its handle all tacky. These cubed chunks of sliced and diced pumpkin shell were in a dish, waiting to get tossed into the compost, nothing but the negative space of our jack-o'-lantern's eyes and nose, its jagged mouth, all cut out and gathering fruit flies.

That was okay. I would clean up later…

Time for dad to have a little Halloween fun of his own. Maybe a wee bit more trick than treat. I had the night all to myself. Might as well try something new, right? I grabbed that dish and emptied the pumpkin chunks out, filling the bowl to the brim with fun sizes. Then I found an index card. A Sharpie marker. In bold, black capital letters, I wrote: TAKE ONE.

Yeah, *right*, like any kid had enough self-restraint to simply pinch a single candy bar. This was a seasonal litmus test. The Halloween Challenge: I left the bowl on our front stoop, turned off all the lights in the house so it looked like nobody was home…and then hid behind the bushes.

Let the games begin.

I waited—and waited—until that first group of trick-or-treaters wandered up, eyeing the bowl like it was some kind of ancient Aztecan relic and they were treasure hunters sniffing for booby traps. If they followed the instructions and only took one candy bar, they would be safe. Good to go. No harm done. But if some punk thought he could get away with grabbing a handful of candy—

BOOGEDY BOO!

—I'd leap out from behind the bush and scare the ever-living shit out of them. Watch them all crap in their costumes. See them run down the street, screaming their little heads off.

Come again next year, kids!

I'm here all night, folks . . .

But I got bored behind the bush. Popping a squat for that long was really doing a number on my knees. My body wasn't made for this kind of stakeout anymore. Plus, it was getting cold out. I just ended up leaving the bowl on the stoop and went inside. *I should clean up the kitchen,* I thought, but I watched a bit of the creature feature on TV until Jasper came back.

"Welcome home!"

"Hey."

"How was it, bud?"

"Good."

"Just good? Did you guys have fun?"

"Yeah."

These monosyllabic answers were killing me. "Nice haul?"

"Yeah." He was still wearing his costume, that mask pulled up to his temples, so it looked like he had two sets of eyes. The top ones were much larger, saucer-like, unblinking. Staring at me.

"Anybody doling out king size candy bars this year?"

"No."

"Any toothbrushes?"

"No."

"Alrighty, then. . . Hand it over." My Dad-Duty included divvying up the candy. Before that first bite, I had to parse through Jasper's stash to make sure there wasn't anything. . .*unsavory.*

I cleared a space on the countertop, pushing the pumpkin chunks back so I could get straight to work examining his candy.

In and out. No fuss. I just needed to make sure there weren't any hypodermic needles or candy apples laced with rat poison or razor blades embedded in chocolate bars.

Nobody *actually* expected to find any of that stuff, not really. But my own mother—Jasper's grandma, God bless her—caught some segment on Fax News about whacked-out addicts slipping rainbow-colored fentanyl to kids during Halloween, which, I'm sorry, sounded like absolute horse shit to me. Why would anyone dole out their own drug cache to trick-or-treaters instead of, you know, taking them? Everybody was always looking for a good scare on Halloween. Even the 24-hour news cycle got in on the fun, freaking out all the ol' grannies with fresh renditions of rehashed urban legends, recycling the same crap I heard when I was a kid.

Same story, only with shiny new packaging: *Watch out for frightening fentanyl, kiddies!*

Jasper had himself a pretty impressive stash. Seemed like a good year: Snickers, Baby Ruths. Tootsie Rolls, Dum-Dums… Christ, who still gave out Dum-Dums these days?

Nothing out of the ordinary. No tampered wrappers. No unpackaged snacks, no Rice Krispy treats. No needle marks. "Looks good to me," I told Jasper. "All clear for consumption!"

Hold on a sec. Wait.

What is that?

There. Right there. Nestled between a Milky Way and a Skittles packet.

A fuzzy lump.

A tumor.

First diagnosis: *That's gotta be a Peep, right?* One of those marshmallow chicks out of its packaging. All spongy. Yellow. Nope—strike that. This was creamsicle colored. Orange. It could've easily been a piece of pumpkin shell from the color of it all, a soft section of an eye carved out from a jack-o'-lantern. Somehow, it must have slipped into Jasper's bag by accident.

I plucked up the chunk, pinching it between my fingers. It wasn't shaped like a chick at all. It certainly wasn't a shard of pumpkin shell. It was just a square hunk of sugar. A squishy cube, all pink hued. Sorry, make that lavender. I couldn't quite pin its color down.

Okay, so maybe it wasn't a Peep… Then what the hell was it? I tested its consistency, gently pressing down on it. The puffball inflated back to its original dimensions after I let it go.

Jasper didn't need to eat this…whatever this was.

Into the reject pile it went.

"All yours, champ…" I handed the bag over.

Jasper grabbed his stash and rushed for the living room, so he could parse out his bounty into different piles. Chocolates over here, hard candies over there. He was so systematic about it, so color-coordinated. Killed me. Where did this kid get his organizational OCD from? Definitely not from his father.

Suddenly my sweet tooth kicked in.

All this surveying of candy left me craving something yummy. I wasn't feeling particularly picky. Just needed something to sate the seasonal need for treats.

All I had was the crap I cut out from Jasper's stash. So I eyed the reject pile. The bottom barrel discount sweets. The off-brand candy.

What would one hurt? I deserved a little something for my trouble, didn't I?

Treat thyself, good man…

I picked up the weird one. The not-Peep or whatever you call it. Don't ask me why, but it felt warmer. Warmer than before. Like I'd had it in my hand all along, heating the chunk up with my own body temperature, until it was all hot and sticky. Kind of felt like flesh.

Who would actually eat something this sticky?

Christ, who'd hand a candy like this out?

There was this one family up the block—the Lindens. A little granola-y, if you get my drift. Lots of crystal windchimes. Instead of handing out fun sizes for Halloween, they made their own sugarless snacks for the kids. Little Ziplock baggies of homemade trail mix. That sort of thing. I could totally imagine them whipping up their own batch of gluten-free marshmallows or whatever the hell this nubbin was. This had their little hippie-dippy recipes written all over it.

So. Marshmallow. Obviously. Dangerous? Hardly. I simply popped it in my mouth and—

angels

angels

angels

angels

angels

angels

angels

angels

angels

angels

—bleeding all of a sudden. I must've bitten my tongue because there was red all over the countertop now. A slender thread of pink drool dribbled down my chin, suspended like a shimmering pendulum on a grandfather clock. It swayed and snapped and splatted against the tile.

What the hell just happened?

Where did I go?

I had no idea how long I blacked out. I'd lost hold of myself. Of time. My grip on the moment had slipped. I still felt dizzy. The kitchen wouldn't stop spinning. I had to grab hold of the counter to balance myself. Stay upright. All my senses had silenced themselves, save for taste.

Sugar. On my tongue.

In my blood.

My body.

The sweetness reached all the way in—I mean, down deep—to the core of me. My very being. I had never tasted, never experienced, anything as honeyed as this.

How could a chunk of sugar make me feel so insignificant? Like nothing else mattered?

What's the sweetest thing you ever tasted?

Pixie Sticks?

Fun Dip?

Those are nothing but pure processed sugar.

Go further.

Sweeter.

Take the sweetest thing you've ever tasted.

Now multiply it.

By a million.

You're still not even close. I'm talking about a transformative experience here, where the second that confection hits your tongue and your taste buds activate, you are no longer the person you were before. You'll never be that person ever again. That person doesn't exist anymore. The flavor alters you. *Converts* you. There's no going back.

Fentanyl was the furthest thing from my mind. Mesh all the

meth, the heroin, whatever drug of choice, it still couldn't match the impact of that heavenly confection. Not even close.

All I could think about was that sweetmeat.

The most delectable treat.

I had never been one for religion, but this truly felt like some BC and AD kind of shit. From there on out, I could mark my existence to what my life was like before I tasted that sweetmeat…and then everything after.

One simple swallow, that was all it took. This was a spiritual awakening. An edible epiphany. A lightning bolt to my tongue.

A cosmic marshmallow.

Manna from Heaven.

Where did this sweetmeat come from? Whose house was doling it out?

How could I find more?

Poking my head into the living room, I spotted Jasper's haul all lined up in neat piles. The candy bars, the lollipops, Jolly Ranchers—just looking at them all made my stomach twist.

Those weren't sweets. Not really. His stash was nothing but saccharine ash.

"Hey, Jasper… Quick question for you. Which, uh…which houses did you hit up tonight?"

He glanced up at me like this was all some kind of trick (or treat) question. "Why?"

"Do you remember your route?"

"We just went up the street."

"Our street?"

"Yeah."

"What about the rest of the neighborhood?"

"We didn't leave the—"

"I know, I know. It's not that. I just—I just wanna know which houses you went to."

"Why?"

"Just tell me which houses."

"I don't know..."

"What do you mean you don't know?"

"I don't know!"

"You don't remember or you just don't want to tell me?"

I needed to find the sweetmeat. One of our neighbors had given it to him, right? It couldn't have just magically materialized in his candy sack. Whoever doled it out had to be in our neighborhood.

I just had to figure out where. Who. And fast. I could feel myself crashing. The celestial sugar rush was already ebbing away from my bloodstream, leaving me feeling empty. Hollow.

"Do you think it might've been—"

A punch in the gut abruptly forced me forward. My intestines clenched.

"Dad?"

"I'm fine. It's okay."

"Are you—"

"I'm fine, I'm fine. I just need to—need to—"

I'd been dosed. That was what this all was. Perhaps it actually was fentanyl after all. Mom was right. Fax News was right. *Fuck*, I thought. *Oh, fuck. I'm high right now.* The urban legend was true. Someone in our neighborhood really had tampered with the candy and I was tripping my balls off. What could I do? Call 911? I simply ran into the bathroom and gripped the edge of the sink, staring down my reflection in the mirror as my brain launched into the cosmos, hitting the stratosphere at eleven kilometers per second, twenty-five thousand miles per fucking hour.

What do I do what do I do what do I—

My first tooth fell out. It slipped past my lips and hit the tiles, a shooting star.

Well, that was unexpected…

I leaned into the mirror and pulled back my upper lip. Sure enough, it looked as if I hadn't brushed in months—Jesus, *years*. These cavities were wreaking absolute havoc throughout my mouth. My teeth wobbled about the gumline, tipsy passengers onboard a pink cruise liner in the middle of a monsoon, all of them falling overboard.

This isn't real none of this is real none of this is really really happening—

I pinched a cuspid. Without as much as a wiggle, the tooth uprooted itself…and dissolved. The enamel, the very bone, had gone all soft, smearing into this off-colored paste.

I'm high right now; that's all. I'm hallucinating. None of this is real none of this is real—

I still found myself craving it. I needed more.

Just one more bite.

One simple nibble.

You just don't get it. You can't understand. There is no word in the human lexicon that can register the saccharine caliber of this candy. Explaining the taste to someone who's never tried it is simply a waste. The sweetmeat opens your senses. Expands your tastebuds. There are flavors that go beyond the monosaccharide spectrum. Beyond *sarkara*. Beyond *shakar*. Beyond *sucre* or *jaggery* or *jagara* or *cakkara*. This sugar doesn't come from our world. It isn't meant for our mouths. Our blood. To taste it is to lick from the cosmic Fun Dip of the gods.

Jasper called out to me from the living room, and I snapped back to our realm. "Can I have another candy, Dad?"

"How many have you had already?"

"Three?"

"That's enough sweets for one night, son…"

Not enough. Never enough.

"Please? Just one more?"

"I said no." I lifted my voice a little too much for my own tastes, my temper flaring fast, punctuating the 'no' with another tooth spilling out of my mouth and tumbling into the sink.

"Pleeeeease?"

"What did I just say? No more candy, damn it!"

I couldn't control myself. This empty-calorie rage just came out of nowhere. I felt like I'd eaten nothing but crappy candy all night. All day. This was withdrawal. It had to be. I was crashing fast. Too fast. Like falling out from the sky. A migraine ice-picked my temples. I hadn't meant to snap at Jasper. I needed to settle my stomach. Needed something more than just—

sweet

—sugar in my belly. I had to get out of the house. Had to find the—

meat

—house where this candy had come from. Just to know what I'd taken. What it was doing to me. How to make it stop. Make it all stop.

Jasper didn't lift his head from the floor when I told him I was stepping out, which was a relief. Small blessings. If he happened to glance up at me as I slipped through the door, he would've seen this drooling lunatic with flapping gums. Luckily, most trick-or-treaters were already home. Halloween was coming to a close for another year. That left the streets to me.

Look, you don't have to tell me how weird it is for an adult to be wandering up and down the block by himself. I know how this looked. How I looked. But I needed to see. Needed to try.

Which house was it?

Who drugged me?

Already my stomach was twisting. The cramps came on quick. Felt like a punch to the gut. I was hungry. So fucking hungry. But the thought of food made me sick. All I wanted was—

angels

—that candy, that sweet sweetmeat. I found myself doing this odd cramped crabwalk, hobbling down the block while holding my stomach, just trying to keep everything in place.

I'd given up on wiping my face, letting the drool funnel down the chin. I could hear my own lips smack against my swollen gums every time I breathed through my mouth.

I knocked on doors. All the way up our block. *Hey, uh…this is a weird one for you, but…I'm curious. What kind of candy did you hand out tonight? Was it a marshmallowy-type thingy?*

Though, truth told, it came out sounding more like

sweeeeeeeetmeeeeeeeeeaaat

sweeeeeeeesweeeeeeeesweeeeeeeeeeeeeeetah-tah-taaah

mmm-mmm-mmmmmmmmeeeeeeat

I was the one trick-or-treating now. Look at me, in my spooky costume! Listen to me, asking for candy! Gimme gimme a treat! Please! Just one sweet… But not just any candy, no.

I needed that majestic sweetmeat. Need more more more. Need it noooooooow.

Was it this house?

Or this one?

Or this?

Of course, my neighbors looked at me like I'd gone mad. I was going door to door, interrogating them about a candy I couldn't explain, couldn't articulate. That was because they hadn't tasted it for themselves. They didn't understand. How could they? How could anyone?

They wouldn't know. They could never know.

You haven't tasted it, I can tell. You'll never taste it. Never get your hands on a yummy morsel. Never perch a chunk on your tongue, sealing your lips over it, closing your eyes and taking a deep breath through your nose before letting your saliva saturate that sweetmeat.

Eat, for this is my body.

You'll never know what it's like to taste a slice of heaven. If you did, you'd be just like me. You'd dedicate the rest of your miserable existence trick-or-treating to the ends of the fucking world, knocking on every last door on this goddamn planet, every day, all year long, until your feet are nothing but bloody stumps, your body nothing more than skin and bones…

Someone might've called the police. A cruiser swept down the street. I hid behind a bush, crouching low, where they couldn't find me. The morning sun softened the horizon. I'd gone to the outer borders of our suburb and back again, winding throughout our neighborhood.

There weren't any houses left. I'd knocked on every last door.

Save for one.

Every neighborhood has that one house. The house that doesn't take part in the holiday. I would've walked by without giving it much thought. There were no lights on. It looked empty.

Funny, I thought, *it looks a lot like our house.*

I had found it. Finally found it.

The front stoop of a temple. The very gates of Heaven. A dish on its steps. A note written by the angels—

TAKE ONE

I was weak. I had always been weak.

This gift. It was too much for me. I had been granted access to the sugar cane of angels; I had tasted it. It'd been on my tongue. I licked it. Swallowed it. And now I was willing to sacrifice everything, everything I had in this world, for just one more mouthful.

One more taste.

Sweet.

Meat.

Maybe they had more inside. Something told me to sneak a peek through the window.

Just in case. Just to see.

There. Right there. On the floor. I could barely make it out through the glass, but lying in the hallway, deeper into the house, was...was...

A body. A body on the floor.

A kid.

Christ, I thought, *there's a child on the floor. He's still wearing his Halloween costume. A cartoon character of some kind. He's not moving. He's just there, on his back. I have to—*

Have to—

The door was unlocked, so I slipped in. Raced to this—

This—

angel

angel

angel

angel

angel

angel

angel

angel

angel

angel

Sections of its flesh had been sliced and cubed. The negative space of its eyes. Its nose. The jagged slash of a jack-o'-lantern's mouth. All in piles. You could see where the cutting had stopped around its ribcage. All the colors were bright. Fluorescent. The colors of a Saturday morning cartoon. Purple and pink muscle tissue. Orange and green bones. Blue organs below.

Sweetmeat. Here was the sweetmeat. I had finally found whose house it had come from.

I noticed the knife just next to the body, its handle all tacky. Sticky.

I poked the body.

My fingertip simply sunk deeper into its spongy mass. When I yanked my hand back, the impression left behind by my finger slowly started to spring up into its original shape.

Someone had carved it into small portions. Someone had plopped those pieces into a dish and left them out on the doorstep. Someone had written in Sharpie on an index card:

TAKE ONE.

But who has that kind of strength? That level of self-restraint? Who could resist the gravitational pull to grab as many as they could and stuff them all into their bag?

Jesus, how many kids in the neighborhood had taken a bit of this angel home?

How many had already eaten from its flesh?

I hadn't realized my mouth was watering. Not until the drool dripped to my knees, soaking into my slacks.

The knife was right there. All I had to do was pick it up and cut off a piece. Just a small slice. Right where they left off, whoever they were. What would one more chunk hurt?

Why bother with the knife at all? I could just lean in and take a bite right off the bone.

Gimme that sweet, sweet meat. Lord, it melts right in my mouth.

THE MAGIC TRICK

by Gregory L. Norris

1. The Little Magician

On a Halloween night much closer to the end of my life than the magical All Hallows at the start, I answered a knock at the front door of the modest little ranch house located far from the bungalow where I grew up, and discovered I'd been visited by the tiniest of sorcerers.

"*Abra*—" he declared.

In the fraction of a second before he concluded his spell, his black walking stick-turned-magic wand aimed at me, I absorbed his presentation through what remained of my eyesight. Not more than four feet tall, he was decked out in black tails and trousers and a crisp white tuxedo shirt, a red bow tie that matched the satin lining of his cape, and top hat on head that contained the results of an unknown number of incantations—rabbits and doves, playing cards, and cosmic dust among them.

"—*cadabra*!"

I applauded. "Bravo!"

The magician bowed. "Now, make with the candy!"

I picked up the orange plastic jack-o'-lantern filled with chocolate bars and let him take two, even as my breaths came with ever increasing difficulty and the area beyond the bald glow of the porch light where the little magician's parents waited blurred. He stuffed the candy into a velvet bag already heavy with the spoils of other performances held across our neighborhood whose windows and shrubs glowed from strands of vibrant pumpkin-colored lights and a waning October moon staring down through its narrowed Cyclops eye. Not far away, an entire cast of creature features frolicked—skeletons, witches, vampires with plastic fangs, and zombies cursed to roam the Earth…at least until eight o'clock, the town-mandated end of trick-or-treating.

I closed the door and returned the candy bowl to the hall table before it spilled from my shaking hands. I made it into the kitchen and splashed water on my face, aware of another knock on the door.

"On my way," I said in a voice barely there.

The knocks that followed grew louder, more insistent. My next sip of air clotted in my throat, and the world slipped out of focus.

I hadn't thought about Warren and what happened in…years, was it? *Decades.* I'd entombed the memories behind mental brick and mortar. Around me, time lost cohesion, and the past superimposed over my present. Space distorted with it, and the rapid knocks transformed into thunder, heartbeats. The knocks—

2. THE OTHER LITTLE MAGICIAN

Increased, becoming frantic. I hastened from the tiny bedroom wedged at the back of the bungalow, where my face had been stuck in a book, my consciousness transported to another planet and reality. The house sat chilly from the October Saturday that projected beyond the windows deceptively bright in strokes of sunny yellow, pumpkin orange, and blood red thanks to the foliage. But the temperature had plummeted here at the end of the universe, and the morning had woken to the season's first frost.

Warren stood outside clad in shirt with short sleeves and the same ill-fitting hand-me-down pants with the stripes he wore six out of seven days every week. He shivered in that instant before our eyes connected through the door's window glass, and I wondered if the cause was weather-related or something other. Then I saw the fresh cut on his mouth and easily imagined the source. As stated, it was a cold Saturday morning in October. Friday night meant his father had gone a few rounds on him in celebration of the arrival of the weekend with a six-pack or several.

I opened the door. The frigid morning air swept in, smelling of autumn and the sourness of Warren's clothes.

"Come on," Warren said, so excited he didn't react to my look of horror over his split lip crusted with a scab of dried blood. "I have to show you something!"

"What?" I asked.

"Can't tell you. Gotta show— It's *magic*."

The strange cosmic energy I often experienced living in the rural town far from all that had once been familiar ignited within me. In that previous summer, Warren and I had spotted a snake we swore stretched out to the length of a horror from Loch Ness slithering through the meadow across the road where we picked flowers for my mother. The rush of terror had also been electric. Up past the deep woods, near the new interstate going in, was an abandoned farmhouse. Just the image of it, glimpsed whenever Warren got me to challenge my mother's strict order to not go that far from our front door, unleashed wonder in my belly. It was an empty old house, but to me it was a haunted castle.

Lost in my excitement, I was halfway down the flagstone and cement walk, crunching through fallen leaves, before I realized I was still in my stockings.

Following my mother's departure from the relationship with the man who was my father in biological terms only, we went to live in that small bungalow in a strange town located at the end of the galaxy. We arrived in the spring—May, on Mother's Day, which now seems incredibly fitting. The tiny house, a winterized cottage that had once been a seasonal camp, was part of a necklace of small oases laid out along a single-lane paved road running through meadow and dense woods.

Our place was next door to Richard Hollings and his son, Warren, who was one year older than my six, and the best friend I ever knew.

We crept silently past Warren's father's old truck and through the back door whose window was cloaked in a heavy bath towel. All the windows in that house were shrouded against prying eyes and to keep in secrets. It was the late 1960s, and people didn't talk about the abuse kids suffered, even when the proof was left in the open. We certainly didn't at that moment; our voices could have roused the monster passed out in the bedroom at the front of the house. Our destination was Warren's tiny hovel, which mirrored mine. Even so, we heard the monster's snores through the otherwise throbbing silence in that dark tomb.

"*Over here,*" Warren whispered.

I pursued him past the single mattress on the floor that was his bed, no frame nor box spring, to the three built-in bookshelves that bore no books. On this morning, however, the shelves weren't empty. On the top, a single playing card was arranged upright and facing out—the King of Diamonds. On the middle and bottom shelves, intricate houses made of the rest of the deck had been constructed. The nervous energy rippling off Warren in concentric waves and spilling into my soul intensified.

"*Behold,*" he said.

I wasn't sure what I was looking at and told him so.

"A magic trick," Warren said in a voice that dared rise above our cautious whispers.

Magic? Despite our immediate surroundings, which had bottled the odor of sweat and a mildewed funk and something far worse I now realize was despair, I was again reminded of the many wonders of this place.

In one of the houses beyond ours was an elderly couple who owned an old beagle who was missing a front leg. We called her "Peggy, the Three-legged Dog," and she was so sweet, you couldn't help but understand she was too happy, too filled with life, to regret that one defect. Not far from there was a multi-limbed tree with a million climbable branches that soared up to the clouds that we'd named "Yggdrasil" after the legend in an old Norse mythology book my mother scored at a yard sale. And as for clouds…

One summer afternoon, it rained when the sun was still out, and while Warren and I splashed through puddles, a cloud drifted down from the sky, and we'd both touched it.

I already believed in magic.

"You ready?" he asked.

I said I was. Warren rubbed his hands together, and, at any second, I expected electricity to crackle from his fingertips. He held his breath, steeled himself, and stepped closer to the built-ins. Warren stood on tiptoes, aimed his right pointer at the King of Diamonds, and with the barest nudge, slid it through the miniscule gap at the back of the shelf.

The playing card slipped through empty space. On the way down, it clipped the roof of the first house of cards and sent it tumbling in a domino sequence. But the trick was far from over. The lone King continued down past the *second* gap and landed on the house built across the bottom shelf. Before the first flimsy construction project completed its fall, the second collapsed.

I was blown away. I raised my hands to applaud, going on instinct. Warren caught me in time before the thunderclap emerged to possibly wake the sleeping horror in the other bedroom.

We sat outside and ate cereal in dry handfuls from the box my mother had bought the day before when she shopped two towns away. I wondered when Warren had eaten last.

"That was *excellent*," I said, stressing my favorite new catch phrase for things extraordinary.

Warren beamed. "Took me seven tries to get it just right."

"Lucky Seven," I said. Then, my mind, which was wise beyond its years, sent a dark cloud over my exuberance. *Lucky?* I imagined the blow from his father's fist, the blood, and a kind of insane terror that had made sleep impossible for my best friend, so much so that he went in search of legerdemain as a way to cope and pass the time.

"I'm gonna learn magic—the real stuff," Warren said between crunches. "I'll be better than Svengali or Houdini."

The brisk October wind gusted and clanked chains made of fallen leaves, its ghostly moan timed perfectly to Warren's promise. And I believed him.

On Monday morning, we hiked to the bus stop and waited. Boarding, we sat huddled together on a seat near the front. The location spared us no less of the taunting from the other kids than our situations at home. We were the easiest of targets—the nerd with a single mother when they all had dads, and the kid who wore the same sad rags every day. Warren had a father, God help him.

Only God didn't.

Halloween neared. The days grew colder and shorter. Night arrived even earlier. A strange kind of magic carried over the world on chilly breezes that smelled crisp from dead leaves. And a monster worse than anything I watched in the creature features viewed on the ugly, boxy TV set connected to the rabbit ear antenna continued to brutalize my best friend.

3. Escape

"I'm running away," Warren said.

I couldn't see his new wounds except for the proof of them in his eyes.

"I'll go with you."

The words were out of my mouth before I could rationalize what I was saying. I very methodically walked into the house. My mother sat at the secondhand dining table with two mismatched chairs she'd gotten at a garage sale, sipping her coffee from a glass mug and lost in a paperback romance novel.

"I'm running away with Warren," I calmly announced.

She didn't look up. "Um-hum. Pack extra underwear—and stay away from the interstate. What do you want for dinner?"

I marched into her room and pulled the empty hatbox luggage, round and robin's egg blue and smelling of a hint of faded perfume, from the closet. In it, I packed four paperback books—all with thrilling covers that showed rocket ships and men in spacesuits, a change of clothes, my favorite stuffed bear Teddy, and a box of crackers, two glass bottles of soda, and another full box of cereal. The latter was too big to stuff into the case as was, so I removed the bag from the box and zipped everything up.

We cut across the road and into the woods, where we picked up a trail long ago beaten into the ground by hikers, explorers, and, perhaps, other refugees. Warren and I followed the ancient farmer's wall, the boulders covered in gray-green lichen, up to the first ridge from which we could see the roofs of our houses through breaks in the naked tree branches. We snacked. At that point, we were both still too hot from adrenaline to consider that running away without heavy coats in a Northern New England October wasn't exactly the smartest of moves.

For Warren, it was the only one.

"Where we going?" I asked.

He didn't answer, but I knew.

The house appeared before us, gray and weathered like a ghost against the backdrop of conifers that no longer looked fully green in the overcast. The state had appropriated the land. Torn-up pasture had become parking lot for heavy construction equipment and vehicles as the new interstate plowed forward through the countryside.

A mix of excitement and dread filled me. That house was a wonderland from the territories of my imagination. But it had also become real now that we'd reached the forbidden boundary of my world.

"Come on," Warren said, shattering the spell of thoughts I'd fallen victim to.

It was the weekend, so nobody was around. Still, we crept closer to our destination. My flesh prickled with worry that, from either the house or surrounding woods, we were being watched. We rounded the sagging front porch, cut through the brambles covering one side, and made it to the backdoor. The door was unlocked. Nobody lived here anymore, just wildlife and now two runaways.

The old farmhouse wasn't much warmer inside than it was beyond its decrepit walls. Numerous windows had been broken. Leaves had found their way into the place along with animals. We discovered acorn shells gnawed open and shredded pinecones on top of the dirty table and counter. The place exuded a pungent yellow smell from mice and other intruders.

It wasn't some castle from the distant realms of Scotland or Bavaria. Still, I stared about with breathless, wide-eyed curiosity. Past the kitchen was a parlor whose ratty old furniture had been chewed through by rodents. From there, wooden stairs led up to the second floor. While I gaped, Warren hopped onto those stairs, which groaned, and scaled them.

"It's safe," he said.

I thawed enough to pursue him and held my breath, expecting the old risers to give out beneath my weight with every advance higher. At the top of the stairs, the floor continued ahead warped and uneven to the point where you could roll a ball on gravity alone, past another window, and to three doors. Two stood open—a bedroom with a wooden four-post frame, no mattress, and an ancient dresser whose mirror lacked glass at the left, and a bathroom on the same side.

Warren wrestled with the knob to that third, closed door. The wood had warped. Grunting with either anger or desperation or a mix of both, he shouldered the door open. It complained and surrendered. Beyond was a back bedroom that looked only slightly less ravaged by time and the elements than the rest of the place.

My sense of wonder returned, fed by the room's contents. Here there was a full bed—single, with four tall posts, all of them capped in carved pineapples. An intact mirror hung on the wall. An old steamer trunk sat at the foot of the bed. While Warren struggled with the trunk's latches, I wandered in a daze over to the window, which gazed down at the rear of the property. From my vantage point, I could see the clean corridor of the new interstate that had bitten its way through the trees. A salmon pink and white land boat, one of those cars with plenty of fins, motored north. Closer, the maple and birch trees had shed their leaves and clawed at the overcast sky like skeleton hands with long, thin finger bones. A squirrel's nest braced the palm of an oak.

My focus drifted down to the ground. A square of ancient

wooden slab appeared not far from the back of the house where we'd committed our invasion. I only saw it briefly.

"Look!" Warren called.

I turned from the window. He'd successfully opened the trunk and plundered its contents. Inside were clothes. Warren held up a pair of black trousers, a white tuxedo shirt, and one of those elegant black bowties you saw on performers who sang or made music on album covers.

"*No way!*" Warren added.

He held the trousers to his waist. They were too long.

"I'll roll up the cuffs," he said as though reading my thoughts. "And I'll tuck in the shirt!"

"What about shoes?" I asked.

He examined his dirty sneakers. "These'll do."

I was glad for him, because he seemed so happy in that moment. When he changed into them, I had to admit the only things missing were the top hat, cape, and magic wand.

"Excellent!" I said.

Evening descended, cold and silent apart from the drone of the occasional car traveling the new asphalt of the interstate or the cry of a night bird. On our backs, we stared up at the early dusk, our stomachs filled with cereal and soda, our eyes wide from nerves.

"Do you think there are monsters out there?" I asked. "Giant lizards in Loch Ness, Sasquatches in the wild woods, vampires and mummies and werewolves?"

"Not those kinds," Warren said. And then he went silent.

We buried our gazes in the sky and what remained of the moon, and the breeze gossiped through all the mysterious and secret corners of the forest that surrounded us.

In my mind, I was in Warren's room, asleep on that bed but also conscious. The wind blew a kiss, and the trigger card fell. Right before it dropped, the King of Diamonds spoke my name. Then, while falling, a swipe of his colorful cartoon ax and the first of the houses made of cards collapsed.

The Hollings house trembled in sympathy around it.

As the King continued his demolition, I caught movement from the direction of the bedroom door. Something gigantic and monstrous had arrived. I noted the flash of light reflecting off scales, the terrible glow of red eyes, and heard the deep, juicy labor of its breaths. It was coming for me.

My astral self broke focus and darted a glance down at my sleeping body. Only it wasn't me slumbering unaware of the monster's arrival.

"*Warren,*" I tried to call out.

The house shook. The King swung his ax, and the second stage of the magic trick kicked into action. The door flew open, and the monster surged in.

I bolted awake and screamed. The house continued to quake, and, as dark figures and shadows streamed toward us, the monster again spoke my name. I sucked down a deep breath and realized my mother stood beside it.

The policeman wrapped the blanket around me—one of those old surpluses from the army, drab green, and scratchy. My mother did her tiger's dance dressed in a robe over her pajamas and slippers. She wore curlers in her hair.

"—how worried I was? When you told me you were running away, I thought you'd be back in time for lunch!" She pulled me into her arms. Then she released me and gave me a shake. "Don't you *ever* do that to me again!"

From the cut of my eye, I saw Warren being led away to his father's truck, which was parked among two police cars and all the heavy equipment.

"This house isn't safe, son," the cop who'd wrapped the lousy blanket around me said.

I wanted to bark at him that he wasn't my dad, and I sure wasn't his son. But my gaze connected with Warren's, and for the first time, I really felt the cold. The monster walked him away into darkness, and I saw the desperation in his eyes.

"No," I said to the cop, the monster, and the universe.

But Warren was already gone, swallowed whole by the night.

I laid in the shadows on my spine and stared at the ceiling, frozen in place by my fears for Warren. Fears for myself. Fears that the magic of the world had been corrupted and taken a decline toward oblivion like the dodo birds I'd read about in one book and the saber-toothed tigers and mastodons before them whose artwork graced the pages of another.

My mom punished me by forbidding me to go trick-or-treating, and I was mostly okay with that. But as the night arrived on the calendar, she warmed and relented.

"I don't have a costume," I said in a flat voice.

"Throw a sheet over your head and go as a ghost."

"No, I'll have to cut two holes for the eyes."

I sensed my mother's guilt as she fished an old sheet off the top shelf in her closet. "Use this one."

"But it's *pink*," I protested.

"Nobody will notice in the dark!"

I surrendered and cut. She offered to take me. I told her no, I was okay.

"I don't want you going that close to the highway again."

"I won't," I promised.

She hugged the little pink ghost and, at twilight, I set out into the crisp, October Halloween darkness, pillowcase in hand, silly ghost costume cloaking my identity.

I scurried past the Hollings's driveway. Warren's father's truck was gone. From the shadows of the front stoop, another ghost appeared, this one dressed in an ill-fitting magician's uniform pilfered from an old steamer trunk in an abandoned farmhouse.

"Warren," I gasped.

I hadn't seen him in days. His face bore fresh wounds, but the eerie calm in his voice when he addressed me spoke that he was well past feeling his father's beating. I wanted to hug him. I didn't. A strange energy emanated off his body like a magical aura.

"Let's go," he said.

"Trick-or-treating?" I innocently asked.

"No, far away. It's time to escape."

He tipped his chin in the direction of the deep woods.

"I can't," I said. "I promised my mother."

He hung his head but only for a second. Then, Warren marched across our single-lane road. I hurried to catch up.

"Wait," I called.

He stopped though only half-turned toward me. "I've been practicing."

"Practicing?"

"Magic. The legit stuff. None of those stupid card tricks. I'm talking the kind of hocus pocus where a kid can disappear and never be seen again unless he wants to. Goodbye."

I struggled to answer. I willed my legs to pursue as he continued forward, *gliding* as though his soles levitated above the earth. And then my best friend was gone.

I never saw Warren again.

4. The Famous Disappearing Act

Magic.

Warren did it. He walked up and into those woods on the most magical night of my boyhood and vanished from our lives, entering other dimensions and worlds of mystery and wonder.

One pink ghost alone wandered from house to house, collecting candy and plump autumn apples in a daze, convinced Warren would succeed. He was a magician, and there was real magic in this world.

Of course, I was questioned, but I told them nothing. I hadn't seen Warren since the night they found us in the old farmhouse. The common theory, at first, was that he'd made it to the new interstate and had hitched a ride away with some stranger who, perhaps, drove one of those land boats with so many fins.

I knew differently. Warren had snapped his fingertips, spoken the secret incantation, and had woven a spell, disappearing in a puff of smoke. The truth was, he'd—

5. GHOSTS

—Walked, in the darkness, over that square of old wood I'd seen hidden at the back of the house, cracked through the rotten planks, and had drowned in the old farmhouse's well. They found his body the following spring.

6. THE LITTLE GHOST

I came out of the spell and once more entombed most of what had been exhumed on the Halloween night closer to the end of my life than the start. I was old, and what had happened with Warren Hollings was a very long time ago.

Composing myself, I picked up the plastic pumpkin filled with candy and answered the next excited knock at my front door. Standing outside was a little ghost in a sheet with two holes cut out for eyes.

"Trick or treat," the ghost squealed and held out its bag for candy.

And, for a terrible instant, I wondered if I was staring at myself. Time had already twisted in reverse on this Halloween night. For all I knew, it had again, and I was in the center of yet one more paradox, my past self facing my present unthinkable decades later.

No, I decided.

I tossed two candy bars into the little ghost's bag, one for the apparition, another for the ghost of Warren, and, smiling, quietly closed the door.

THE TREAT-OR-TRICKER

by Evans Light

It was nearly nine-thirty when the doorbell rang.

Awfully late for trick-or-treaters, the man thought. The last group had stopped by almost an hour ago, and he'd just gotten comfortable in his recliner and lost in a TV show.

Teenagers, he guessed, making their final rounds. Cleaning out leftover candy.

He set his remote down on the coffee table, grabbed the bowl of Halloween candy from the kitchen counter, and headed for the door.

A little boy, about eight or nine years old, stood alone on the porch.

He was not wearing a costume.

"Treat or trick?" the boy said.

The man didn't recognize the boy from around the neighborhood, and no car waited on the street.

The boy held a clear plastic bag full of candies. They were all the same kind, not the hodgepodge assortment one would expect a child to have toward the end of Halloween night.

A small cardboard box sat on the porch beside him.

"Treat or trick?" the boy said again.

The man laughed.

"'Treat or trick?' Don't you mean 'trick or treat?' Where's your costume?"

The boy didn't flinch.

The boy didn't smile.

"No, I said what I meant to say. Do you want a 'treat' or a 'trick'?"

The absolute seriousness of the child surprised the man. It was amusing, so he decided to play along.

"Well, let me think… No one really likes a trick, except the person playing it. So I suppose I'd rather have a treat."

"You do know tonight is Halloween, right?"

"Why of course," said the man.

"Then you should also know that you need to be wearing a costume. You do know that, right?" asked the boy.

"But I don't have a costume."

The little boy sighed, as though immensely burdened.

"I figured you wouldn't. That's why I've brought some with me."

The boy unfolded the flaps of his cardboard box and withdrew two large rubber masks. One was a zombie head with an eyeball dangling onto the cheek. The other mask was some sort of tree monster with a very long twig for a nose.

"My, aren't those frightful!"

"Please pick one quickly. I have many houses yet to visit," said the boy, all business.

"You want me to wear a mask?"

"Yes, please. Halloween must be done correctly or else it's not Halloween."

The man scratched his head, puzzled. "I've got some candy left over. You can have the rest of it if you want," he offered.

"I asked you first," said the boy. "I asked if you wanted a 'treat' or 'trick' and you said 'treat.' Now, please pick a costume. As I said, I have the rest of the neighborhood to visit this evening."

The man wondered where the boy's parents were, why he was out so late all by himself. He considered dropping a candy into the boy's bag and shooing him away. But the child was so earnest, he decided to continue playing along. Doing otherwise appeared as though it might cause the boy great stress.

"Okay," said the man. "I'll be the zombie."

"Excellent choice," said the boy. He gave the mask to the man and waited for him to put it on. The man adjusted it until his eyes blinked out from behind cut-out holes.

"Arrggh!" said the man, dangling his hands from outstretched arms as though he'd joined the ranks of the living dead.

"Very nice," said the boy. "You really scared me. Now, what do you say?"

"Thank you?" guessed the man.

"No, not 'thank you.' By your age, I'm surprised you don't know how this works. To get candy, you should say, 'trick or…'"

"Oh right!" said the man. "Trick or treat!"

A broad smile spread across the boy's face. The porch light reflected in his eyes, twinkling like a swarm of fireflies. The boy reached into his sack, extracted a single piece of hard candy, and handed it to the man.

"Happy Halloween," the boy said.

"Happy Halloween to you, too," said the man, his voice muffled inside the rubber mask.

"Well?" said the boy.

"Well what?" said the man.

"Aren't you going to eat it?"

"Right now?"

"Yes, right now. I want to see if you like it."

The man held the candy up to the mask's eyehole to get a better look. It was red and round and individually wrapped. The man had eaten none of the treats he'd passed out that evening. He'd specifically purchased candies he didn't like to avoid temptation. One little piece of candy wouldn't hurt. In fact, it looked like something he might enjoy.

"You can eat it through the mouth-hole, if you want to," the kid said, his voice suddenly bright and full of cheer. "It's funny-looking to see a zombie eat candy."

What the hell? Why not? thought the man. He popped the candy from its cellophane wrapper right through the rubber hole, into his mouth. His tongue explored the raised ridge that ran around the middle of the confection. It had a strong cherry flavor that was thrilling and delicious.

"Thank you," the man said. "It's wonderful."

"I'm glad you like it. Can I please have my mask now?"

The man pulled off the mask and returned it to the boy, who packed it neatly into the box, carefully folding each flap back into place. Once done, the boy collected his things and bowed slightly.

"Enjoy the rest of your Halloween," said the boy.

"You as well," said the man. He closed the door and headed back to finish his television show. *What a weird-ass kid*, he thought as he bit down hard, crunching the candy.

Foam filled his mouth as the sweetness of cherry gave way to caustic bitterness, making him gag. He jumped up from his chair and took two steps toward the kitchen. Then he fell down and lay dead on the floor.

A t the house next door, the doorbell rang.

A man and his wife exchanged puzzled looks. She grabbed the bowl of leftover Halloween candy from the kitchen counter and headed for the door.

A little boy, about eight or nine years old, stood alone on the porch.

He was not wearing a costume.

"Treat or trick?" the boy said.

TUTTI I MORTI

by Steve Rasnic Tem

All dead. All gone.

It was late, darkness a smear outside his bedroom window, yet he decided to go out for a walk. His son would not have approved, but his son was asleep, and Lorenzo was a grown man, an old man capable of making his own decisions, despite what anyone else believed. He had nothing to do, no responsibilities, no tasks he needed to perform. At this stage in his life, he preferred the night. His mind was clearer after the sun went down, and he'd become self-conscious around other people. They were always eager to tell him he'd made some mistake.

He didn't know how far he needed or wanted to go. He had no plan. He would have called a taxi, but he no longer had credit cards or cash of his own. His son bought him a cell phone, but he never learned how to use it.

His son controlled everything. Yet his son couldn't keep his house clean. As Lorenzo moved through the house, he was alarmed by the layers of dust over floors and furniture, the cobwebs, the widespread disarray. Something trickled down his cheeks. He wiped it with his finger and looked. Was that perspiration or blood or tears? He honestly didn't know.

As he left the house, he was surprised to discover the front door had been tagged with black spray paint—an X or a lopsided T. The homes across the street bore similar signs of vandalism. The lack of civility troubled him—yet another indication he'd lived past his expiration date.

The remains of shattered pumpkins littered the front yard. Lorenzo remembered his childhood in Italy, how they carried pumpkins carved with the shape of a cross with lit candles inside as lanterns. They called them *cocce de morte*, dead people's heads.

She joined him out on the sidewalk. He wasn't sure exactly who she was, and he wouldn't look at her, but it seemed quite right she should be the one to accompany him. They strolled past the small houses at the end of this row, each one dark as a blinded eye, around the library, and beyond.

Many more people were out at this hour than he'd expected. Teens and twenty somethings. Maybe thirty somethings, but his ability to estimate age had deteriorated over time. People were now either very young or very old.

A tall man stood in front of them, his bare face tattooed into a hideous mask. The man's coat fell open, chest exploded, heart visible inside the rib cage. Then Lorenzo realized it was simply a T-shirt design. The man wouldn't yield so they had to push around him. Lorenzo never would have tolerated such rudeness when he was younger.

Many in the crowd were elaborately costumed. Bright scarves and hats, voluminous suits and dresses, faces painted or masked or both. Some carried lumpy bags. A few were in high spirits, but overall there appeared to be a solemnity to the occasion, whatever it was.

"Perhaps it's a festival. A big one, from the looks of things." It was the first time Lorenzo had spoken to her since they started walking.

"It's Halloween, dear. Don't you remember?" He'd always loved the sound of her voice.

"Is it, already? It's that late in the year?"

She laughed so softly he barely heard her. "Look at the trees. The leaves are almost gone. It's too late for the little goblins, but the older ones are out. I imagine they still have parties—don't you think? You used to love parties."

"I *hate* parties. I never know what to say. Especially when they ask me how I'm doing. They're just being friendly, I suppose, but how do you answer such a question? Do you tell the truth?"

She didn't answer. He wasn't surprised. No one wanted to talk to a complainer. He'd always been a moaner, but in his advanced years he was worse.

Trick or treat. That's what they called it, what they did on Halloween. Extortion was what it was. *Cosa Nostra* business. When he was a boy in Italy, they did not trick-or-treat. What Italian parents would allow their children to wander into strangers' homes? There it had been a religious holiday, *Ogni Santi e il Giorno dei Morti*— All Saints and All Souls. *Novembre 1 e 2*. He remembered all the lit candles and the crosses. They left out a lamp, a bucket of water and a little bread, so the dead might find their way home, then eat and drink. In some houses the fireplace was kept going for the whole night and the table was set with plentiful food for the dead so they might feast.

Was the food gone in the morning? He could not remember.

Perhaps his parents hid this from him. He thought of huge meals left on tables for days, rotting and swimming in sour liquid, all because the families could not let go.

It seemed they had left the crowd behind. They passed through a neighborhood which was completely dark, the houses seeming more like tombs than dwellings, except for an abundance of lit candles on the porches, the sidewalks, collected into large groupings on the lawns. Some of the candles were tapers as thin as flaming fingers. Others were long and thick and waxy like severed limbs set on fire. The largest tabby he'd ever seen erupted from the bushes in front of them and scattered dozens of the candles as it raced through a sequence of lawns. At one point it may or may not have caught fire, and Lorenzo screeched in dismay. The cat vanished before he could ascertain its fate. Lorenzo tasted ash and tried to spit it out. But once you have acquired such a taste it never completely goes away.

Across the street an angry couple herded their two children along. *Where were you? We've been searching everywhere!* The boy was throwing a tantrum, making it quite clear he didn't want to go home. Lorenzo would have gotten a beating for behaving that way.

Lorenzo looked around and could not find her anywhere. She'd abandoned him again, all because of his sour attitude. He would try to change. He would try to do better. How many times had he promised her that?

He felt a flutter of panic deep inside his throat. Was he going to cry? Old men tended to weep. They could not help themselves. He didn't know if he could find his way home without her.

He turned the corner and was confronted by the crowd again. The size of it alarmed him. He couldn't guess the total number, but it had to be in the thousands. The territory the revelers occupied had expanded. All he could see were costumed figures filling the streets, the yards, the public parkways. A giant street celebration, he supposed, for the holiday. It was all so—what was the word—theatrical? Some costumes appeared commercially made, perhaps based on popular cultural icons, but since he didn't go to the movies or watch television, he had no idea which ones.

Someone had covered themself with a white sheet and cut two eyeholes to fashion a makeshift ghost. The sheet appeared to be spotted with bloodstains.

A large number had rough brown sacks over their heads. Lorenzo thought of them as sack heads, and under any other circumstance he might consider them comical or ludicrous, but not tonight.

Deeper into the crowd the costumes became more frightening—cloth ripped and painted to suggest decay, masks and prostheses bubbling with disfiguration, mutation, and extensive injury. A few of the characters featured missing limbs and other random amputations. The mob was thick with drunkards. Every few minutes some merrymaker would fall over, intoxicated, or dead—it was difficult to tell.

He reached out for her hand and found it. She'd come back. But had she forgiven him? Her fingers were stiff at first, then gradually relaxed and intertwined with his.

"It seems in poor taste," Lorenzo said, but stopped. He didn't want her to perceive him as someone with no sense of humor. He had no idea if any of this was in poor taste or not. Fashions change, and he had lost the ability to tell. But he had never liked being reminded of people's misfortunes. Everywhere people were suffering, their fates inescapable. This was nothing to celebrate.

The density of costume made him uncomfortable. This was no minimalist masquerade. Faces and arms, hands, were painted, and on top of these, masks and layer upon layer of personalities were applied.

Risqué outfits were much in evidence: exposed bellies and butt cheeks, bare breasts, an abundance of naked skin for such a cold night. These costumes would have been taboo when he was a young man. He hadn't realized they were considered acceptable now. He tried not to stare, but these forbidden delights were everywhere he looked.

Someone started a fire near one edge of the crowd. Certainly, it was a chilly evening, but this seemed unwise. He should have brought a coat. His shirt and pants were much too thin. Or perhaps he was still in his pajamas. Lorenzo wasn't sure.

Setting a fire close to so many people was a reckless thing to do. He couldn't see them well, but a circle of costumed figures danced around the fire, at times practically touching the flames. One towering figure appeared to be toasting its long fingers.

For a moment, they stopped moving, and that portion of the crowd became a frightening tableau of fire and burnt silhouettes. The mob began to shift direction, perhaps as people realized the danger, or maybe as part of some drunken, communal sway. Lorenzo pushed against the prevailing traffic. He didn't want to be trampled, but he was also desperate not to be trapped. Finally, he had to give into the tide and allowed himself to be swept away.

She'd let go of his hand. There was nothing he could do. He'd promised he would take good care of her, and yet he'd let her down repeatedly. His tender feelings for her had never gone away, even after all these years without her.

The flood of carousers appeared to turn in a circle, then split into several disparate arms. His group was forced down a narrow street, bodies pressed tightly against each other. His body began to tilt. He struggled to remain upright. The pressure of the other bodies kept him from falling, but he couldn't stand either. He traveled this way for some distance, carried along without his feet touching the ground. A murmuring arose deep within the horde, its tone darkening, becoming more animal-like.

When the street ended, Lorenzo was vomited out into an open space. He didn't recognize the area but thought it might be a park or athletic field. Fallen leaves were everywhere, wet and sticking to his shoes. A thick layer of filth accumulated over the lower part of his body, giving his legs a ruined appearance.

Broken masks and bits of costume lay scattered across the ground, stained, tainted. Yet he was still tempted to pick them up and examine them to make sure they were pieces of costume and not flesh and body parts. Each time, he managed to stop himself from acting on this bizarre impulse, realizing he might become infected with some terrible disease.

Someone was walking next to him. He was hopeful it might be her. He heard the tap tap tap as the bearded man passed, as if the fellow had a cane. But when Lorenzo looked down at the man's legs, he could see the fleshless skeletal feet. He looked back at the man's head and now his beard consisted of narrow threads of skin hanging from his chin.

A hand grabbed Lorenzo's. "I'm so glad you came back," he said. But glancing her way he realized he was holding a hand severed above the wrist. He shook his arm repeatedly until the hand let go.

A man approached, waving his handless arm. Lorenzo tried to tell him he didn't have it anymore. The man shouted and his tongue detached, flying over Lorenzo's head.

The field, ankle-deep in the debris from assorted carnage, resembled a massively messy meal, the plates and silverware buried beneath the leavings. The path through the wreckage was long and torturous. Lorenzo avoided touching the bits as much as possible, but the wet, gooey texture of the ground was inescapable.

Straggling survivors from the crowd drifted out of the mouths of the surrounding streets, dazed and wounded, but apparently still seeking comfort in the company of others. Some huddled standing and weeping. Others collapsed into piles, using one another's bodies for protection from whatever threats remained.

A trumpeting sound filled the air. Panic gripped the survivors, some fleeing, others clinging to each other for reassurance or resigned to share the same fate, their limbs and bodies twisted together.

Out of the tall trees bordering the field a series of narrow legs emerged—four or six or eight—so tall and narrow they disappeared into the darkness above. Lorenzo could not see whatever they were attached to, mammoth insect or beast or something even less imaginable. Sharp, blade-like appendages. The number of legs changed as the seconds passed and the legs came down on people and destroyed them, severed them, or mashed them into the ground. Then the arms came down out of the darkness, equally long and narrow and deadly, ending in claws which snatched and grabbed and tore bodies apart. Lorenzo kept looking up, still unable to see a body or a head or a physical source.

It harvested what remained of the crowd. No explanation. No trial. No reprieve. No interest in their desperate pleadings.

Lorenzo trembled as the thrashing legs and arms grew closer. He felt too old, too sad to run. Then her hand closed on his and she was there again, urging him on, practically dragging him out of the field. When and how had she gotten so strong? He remembered her always as a fragile, delicate creature.

They didn't talk for some time, but she maintained a firm grip on his hand, guiding him through the dark streets. He still couldn't bring himself to look directly at her. He didn't know why. Perhaps he was afraid of what he might see.

Lorenzo had no idea what time it was. He wondered if his son missed him yet. Trash covered the trees, the bushes, the houses.

His grandmother in Italy always had tales about this time of year. He never knew if any of them were true, but it felt disrespectful to doubt her. He remembered her saying if he were good and prayed for their souls, the dead would bring him gifts. But everything had been taken from the dead. What did they have left to give?

Lorenzo didn't understand how it could still be dark out. He'd left quite late, and he'd been gone for many hours. He could see a dim glow just above the distant horizon, but the sun appeared stuck there, unable to rise.

Lorenzo watched as scattered shapes still in their Halloween costumes returned home. Some reentered their houses without bothering to open doors. Of course, he no longer owned any doors. But what would happen when he reached his son's house?

Somewhere along the way he lost the comfort of her touch again, but she was there waiting for him in the open doorway.

"I don't know about you, but I'm famished," she said.

He gazed at her for some time. His wife appeared much as he remembered her—her wide smile, her large green eyes. But there was a fatigue in her face he had never seen before.

They sat at the massive spread laid out for them, enough food for a dozen people for a dozen meals. He tried to eat a little bit of everything, although sometimes he found the skin tough and difficult to chew.

THE LAST HALLOWEEN

by Larry Hinkle

Connor knows it's over from the way she averts her eyes when he asks if she's excited. The way she ignores his questions about what she will wear, or if her friends are coming. He knows this is probably the last year Gabbi will tolerate the embarrassment of trick-or-treating with her dad. His little girl is growing up too fast, and it cuts sharper than a razorblade hidden in an apple.

As they leave their house, a trio of shooting stars streak across the night sky.

"That has to be a good sign, right Gabbi?" He points up as the stars flash over the horizon.

"I guess," she says, eyes glued to her phone.

Kasey and Debi, Gabbi's two BFFs (this week, at least), are waiting for them at the end of the driveway.

She doesn't speak to him for the next half hour, splitting her attention instead between her friends and her phone. At least she still says "trick or treat" at each house—well, mumbles it, really. Still, it's better than nothing. And he'll take any good parenting points he can get right now.

Ding!

Another text from his wife, Traci, who volunteered to stay home so he could chaperone Gabbi and her friends. She's been texting him since they left, sending pictures of kids in memorable costumes and an occasional sneak peek of the special ensemble she's wearing *beneath* her passing-out-candy outfit, the one he can't wait to take off as soon as Gabbi goes to bed.

(TRACI) Pretty dead here now.

She's attached a photo of their empty porch.

(CONNOR) Just wait. The monsters will be on Maple Street soon enough. Lots of 'em out heading your way.

He sends a couple pictures of random trick-or-treaters gathered on the curb. Mixed among the usual killer clowns, ballerinas, and superheroes are two kids wearing identical alien outfits.

Awkward, he thinks, remembering the Halloween he was one of three homemade mummies in his third-grade class while watching them pass.

None of the kids' costumes had lasted past their first bathroom break that day, but these alien costumes are good. Great, actually. These kids look like they've just stepped off a star cruiser. Their eye stalks track his movement, while their tentacles sway independently of one another. He can't see any strings, no matter how hard he looks. He figures they must be wearing some sort of little robotic rigs. Their ray guns, meanwhile, look downright dangerous, covered in scuffs and burns. Whoever made these costumes belongs in Hollywood, not banished out here to Bumfuck, Ohio.

"Y'all see those meteors earlier?" Kevin Burke asks as he drops some candy in Gabbi's bucket at the next house. "Reporter on the news said they probably hit the ground a few miles from here."

"That would make them meteorites," Connor says.

"Huh?"

"They're meteors if they burn up in the atmosphere, and meteorites if they reach the ground."

"Whatever, Carl Sagan." Kevin laughs. "Either way, it's pretty cool. Bet the area'll be crawling with Poindexters for the next few days. Hope so, at least. Our coffee shop could use the extra business."

"Hear that, Gabbi?" Connor asks. "Meteorites on Halloween. I told you tonight would be special."

She looks up long enough to roll her eyes, then returns her attention to her phone. She and the other girls start walking toward the street.

Kevin snorts. "Kids today. Noses always buried in some sort of device. Wouldn't see a meteor—sorry, *meteorite*—unless it landed on their head."

Connor laughs. "Guess us old folks are the only ones who pay attention to the stars anymore, huh?"

"Who you calling old, old man?"

"Sorry, just feeling a little sorry for myself tonight. I'm afraid this'll be the last time Gabbi lets me take her trick-or-treating. I still remember that first year like it was yesterday. Me pushing her in the stroller, her plastic pumpkin in her lap..." He sighs. "Time goes by too fast."

"So, who's that with Gabbi?" Kevin asks as the kids wait at the end of the driveway.

"Kasey and Debi."

"Thought that might be them, but I wasn't sure. You're right, they do grow up fast. But then who are those two?" Kevin points at two aliens standing next to Kasey on the sidewalk.

Connor does a double take. "No idea. Guess I picked up a couple of stragglers." Are those the same kids he'd seen a few minutes ago? They'd been heading in the opposite direction when he'd snapped their picture.

Ding!

"Talk to you later, Kev. That's Traci."

A picture of Twizzlers tucked into his wife's cleavage pops up on his phone.

Shit! He scrolls down to hide it.

(CONNOR) You trying to get me arrested? The little aliens could've seen that.

(TRACI) Who?

(CONNOR) Couple kids in alien costumes. Not sure who they are. One of the girls must know them.

He sends her a picture of the kids standing together. Gabbi's short for her age, yet she still stands a good six inches taller than the aliens. Unless you count their tentacles, that is. *Wouldn't mind having one of them guarding the net on Gabbi's soccer team*, he thinks.

(CONNOR) Their costumes are amazing. They won't break character, either. Just make weird little squeaky noises.

(TRACI) Bet Gabbi loves that.

(CONNOR) Don't think she's even noticed. Night's not exactly going how I'd hoped.

(TRACI) Sorry. I've seen a few kids wearing that same costume, too. Must be from a movie we missed.

He watches Gabbi and her friends turn up the next driveway, then sends Traci another text.

(CONNOR) Gotta go. We're hitting the Emerson's now. They've gone full tits gonzo this year. Surprised you can't hear it back at the house.

He catches up to the kids as they're coming back down the front walkway. Kathy Emerson sets her bucket of candy down on the porch and waves. She's wearing a homemade zombie costume. Connor's glad she hadn't tried for a sexy zombie.

"Nice job on the decorations this year, Kath," Connor says. A fog machine blows mist through backlit tombstones in the front yard, while scary music plays from speakers in the bushes. They've set up a projector to play *Night of the Living Dead* on a sheet hanging over the front window. The sound is down, but Connor knows the dialogue by heart.

"Thanks," she says. "But I think we missed out not doing a spaceship this year, what with the shooting stars and all these little aliens. I've counted fifteen of 'em so far tonight. Almost feels like we're being *Punk'd*."

"Weird, huh? A couple of them glommed on to us, but I have no idea who they are. They don't talk at all. Just make little squeaky noises."

"A couple? Guess again, Einstein. I count five of them down there with the girls."

Son of a bitch! Three more had joined up when he wasn't looking. It had to be from a movie they'd missed, like Traci said. Maybe those Minions finally went to outer space? Or maybe it's from some viral video. God, when did he get so old and out of touch? He says goodnight to Kathy, then walks back to the street where the kids are waiting.

He taps Gabbi on the shoulder. "Who are your alien friends?"

"Don't know." She looks up from her phone for a second and grins, giving him a glimpse of the woman she'll become. *Is becoming,* he reminds himself. "I thought they were friends of yours," she says, then turns her attention yet again to her phone.

"That's funny." He reaches to put his arm around her shoulder, then remembers she doesn't like to be touched in public. Not by him, at least. He wonders if Kasey and Debi's dads get the same treatment. Connor steals a glance at her feed instead. It's full of too-young girls dressed as sexy something-or-others. He blushes and looks away.

Something tugs on his sleeve. "It's just us, Mr. Rae!"

Connor looks down. Two of the aliens have taken off their helmets. He smiles at the Baker twins. Mystery solved.

"Oh, hey Timmy, Kimmy. Nice costumes."

"Thanks." Kimmy says. "But they're not nearly as neat as some of these other ones."

"They're fine," Connor says. "I didn't recognize either of you, and that's the important part, right?"

"Right!" Timmy says as the twins put their helmets back on.

Ding!

This time Connor makes sure there are no kids in eyeshot before he opens Traci's text.

(TRACI) Friggin' creepy.

The attached picture shows maybe a dozen aliens huddled on their front porch.

(TRACI) I looked up and they were just out there. Never rang the doorbell. And when I opened the door, they just stared at me. No "trick or treat" or anything. They don't have candy sacks, either. Just scary looking ray guns. Think you can come home soon?

(CONNOR) Yeah, we're almost at the end of the block. Two more houses, then we'll head back. I think Gabbi's tired of me, anyway.

(TRACI) Thanks. I know this night meant a lot to you, but these kids are freaking me out. I promise I'll make it up to you.

The attached photo shows a candy bar tucked into her garter belt.

She must not be too scared, he thinks.

The kids had gone on without him. He doesn't want them to get too far ahead, so he picks up his pace. He walks past the Godfreys' place. They usually pass out great candy, but tonight their house is dark. So is the Carmens, the Williams, and the Schmidts. It makes him sad to think the neighborhood is outgrowing Halloween, too.

Finally, he sees the girls further down the street, now walking with a group of eight or nine kids in alien costumes. Gabbi looks back and waves for him to join them. Her wave is a little too fast. Is she worried about something?

Her phone probably died and she wants to borrow my portable charger, he thinks as he sticks his phone in his pocket and starts to jog. That, or one of the aliens is playing grab-ass.

"Hey, wait up!" he yells, a little too loudly.

The *thwup-thwup-thwup-thwup* of a helicopter grows louder. He stops and looks up as a spotlight illuminates the street between him and the girls. The pilot is searching for someone on the ground. Connor watches as it circles overhead, the light sweeping across several of his neighbors' yards. The helicopter makes two more passes, then the light winks out as it flies off in the direction where the meteorites would've landed.

He looks back down the street for Gabbi. Either the girls were too busy on their phones to notice, or they weren't interested, because they'd kept walking and were almost two blocks away now.

He runs after them.

By the time he catches up with the group, Gabbi and her friends are gone. Now it's just the aliens.

"Hey kids, where's Gabbi?" He wheezes, struggling to catch his breath. His stomach rumbles at the smell of barbequed meat. Maybe next year he'll drag their grill out to the front drive and pass out hamburgers and hot dogs to the parents. It would be nice to have a new tradition. He just needs to find Gabbi first so he can go home and rescue Traci.

The aliens stare up at him.

"Gabbi, where are you? Kasey? Debi?" His voice raises a little with each name.

Nobody answers.

He calls her phone, but it goes straight to voice mail.

"Ha, ha, very funny, girls," he says. They're probably hiding behind the bushes, having a good laugh at the old man. Or even worse, filming him. That'd be the perfect capper to the night.

He moves to push his way past the nearest alien. "Come on, Timmy, Kimmy, whichever one you are, scoot out of the way." One of its tentacles smacks him. Hard. "*Fuck!*" He yanks his hand back. There's a sucker mark on his wrist. The alien looks up at him and lets loose a string of squeaks.

"You're not Timmy," he says, staring down at the alien who hit him. He sweeps his gaze over the group. Timmy and Kimmy aren't there, either.

"Okay, this has gone far enough," he says. "Where's my daughter? Where are the other kids?" He stands tall and puts some extra bass in his voice, in full adult mode now. He can't let these kids know he's a little spooked.

But what if they're not *kids?*

The street's gone quiet. Even the Emersons' scary music has stopped.

The aliens form a loose circle around him. "Please, did any of you see where they went?" His voice cracks, but he doesn't care. His daughter is missing, and finding her is all that matters.

Ding!

He nearly drops his phone. It's a video call from Traci. There are aliens pressed up against every window. Their eye stalks sway as they peer into the house. The tips of their lasers glow a fiery orange.

"Help," she whispers. "They're all around the house now. I turned out the lights, but I'm afraid to move. I don't want them to know I'm in here alone." She turns the phone to her face. *"Come home now!"* she says through clenched teeth. He hears glass break. Traci screams as a brilliant white light fills the screen.

The call disconnects.

Fuck! Traci needs him, but he can't leave without Gabbi. He tries calling Traci back. His phone beeps, then disconnects again. He tries calling Gabbi, but this time his phone shuts down.

"What the hell?" He smacks it a couple times, but the screen stays dark.

"Gabbi, your mom's in trouble," he yells. "We have to go!"

He turns to run, but the aliens have closed tight around him. The tips of their lasers glow orange as they take aim.

Overhead, the sky is filled with shooting stars.

KATRINA'S HALLOWEEN CANDY JOURNAL (2023)

by Patrick Flanagan

Octtober 31 2013, Katrina G Fonderbirg recording, Age 11. Costume is Pumpkin Princess, design copywrite Katrina G Fonderbirg. Starting address is 2117 El Dorado Lane.

Other trick-or-treaters:

-Jessi Maxwell, costume is A Cowboy (but not Woody), also no Gun

-Janelle DiMartino, costume is Wolverine but as a girl

-Kiria Sands, costume is Princess (blue dress)

-Holly Daniels, costume is Princess (green dress)

-Maureen Smith, costume is An Elephunt

Katrina established the marching order like an air traffic controller lining up Airbuses over O'Hare. Jessi was first in line on the sidewalk, the scout. She separated the princesses with Janelle because she wanted to show off the group's variety and three princesses in a row was too much for her to handle.

"But you're not a princess," Kiria mentioned casually.

That threw her into a Class 4 tizzy. "*I am so!*" she said through gritted teeth. "I'm a *Pumpkin Princess.*" She said it as if she were almost embarrassed to have to point out such an obvious fact, even though Pumpkin Princesses hadn't existed two days ago when she first thought the concept up. Her faded orange jack-o'-lantern costume was draped over her like bad upholstery, but she strode around in it like she was Catherine the Great. "What's the big, anyway?"

The ordinary, non-vegetable-based princesses carefully did *not* exchange a look, at least not before Kat turned her back to them. *What's the big?* was Katrina for *Just shut up and do it my way.* Which more often than not, they did.

Janelle was fully in character by this point, although she seemed to confuse Wolverine with a werewolf, because she kept growling and raking the air with her plastic claws. Maureen, Katrina's weirdo fat cousin from Delaware who they'd all just met tonight, stood silently in the rear. Her elephant mask was listing to the left.

"Let's *go*," Katrina ordered, and Jessi dutifully snapped to and took them out of the driveway. Katrina wanted them marching on the sidewalk because she thought it looked cuter and what's the big, anyway. "I'll film it for us."

So stay off your *phones*, Holly thought at Kiria, who seemed to intercept the thought with another smirk.

Katrina was in Seventh Heaven. *Finally,* they had graduated from having to go to "Trunk-or-Treat" in the high school parking lot with all the babies. She had been working on Mommy and Daddy for over a month to get permission to trick-or-treat through the whole development by themselves, and her efforts had paid off. As much as her friends found her annoying, they had to admit that she got her way a lot.

Maureen had helped, with her You Know What, but Katrina didn't see why she had to share that with the group.

1) *Van Vliet house – Candy was 2 Hershey miniatures each. I picked 2 Mr. Goodbars because they are best. Mrs. Van Vliet was friendly –* <u>*NO COSTUME*</u>*, might return*

2) *Kennedy house – No answer, lights on inside. Hiding?? Will* <u>*DEFFO*</u> *return later*

3) *Wong house –* <u>*GREAT YARD, giant spider and cemetary stones, skull on front porch*</u>*. Mrs. Wong had spider costume thoguh, which is bad (repeatition). Candy was Skittles which is GOOD*

4) *Parsons house – no answer, lights off. Excused*

They suffered their first casualty at the end of the first block. Jessi's cell phone began singing "Thank U, Next" and she stepped out of formation to answer. In less than a minute, she was telling her mom she was on her way home. "Sorry, thanks," she yelled without turning around, already across the street.

"She didn't even *put up a fight*," Katrina said, exasperated.

Kiria and Holly thought the same thing at one another. *Why didn't I do that??* Now they were stuck with Kat until she got bored with the whole thing. *Actual* trick-or-treating had sounded fun at first when Katrina had brought it up earlier in the week, but the princesses had quickly gotten bored. It was basically begging, and it was a lot easier to just have their parents *give* them the candy so they could stay home and game. Even Janelle had dropped the growling bit and was now just swinging her claws jauntily. She'd scratched one of her sideburns off because the glue was too itchy.

Beneath her crooked pachyderm head, Maureen wheezed. Or… coughed. They weren't sure what the sound was. It was wheezing, nasally. Like trying to snap a bundle of wet twigs that are too soggy to break, so they just crack and grind together.

Katrina reached out and took her flopping felt glove in her hand. "Everything okay, Mo?"

Wolverine and the princesses watched Maureen not nod.

It was kind of weird that she hadn't taken her mask off, actually. It was warm for October, and it looked like it would be really hot inside that thing.

But finally, her trunk twitched as she rocked her head back and forth a little bit, which Katrina took as an *All is well*.

Maureen began to cough something up, but nobody turned around to look.

Almost over. It was almost over. Kat would get bored soon and release them. Had to.

5) *Fontaine house – Bazooka gum, YUCK. No costume!!*
   VISIT LATER

6) *Hart house – NO ANSWER! VISIT!*

7) *Fishbein house - <u>!!!TOOTHBRUSHES!!!</u> – UNACCEP-*
   TIBLE!!!

8) *Kyle house – NO ANSWER!!! CAN SEE PEOPLE*
   INSIDE

Kiria was the next to rebel, and Katrina quashed her defiance immediately, but it didn't last. As they reached the twin shrubs which guarded the end of Hauser Lane, Katrina's group disintegrated on her. She used all her considerable willpower and yes, charisma, if it could be called such, to keep them in line, but the rebels had a trump card.

"It's getting dark," they kept repeating. And it was—darker by the minute.

"One more block," Katrina commanded, but she could hear the pleading in her own voice.

Behind her, Maureen shuffled her big elephant feet uneasily. Katrina shook her head ever so slightly.

Wolverine almost…*almost* backed down, but the princess twins were united.

"My mom will be *mad* at me," Holly said, as if proud of the fact. "I'll see you tomorrow in school."

And with that, the group collapsed.

Katrina told herself she wouldn't scream. For whatever reason, she had gotten it into her head that tonight would be some kind of epic quest for candy, that they would break out of the usual neighborhood confines and discover some mythical, fairy tale housing block. One her parents never drove through while she sat in the back seat. One where it was Halloween every week and all the grown-ups wore costumes and each yard was haunted by gigantic papier-mâché monsters and festooned with cobwebs thick as cotton candy. And every house handed out full-sized candy bars or giant bags of gummies.

Katrina's mom delighted in pointing out how *big* she was—it was one of the few subjects which banished the bossy, assertive Katrina back to the shadows—and she should have known that if such a magical neighborhood was within marching distance that her mom and dad would never let her trick-or-treat there by herself. Well, maybe with Maureen's help.

It was a dumb baby idea, she concluded, trying to scrub away her disappointment.

But walking back home, passing all the houses with empty bowls on the porch and front yards unblighted by tombstones or scarecrows, the disappointment curdled into anger.

No. Halloween. Spirit.

Didn't people *understand* how important this was to Katrina Geraldine Fonderbirg from late September to early November? Didn't they *care*? Why were they acting like she wasn't *important*?

Maureen gurgled, perhaps sympathetically.

Back home, Ed and Ellen Fonderbirg sat motionless at their kitchen table. The lights hadn't been on when the girls had left, and the house was getting dark. A few kids had knocked on the front door, but they hadn't gotten up to answer.

An ant crawled up Ellen Fonderbirg's arm. She could feel it, but it marched up past her elbow inside her shirt, out of view.

Katrina didn't go home, not to her home anyway, but to Maureen's home. Maureen lived in the woods past the end of Geller Lane, the place her dad always called *"Tragically Undeveloped Real Estate."* When Dad said things like that it made Katrina grin from ear to ear. She loved using special names for things like that. She could hear The Capital Letters. She really loved it when Dad said *quote and quote* before giving something a special name. But the forest, the Tragically Undeveloped Real Estate, that was where Katrina had found her a week ago. Maureen wasn't really her cousin from Delaware, that was just The Story she told her friends. When Katrina lied, it wasn't really a lie; it was just The Story.

"Sorry, Mo," she said to the elephant. "I thought we would really clean up tonight, but this neighborhood sucks. You saw, right?"

Maureen didn't nod, but Katrina felt her respond. *Yes. Saw.*

"Less than half of the houses had decorations!" Katrina stomped through mounds of dead leaves and sticks. She waved her composition book, containing all the evidence she'd gathered of the neighborhood's undeniable and unforgiveable misdeeds she'd ever need. "And little bags of candy? Not even full-sized?"

You're already *full-sized as it is, Katie,* her mom would have said, bringing tears to her cheeks.

"I don't *care* if I'm Full-Sized, Mommy. I *want—my—candy!*" The Feeling had a hold of her now, had wrapped its thin red fingers around her and was squeezing the rage out of her body. When things got bad and she couldn't change them, she got The Feeling. An incoherent, wordless, blinding helplessness. It was the worst feeling in all the world, The Feeling, and the only way to banish it was to scream and kick and break something and hit somebody. She couldn't stand not being in control of everything.

Under her costume, Maureen began shuddering. It took every iota of self-control not to tear off the coverings the human had draped over its form. The link was strong, and not easily severed, and Maureen was getting the Feeling now, too.

Katrina was the only real person in the world, so bad things weren't bad when she did them; they were something else. It was easy to think about when you looked at it like that. Like when Mommy's cat, Angie, had run away. That wasn't true; that was The Story she told Mommy and Daddy. Daddy didn't care, but Mommy was upset. So Katrina thought up The Story to keep her from getting really mad. It was better that way. She had gotten The Feeling when Angie had scratched her, and then later, she fixed it. And Mommy had never found out. That was an eternity ago, almost two whole years. Back then, The Feeling never came on as it strongly as it did these days.

Katrina Geraldine Fonderbirg, age eleven, the Pumpkin Princess, threw her head back and howled. Not yelled, not screamed. Howled. An animal's sound. She closed her eyes so tightly she could feel them bruise, and howled until her throat felt swollen and raw.

She opened her eyes…and saw through Maureen's eyes, too.

It had happened for a second back home, when Mommy had tried putting her foot down, and even Daddy too. No. That was the word that gave her The Feeling more than anything else did. They told her "No," even though she had *patiently* and *politely* explained the quest for candy to them, how she was certain it would be magical, but "No…" They had said "No." And she had screamed, and Maureen, who had been sitting in the closet for over two hours, had walked into the kitchen and did it to them.

Katrina had blinked and was back in herself and blinked the pain out of her eyes as she looked at her parents, trapped in psionically-induced paralysis. She had poked their cheeks and giggled as her parents just sat there. Just sat there and did nothing. It was *the best*. She had almost showed Kiria and Jessi and the rest, but she didn't want to start trick-or-treating late.

It had lasted for a second and then gone away. But not now.

She was in Maureen's brain—or in the spongy, gelatinous organelle which passed for its brain—and Maureen was in hers. And The Feeling... *The Feeling* was in both of them—bright and fiery and awful as the midday sun.

Katrina's feet were moving without her realizing it. Maureen was leading her now. And Katrina realized, as she climbed down into the muddy depression just past the mighty skeletal remains of the huge uprooted tree, that the hole was a lot bigger once you ducked down low enough. That there was a big, big hole under the ground. Not backyard big, but garage big. Big enough for Maureen to hide what she'd been hiding.

It didn't look like a *real* spaceship, shiny and metal like in the movies, but Katrina trusted her friend. It was gray, the color of mud, or dishwater, or dead skin. And rough to the touch. Lumpy, uneven. But there was room enough for the both of them.

Katrina didn't even get to say, "Blast off!" Which disappointed her. But not for long.

9) *Donohoe house –* NO CANDY, NO DECORATIONS. MR. DONOHOE IN THE LIVING ROOM!! *Blew up whole house, car melted with laser-ray*

10) *Krieger house – Mr. Krieger smelled bad, only gave one mini candy per person – blasted off wall, shot him with laser-ray – burned – let Jason and Mrs. Krieger go, theyre nice*

11) *Gelbwasser house – pulled front off of house, fired missile inside – house collapsed – NO DECORATIONS*

12) *Carmichael house – no deocrations, Mrs. Carmichael was mean when I wanted more candy than one – used spaceship arms (tenticles?), grabbed and pulled her up and then into parts*

13) *Sizemore house – was excused for good decorations BUT!! Mr. Sizemore shot his shotgun at us – laser-ray – exploded*

14) *Dunlop house – full Nestle bars – excused*

Katrina's chubby face was ruddy with excitement, her eyes crinkled with laugh lines. This was what she had wanted! She was in control now. All the people who had not done what she wanted, not behaved exactly how she wanted them to, would be gone soon. It was like the best video game, where somebody wins it and then handed her the controller and said, "You won! You won, Katrina!"

She was! She was winning now! The entire neighborhood was burning down. There were police down below, clearly unsure what they were seeing but shooting their stupid guns anyway. Not that they did anything. Katrina couldn't even hear the bullets bouncing off the ship. And *there* was the Wingfield house on the next street. Their candy had been great, Kit Kats and mini Twixes, take as many as you want...and she did. But Mr. Wingfield called her *pudgy* once. He hadn't known she'd heard him, but she had. She squeezed her eyes and her face and The Feeling bubbled up again. And she felt Maureen's hands—her hands—working the controls, setting the squiggly targeting crosshairs directly on the Wingfield's stupid German shepherd.

She was so ecstatic that she didn't even mind Maureen touching her head. At least it felt like she was. Katrina didn't fully understand what was happening, couldn't understand that spaghetti-thin strands of nerve endings coated in an anesthetic slime had already pushed through Katrina's optic and nasal cavities and were already rummaging through her temporal lobe, sniffing out that resentment-engorged amygdala. Once the harvesting was complete, it would be easy enough to pry off the roof of her skull and finish the absorption process. A strong, healthy bipedal form, with a cerebral cortex dripping with unused potential, could serve Maureen as a host body for decades.

But first, another Butterfinger. Or perhaps two. Maybe Katrina didn't want the ones in her bag.

THE WIND

by Brennan Fredricks

I t's just the wind. Deep breath. It's just the wind. Light a cigarette if you can. Put a lip in if you can't. Sip your energy drink. Stay calm. Stay awake. Keep moving. Keep looking. Keep listening. Keep smelling. It's just the wind. Stay calm.

Soon the watch will be over. Soon you'll hear your buddy stirring. Or soon it'll be five 'til and you can kick him awake yourself. Then it'll be his problem. Then you can go back to your warm sack. And in the morning, the only thing to dread is another fifteen-mile foot march. Soon.

Stay awake, stay calm. It's just the wind. It's just the goddamn wind. It's always the wind. If it's not the wind, it's an animal. And if it's not an animal it's…

It's just the goddamn wind. It's always the wind.

The wind is always against you. It makes cold colder, and hot hotter. When it's wet, it pelts you. When it's dry, it burns you. It gives chaos to peace, and peace to chaos. It chaps, and bites, and gnaws, and bludgeons you. It exposes you and conceals your adversaries. It forges new adversaries in the darkness. The wind is always against you.

So, you light your cigarette. You lip your chaw. You sip your energy drink. You steady your optics, and you gaze out across the empty desert. Is that movement? Are those footsteps? Are those whispers? Shapes manifest in the darkness all around you. You can't see them, but they're there. And they most definitely see you. They always see you. But you will never see them. And they know you. They know beneath all that gear you're just a scared little kid. They know those high speed NVGs and that thermal scope make no meaningful difference. They know that weapon in your hand is useless. They aren't tools; they're symbols. And here in this darkness, those symbols are meaningless.

The wind is still at it. Those shapes are moving closer—whispering, plotting, pointing. If you don't wake up your team leader, you'll all be dead. If you do wake him up, he'll make you wish you were dead. The wind knows this. The shapes in the darkness know it, too. And most of all, you know it. It's a shared understanding between the three of you. The game you play.

You aren't guarding anything. You aren't watching anything. Like your tools, you too are nothing more than a symbol. A sculpture. A banner. A scarecrow. You'll never spot them. You can't fight them; you can't stop them. You can only outlast them. You can only wait silently, all the while knowing they're here and they're coming. One more hour. Can you make it? Stay awake. Stay calm. Light a cigarette if you can, put in a lip if you can't. Sip your energy drink. Adjust your optics. Move. Stop, listen, look, smell. Think. Think back.

You're nine years old. It's Halloween. You're all alone walking the streets of your sleepy, Southern plantation-style suburb. It's getting late. The other kids have already retreated to their houses for the night. Treat time is over. Now it's all tricks. And spooks. And darkness.

The long, lonely stretch of road that passes between the front and back of the neighborhood. Where the streetlights and houses end, and the forest begins. Its dark, twisted limbs overhang the cracked and potholed pavement like a canopy, trapping it in shadow.

You're reaching the edge of the light. You see the stretch of gloom before you. Calling you to it. Taunting you with a thin whisper. You hear the sudden hoot of an owl in a tree somewhere, obscured. The howls of coyotes somewhere not so far away.

You're alone. Where is your brother? He said he'd meet you here by now. He said he wouldn't make you walk alone.

Earlier in the evening, after your parents had left for the night to attend their own Halloween festivities, your fourteen-year-old brother, your caretaker for the night, had treated you to your first horror flick—a bootleg copy of *The Legend of Sleepy Hollow*.

He called it hokey and stupid, and laughed his way through the antics of Johnny Depp's Ichabod Crane, and the headless Hessian horseman. He laughed even harder as you gasped, and cringed, and hid your eyes as the horseman tore through the twisted forest trail chasing his prey toward the bridge.

That dark, twisted forest trail that looked not unlike the one now before you. You stop there on the edge of the light, just before the shadow, peering down the long dark. A few meters away, there's a creek. The road dips down across it, then slopes up again into the forest trail. The dark, despairing, twisted branches that encircle it shrink in over the road as you peer into them.

You wait. You're not going alone. One minute. Two minutes. Five minutes. You're not going alone. Ten minutes. Nothing. No one. No choice. You take a deep breath. You shudder; you sniffle. You try not to cry. You take a step and start the long dark trek.

Alone.

It's not all bad at first. Quiet. Gloomy. You feel your heart beating steadily, but not racing. Not yet. You start down the slope in the dip of the road. You reach the bottom and gaze over the guardrails into the creek.

You go on. Into the forest canopy. The stars disappear in the gloom. There's no moon. No light. No sound. Just your breath and your heartbeat growing faster.

Fifty yards in or so the sounds begin. Creaks. Cracks. Snaps. Rustling. It's just squirrels. You press on. Chirps, and hoots, and gasps. It's just the crickets. Just the birds. The bats. Just the sounds of the forest. Your heart's beating faster. You keep walking.

You're cursing your brother now. Where was he? He was supposed to be here. He was supposed to take you trick-or-treating and then walk you home. But he'd abandoned you early on and told you to walk with other kids. He'd gone to hang out with his older friends. You told him you didn't want to walk this road alone. He told you he'd meet you at the last house at 9:00. Now, here you are, alone.

And suddenly you hear a shrill cry in the air. A whisper. A breath. It bellows behind you, forcing its way through the twisted overhang of dead limbs and branches. You hold your breath. It passes. It's just the wind. It's just the wind. Your heart's beating faster. You keep walking. It's just the wind. Another gasp wisps through the trees behind you. You feel its cold respirations against your back, against your skin. Against the hairs that are standing up on your neck. It's just the wind.

You can see the light again now, at the end of the long, twisted road. You're nearly out. You're nearly safe again. Just another hundred yards or so. You start to feel relieved.

Then it hits you again. The whisper. The gasp. The hollow shrill breath passing through the dead, gloomy trees. But it's just the wind. You're fine. It's just the wind.

But you notice the sound is different now. It's not a whisper. It's a whine. An eerie, buzzing whine. You turn to look behind you. Nothing to see but the gloom. It's…it's just the wind.

Keep walking. But the whine grows louder, closer.

You turn again. Now you see it—a pale glow some few hundred feet behind you. Your heart skips. You feel a cold icy terror flow through your entire body. It's getting closer. It's coming.

In your mind you see the fiery pumpkin head of the headless horseman. You hear his shrill cry, chasing you. In terror, you begin to run. You sprint for the light, for the houses, for safety. Like Ichabod sprinting for the bridge. The sound chases you. You don't dare look back.

As you run for your life, you hear its whine become a voice. It's calling for you. It's calling your name! It's after you! Run!

You're almost there, but it's right behind you. You have to make it to the light!

Then, just before you pass into the light, you hear the voice become familiar. You hear it shouting your name in frustration. You turn to look and see the pale glow of the golf cart's headlights. You see your brother in the passenger seat, next to his friend, driving the golf cart.

"What the hell is wrong with you kid? I told you to wait at the other side!"

Wake up. Are you sleeping? Were you asleep? No. Maybe. Who knows? Shit. They can shoot you for that, y'know. What did you miss? Look down in the valley. Look at the road. Did something pass by? Slap yourself. Sip your energy drink. It's all gone. Damn it. It didn't do a damn thing for you, anyway.

Light a cigarette. Look out. Stop. Listen. Look. Smell. Is that a glow in the distance? Is that a fire you smell? Are those whispers? Those shapes in the darkness have moved even closer by now. Look at your watch. 0335. Twenty-five minutes 'til the witching hour is over. Twenty-five minutes 'til your shift is over.

Another huff of wind assaults you at full blast. The sand strikes you in all the most inconvenient places. All around you, in the darkness, the desert is warping to the shape of the wind. In the morning, that whole valley will look different. In the morning, that whole valley will be gone. Either buried in the sand or taken away with the wind to another spot, another valley, another dimension. Pray it doesn't take you away with it.

You shiver and scratch and rub your eyes. Fuck this.

Fuck this.

You're sixteen. It's Halloween. You're Bob Dylan, but nobody gets it. The loud music and ambient sounds of twenty or thirty different voices drone out the sound of the TV. You're on the couch between two other dudes who are either too stoned, too drunk, or both to move. You're watching Halloween. The original. You've never seen it. Your family has a thing about horror movies. Despite this, you don't find it the least bit scary. But Mike Meyer's mask is sick. Even you must admit.

The newest girl of your dreams is making out with one of your best friends somewhere a few meters behind you. You're stuck there on that couch, paralyzed with dope, alcohol, depression, and angst. You can't look at them. And you can't leave.

But you can go outside. Onto the porch. You can light a cigarette and play the wounded, brooding, stranger. So, you do.

Outside there's two girls talking. You ignore them and master the scene. Light a cigarette. Stare into the distance. Somewhere there are more important things going on. There are problems waiting for you to solve them. There's a war in Afghanistan. There are children dying in the streets all over. There are unanswerable questions and impossible feats waiting for you. Let your friend have the girl. You have more important things to worry about. You have deep questions to answer. You have a world to save.

One of the girls goes inside. An awkward moment of silence follows as one remains. She's pretty. You've seen her before, but you don't know her name. She's not the girl you want—the one making out with your friend. But she's a decent distraction. And suddenly she's buying your whole act. She's asking what you're thinking. You're giving her an answer that will make you cringe several years from now. But right now, it's working. Then she's kissing you, and you're kissing her. And touching her. And feeling her. It lasts only seconds, but to you, it feels like hours. To you it's time eternal.

But, like all good things… The door opens. The session ends. You turn to see the girl of your dreams hanging out the door. Her face is ambiguous. Is she surprised? Is she impressed? Is she jealous? She's telling what's-her-face it's time to leave. You don't even catch her name before she's abandoning you on the porch. But it doesn't matter. You're still on cloud nine. You light a cigarette and savor the moment. Suddenly, those problems in the world don't seem to matter so much. And, before long, your friends pop out the door and tell you it's time to scram, too.

You start the long walk home still on cloud nine. You talk. You light a joint. You walk. Your friend is talking about the girl of your dreams of yester-hour. They're gonna hook up soon. Maybe tomorrow. An hour ago, this would have torn your world apart. Now, it doesn't matter at all.

You're nearing the crossroads where he will split to his abode and you to yours. You're looking forward to a long walk home, in the blissful, doped up company of the Stones, Dylan, and a few dozen indie tracks on your iPod. Maybe even some Miles Davis if the mood strikes you. But your friend has one last trick up his sleeve. Or rather, in his backpack. A fresh roll of duct tape.

His eyebrows raise along with his smile as he holds it out to you. Tradition. You can't help but smile back and nod in full-hearted agreement.

Quickly, you set about laying the first strip across the road, before dashing as fast as you can to the knolls of the golf course that borders the roads just fifty meters off or so. You wait. Five minutes pass. You're starting to get bored. And then you see headlights riding the curves of the road just a little ways off. Game time.

The car pulls around the bend. It never has a chance. All at once, you hear the satisfying click-click-click of the tape wrapping itself around its target. The car slows to a stop just a few feet ahead. The driver steps out. Looks. Curses. Swears vengeance.

But he's tired. He probably just got off a long shift at a job he hates. Something you couldn't understand. Something he likely didn't understand, either, just a few years ago. But now he's piling back in his car, and driving, and clicking his way down the road, 'til he passes out of sight and sound. And you're laughing, and high fiving your buddy.

You repeat the ritual a second time to the same effect. Same slow stop. Same puzzled look. Same curses. Same swears. Click-click-click. Laugh-laugh-laugh.

One more? Of course!

But this one is different. This one is an old van. Dim light. Worn, black paint. Serial Killer van. Driver in generic coveralls. Pale face.

Silent. No curses this time. No swears. Just a pale face staring across the fairway. Your heart races as he looks. And not in the fun way. Seconds of staring. Minutes, hours, nights, years. An eternity.

You're not looking anymore. Neither is your friend. You're looking at each other in unspoken terror. Suddenly, it's not fun anymore.

You feel a great relief as you hear him climb back in his van. There's another click-click-click but no laughs this time. Just relief.

"All right, man," you both say to each other. "Enough for tonight." Handshake. Hug. See you tomorrow, brother. And out of nowhere the wind begins to blow.

Walk.

Down the road, headphones in, vibing. Peace. Serenity. You're high as a kite. Your thoughts race between passionate scenes that flow with music, and the lips of some angel on someone's back porch. All is right in the world. No problems to solve. The problems can go to hell. You're in heaven.

All at once it's dark. The streetlights end, and you're staring down a dark twisted road. You're looking at that dark forest canopy. The way it caves in across the road, filling the void of the shadows. You feel small. It's dark. It's twisted. It's long and lonely. It's quiet. It's gloomy. You're at the edge of the light. You pull out your headphones, and suddenly you're walking in silence.

But it's not silent. Not really. In fact, it's loud. Louder than your headphones. A steady flow of white noise from the wind blowing at your back, through the shadows, through the dead and twisted trees. Owls hoot. Coyotes howl. There are noises in the trees. Is that movement? Is that the wind? Is that the last of the autumn leaves shedding their foundations?

You're getting closer to the end of the shadow. You can see

the light now. Soon you'll be out of the darkness, and you'll pop headphones back in. Soon the music will play again. Just walk.

The wind is getting harder. Getting louder. Getting scarier. It's not steady either. Not a flow, but a gasp. A breath. Coming in rapidly. Blowing out slowly. The trees groan. Twigs snap. Invisible creatures stalk, and scurry, and slither.

The breaths of wind grow stronger, mimicking your own. Your heart begins to race along with your mind. They bounce around looking for hope. Looking for a future. An adventure, a journey, a challenge, a prize. A girl on a porch. A girl hanging out the door. Was she jealous?

A loud and crashing gasp. A van. Coveralls. A thousand-meter stare. A pale face. A mask. Silent. Still. Ominous. A knife. Blood. Stalking you. Always there, never seen. Never heard. Until…

There's a noise in the distance. Behind you. You tell yourself it's the wind, but in your soul, you know it's not. It's coming. Closer. You hear it crossing the dip in the road, over the creek. You hear the whine of the engine. You recognize it. Click-click-click.

Now you see it. Headlights. It's coming. He's coming. He's coming for you. And no girl on any porch can stop him. But don't be silly. Don't be ridiculous. You're no longer a child. You're not going to run.

But it's getting closer. And going faster. You hear the engine rev. You hear the axle turning. Click-click-click. It's coming for you. It's going to get you. Don't be silly. Don't be ridiculous. You're no longer a child. Run!

So you do. You run for the light. You run for your life. The engine revs behind you. It's right there. It's almost on you! Run!

You're looking for a ditch. You're looking for safety. Looking for a back porch, and a cigarette, and a girl kissing you. And another girl hanging out the door. But it's not there. Only the headlights are there. And the engine whining. And the axle. Click–click–click. The lights are bearing down on you. You're running for your life. You see them glow and grow on you. Spotlighting you. Exposing you in the pale-yellow glow. And all at once…the pale-yellow changes. Suddenly, its red and blue.

The engine slows. The whining stops. The clicks dissipate. The vehicle pulls beside you. 'Constable,' reads the letters on the side of the white SUV. A stern face leans out the window.

"What the hell are you doing kid?"

Another breath of wind shakes you. The desert trembles underneath you, and you tremble with it. You shake yourself and find you can no longer tell which shivers are voluntary and which are compelled. You try to steady yourself against the wind, but it's too fierce. You hide your eyes beneath your arms as the sand whips you with ten thousand microscopic lashes.

It's over now. The darkness is upon you. The shapes are closing in. They caught you slipping. They caught you sleeping. It's all over now, baby blue. Prepare yourself. Grip your rifle. Stop. Listen. Look. Smell. Get ready.

All at once, a voice calls above the wind. "Yo, Fred."

With the call, the wind seems to subside. The desert settles. The darkness falls back. You hear the voice again. "Yo, Fred!"

You turn to see your buddy walking up to your position on the hill. "Sorry I'm late, man. I just couldn't tear myself out of my sack."

You look at your watch. It's 0405. The witching hour is over. The shift is finally done.

"It's all good, man," you say, letting your hatred stay silent.

He sets up beside you and looks around, shivering. "Happy fucking Halloween, brother," he says. "Anything going on?"

Just then another howl bellows through the vast of the desert. For a moment, it feels like the very foundations of the earth might shatter. The dust swirls. The bushes flail. The body trembles. The darkness closes in on both of you. The shapes set in. Ready to fire. Ready to kill. Then at last, once more, the gasp subsides. The dust settles. The earth steadies itself.

You light your last cigarette and look at your buddy. "Nah, man," you say through a puff of smoke. "Just the fucking wind."

FREE CANDY AND TELESCOPE VIEWS

by Red Lagoe

Estelle had never been in detention before, but questioning her fifth grade teacher's intelligence on the pronunciation of Uranus was apparently a one-way ticket. She'd moved to town last week, and with Dad being overly critical of every little thing, she didn't mind staying after school if it meant not going home.

In detention hall, she sat beside a boy named Van, who she wasn't permitted to talk to, so she had no idea what kind of person this kid was. Not that it mattered; she'd befriend anyone if it meant she didn't have to go home. When the bell rang, they headed out, and Van flipped off the teacher while her back was turned.

Estelle forced a laugh and walked alongside him. "That was boring."

Van's face soured.

"Are you going trick-or-treating tonight?" she asked.

"Nah. That's for babies."

"Yeah, but it's candy. When else do grown-ups give us candy for no reason?"

Van wasn't impressed. He swung open the school doors and they stepped into the brisk autumn air. Thick, dark clouds loomed overhead, obscuring any chance of seeing the stars tonight. When Dad lost his job in the city and dragged her to a trailer park on the outskirts of this tiny town, the open skies and promise of no light pollution was the only thing she looked forward to. Without her friends as an excuse to get away from home for the evening, all she had was her love of astronomy. She fully intended on sleeping in the truck bed all night long under a canopy of stars. But since she moved here last week, there hadn't been a single clear night.

She lowered her eyes back to the earth, where crunchy maple leaves shattered into pieces underfoot, and hurried to catch up with Van. "Everyone loves candy."

"Yeah, but this town sucks."

Estelle desperately wanted to go somewhere tonight and wouldn't mind having someone to run to when things at home got bad. Making a friend was a necessity. "Then forget the candy. It's called trick-or-treat for a reason. The *tricks*."

Van trudged through the ankle-deep layer of fallen leaves. "What kind of tricks? Like egging houses and stuff?"

"Sure." She'd rather cook up the eggs and eat them than waste them on a prank, but despite her rumbling stomach, she agreed.

"We should egg Ms. Roberts' house." Van's eyes narrowed as he grinned.

Seeing that made her insides uncomfortable. Estelle buried her gut feeling. "Let's do it."

"It's payback time," Van said. "I'll meet you at the fountain when it gets dark."

She headed downtown, zippering her hoodie against the chill in the air. The public library was open, so she meandered in to pass the time by exploring the science shelves.

It was much smaller than the libraries she was used to, but it would have to do. She ran her fingers along the dusty spines, her fingers passing over titles about math, geology, chemistry, and… *yes*, astronomy. Tucked into the same section were just as many witchcraft books. This made her laugh a little to herself.

She sat with a book on stargazing, then skimmed through an astrophysics text she didn't understand. When it was time to go meet up with Van, the librarian stopped her at the door. "You best not be stealing any books!"

Estelle shook her head. "I'm not."

"So, you don't mind if I look in that bag of yours?"

She did mind, but she didn't know how to say no to a grown-up. Estelle clutched her straps and shook her head.

The librarian, an older woman with ice-blonde hair, approached her with high-arched eyebrows. She rummaged through Estelle's backpack with a ruler.

"I didn't steal anything."

The woman looked down her nose. "Socks and underwear…a toothbrush." She stepped back and crossed her arms. "You running away?"

"No." Estelle jerked away and zipped her bag. "I gotta go."

Estelle and Van had canvased the entire town, and since they were without costumes, several people refused to dish out the candy. Van said he was making a list in his head of all the places he needed to egg later. They ended the night at the edge of town, in front of Ms. Roberts' house, where Van had stashed a dozen eggs.

It was getting late. The streets had emptied of trick-or-treaters and their helicopering parents, and Estelle sat on the sidewalk digging through the bottom of her backpack for candy, gobbling down anything to quell the hunger.

Van chucked an egg at Ms. Roberts' house and ducked behind the overgrown shrubs to sit with Estelle.

She drew her knees to her chest, dreading the end of the evening—that moment when she'd have to tiptoe into her house, hopefully unseen. Best case scenario, Dad would be drunk and passed out, but she feared 9:30 p.m. wasn't late enough for that.

Before they moved to this town, she could easily stay the night at her friend's house to avoid her dad, but now she had nowhere to hide. The bruises on her wrist were hidden beneath a bulky sweatshirt where nobody would see them, but as she reached for the candy at the bottom of her bag, they rubbed against her notebook, reminding her of the raging, drunken fury she'd face later.

"Told you it sucks here on Halloween." Van inspected his plastic grocery store bag. "Bit-O-Honeys, Tootsies…ewww… a homemade popcorn ball…"

He pulled the sticky mess out of his bag and threw it across the street. It rolled to a stop by a small sign adorned with fairy lights that read: "Free candy and telescope views." An arrow pointed to a dark, unmarked street leading uphill through the woods outside town.

Estelle wiped the dirt from her butt and ran across the empty street under a pool of lamplight. "Telescope views! I wonder if they're doing sidewalk astronomy?"

Van sat unmoved from his position, unwrapping a piece of unidentifiable candy. He shrugged.

"I read about it. Astronomers set up telescopes on busy streets then let people look at planets and the moon and stuff. Some people even do it on Halloween for trick-or-treaters. I bet that's what it is!"

Van's brow furrowed. "So, are you, like, a nerd or something?"

"I just like space."

His raised eyebrow indicated he could see right through her cool-kid façade. " I'm not going up there." Van stood and nodded toward the dark, mysterious drive leading into the woods. Tall, naked-branched trees towered on either side and there were no streetlamps to light the path. At the top of the rounded hill, a break in the clouds allowed a view of the black, star-studded sky beyond.

"Look! The clouds are breaking!" Estelle's heart swelled. "That bright one is Jupiter!"

"You don't know that."

She pulled out her star app and lined it up with the sky, leaning closer to Van. "Right there. Jupiter."

Estelle didn't wait for Van to follow. She flung her backpack over her shoulder and headed into the darkness.

"That's a stupid idea!"

"Candy and telescopes! That's the best idea ever."

Van's sneakers smacked against the pavement as he caught up. "Seriously... The woman who lives up there is crazy."

Estelle slowed. The looming trees on either side seemed to grow taller, cloaking them in shadow.

"It sounds fake," Van said, "but everyone says she's, like, a witch or something."

It was so dark on this street that Estelle couldn't make out his features, but the steely silence that followed was enough for her to know he was serious.

"The whole town says it... They say she eats children."

Estelle burst into laughter. "If you're trying to scare me, it won't work."

Van grabbed her wrist. The sharp sting of pressure on her bruises made her wince. She yanked it away with no more than a flinch and flared nostrils. She continued her climb up the steep hill, and a soft yellow glow came into view as she neared the top.

Van kept up. "Last year on Halloween, my best friend Mark came up here and never came back. And the police didn't find nothing."

"Maybe they didn't find anything because..."—she wiggled her fingers creepily—"the witch ate him!" She fought a smirk.

"Fuck you."

"I just don't believe in witches and stuff..." She sighed. "I'm sorry your friend went missing. What do you think happened?"

"They said he ran away, but no way... Mark wouldn't do that. She *did* something to him."

Estelle patted him on the back, but she wasn't very good at consoling people. How could she genuinely feel bad for a kid who had run away from home when she wanted so badly to do the same? Tonight, Estelle would go home to a slap in the face, or more likely be shoved against the wall so hard the drywall would crack. In her eyes, this Mark kid was lucky.

"We could egg her house if it makes you feel better." She faced him, but he was nearly invisible against the black void of the street behind him.

"What's the point?"

"Are you scared?"

"No!"

"Then come on! I'm not missing this." Estelle marched up the hill to where the trees opened to a clearing and the street ended. There was only one house—a quaint, split-level home with vinyl siding and a warm yellow glow emanating from the windows. It was the kind of home she always dreamed of, one that welcomed and invited.

A sign identical to the one at the bottom of the hill directed them around the side of the home to the backyard. The clouds swirled black and purple at the edges of the hole, as if the sky had opened just for her. With her chin up, jaw hanging open, her foot caught on something soft—an animal—and Estelle nearly fell face-first, crashing to her elbow and scraping it to avoid stepping on the poor little creature.

Van stayed a few feet behind as a black cat cried out and darted away.

"I'm sorry, kitty!" Estelle brushed herself off. "I didn't see you!"

Van groaned. Part of her was desperate to make him like her, but another part was okay with letting him go. There was a meanness to him she couldn't stomach.

The black cat returned to Estelle. "Are you okay, kitty?"

It cautiously rubbed its face against her outstretched hand. As the cat circled, its body came into the light. There was no fur, only dark gray scar tissue covering the entire half.

Estelle pulled her hand away, afraid she might hurt the cat, but the leathery skin seemed to have healed long ago. "What happened to you?"

When it saw Van, it arched its back, growling and hissing, then sprinted away, disappearing behind the house.

"He doesn't like you." Estelle laughed.

"I don't care."

When Estelle looked in the direction where the cat had run off, a woman stood in shadow with her hands on her hips. She was tall, at least six feet, wearing jeans and an orange bubble vest. Hardly the pointed-hat, child-eating witch Van had spoken of, she clasped her hands together and smiled. "You trick-or-treaters are a little late. Before I pack up my equipment, do you wanna see Jupiter?"

"Yeah!" Estelle headed toward her

The tall woman gestured for them to follow, but Van lingered behind.

"What's the matter?" she asked.

"It's past my curfew. I gotta head back."

"Vaaan!" Estelle said. "Come on! I've never looked through a telescope before. My dad wouldn't let— One quick look and then we can go."

Van groaned and lumbered toward her, seemingly out of a need to act unafraid, rather than genuine interest in what she wanted to do. His eyes were locked on the woman in the orange vest like he was a predator ready to strike.

"Just around back. It'll only take a sec." She led the way, Estelle right on her heels, eager for what she was about to see.

"You don't look familiar," the woman said to Estelle as they rounded the corner into a dark backyard lined with red rope lights along the ground. "Are you new in town?"

"Yeah…"

"What's your name?"

"Estelle."

"I'm Marietta." She turned to Van who stood with his arms crossed. "Hello, Van. I'm glad you came tonight."

"How do you know my name?"

Estelle's eyes took a moment to adjust to the darkness. Red lights marked a perfect circle in the grass. Straight glowing lines led toward the center where a massive black tube stood tall and wide like some kind of circus cannon. It was a Dobsonian telescope—a simple tube structure with a big mirror in the bottom to collect light from the stars. The eyepiece was at the top, so high up that a step ladder was needed to look through it.

She'd read all about these types of telescopes, but this one was different. It wasn't a classic, manual design. Nor was it an elaborate electronic one with wires and cameras and Wi-Fi connections. This telescope was adorned with brass gears and, when she looked closely, they turned and clicked like moving clockwork structures. It pointed near the edge of the cloud cover, ticking with each second that passed, but didn't appear to be locked on Jupiter. It was aimed at a different patch of sky. Beside the telescope, a silver, curved satellite-like dish was aimed in the same direction.

Estelle gawked at it. "I've never seen one like this— "

"I asked," Van said, "how do you know my name?"

The woman ignored his question. "That's because there is no telescope like this one. I built it."

"Wow!"

"Well, technically my ancestors did, but I've made some tweaks of my own."

"Can I look in it?" Estelle asked.

Marietta held up an arm to block Estelle. "It's not ready yet. She gestured to a smaller telescope near the shed at the edge of the circle. It looked like one of the Schmidt-Cassegrain designs from the telescope magazines. This one had all the modern wires and connections. "Go take a peek through that one. It's tracking Jupiter."

Van raised his voice. "I asked—"

"I know your name because you've been to my house before."

"No, I haven't."

"Don't lie to me…"

A knot formed in Estelle's gut, which she ignored. This was her chance to see into space, to see Jupiter, some 400 million miles away. She leaned over the eyepiece and a small tan disk with cloud bands came into view. She soaked up everything and tried to lock it into her memories in case she never got the chance again. It made having to go home all the drearier. Tears blurred her vision, but she choked them back.

"You and your friend, Mark," Marietta said. "You were here a year back or so."

"What are you talking about?" Van said. "Estelle, let's go."

"Van, you gotta see this! I can see three…no, *four* of Jupiter's moons!"

"So what!" Van said. "I don't care about some stupid moons. This lady is fucking crazy."

Estelle's heart raced. She hated conflict more than she hated being hit, because conflict usually led to a beating. And while she didn't think Van or Marietta would start throwing punches, that worrisome feeling overwhelmed her.

"I'm sorry," she said to Marietta. "He's just a little nervous because his friend went missing last year."

"Understandable," she said, eyes locked on Van. "I'm sorry for your loss."

"I didn't lose him! He came here."

Estelle broke the discomfort the only way she knew how. "He thinks you eat children." She giggled nervously, hoping it sounded like a joke, but nobody laughed.

After a moment, Marietta sighed. "I know people in this town say things about me, and I don't care…" Her eyes drifted to the sky. "You know what I do like to eat?"

Estelle shrugged.

"Spaghetti." Marietta smiled.

"I like spaghetti, too. It's my favorite."

"I knew I liked you the moment I saw you." Marietta smiled, and it was as warm and inviting as the windows of her home. "Seamus likes you, too."

The cat walked a figure eight between Estelle's calves.

"Before you leave," Marietta said. "Take a look through the special telescope."

"Really?"

Marietta nodded. "Van...please take a look at Algol."

"Algol?" Estelle asked. It didn't sound familiar.

Van crossed his arms in defiance.

"If you won't I will." Estelle took a step forward but was stopped by an outstretched arm.

"Not you." Her words could've been daggers.

Estelle fell back sheepishly and quieted herself.

Marietta tilted her head and smirked. "Not yet, Estelle. The first view will be for Van—a peace offering."

"Van, just look already so I can," Estelle said. "Then we can go."

"Fine." He approached the step ladder and climbed to reach the eyepiece.

Marietta let out a long sigh. "There...that wasn't so hard."

Estelle swiped open her starry sky app and looked up Algol so she could know everything about it before she viewed it. It was a star.

"Van, I know your name," Marietta said while Van remained glued to the eyepiece, "because you and your friend Mark were playing in the woods behind my house a little over a year ago."

Mark remained still, eyes gazing through the telescope with his back to Estelle.

Marietta continued. "Though, I wouldn't call it 'playing.' What you were doing was downright evil, don't you think?"

"What happened?" Estelle asked, looking up from her phone. "Van, what'd you do?"

He didn't budge.

"How well do you know Van?" Marietta asked.

"I met him today."

"Then it should alarm you to know he and Mark were behind Seamus' scars."

Estelle gasped and knelt to pet the cat, wishing her touch could take away the pain.

"They set him on fire…"

Tears welled in Estelle's eyes. "Van! Is that true?"

He remained statuesque.

"I'm afraid so," Marietta said.

"Van!"

Marietta stopped Estelle. "You should stand back."

Flashes of red and green light shot into the telescope. Estelle froze as the telescope ejected colors—reds and pinks, blues and greens—into the sky. The hole in the clouds swirled and pushed outward, as if a rocket had just pierced them. Algol grew brighter and then dimmed as the light pouring out of telescope burned bright as the summer sun.

When it cleared, Van was gone.

"Halloween is a very special night," Marietta said.

Estelle couldn't speak, her phone clutched in a tight grip, wondering if she needed to call for help.

"Van was not a good person," Marietta said.

Estelle nodded, looking back to the nearly hairless cat. "Did he really do this to Seamus?" Her chin trembled, fighting tears.

Marietta's lips tightened into a straight line. "Some people are not meant to live among humans. Some are born with too much evil."

Estelle hugged her abdomen, reminded of the bruises on her wrists and the evil sitting at home waiting for her to return.

"Van is an offering to Algol." Marietta nodded to her phone. "Go ahead and read more about it. If you decide to call for help, I won't blame you."

Estelle swiped open the lock screen, bypassing the emergency call feature, and headed straight back to her sky app. She clicked on the information about the eclipsing binary star.

"Algol is 89 light years away…" Estelle didn't understand much about space travel, but she knew it would be impossible to send a person to it as an offering. Even at the speed of light, it would take a long time—eighty-nine years to be exact, but she kept that to herself and continued reading. "Also known as Beta Persei, or…the Demon Star." Her voice shook and she lifted her eyes from the phone, realizing now that she stood in the center of a massive glowing red circle of lights. The straight lines that crisscrossed at the center, around the telescope; they were in the shape of a five-point star.

Marietta used a green laser pointer to shine a beam into the air. She whispered some mumblings Estelle couldn't decipher and, within seconds, something whooshed past her and smacked into the satellite dish. There she saw a heap of slimy goo.

"Algol takes what it needs—the souls of the evil ones—and sends back what it doesn't as a"—she tilted her head—"sort of appreciation gift."

"But how? It's impossible to travel—"

"I have my theories," Marietta said. "It's not light travel. That would take too long. But judging by the look of what's returned… Well… Have you ever heard of what would happen to a person if they fell into a black hole?" Marietta shrugged. "It's all theoretical, of course. What matters is that it works. I don't need to know all the science."

Estelle drew closer to the dish and saw long strands of pink, red, and white piled on top of each other. She recalled skimming over the section about black holes because it was way over her head, but there was one part she'd never forget. "If a person were to fall into a black hole or something, they, like, stretch out into long strands."

Marietta scooped a handful of the remains onto a plate. "Scientists call it spaghettification." She pulled a long thin noodle of Van's viscera from the pile, held it over her mouth, and lowered it in. It slurped and slithered through her lips as she sucked it into her mouth. The noodle wriggled like a dying worm against her cheeks, splattering them with red. "Not bad." She licked her lips. "Not anymore."

Estelle stammered, mouth moving, but unsure what to say.

"If you must call the police, you can. I won't stop you. But they won't believe you." Marietta's eyes were soft, her face honest and sincere. "I only have to do this once a year, on All Hallows' Eve… It's the perfect timing for Algol's eclipsing cycle."

Estelle chewed her lip, still unsure what to say. For some reason, she calmed the longer she listened to Marietta talk.

"If it makes you feel any better," Marietta said, breaking the silence. "I only pick people who are *really* bad." She cradled the plate of Van's remains in her elbow. "You're not running away from me, so I take it you don't want to go home."

Estelle shook her head.

"Are you hungry? You can come inside and have a bite."

Her stomach churned.

"Don't worry. I have *real* spaghetti too—with pasta noodles. Vegetarian friendly." Marietta laughed.

Estelle reluctantly took a step forward, stomach desperate for anything other than sugar.

"Come. I'll teach you a few things."

"Like…" Her teeth chattered, finally able to spit out a few words. "Like about Jupiter?"

"Sure!" Marietta extended a hand. "And we can discuss who you think we should offer to Algol next year. Only the worst people, of course."

Estelle clutched her backpack to her belly, thinking about thrown beer bottles, screaming, fresh cuts and bruises, and she followed Marietta into the warm yellow glow of a home where she could disappear, never to be found by her father again.

THE HALLOWEEN LOST

by Frank Oreto

My jack-o'-lantern is one of those plastic plugin numbers. The cord shorted out a few years ago, so I cut a hole in the back and shoved in some Christmas lights. I had no choice, because they had banned the sale of pumpkins between September first and November 31st back in 2026. Most farms stopped growing them by then, anyway.

I carry out the basket full of treats—small grease-stained paper bags full of popcorn. The bags could have been full of old potatoes or stones. But you got to make an effort, right?

"What are you doing?" The woman from across the street's face is lined, her steel gray hair cut close to her skull. The look she gives me is more severe than her hairstyle. "You trying to prove something? That you're the only one who cares anymore."

I've dealt with this before. From old neighbors, friends, even from Barbara before she packed up and left me four Halloweens ago. The old woman just moved in this year. I don't even know her name and feel no need to justify myself to a stranger. I ignore the woman's questions and go about my business. The jack-o'-lantern goes on one side of the step, the basket full of popcorn bags on the other. I sit down between them.

The old woman crosses the street. She stands at the bottom of the cement stairs looking at me as if she's stumbled across Norman Rockwell's shittiest Saturday Evening Post cover. Up the steps she comes, far enough to give the treat basket a sniff. "Popcorn?"

I nod.

"My sister used to give out bags of popcorn for Halloween. There I'd be, slinging full-sized freakin' Snickers bars and the kids would all be telling each other about the lady down the street giving out popcorn. Ungrateful little shits."

I actually chuckle.

The woman launches back into her interrogation, as if getting a smile from me means I have to answer her questions. "You know they're not our kids anymore, right?" Not since the first time back in '24. We just didn't know it then."

"Where were you?" I ask. The question just pops out. The question we all ask when we meet someone new. Where were you on October 31st, 2024, when the children disappeared? When the world ended?

I see a blue gauze skirt and a plastic wand with a star on the end that lights up. A fairy princess dancing across my living room, full of laughter and still smelling of the cool October night. Then the room is empty except for the pile of Smarties, Nerds, and fun size milky ways on the coffee table. The house echoes with my shouts of her name—a name I haven't said out loud in years. Other voices call other names outside.

"Sammy, Kristin, Jackie boy—quit this foolishness or you're going to be in big trouble." No one answers. No one ever will.

The old woman's voice pulls me back to the now.

"I was in Hope's Rest, Tennessee." She pauses, looking at me closer. "You okay?"

I'm not, but I nod anyway. These days, everyone knows questions like that are rhetorical.

"It was like one of those television show nightmares where you keep waking up then realize you're still dreaming. First, I thought the only ones missing were my grandkids, Rodney and Troy, my little bucktoothed wonders. They both wanted to be Batman that year. What a fight that was." The woman shakes her head as if to dislodge the nostalgia. "Then the phone starts ringing. Have you seen Mary? Have you seen Tim? Sarah? Todd? Jimmy? And I realize, my God, it's the whole town. How could a whole town worth of kids just disappear?

"I have my coat and scarf on then, about to walk out the door and join the parents already searching the streets, but I turn on the TV first. You know, just to check the news. It wasn't just Hope's Rest. Not even just the U.S., either. Countries that didn't know Halloween from Arbor Day were reporting their kids gone, too.

"But it *was* Halloween. Even in Timbuktu or wherever. All over the world kids had got dressed up in whatever makeshift costumes they could come up with, went trick-or-treating and then just disappeared. That's why I don't get this." She points at the glowing jack-o'-lantern. "It was Halloween that took them."

I'm pretty sure they've heard of Halloween in Timbuktu, but I get her point.

We're both quiet for a few minutes. This is also part of the *conversation.* You start with where were you when they disappeared, then you think about the waking nightmare of it all. The constant searches even though you know damn well there's nowhere to hide every kid on the planet between five and ten years old. The articles and news shows—self-proclaimed experts or holy men blaming God, the commies, or cosmic rays. Sometimes all three.

Then it's, *"Where were you the next time?"*

I feel the tears threatening. Twelve years and I still feel so raw. We all do. I think of the joy and near madness of that next Halloween. No one had Jack-o'-lanterns on their porches. No kids were allowed to go near a costume. But suddenly the streets were full of our lost children—princesses, pirates, monsters, and superheroes.

They came back.

But they didn't stay.

We grabbed them off the sidewalks, locked them in our houses. Police drove along the roads, shoving costumed children into cruisers. But you'd turn around, look away for only a second, and they were outside again knocking on doors, saying 'trick or treat' in whatever language was used in that part of the world.

Then they were gone again, along with every child who had turned five since that first Halloween. That's when we all sort of gave up. Well, maybe not on that second Halloween, but by the fourth and fifth, hope had definitely fled. Why have more kids when you know you'll lose them in five years?

I see one on the corner—a child. They *are* only children, despite what my new neighbor says. This one wears a white cowboy hat and checkered vest. The six-guns at his hip shine in the last light of the setting sun. More trick-or-treaters appear. A tiny sheet-covered ghost clutching a pillowcase treat bag. An older girl—nine, maybe ten—comes around the corner. Judging by her ripped clothes and makeup, she's either a punk rocker or a zombie.

They march up on to porches, ring bells, knock on doors. The porches are dark. If there are people inside, they don't answer. I'm the only house with a jack-o'-lantern. The Ferguson's down at 1472 used to put one out. A big ceramic number with a flickering candle inside. But Norm Ferguson moved away to Milwaukee after Mrs. Ferguson took a nap in their Buick with the engine running and the garage door closed tight.

The squeal of tires cuts through the night and my thoughts. A truck practically slides around the corner onto our street. It rides half on, half off the sidewalk. The tiny cowboy goes down first, pulled under the tractor sized wheels. Spinning rubber yanks the ghost's sheet away. I can see the pale face of the boy beneath for a moment, then the truck rolls over him. The crack of small bones is as loud as the truck engine.

I run across the street without thinking, waving my arms and shouting. For a moment, I think I'm going to share the same fate as the costumed children. Then the truck screeches to a halt, the grill inches from my chest. The horn blares.

Doors swing open, and two kids in their early twenties pile out of the truck cab. One gets nose to nose with me right away. The other, his head covered in a checked hunting cap, hangs back a bit.

"You want to get run over too?" The boy is tall and fat with a flat face and breath that screams cheap beer and bad teeth.

Fear blooms in my chest, pushing away my anger. These *kids* are half my age, twice my size, and looking for trouble. They could easily put me in the hospital. A screen door slams, and I hear footsteps behind me.

"Fuck," says the boy in the hunting cap, his high, fearful tone a warning.

The flat-faced boy pulls his nose from mine and looks over my shoulder.

My neighbor stands on the sidewalk with a double-barreled

shotgun. The polished mahogany stock is pushed tight into the crook of her shoulder and her eyes squint down the barrels. She looks like she knows her business. I move to her side.

"Boy, I couldn't miss from here if I wanted to." There is no fear or even anger in her voice, just a weary certainty.

The companion is already back in the truck. The fat kid stands stock-still, but defiant. "We could just run you over too, bitch." His words are an angry hiss.

For a moment, I think she's going to do it. I imagine the ear-ringing blast of the first barrel going off. I see the angry young man tossed back against his pickup, his chest nothing but blood and shredded flesh.

Instead of pulling the trigger, the old woman slowly lowers the barrels. Her hard face sinks into sad lines. "How old were you, son? Eleven, twelve? Did you have a little brother you were supposed to keep an eye on that night? Maybe a five-year-old sister who thought you were the biggest, strongest boy in the world and wouldn't ever let anything happen to her?"

The boy whips his head back as if someone had punched him.

"Did you wish you'd been taken too? Did you pray for it, when you laid in bed, no kiss, no story? Your parents downstairs, sitting alone in separate rooms, drinking, crying, or both."

"Hold this for a minute." She hands me the shotgun, then walks over and takes the boy in a rough embrace. "It wasn't your fault, not a bit of it."

The boy stands stiff for a moment, then melts into her. Tears and sobs gush out of him in a wave. She whispers something else to him, and he nods. A minute or two later, he's back in the truck. They back down the street slowly, turn at the stop sign, and disappear into the night.

My neighbor wipes her eyes, then takes the shotgun from my hands. "My name's Anna Lewis. Friends call me Button."

"As in cute as a..."

Button nods and graces me with a hard look.

I hold my hands up. "All right then. Button, my name's Terry."

We cross the street back to my stoop. The children fill the sidewalks now. So many. The cowboy has gotten to his feet, straightening his limbs back into proper shape. The ghost pulls the tire-marked sheet back over his head. They join the rest.

Button lays the shotgun on the porch behind us, then sits next to me as the children walk up to my basket. The night echoes with their sing-song mantra—"Trick or treat."

Button leans her head against my shoulder and gives a tiny sob. Tears flow from behind her thick-lensed glasses.

I put an arm around her and try to give what comfort I have, but I don't cry. I can't afford to. I have to keep an eye out for a couple of Batmans—Batmen?—with buck teeth, one shorter than the other. Mostly though, I look for a fairy princess dressed in a gauzy blue skirt and butterfly wings that hang down so far, they almost drag the ground. She'll be holding a plastic wand with a star on the end that still lights up after all these years.

I can't wait to see her.

TATE

by Ronald Malfi

She had been dreading this night for weeks. This night of all nights, a year-long string of them, each one carving a hash mark into her brain—that fingernail-on-a-chalkboard *skrrrrit* that set her back teeth to grinding.

Nick had insisted on buying candy. She didn't argue, but instead studied him as he crawled into his jacket in the front hall, a forty-year-old man ambulating with all the *joie de vivre* of a death-row inmate. A corkscrew of hair at the back of his head and several days' growth darkening his jowls, Alice wondered if this was a good thing, him leaving the house to purchase bags of fun-size candy bars and brightly wrapped balls of candy. Leaving the house, today of all days—*skrrrrit.* She helped him along, kissing the side of his slack, unshaven face, as if for good luck. He was like someone going off to war.

When a half hour passed, Alice began to grow nervous. It was a five-minute drive to the grocery store in town. Maybe they were out of candy and he had to go someplace else? Maybe the Walgreens out by the highway? Tonight was the night, of course—Halloween night—so what fool waited until the last minute to stock up on goodies?

At least he got out of bed and brushed his teeth, Alice told herself as she hunted through the refrigerator for something to prepare for dinner. *At least he got out of the house for a change.*

When two hours passed and still Nick hadn't returned home, she dialed his cell phone. It rang a handful of times then went to voicemail. Nick's cheerful, alien voice invited the caller to leave a message. Or maybe the current Nick was the alien version, while that cheerful voice on the recording was the genuine article.

When some early trick-or-treaters came to the door, Alice smiled apologetically, then distributed to them a handful of mints she'd found at the bottom of her purse. As the kids each thanked her, she stood wondering if she should call the police and report Nick missing. She imagined a pair of police officers discovering Nick's Corolla down by the reservoir, front door slung open and chiming, keys still dangling from the ignition. Nick's clothes would be folded neatly on the driver's seat, his wallet and cell phone atop the pile like the toppings of this morbid sundae. After a brief search, they'd locate his body beneath the motionless, coal-black waters of the reservoir, his skin fishbelly-white, his eyes gone to jelly in their sockets.

She made herself a drink to quell her nerves. Was she overreacting? Or was she just unsettled by the anniversary?

We shouldn't have stayed here…

She was just about to dial 911 when she heard the Corolla pull into the driveway. Alice hurried to the kitchen window and watched as Nick climbed out of the car. He was clutching a bag of candy to his chest, pressing it against his body, his pale fingers digging into the plastic. Nick was tall, about six-four, but he'd lost so much weight over the last year that he looked every bit as skeletal as the plastic Halloween novelties on the Fabers' lawn across the street.

"What took so long?" she asked him as he came into the house, stomping his boots against the jamb. "We've already had a few eager visitors." She tried to sound light and airy.

Nick made a noise that could have been a humorous grunt, could have been indigestion. Still in his jacket, he shouldered past her and shuffled into the kitchen. A pot of spaghetti was boiling on the stove; Nick glanced at it, then reached above to pull down a large plastic bowl from the cupboard. He set the bowl on the counter, tore open the bag of candy, and emptied the bag's contents into it. They were Tootsie Rolls, Alice saw, and not even the big ones. Was there a more boring Halloween candy than those cylindrical brown turds?

"It was all they had left at the store," Nick said, as if reading her mind and finding it necessary to proffer an excuse for this sad display.

"Maybe we should have gone someplace," Alice said.

Nick picked up the bowl of Tootsie Rolls. He glanced at her, his eyes a smoky, distant black. There was some white crust—toothpaste?—socked in one corner of his mouth. "Gone someplace?" he said, his voice deadpan. As if they hadn't discussed this already.

"You know," she said. "Anywhere. Just...not to be here."

"Oh."

"It's not too late. We can throw some things in a duffle bag, get in the car—"

Just then, the doorbell sounded, an electronic ding-dong that made Alice jump. Nick actually laughed—did he take some small pleasure in her unease?—then headed down the hall to the front door.

"Trick or treat!" That singsong chorus channeled all through the house. It made Alice feel cold, as if their chant was carried to her on the crest of some frigid wind.

On the stove, the water boiled out of the pot and onto the burner, where it sizzled and spat. Alice lowered the temperature, then went quickly to the bottle of Old Forester on the counter. She poured herself another finger from the bottle—her third since Nick had left the house to buy candy—and knocked it back with a grimace. Then she poured a glass for Nick, dumped in a few ice cubes, and carried it down the hall to the bathroom. She took down a bottle of Xanax from the medicine cabinet. An ER nurse by trade, she could have pilfered something more potent from the hospital, but she knew the Xanax worked just fine, and she had a prescription for it. She crushed one tablet beneath the glass then swept the powder into Nick's drink.

The trick-or-treaters had gone, and Nick was no longer in the foyer with his bowlful of lousy candy. He wasn't in the living room, either.

"Nick?"

The house was silent. She carried the drink to the stairwell, pausing to glance out a window to confirm that the Corolla was still there and that he hadn't left again. It was. Upstairs, she peered into their bedroom, but it was empty. Ditto, the adjoining bathroom.

"Nick? Honey?"

She caught a shadow slide across the threshold of the open doorway at the far end of the hall. Tate's room.

We should have left town for the week, she thought again, creeping down the hall toward Tate's room. *We could have gone to the Poconos. We could have gone to Florida, where it's bright and sunny and warm.*

Nick was sitting on Tate's bed. He was still in his jacket and still with that cowlick of hair standing up at the back of his head, but he was now cradling one of Tate's pillows between his knees. Turning it over, running his fingers across its sports-themed pillowcase. Kneading it like dough, like the way he'd kneaded that bag of Tootsie Rolls. As Alice looked at him, the ice in the glass clinking as her hand trembled, he brought the boy's pillow to his face and inhaled with his eyes shut.

"This isn't healthy, Nick. Please."

"Oh," he said, his voice soft. That was it—*oh.* As though she'd just passed along some casual bit of wisdom.

"I made you a drink. Come on down and drink it. Dinner's almost ready, too."

"I went to the cemetery," he said. "That's what took so long."

She felt a finger of agitation press against the back of her throat. "Come," she told him. "Dinner."

They ate in relative silence, interrupted only when a group of children would ring that awful, mechanical doorbell. "I'll get it," Alice kept offering, but it was Nick who kept ratcheting up from his seat to do his mummy shuffle down the hallway to the front door.

"Trick or treat!"

"What do we have here? A ghost? A zombie?"

He almost sounded ebullient. Maybe it was the bourbon. Or maybe it was the Xanax, making him loopy. Alice got up and fixed him another drink. A double.

"Thank you, mister!"

"Be safe! Have fun."

Alice sat, twirling overcooked spaghetti around her fork, waiting for Nick to return. When he didn't, she set her fork down, got up, and wandered down the hall. She could hear the TV on in the living room. Poking her head in, she found Nick on the sofa, gazing dazedly at the television. *The Jack-o'-Screams Halloween Spooktacular,* that horrible holiday special, was on, and Nick was staring at it with a glazed expression.

"What about dinner?"

Slowly, he rotated his head in her direction. When she met his stare, something at the back of her throat clicked, and for one moment, she wondered if her daydream about the police finding Nick's body floating in the reservoir wasn't in fact a reality, and there he was, dead and mindless and hollowed-out, yet right here at the same time, staring at her with eyes as lifeless as tack-heads.

"This was his favorite," Nick said, motioning with one hand at the television. "We'd watch it together every year. Ever since he was a toddler."

Alice swallowed what felt like a golf ball. "Nick," she said. "Why'd you turn that on? Don't do this to yourself."

"I didn't," he said. "I didn't turn it on. It came on by itself."

On the TV, Jack-o'-Screams, that hollow-eyed, pumpkin-headed puppet, turned to the camera and said, "What kind of *caaaan-deeee* do *you* like?"

Alice shivered.

The doorbell chimed—*zzzing-zzzong.*

They remained staring at each other for the length of three heartbeats. Then—

"I'll get—"

"No," Nick said, shoving himself off the sofa. He brushed by her and shambled down the hall just as the children on the porch, overzealous and sugar-fueled, rang the bell again.

On the television, Jack-o'-Screams unhinged his jaw and made a clicking sound, as if he had teeth back there somewhere in his squat, empty pumpkin head. Canned laughter crackled, tinny and vacuous. Batty Witchmas dropped from the rafters on her marionette strings, her silver eyes gleaming.

"Knock-a knock!" Batty Witchmas shrilled. For some reason, she spoke with an Italian accent.

"Who's there?" said Jack-o'-Screams, his jaw flapping.

"Boo!"

"Boo who?"

"Aww, Jack-o, why you's a-cryin'?"

More canned laughter.

Alice dug the remote out from the sofa cushions and switched off the TV.

It wasn't silence that followed, but a muffled whimpering sound that came to her from the front hall. She turned out of the room and peered down the hallway and into the foyer. The front door stood open, and there was Nick kneeling before the threshold, head bowed, shoulders slumped. He was sobbing. It had grown dark, and no one had replaced the porch light in over a year, so Alice could only make out her husband's silhouette at first…but then she could see there was something *wrong*. A smaller head rested stiffly on one of Nick's slumped shoulders.

"Nick, honey," she said, moving quickly to him.

He knelt there, arms wrapped around a child, a solitary trick-or-treater who stood motionless, perhaps even paralyzed, within the confused tangle of Nick's grief-stricken, clumsy embrace.

"Let him go, Nick. Let him go."

She grabbed a fistful of Nick's collar, tugged him backward. The boy he was embracing kept his head on Nick's shoulder, though his eyes—moist, pearlescent little orbs—shifted in Alice's direction.

"Let him go, Nick."

"Look!" Nick brayed, his voice cracking. "Oh God, Alice! Look at him, will you? He's come home!"

"That's not Tate."

"My God, Alice…"

"Please, Nick. This boy is not your son." She peered out beyond the porch, down the length of the flagstone walkway, out to the street, searching the night for signs of this boy's parents. But there was no father waiting on the walkway, no mother with her arms folded impatiently waiting in the street. There was no one else out there.

She tugged at Nick's collar more forcefully.

"Goddamn it, Alice, *look!*"

And it was then she realized he wasn't sobbing, but *laughing.* Yes, tears still streamed down his face, but Alice saw her husband was nearly hysterical with laughter. Somehow, that made her feel even more uncomfortable.

She looked down at the boy, saw he was about seven or eight—Tate's age when he'd died—and possessed the overlarge, beseeching eyes of some curious woodland creature. For a costume, he wore a plain white frock with a hood, although the hood was turned down, exposing his pale, bland face and his thatch of straw-colored hair.

"Nick, this isn't Tate. Tate is dead. Please, honey."

Nick bolted to his full height. Breath shuddering from his lips, he swiped the tears from his eyes with the heels of his hands. Then he lowered one hand and gripped the child delicately around the neck. He drew the boy to him, kissed the top of his head…then gathered him up off the floor and into his arms.

"Nick!"

He ignored her; he carried the child down the hall, his gait determined yet unsteady. Plodding, like Frankenstein's monster trudging through a wooded swamp.

Alice hurried out onto the porch, shouted, "Hello?" Surely this kid hadn't been out here alone. If not with parents, then there must be a group of other kids out here looking for him. She saw someone across the street, standing on the Fabers' front lawn, and so she called to them and began furiously waving both arms above her head. But when the figure didn't wave back, she realized she was signaling to one of the Fabers' life-size plastic skeletons dressed up in old work clothes.

She went back inside, where she shut and bolted the door.

Nick and the boy were in the kitchen, seated together at the table, the boy in Nick's lap. Nick was groping and pawing at him, his unshaven face buried in the crook of the boy's neck as he wept delirious, ecstatic tears.

Alice stared at the boy. Opened her mouth to offer some version of an apology, or perhaps to tell the child this was all a misunderstanding and he wasn't in any danger…but then something froze her tongue to the roof of her mouth.

She could see him better here in the lighted kitchen, his pale round face and large eyes, his small, pursed lips, the tawny rake of bangs across his gently-furrowed forehead. He was done up as some sort of ghoul, his skin a faint, icy blue, and with those large, staring eyes peering out from deep pockets in his skull. She could see the faint spidery network of veins along his temples, delicate work, as was the spongy mold that bristled out from behind his left ear. The boy cocked his head to one side, and there it was, right there—an undeniable bulge along the left side of his throat, no bigger than a thumb pressing against the wall of his windpipe.

"Hey," she said to the boy, her voice raised a notch. "Who made you up like this? Who are you supposed to be?" When the kid didn't answer, she reached out and planted her fingers into one of his narrow shoulders, gave him a shake. "Who are you supposed to be?"

Nick swatted her hand away. "He's Tate, goddamn it. What's the matter with you?"

"What's the matter with *me*? Nick, Tate is dead. This isn't Tate. This is someone's..." She wanted to say *someone's idea of a terrible joke*, but the words dried up in her mouth. The boy kept staring at her and it was making her feel ill.

Nick's anger at her faded the moment he turned back to look at the boy perched in his lap. A runner of snot descended from one of Nick's nostrils, shiny as quicksilver. As he ran a hand over the boy's hair, he said, "I don't know how this...how this could happen...I don't..." He sucked that snail-trail of snot up into his nose. "My boy, my boy," he said, pressing his sweaty forehead to the side of the boy's face.

The boy brought up one pale hand and caressed Nick's stubbly cheek.

"Nick," she said, her voice just barely audible. "Please..."

Nick slammed one hand on the tabletop, and the utensils in the spaghetti dishes jumped. "This is him! This is my son!" He gripped the child about the chin, squeezing the flesh to a dimple. "Can't you see? Can't you look at him and see?"

She was looking; she could see.

"You don't know because he's not your son," Nick said. "He's not your flesh and blood like he is mine. You don't know because you're not a mother. You never wanted to be. But *I* know. *Look at him*!"

"Enough of that," Alice said. She tried to sound calm and collected, but her voice came out too small, too inconsequential. "That isn't fair to say to me."

Nick slammed his hand down on the table again. "He's hungry!" He looked at the boy, who was still staring at Alice. "Are you hungry, son?"

The boy said nothing.

"My God, my God!" Nick shouted. He kissed the side of the boy's face, then hoisted him off his lap and set him in a neighboring chair. Nick staggered toward the refrigerator, tore it open. He began piling deli meats, leftovers, fruits and vegetables onto a plate.

The boy just stared at Alice.

And Alice, in turn, kept staring at that conspicuous protrusion along the left side of the boy's throat.

"A celebration!" Nick shouted. He was crying again, happy tears, his hands jittery as they stacked random bits of food onto the plate. "That's what this is, all right. A homecoming. An honest-to-God, according-to-Hoyle miracle! We're blessed!"

"Nick," Alice said, her husband's name sticking to the roof of her mouth. It seemed all she was capable of saying, and nothing more.

In the living room, the TV burst back on. Alice heard Jack-o'-Screams shouting: *"Look at all that caaaannn-deeee!"*

"Here-here-here," Nick said, dumping the plate of random food on the table in front of the boy. "My kid's hungry. It's been a year. Eat up, son." Nick snapped his fingers, then hurried to the cabinet and took down a glass. He filled it with 7-Up from the fridge, spilling some down the side of the counter and onto the floor, then spilling more as he carried the fizzing glass of soda to the table.

"Ha ha!" Nick clapped his hands, stomped his feet. His face was beet-red and shiny with tears. "My God, Tate. My good boy. I'm so sorry, son. I've missed you so much." He dropped to his knees before the boy, burying his face in the child's lap.

As Alice watched, the boy brought one hand up from beneath his frock and proceeded to stroke Nick's hair. The boy's fingers were grimy, the nails rimmed in black, the nails themselves an unnatural seawater hue. Alice saw that the boy's other hand clutched a bustling burlap sack, big as a softball. Tendrils of cobwebs seemed to cling to the satchel, wafting about like smoke, but when Alice blinked, the cobwebs or whatever they had been were gone.

Nick looked up at the boy. "What is it, baby? Aren't you hungry? What do you want?"

The boy's eyes shifted from Alice and scaled the far wall. He turned his head, exposing that hideous knob of flesh poking from his neck as he did so, and peered out into the hall, toward the sounds of the TV. From the living room, Batty Witchmas cackled, then shrilled, "It's about to get *verrrrrry scaaaaary,* boys and ghouls," which was met with thunderous applause and laughter.

"Yes!" Nick boomed. He stood so quickly that Alice, who was clear across the room, took an instinctive step back. "Your favorite Halloween special! Of course! It's on. Let's watch."

He gathered the boy up in his arms again and squirreled him away into the living room.

Alice stood there motionless, her body feeling like a lightning rod that had just been struck. When she felt capable of doing so without falling down, she returned to her seat at the table. She could no longer eat, so she raked at the spaghetti, dragging the tines of her fork back and forth along the plate. She finished her drink, then sat there feeling cold and confused while Jack-o'-Screams and his puppet pals gibbered in the next room.

She got up and went out the front door. She had given up looking for this child's parents—she kept thinking about the bulging knot at his throat—and instead went around to the side of the house, where low shrubbery hugged the siding and a plastic bird feeder swayed from the eaves in the night. Alice peered into the living-room window.

They were seated together on the sofa, the bluish glow of the TV flickering in their eyes. Nick was squeezing one of the boy's pale, mottled hands, his head tipped back against the sofa. He wore an ear-to-ear grin and his eyes still leaked tears, but the Xanax had dulled his expression and blunted his enthusiasm.

The boy turned to the window and stared out at her.

Alice staggered backward, scraping her arms against the twiggy bushes.

I could get in the car and drive away, she thought. It seemed completely reasonable—necessary, even, given the circumstances— but for some reason she found herself walking back into the house.

"Come join us," Nick said, once she appeared in the doorway of the living room.

She came around and sat beside Nick on the sofa. The boy's eyes followed her the entire time. He watched her still, peering at her beyond Nick's profile. The boy's eyes looked yellow and rotten, faintly backlit by some unwholesome, otherworldly radiance. She kept staring at the swollen knob at the side of his throat. In her mind, she kept seeing the way Tate had clutched at his throat and kicked his feet. Kept hearing the *reeeet-reeeet* of his sneakers skidding along the linoleum.

Skelly-Belly, Jack-o'-Screams's best pal, bolted onto the screen. He had a pair of wild, bejeweled eyes in his skull, and they swished furiously back and forth like the frantic, lunatic eyes of a Kit-Cat Klock.

"Is it time for more *caaaannn-deee*?" Skelly-Belly shrieked. Then he pitched back his puppety head, and his jawbone swung open. A flurry of colorfully-wrapped candies rained down from the sky as Skelly-Belly gobbled them up. Behind Skelly-Belly's ribcage was a translucent bladder that swelled comically with air as he munched the candy.

"Uh oh," said Jack-o'-Screams, sliding into frame.

Nick laughed, startling Alice. She looked at the boy, who was still staring at her.

"Looks like someone's fixing to have a *tummy ache*!" Jack-o'-Screams hollered…and then he produced what looked like a long, gleaming knitting needle.

Nick slapped one knee and kept laughing. He had one arm slung around the boy now, and he squeezed him tight. Tears kept spilling down his red, heated face.

Batty Witchmas popped up on the screen, her green felt hands pinned to her face. "Oh, Madonn'!" she cried, eyes wide.

Jack-o'-Screams jabbed the knitting needle between two of Skelly-Belly's ribs, bursting the rubber bladder. Animated explosions filled the screen, set to a soundtrack of children laughing.

Or are they screaming? Alice thought.

"Enough." She jumped up and switched off the TV.

"Oh, hey," Nick said, his speech slurred. He looked like he was struggling to keep his eyes open.

"No more," she said. "The boy needs to go home."

Nick sat forward, his brow creased in consternation. "Home? Alice, you're not hearing me. He *is* home. Tate's come back. He doesn't…he doesn't *blame* you, honey…"

She felt a jab of pain in the center of her chest, as if Jack-o'-Screams was giving her the old knitting needle treatment.

"I don't blame you, either. It was an accident. A terrible accident. But it's okay now. We're all back together now." He turned and faced the boy. "Aren't we, son?"

The boy did not look at Nick; his cold, faintly luminescent eyes held Alice in their gaze.

Nick kissed the side of the boy's face. "You've come a long way to get back to us, Tate, and you must be tired," he said. "I'm tired, too, son. I've been tired and sad for such a long time. But now it's time to rest. Come on, Tate."

Nick stood from the sofa and the boy stood with him. He was still holding Nick's hand, still clutching that grimy burlap sack in the other. Alice could see streaks of dirt and smudgy grass stains along the front of the boy's hooded white frock.

Nick led the boy from the room. A moment later, she could hear their languid footfalls on the stairs. She waited, holding her breath until she could hear them no more. Then she went to the bathroom medicine cabinet, dry-swallowed a Xanax of her own, then poured herself another glass of bourbon once she was back in the kitchen.

Her mind began to feel fuzzy and unanchored as she cleared the kitchen table, dumping the uneaten spaghetti into the trash then stacking the dirty plates in the sink. By the time she'd wiped down the tabletop and swept the floor, her mind was floating somewhere above herself. Xanax and alcohol did not mix. Neither did alcohol and her psyche meds, although she couldn't remember if she happened to take them today or not. Anyway, what did it matter? She was thinking now that she had probably just imagined the whole thing.

It's been a rough year, she rationalized, pouring herself yet another drink. *We both knew tonight was going to be hard. It's the anniversary, after all…*

She climbed the stairs to the second floor. The hallway light was off and she didn't turn it on. A soft glow shone at the end of the hall, emanating from Tate's partially closed bedroom door. She paused before entering, taking a deep breath, then pushing the door open wider.

Nick lay on Tate's bed, his head turned to one side, snoring loudly. The boy was gone—and had he ever really been here?—and this caused a tidal wave of relief to wash through her.

"Alice," Nick said, startling her. It took her a moment to realize he was talking in his sleep. Or so it seemed. "Don't…blame you…"

Downstairs, the TV came on. A finger of ice traced down Alice's spine. She crept back out along the landing and hesitated at the top of the stairs. All too clearly she could hear the sour, discordant theme music that signaled both the start and the conclusion of the *Halloween Spooktacular*—all harpsichord and wolf howls.

She moved slowly down the stairs. By the time she reached the bottom, her heart was hammering in her chest and a fine sheen of perspiration had broken out across her brow.

The light from the TV played against the opposite wall of the hallway. In it stood the shadow of the boy.

Alice stepped into the living room to find the boy waiting for her. He stood in the center of the room, the frenetic lightshow of *The Jack-o'-Screams Halloween Spooktacular*'s closing credits painting his otherwise pale flesh and white frock in a slipstream of psychedelic colors.

"Who are you?" she asked the boy, her voice unsteady.

The boy said nothing; he merely watched her with those dull, dimly glowing eyes.

"What do you want? Why are you here?"

On the TV, Jack-o'-Screams made an encore appearance. His foam jaw gyrating, he shrieked, "Hey! We are still here for *caaaannn-deeee!*"

"It was an accident," Alice said. "You…you choked on a piece of…"

"Caaaan-deeeee!" Skelly-Belly echoed from the TV.

Alice's eyes ticked toward the screen just as Batty Witchmas joined the other two characters. Her green felt hands were still pinned to the sides of her face, her eyes still wide in mock surprise. "You didn't want the boy," said the witch. "You never did."

"It's true!" shouted Skelly-Belly. "Yes, the boy began to choke—*bwah-ha, bwah-ha*—but do you know what Alice did, boys and ghouls?"

A collective *"What did she do?"* came from the studio audience.

"She did *nothing,*" said Skelly-Belly, who followed that up with his signature guffaw: *"Bwah-ha, bwah-ha!"*

The studio audience began to boo her.

Alice shook her head, but she knew they were right. Tate had started choking on a piece of candy, had fallen to the floor clutching his throat, kicking his legs, thrashing about. Alice had been with him, had watched it happen. A simple abdominal thrust would have most likely dislodged the obstruction—Alice was well-versed in performing this maneuver, having done it countless times while on shift at the hospital—but instead of springing to action, Alice merely watched it happen. When Tate's eyes began to bug out, she sat on a kitchen chair and studied him. When his face went from red to purple to blue, she crossed and re-crossed her legs, and took a sip of the wine that she had only moments ago poured herself after returning from trick-or-treating with the little brat. She wasn't even his biological mother, yet here she was. Once he stopped moving, stopped breathing, she got up, stepped over his body, and poured herself another glass of wine. Then she worked herself up in a frenzy in front of the bathroom mirror before calling 911.

"It's all so *terrible,* boys and ghouls," Jack-o'-Screams said, his large pumpkin-face filling the screen. His triangular eye sockets looked unfathomably deep and accusatory. "It's all so *cruel.*"

"Is it *time?*" Skelly-Belly screeched, his jawbone chattering.

"Yes!" cackled Batty Witchmas. "Is it? Is it time, Jack-o?"

The boy—Tate—extended a hand to her. It was the hand clutching that dirty burlap sack. As Alice stared at it, the sack appeared to swell then deflate, as if respiring. Those strange cobweb-like tendrils were back, floating like strands of gossamer around the satchel.

"You know what, boys and ghouls?" Jack-o'-Screams said, his voice a low growl now, his face so close to the screen that it was a fuzzy orange blur. For a moment, one indistinct triangular eye swam across the screen, empty as a void. "It *issss*," Jack-o'-Screams hissed. "It is time for *caaaaaannn-deeee…*"

The kids in the studio audience cheered, but Alice hardly heard them. Like someone else in control of her body, she reached out and took the burlap sack from the boy, opened it, and began to eat her Halloween treats.

A PERFECT NIGHT
FOR A PERFECT MURDER

by Jeremy Bates

I f you're going to commit murder, I highly recommend it be the premeditated kind.

All other types—second degree, felony, manslaughter—are just amateurish in comparison. A rowdy asshole who gets into a barfight and kills another rowdy asshole with a broken bottle: second degree murder, amateurish. A drunk driver who runs over a pedestrian: felony murder, amateurish. A boyfriend who strangles his girlfriend to death in a heat-of-the-moment argument: voluntary manslaughter, amateurish. A nurse who administers a lethal dose of the wrong drug to a patient: involuntary manslaughter, amateurish. In each of these cases you're more likely than not going to get caught. You're going to get locked behind bars. And you, my friend, will forever be labeled by me as an amateur.

So I'll say it again. Premeditated murder is the way to go, take it from an expert.

Why premeditated murder?

Quite simply because it involves thought, it involves planning and caution and calculation, and if you're even half-intelligent, you have a good chance of pulling it off.

Especially if you follow my three rules.

But first let me start with a few words on what I find to be one of the biggest perks of premeditated murder (aside from getting away with the murder, of course). It's something would-be murderers don't think much about, and that's the anticipation of the kill. I like using a metaphor to illustrate what I'm talking about. You can buy a juicy, artery-clogging kebab and fries on the spur of the moment when you walk by a kebab shop.

I wouldn't blame you for doing exactly that after you get a whiff of the lamb on the rotating spit, the Madras curry powder, the frying oils, the toasted waffle bread. But me, folks...well, I suppose I have a bit more self-control than most. Because all those smells, as tempting as they might be, won't lure me into the shop.

You see, if I'm going to indulge in such a guilty pleasure as a lamb doner and fries, I'll give myself a few hours to let my anticipation simmer before I go out and buy the meal. That way, when I finally gobble down the kebab, it won't simply be five minutes of guilty pleasure, will it? Because I've also had those three, four, five hours of looking forward to the meal to make it all the more satisfying and worthwhile, to make it feel...less cheap, if you can dig what I'm saying.

Really, I can't tell you how rewarding this kind of build-up is. And if it applies to a kebab, folks, it sure as hell applies to bloody, old-fashioned premeditated murder.

With that out of the way, I'll get to why you're all here, what you really want to hear me speak about. My three beautiful rules to increase your odds of successfully committing premeditated murder and avoiding the legal consequences.

So without further ado, here's Rule #1: Get rid of the body.

To be clear, if you're driving back from the bar intoxicated late at night, and you run over some kid crossing the street, my advice to you would be to leave that fucker right there and drive away as fast as you can. But that's not what we're talking about. We're not talking about felony murder. We've just been through this. What we're talking about, my friends, is cold-blooded planning; hot-blooded malice; all the good stuff only humans are capable of.

Premeditated murder.

And the last thing you want to do after you've intentionally killed someone is to leave their body behind. *But why, Bob?* you're thinking. *I'm smart. I'll spin a tale about a break-in gone wrong, some shit like that. I'll outwit the cops.*

No, you won't. I don't care how smart you think you are, how good a liar and actor you think you are. Homicide detectives are excellent at what they do. They've devoted their lives to putting people like you behind bars. So don't—I repeat: *don't*—give them the crime scene on a silver platter. And that's exactly what you're doing when you leave the body behind. You're giving them the time of death. You're giving them the modus operandi. You're giving them the murder weapon, and of course you're giving them the location where the death took place.

They'll search every inch of that place, wherever it is, looking for fingerprints, hair, DNA. They'll talk to any and all potential witnesses. They'll check every goddamn doorbell camera in the neighborhood. And regardless of whether you even knew the victim well or not, they're going to figure it all out. Because you handed them the crime scene on a silver platter.

So dump the body. No body, no crime scene. And how does one solve a murder without a crime scene? Chances are, my friends, one doesn't.

Having said all this, how you get rid of the body is up to you. Needless to say, put some thought into it. Tossing a corpse into a dumpster behind your local Walmart is not a great idea. You might think the body will remain hidden beneath all those black Glad bags full of trash. But corpses smell. After a couple of days, they stink. Chances are someone's going to wonder about that smell and go digging through that trash.

Tossing the corpse in a lake is a no-no, too—tossing it in any body of water really. Corpses float. They'll wash back up on shore. Even if you weigh one down with rocks or what have you, flesh decomposes, muscles and sinew fall apart, fish eat that stuff, and a dismembered leg or foot or something could make its way back to land. So all I can say is be creative here, folks. Think outside the box. Just remember—if there's no body, there's no crime scene. No crime scene, no murder. From an investigative standpoint, anyway.

All right, let's keep moving. Let's jump right into Rule #2: Wear gloves and a mask.

Gloves are self-explanatory, aren't they? The worst evidence you can leave behind at a crime scene is your fingerprints (actually, the worst evidence would probably be your mobile phone or wallet, but if you're dumb enough to do something like that, God help you, sir or ma'am, you're in the wrong business, and all the tips in the world aren't going help you, I'm sorry to say).

Now, if you're a film aficionado like me, you've no doubt seen a scene in which a murderer wipes down the interior of the car after he murders the driver. Or maybe you've seen one in which a burglar shoots Mr. and Mrs. Perfect between the eyes (still clad in their matching pajamas because they heard glass break downstairs and unwisely decided to investigate) and then goes around the pretty suburban house wiping down all the surfaces that he (and let's be honest, folks, burglars are rarely ever female, are they?) might have touched.

My point is: leaving fingerprints in the first place is just sloppy business. Because fingerprints, I shouldn't have to point out, are damn near invisible. You're almost guaranteed to miss one here or there. Moreover, all that wiping down takes time…and time is not on your side when you've just fired two gunshots in a well-to-do neighborhood at two in the morning. So gloves…yeah, don't leave home without them. There's nothing more to say about them than that.

A mask, on the other hand… Well, the necessity of wearing one might strike some of you as a bit more controversial. However, I will argue to my grave that it's absolutely essential for the very simple reason that it guarantees anonymity. Yes, I know what you're thinking: *I can't exactly walk down the street wearing a mask like I can a pair of lambskin gloves without drawing attention to myself, can I?* And if you leave the mask off right up until you pull the trigger, twist the dagger, or do whatever dastardly deed you're going to do, what benefit is it providing you? Chances are you've already been caught on camera somewhere, or someone has spotted you, someone who could describe you to the police, something along those lines.

Which is why, folks, I recommend planning your murder for Halloween night.

Indeed, you heard me right. Rule #3, the final rule that ties everything together, is to plan your murder to fall on Halloween night.

Because on this night—and this magical night only—you can walk around in public wearing not only a pair of gloves but also a full-face mask, and nobody's going to bat an eye at you. On top of this—and here's the kicker—you can dress up the still-warm corpse in a costume. I don't know how many of you—and since you're all here listening to me speak, I doubt it's many—have committed premeditated murder before, but trying to get a corpse out of an apartment building, or even a house, is no easy business.

People tend to notice when somebody is dead. And the old roll-them-up-in-a-carpet trick isn't going to fool anybody these days. So what to do? My go-to solution is to bring along a wheelchair and a costume. Once you've slayed your victim, and he or she is good and dead, you dress them up in the costume (with it being Halloween, the scarier the better), plop them in the wheelchair, and roll them out of the apartment or house (or wherever the fuck you've killed them) like the champion you are.

Yes, yes, I once again know what you're thinking: *That all sounds good and great, Bob—gloves and masks and Halloween night and dressing up the corpse, that's all good and great—but planning murder for a specific day of the year is just not practical.* Sure, I understand where you're coming from. But remember, my friends, that we're not talking about felony murder or second degree murder or any of that other amateurish stuff. We're talking about first degree murder, *premeditated* murder. By the very definition of that word, you're planning the murder beforehand, and if you're going to all the trouble of choosing a victim, choosing the weapon, choosing your modus operandi, and, yes, choosing the time and day, why not be a little patient and pick the *best* time and day possible, which is absolutely and indisputably Halloween night?

Okay, I can still hear some of you thinking, *The thing is, Bob, I can't stand my bastard cheating husband. I don't want to wait a month, or two months, or ten. I want to kill him* right now.

Yes, yes, *yes,* I understand and empathize with that too! When you get murder on the brain, you're going to want to commit it as soon as possible. Half of you because you're made up of cinnamon and spice and everything nice, you're only getting your hands bloody out of some sort of perceived necessity, and you can't stand the anxiety and guilt. The other half of you—and I like you bunch better—because you've got a dark side you can't control, and you're a slave to your diabolic impulses.

Either way, whichever kind of dirty little murderer you are, all I can tell you on the matter of waiting until Halloween night is to be patient. Killing somebody is not something you want to rush into, nor is it something you want to screw up. You only get one chance. And if the best chance to commit a successful premeditated murder is on Halloween night—and it really is, my friends, believe you me— then be patient and wait until then.

It's that simple.

Anyhow! That's my spiel, folks. How to commit the perfect murder. Gloves, a mask, dressing up the corpse, All Hallows' Eve. See how it synergizes? How it all works together to give you the best possible chance of success?

Hey, what can I say? You wanted advice from the best, and you just got it…

Fifteen minutes later I left the New York City bookstore where I had been invited to host a writer's workshop. As a bestselling crime fiction writer, I was in high demand for these kinds of things. People liked hearing me spew shit about the writing process, characterization, setting and plot, and yes, my specialty, murder. The truth was, such events bored the hell out of me, but my publisher liked the idea of me communicating with my readers and fans. Which was why I was set to kick off a twenty-two-state book tour next week to promote my latest thriller.

I kept up a brisk pace along Seventh Avenue toward my townhouse in Greenwich Village. The air was crisp and fresh, hinting at incipient winter. Yet Manhattan likely wouldn't see its first snowfall for another month or two. It was still only October.

October 31, to be precise.

The most magical night of the year.

I didn't know the librarian I was about to murder. Not really. We "met" at Butler Library at Columbia University's Morningside campus last week. She worked at the circulation desk, and I asked her what identification I needed to get a library card. She told me my driver's license would do, which I already knew. I simply wanted to hear her speak. She was pretty, had a nice voice, and seemed like a pleasant woman. She was very much my type.

I hung around the library, keeping a discreet eye on her until she finished her shift some five hours later. I never grew bored. The waiting was the build-up.

The anticipation.

I followed her to the Sunset Avenue parking garage. I got in my car, paid the rate at the boom gate, and idled on Sunset until the librarian emerged from the facility driving a green hatchback. If she had parked at the Hinkle Fieldhouse parking lot instead, I would have been screwed, and if she had taken public transportation to work, I would have cut my losses and moved on.

Anyway, I got lucky. She'd parked where I'd parked.

Everything was going according to plan.

It was nearly an hour's drive to her place, most of it on the Eastern Parkway. When she pulled into her driveway, I continued past it, made a right at the corner, and returned to Manhattan.

Now, nearly a week later, on Halloween night, I was back. The librarian's house was a tidy bungalow with white siding and a red roof. A smiling, toothy jack-o'-lantern sat on the middle of three steps that led to the front entrance. The candle inside was no longer lit.

I stood on the bottom step, wearing a white doctor's coat, a stethoscope around my neck, cream latex gloves, and a Mr. Bean rubber mask. I held a plastic bag filled with purchased candy in my hands. My trusty wheelchair was behind me. It was 9:37 p.m. Late enough that most of the trick-or-treaters and their parents had turned in for the night, but not so late that the librarian would be suspicious of a knock at her door.

I knocked a second time, more loudly, and checked my wristwatch again. 9:38 p.m. Had she gone to bed? I was beginning to fear that was the case when I heard the door unlock. A moment later it swung open.

The librarian appeared, just as pretty as I remembered.

She frowned slightly. Although I was a short and skinny man, I wasn't going to fool anybody into believing I was seven years old. However, kids were big these days, and with the full-face mask on, I knew I could pass as a greedy ten- or eleven-year-old.

Anyway, it didn't matter what she thought of my size. She'd already opened the door.

I ascended the upper two steps quickly, drove my fist into her face before she had a chance to react, and closed the door with my foot.

God, I loved Halloween night.

ELEVEN ONE

by Philip Fracassi

Gwen is still dressed like a witch.

She blinks, eyelids thick and crusty with the heavy makeup she mistakenly left on overnight to harden and smear. Her brain is sluggish, her limbs leaden.

Hung over, she thinks. *Damn it. Why am I so...*

Reality rushes in like black smoke, chokes her with memories. Her eyes squeeze shut, wincing from the onslaught.

"Oh no, oh no..." she pleads, and wants to start crying all over again. But she emptied herself of tears the night before, had cried and cried and drank and drank until she puked, then screamed, then destroyed half the stuff in her bedroom, then mercifully...

Then... What? God, did I black out?

She turns her head tentatively, studies her pale fingers resting motionless on the pillow, bitten fingernails painted a thick coat of black. A faded line discolors the base of her ring finger like an accusation, and she grimaces.

Must have passed out… she thinks, shame reddening her cheeks. She looks further along her arm, notices the tight dark fabric at her bicep.

She hadn't even taken off the damned costume.

Gwen sighs and blinks rapidly, fighting against the pull of gummy mascara on her eyelids. Gingerly, she touches a knot of her hair, her scalp sore from the pins put in the day before—an effort to create a bizarre, clumpy coiffure to go with her "mad witch" look. She gasps as she pulls at one large, tangled pin, raven-black strands still clinging to it.

"Owww…" she moans, and tosses the hairpin to the floor.

She lifts her head and the room sways like the deck of a small ship on a swelling sea. Bile burns the base of her throat. She drily, disgustedly swallows it, lies back, and closes her eyes once more; wills her brain to stabilize.

After a few minutes, things settle, and she can think again. Gwen allows herself to slowly explore the events from the day before; gently, as if touching a wound to see how badly it will hurt.

She remembers Robert, the things he said, and it motherfucking *hurts.*

"Oh God…" she sobs, rolling onto her side. Her billowing skirts crumple beneath her weight. She lightly strokes the tear stains on the pillow, wishing life were different, that the last twenty-four hours were nothing but a bad dream she could wake from and forget. Redo.

"Robert…" she whispers.

Gwen wipes the tears away with the back of a cold hand, forces herself to sit up and open her eyes, prays the rocking ship has steadied. Empty bottles fill the nightstand, blurry and judgmental. *I started with the champagne,* she recalls, and there the bottle stands, staring back at her with regal pity.

It was the good stuff. The expensive stuff.

The celebratory stuff.

It was to be their first, and (fatefully) their last, Halloween as an engaged couple.

Best laid plans and all that.

As they'd discussed, Gwen would be dressed as a witch. Robert, a mad scientist. He'd wear a lab coat and carry a large beaker filled with vodka (turned green from food coloring) from which he'd sip throughout the night, bouncing from one party to another. She smiles despite herself, imagining her handsome fiancé in costume—his brown hair matted with gel, thick glasses on his face to bug out his eyes, white lab coat smeared with dashes of red. "For mystery," he'd said when pitching the idea. "What's a mad scientist without a bit of blood on his lab coat?"

She'd laughed and shown him the outfit she ordered online: the Sexy Sorceress.

"Looks more like a witch," he'd said, frowning playfully, for which she jabbed him in the arm while they laughed.

We always laughed, she thinks. *Didn't we?*

There are other bottles on her nightstand, of course. One had been an off-brand vodka that had been mostly empty before she finished it off, but still...

A third bottle, only half-empty—*thank God*—was the nice tequila she and Robert brought back from their trip to Mexico...

And when exactly had they taken that trip? A year ago? Two years?

She can't remember. Her brow furrows with worry.

Gwen looks away from the bottles littering the nightstand, repulsed...and a little frightened. Her memories are a dense fog. She pinches the bridge of her nose—her *I'm thinking hard* tic—and tries to piece it together.

Robert had come over at 8 p.m. sharp, just like they planned. She'd decorated the entire—albeit tiny—house. There was a carved pumpkin on the porch, a battery-powered old crone hung on the front door (if you got too close, the witch would cackle and spit a curse at you, plastic eyes blazing yellow beneath long gray hair and a bent, pointy black hat). Fake spiderwebs flowed between the two posts at the top of the porch stairs, and there was a large (and quite realistic) spider she'd hung with string high above, glaring menacingly at any trick-or-treater who dared look up.

The inside of the house had been covered in less cartoonish décor. She'd draped the lampshades in red silk, so the walls were smeared with a burgundy glow; burned cheap drugstore incense, and placed candles on the coffee table, bookshelves, and along the top of the entertainment center.

The candles were large and black. She'd purchased them from a boutique store that dealt in 'Objects of the Occult and Macabre.' She'd also purchased a bottle of 'Love Oil,' which she had (quite pointlessly, it turned out) smeared on her neck and chest, supposedly causing uncontrollable desire in anyone who dared sniff the rosy scent. The old woman at the register had giggled when she sold it to her and informed her to use it wisely. "Too much of this will make 'im rip the flesh from your bones!"

She'd spoken in such a savage tone that it frightened Gwen, as if the gravelly voice were issuing a true warning. Only the old woman's smirking lips gave her away.

"I'll be careful," Gwen had said.

The old woman had paused, shrugged, then rung up the candles, one by one. Her white-maned head stayed bowed, but after a moment her hazel eyes flicked up to meet Gwen's. "These, uh… recreational?"

"They're appropriate for the season, right?" Gwen said, uncertain what the woman was insinuating. "I mean, yeah, they're decorative."

"They are at that," she'd mumbled, as if disappointed, then bagged the candles and the oil, handed her the receipt with a small bow and more than a little flourish. "Enjoy your things, young miss. Enjoy the night. Be safe."

While stowing the bag into her Prius, Gwen had found the woman's behavior, in retrospect, more than a little odd.

Be safe? she'd thought, shaking her head as she started the car. Then she thought of the ridiculous love oil she'd purchased and laughed at herself, lightening the dour mood the old woman's behavior had provoked.

The memory saddens her now, knowing how things had eventually gone.

Gwen gazes at the clock. The red digits flash zeroes.

Odd.

She wonders when the house lost power, then realizes she could give a rat's ass. Be it morning or afternoon, she's determined to start her day.

Slowly—ever so slowly—she rolls onto her side, drops her legs (covered toes-to-thighs in red-and-black striped stockings) to the hardwood floor. She allows her head to hang until another wave of nausea passes, willing the sickness to dissipate.

After a moment, it does.

She takes a deep breath, stares longingly at the open bathroom door—and the hot shower waiting beyond—with the desperation of a desert wanderer eyeing a far-off oasis. As she stands on shaky legs, she spots her cell phone (tethered to a wall socket by a power cord) lying on the floor next to her nightstand. She considers it briefly, then kneels and taps the screen, bringing it to life. The phone, apparently, survived whatever power outage had occurred while she slept.

To her surprise (and bitter amusement), it's past noon. Her eyes dart to the mail, text message, and phone message icons in quick succession.

No messages.

No calls, no texts, no emails.

Nothing.

Silence.

Gwen frowns, sighs heavily, then lets the phone drop to the floor. As she walks to the bathroom, and the much-needed shower, she begins to remove her witch attire.

S he pukes in the shower.

Not something she's done before, and not something she is terribly proud of. But it happened, and that is that.

As she dries off, she wants to believe she feels better, that the hot shower has been restorative, washing away the dark realities, the shameful response, the inevitable pain of awareness. *Not so much,* she thinks, staring at her puffy eyes in the steam-coated mirror above the sink, angry that some of the black eye makeup has stubbornly refused to be washed away. She feels half-clean, semi-dirty. Blemished, scarred. Broken.

She slaps the mirror with the palm of her hand, wincing at the pain, but not regretting it. It's a chance to retaliate. Vainly and stupidly, sure, but it's something.

She recalls a quote from a philosophy book she read in college:

We cannot fight the universe with fleshly-gloved fists, so we must strike each other with such force that the universe flinches, thereby fortifying our existence.

"Crock 'o shit," she says to her reflection, allowing the steam to blur her visage into distorted blobs of black hair, pale smears of skin.

Fogged by the mist, her eye sockets are nothing but black hollows, and she imagines herself a ghost, or a ghoul. But she is neither of those things.

No no no... she thinks, and smiles for the first time since waking. She's a witch.

Dressed in her favorite stretch pants, black t-shirt and warm, cream sweater, Gwen heads to the kitchen to make coffee, the greatest of hangover elixirs.

Walking through the living room, she notices the staggered black candles are melted, having been left burning all night. The wax flowed over the sides, creating oily waterfalls that settled into fat collars around the bases of the wide candles, now monstrous in their deformity.

With a mental shrug she notes that much of the wax has dripped onto her thin brown carpet, run sloppily over the pressboard sides of a bookshelf, creating stalactites beneath one corner of the coffee table. One candle—the one she'd put on a shelf above the television—has bled down the screen's dead gray surface like long, bony fingers.

She remembers the day she and Robert purchased the expensive flatscreen, giggling about all the nights they would bask in its idiot glare, watching silly shows while sticking fingers between each other's thighs.

Gwen scoffs, then beelines to the kitchen and her new number one man.

Mr. Coffee.

"You're so hot," she says, opening the grounds bin and tossing out yesterday's batch. She smiles sadly at the lameness of her joke, the pathetic sadness of her situation, then pulls a filter from the cupboard above the sink. As she pushes the paper filter into the machine, she ignores the drip of tears that darkens it.

That afternoon, as the nascent November sun slices through her living room—mustard sunlight cuts through her two windows like golden fangs—Gwen cradles her third cup of coffee in one hand, her cell phone in the other.

Across from the couch, the television flickers black-and-white images of *An Affair to Remember*. She stares wistfully at the beautiful dead movie stars, one long, gnarled finger of wax splitting Cary Grant's stupid head in two.

Every few seconds she looks from one screen to the other, staring intently at her lifeless, un-ringing, unwanted, totally forgotten phone.

"Unbelievable," she mumbles, sniffling. A stray tear that had been swimming in her eye makes a break for it, throwing its life away. She imagines it silently screaming as it slides down her cheek, its substance deteriorating with each flesh-traced millimeter, the air clawing ruthlessly at its composition until it halts—dried nearly to nothing—just below her left nostril.

She wipes the watery corpse away mercilessly, spreads it onto her leg, then glares at the phone even harder.

"Damn you, then," she says, and tosses the phone onto the floor, where it clunks on the carpet and lies still. She will not text him. She will *not* call him. He has *destroyed* her life, taken years of her youth like a thief in the night.

She lifts her hand to stare at her fingers, the idiotic black nails, the bone-white line where she'd worn her engagement ring.

She still can't believe he asked for it back.

Filled with resignation, Gwen puts the mug on the table and throws herself onto the crimson cushions of her threadbare couch, sobbing out whatever is left inside until she feels completely and thoroughly emptied.

When Gwen opens her eyes, the television shows static.

She sits up on the couch, blindly reaches for the remote. She presses the channel button, thinking *next, next, next…*

When no shows appear, she clicks off the set in frustration, rubs the sleep webs from her eyes. Before she'd passed out (and after a good bout of tears), she'd retrieved her cell phone from the floor and ordered a pizza.

But looking at the screen, she's surprised to see it's now nearly 5 p.m. She'd ordered the pizza hours ago.

Hadn't she?

Not my day… she thinks sullenly, staring dumbly toward the windows, where the golden light has turned blood-red, leaving the inside of her living room dusky and shadowed. *When the hell had that happened?*

She tries to figure how long she'd nodded off, but time is suddenly flimsy, the day running together like spilled paint. *I was watching the movie, then called for pizza. Then…then…*

She'd apparently fallen asleep, despite having drunk enough coffee to make a sloth twitchy. And now she's *hungry.* Annoyed, she checks to be sure the pizza place hadn't called, perhaps to explain the delay.

How busy can you be the day after Halloween? she wonders, thinking of all the children suffering from sleep deprivation and stomach aches from their overindulgence eating candy the night before.

Gwen didn't hand out any candy. She'd planned to. Had *wanted* to. She always looked forward to seeing the costumes on the little neighbor kids, and because she didn't live in the greatest neighborhood, they usually came nice and early, showing up at dusk and continuing in a steady flow until she and Robert headed out for the night, usually around nine o'clock, to go find their parties. Always the same glorious routine.

She looks across the room, sees the large, orange ceramic bowl by the front door, bulging with treats, and feels a pang of guilt. The kids *had* come—knocking, or ringing the bell—waiting on their just rewards for dressing up and hauling themselves up and down the streets—pillowcases, plastic pumpkins, or grocery bags in their sweaty palms, extended toward each open door. She always thought of them as tiny tax collectors, making their way to every home to collect the dark taxes of their demonic master.

Trick or treat.

Pay or else.

She wants to smirk at the idea, but seeing the candy bowl brings back horrible, scattered memories of the previous night. The way she'd grown so frustrated, then scared, as Robert calmly—*oh so calmly, like speaking to a child*—explained that he was breaking it off. Breaking it all off. Taking back the ring. Ending it. As he spoke, in his infuriating monotone, about the reasons for his sudden change of heart *(which she knew to be complete bullshit because it was clearly another woman… It's* always *another woman),* the door had been thumped, the bell rung. Tiny voices called out from just beyond, demanding entry, demanding dark taxes.

"*Trick or treat,*" they'd yelled, sometimes solo, sometimes in a chorus. A couple times she'd seen a tiny hand at one of the front windows, raised in a curled fist, knocking at the glass like a demon in the night.

At one point she'd abruptly stood, leaving Robert in mid-sentence, strode furiously across the living room—her face already soaked in tears, her stupid witch makeup running everywhere—and slammed her hand against the porch's light switch, plunging the front of her house into darkness. She'd angrily pulled the curtains closed on both windows *(but they're open now, aren't they…)* before returning to the couch, absently plucking at the black folds of her witch costume, waiting for the torturous explanations from his stupid, sniveling little mouth to just stop. Stop. *Stop.*

As he rambled on, she'd thought, *How could I be so stupid? How could I not have seen this coming?* She'd known something was off the second he arrived—*not* wearing the mad scientist outfit, not wearing any costume at all, but dressed in khakis and a T-shirt, sporting trim glasses instead of his usual contacts, his hair neatly groomed.

"Where's your costume?" she'd said upon seeing him, standing in the doorway looking like Witch-fucking-Hazel. Like a bloody idiot.

He hadn't answered. Hadn't said a thing. He'd walked right past her, sat down on the couch, and waited. Waited until she closed the door and went to him, sat with him, not knowing the torture he had planned—the torture she was confident would end in her death. How could anyone live with the amount of pain he was inflicting? How could anyone go on after having their heart ripped out, the blood in their veins flushed with venom, their very soul feeling as if it had been cursed? Forever damned.

Gwen continues sifting through the quagmire of the previous night's horrors, gazing absently at the untouched bowl of candy... when a knock comes at the door.

She checks her phone. It's a bit past five-thirty. No more sunlight comes through the windows. Outside, the evening has curled itself comfortably, like an ethereal black cat, around her world.

She stands with a huff, clicks on the lamp by the couch, its shade still draped in decorative crimson lace. It stains the room red.

"About time," she says, stomach grumbling at the thought of hot food, and goes to greet the visitor.

I t's a goblin.

Or, perhaps, a zombie? The mask covering the child's head has the texture of melted plastic—hairless, gray—and is streaked with shadow and crusted blood. Through the eyelets she sees two bright blue eyes looking up at her earnestly.

Begging.

The goblin...zombie...whatever, wears a tiny blue jumpsuit and clutches a brown paper bag, the local grocery store's logo stamped and faded along the side. His small hands hold the bag wide open, aiming its maw at her face.

Gwen stares down at the boy, no older than ten or eleven, with astonishment. This isn't the pizza guy. This is something else.

She tries to smile, then glances up and around, past him, searching for a group of giggling kids, perhaps a shameful parent making up for a late night at work the day before. It's dark, though. Her porch light had been turned off and the streetlights, although lit, are dull, their usual pooling glow dying somewhere in the dark between fixture and pavement, as if eaten by the night. The street itself is empty—deserted—and she notices many of the other houses are darkened. The Santilli house across the street, usually bursting with light and activity around dinnertime, is dark and quiet. Their kids aren't running in the yard, the television—the one she always sees flashing sitcoms through their bay window—is a lifeless shadow.

Gwen leans forward, peers left, then right. Cars line the street, but none drive down it.

There is nothing. No one.

She shudders, feeling the chill of the moist night air, then reaches her hand to the switch by the door, and flips it. The porch light comes to life, and she can see the boy more clearly. He doesn't react to the light coming on, only shuffles his feet impatiently and shakes the bag a little, as if telling her to *get on with it already*.

"But…" Gwen says, trying to override her confusion. "It's not Halloween. You know that, right?" She smiles at him, trying her best to sound *reasonable*, trying not to sound scolding, or embarrass him.

But the boy just lifts the bag even higher, the blue eyes inside the horrid mask never blinking, never shifting, never leaving her own.

"Well," she says, unsure how to proceed, the boy's stare working on her nerves. "I suppose it's fine. Anyway, I do have some leftover candy."

Gwen reaches back and picks up the heavy orange bowl overflowing with untouched treats. She plucks two items from the top and drops them into the child's bag. She can tell by the sound the candy makes when it hits the bottom—*plunk plunk*—that the bag is empty.

I should think so, she thinks. *No doubt I'm the only idiot on the street giving out candy the day* after *Halloween.*

She has a small laugh at the ridiculousness of the thing, then smiles at the boy kindly. "We good?"

The boy watches her a moment more, then lowers the bag and looks into it. Without a sound, he spins and leaps from her porch, jogs briskly down the concrete walk bisecting her weedy yard, then turns onto the sidewalk. She watches him go for a moment, baffled at the strange occurrence.

As she starts to close the door, she catches a flicker at the corner of her eye. Turning back toward the porch, she notices that her pumpkin—carved to look like a grinning vampire—is lit.

"Huh," Gwen says, and steps onto the porch to look more closely, wondering how it had stayed alight throughout the entirety of the last twenty-four hours.

Suddenly, there's an eruption of sharp, high-pitched cackling from just behind her and she screams, heart leaping to her throat. She spins to see bulging yellow eyes staring back at her. Gwen gapes dumbly at a wrinkled face, stuck in a repulsive rictus, brown plastic teeth snarling.

Its horrid, mirthless laughter rips apart the quiet, gloomy night.

"Holy shit," she says, clutching her sweater with shaky hands.

She stares at the decorative toy witch—and its glowing eyes—for another moment, until the internal timer winds itself out and the eyes dim to silent orbs. The cackling halts abruptly, leaving a silence so complete she feels like screaming.

"You come down soon, crone," Gwen says, and pushes through the doorway.

At the movement, the witch's eyes light again, and the cackling resumes full force. Gwen hustles inside and slams the door shut, leaning her back against it as she waits for the horrible laughter to subside.

"Nasty old bitch," she says, heart pounding in her chest, and unceremoniously drops the candy bowl onto a nearby table.

In the ten minutes that follow the visit of the lone trick-or-treater, Gwen calls the pizza place three times.

No answer.

Then she tries *another* pizza place.

No answer.

"What the hell?" she says, glaring angrily at her phone, as if it were somehow at fault. Starving and frustrated, she eyes the candy. "Well, if we're gonna go that route…" she mutters, then stands up and walks to the kitchen.

Gwen returns clutching a freshly opened bottle of red wine and a stocky juice glass. She sets them on the coffee table and picks out a handful of candy from the orange bowl. Now well-stocked, she falls back onto the couch, giggling at her dinner of wine and chocolate, the rare indulgence almost enough to curb the nettling pain in her broken, hungover heart. She grabs the remote (hopeful the reception has returned) and prepares to watch some bad movies—perhaps a raunchy comedy, something to go with her mood…

There's a heavy knock at the door.

"Are you kidding me?" she says, having already peeled the wrapper off a mini-Snickers, hungrily eyeing the bottle of wine. With a heavy sigh, she gets up to answer.

On her porch are three more trick-or-treaters. One is a girl in a ballerina outfit, her dark hair pulled back from a cherubic face, brown eyes wide and eager. Beside her, a larger boy wears a rubber wolf mask and (somewhat confusingly) a frayed black robe, long enough that it hides his feet.

When she studies the third child, she almost takes a step back.

He's small and thin, seemingly much younger than the other boy, and dressed neatly in a traditional black suit. *A mortician's suit,* she thinks, not knowing why she jumped to that conclusion, but also knowing she's right.

The boy's hair is greased down over his tiny skull, and he wears small, wire-framed spectacles. What she finds especially unsettling, however, is the boy's face.

It's scarred. Horribly so.

His neck appears to have been badly burned at one time in his life, and is now covered in sinewy, pink molten skin that creeps out from beneath the starched white collar of his dress shirt. Riding across his upper lip is a scar so deep it lifts his lips into a permanent snarl, his large white teeth peeking out, as if from behind a red curtain. The side of his face is also badly scarred, but not burned...as though he'd been clawed by a savage animal. Long, jagged red lines run from his scalp, down through his cheek to his jawline. *Looks like the kid was dipped into hot fire while being attacked by a damn bear,* she thinks, simultaneously feeling pity and revulsion, followed by a wave of guilt for her horrible lack of sensitivity.

"Trick or treat," the wolf boy says loudly. Gwen jerks her eyes away from the little undertaker and turns back to the others. The ballerina stares up at her, close-mouthed, eyes greedily wide. Gwen glances blankly at their three open sacks, each made from identical white cloth, the fabric coarse and frayed. *The kind you'd slip over someone's head when kidnapping them,* she thinks randomly, then shakes her head to clear the dark thought.

"I'm sorry," Gwen stammers, confused and still ashamed for staring so long at the poor boy's scarred face. "I'm sorry," she repeats, and again looks toward the darkened street for someone to explain this all to her. For *anyone,* really.

But the street is empty.

"Trick or treat," repeats the deep, rough voice from under the wolf mask, as if growing impatient. As if hungry.

In a stupor, Gwen reaches inside for the bowl of candy, drops a couple pieces in each of their odd cloth sacks.

"You may as well take it all," she says, trying to laugh but failing. "I mean, Halloween is over, right?"

Instead of responding, the ballerina looks quickly to the boy in the mask, who nods sagely—some tacit agreement—and then they turn and walk away.

The little undertaker, however, hasn't moved. She notices the boy is *quivering*; his cheeks shake like jelly, and his still-outstretched hands begin to tremble. He glares at her with what is something akin to pure terror. Gwen starts to say something when the rough voice of the boy in the wolf mask—shouting from the yard—breaks the spell.

"Let's go!" he yells.

As if woken from a trance, the boy in the suit snaps his bag shut, turns on his heel and all but runs after the other two, who are already disappearing into the cold night.

Gwen watches them go, then turns to go inside when the witch hanging on the door comes to life. She yelps and clutches her chest as the witch cackles, those damned yellow eyes glowing with malevolence.

"Think I've had enough of you," Gwen says, and reaches behind the witch's face to find a small toggle switch at the base of the skull, then turns the old hag OFF. The laughter stops. The eyes go dark. Wanting to be sure, Gwen waves a hand before the small sensor in the witch's plastic forehead.

Thankfully, the old girl stays silent.

As Gwen goes back inside, she forces herself to ignore the glow of the jack-o'-lantern sitting atop the front banister, assuring herself it must have been one of those children who had turned the fanged visage around, giving the illusion that it's watching the house.

Watching *her*.

It gives Gwen great comfort to shut the door firmly, sealing herself safely inside the scarlet-tinted living room, ready to drink a hearty portion of the red wine, which awaits her return with the utmost eagerness.

The wine is gone.

Well, the first bottle anyway. A second one, Gwen muses as she pulls the cork, is *untouched.*

The coffee table is covered in candy wrappers and the television plays static, and she couldn't care less. Right now, her mind feels free and fine. She's finally a version of calm and doesn't feel like *thinking,* like *remembering.*

Forgetting is the thing. Yes, forgetting is the *cure-all.*

Just forget... she thinks dreamily, eyes closing, the intoxication from the wine taking over, letting her drift away...

When she hears the *stomp-stomp-stomp* of feet on her porch.

"Oh boy," she groans. Sitting up too quickly, she reels, light-headed, and sits back down, one hand pressed to her forehead, allowing herself a moment. When she finally pushes up from the couch, stumbling a little as the room tips, she walks to the door carefully, as if walking a balance beam. "Let's do this," she says boldly, smiling wide as she swings the door open.

As she looks outside, however, her grin turns into a confused frown.

There are children *everywhere.*

On her porch alone there are at least five: a child covered in a gray sheet pretending to be a ghost, two little witches with pointy black hats, a gauze-wrapped mummy. There's also a boy wearing a hockey mask and carrying a bloody hatchet. Was it Jason? Or Michael? She always gets the two mixed up. He isn't Freddy, because Freddy's the one *(with the burnt skin and the scars)* with the blades on his fingers, and the striped sweater.

As she studies the children on her porch, she can't help thinking that a couple of them seem a little, well...*off.*

The mummy, whose head and body are wrapped in sloppy, dirty bandages—a tuft of black hair sticking from his uncovered pate like a patch of unmown grass—is missing an arm. Where his right arm should be is nothing but a loose, dangling bandage. In the other arm, he holds a plastic candy bag. He's holding it toward her.

How can he even see? she thinks.

There's a deep grunt, and she forgets about the mummy and turns toward the ghost. She notices the feet under the gray sheet are bare, filthy, and covered with oozing red sores. Where a face would (normally) be, two eyes stare back at her through large, jaggedly cut out holes. In the dark, Gwen can't tell what color the eyes are, but they're open astonishingly *wide*, as if the child underneath doesn't have eyelids. His plastic bag, which is empty (and looks like it'd been dragged from a gutter) is held by hands that twitch and shake, causing the bag to rustle like a street beggar's.

They *all* hold their bags up. Waiting, beckoning.

Patiently, Gwen puts candy in each of them, one by one.

When the children turn to leave, she takes a few steps onto her porch and looks up and down the street so she can watch them all walking—so many of them—their small bodies flickering in and out of the darkness as they pace both sides of the street in their strange costumes, like spirits on parade.

She listens closely for the sounds of laughter, or happy screams, or a few parent-inspired calls of "thank you!" from the neighboring homes.

But it's silent. So very silent.

Gwen shrugs. It doesn't matter. As impossible as it seems, it's obviously Halloween again—that much is certain. Laughing to herself, she spins around, reaches behind the witch's face, and flips the switch back to ON.

Then she goes inside, walking fast now, excited to join the fun.

She pours another glass of wine, drinks it down in two swallows, then sets the glass on the coffee table and swoons slightly, giggling as the room sways, then steadies.

The black candles in the living room all burn brightly, their flickering light beating against the walls and ceiling. Gwen's a little curious as to how *that* happened—because *she* certainly hadn't lit them.

Oddly, she realizes that she's not surprised.

Not surprised at all.

"If you can't beat 'em…" she says, hiccupping like a drunk from an old cartoon, and strides purposely to her bedroom, where her costume lies waiting.

Gwen turns on the bathroom light and studies her face in the mirror. Her black hair is pulled tightly away from her face—not in the clumpy fun style she had experimented with the day before, but slicked flat with a firm-hold gel. She applies coal-black lipstick and reapplies makeup to her eyes, putting on the same mascara, eyeshadow, and dark eyeliner she used previously, although now she does it with more precision and a little flourish, curling the eyeliner away from her eyes to create a subtle winged effect. She purses her lips, gazes deeply into her own hazel eyes, and sponges her cheekbones with a stark-white cream.

With one last look at her remade face, she turns from the mirror and walks into the bedroom. Stripped to her underwear, she begins to put on the modified costume.

She'd taken scissors to the dress, cutting the layered frills away and hacking the fabric until it clung in daggers just below her hips. She replaces the striped stockings with fishnet nylons, supplants the clunky black loafers she'd had on yesterday with her best pair of black high heels, the ones she only wears on special occasions.

As she scoops up the pointed black hat that came with the costume—the one item she had felt needed no alteration—her eye catches a shadowed figure by the doorway leading to the living room. She grabs the hat and, unconcerned, takes a moment to study herself in the full-length mirror. She presses the hat snugly over her plastered-down hair, her eyes darkening nicely as her face falls into shadow under the wide brim.

When she finally turns toward the door, she sees there isn't just one shadow. There's three.

Three children—all wearing costumes—stand in her living room, waiting for her. She walks briskly toward them, chin high, spine straight. The children quickly back away, leaving her space to pass untouched.

In the living room, she fills a glass from the second bottle of wine and guzzles it down. Grinning with excitement, she looks at the clock hung over the couch.

7:40

Almost time.

There's a tug at Gwen's waist and she looks down. It's one of the children, of course—the odd undertaker. He holds a long, sharp knife toward her in one tiny, clenched hand. She takes it, smiles reassuringly. She wants to pat his head but sees the bugs crawling through the strands of his greasy hair and stays her hand.

She spins toward another insistent tugging to face the ballerina, her big brown eyes gazing up with the purest form of love there is in the universe—the kind of love you know, without a doubt, will never stray, will never be broken, will never be betrayed.

She holds out Gwen's engagement ring.

Gwen kneels, smiles, and plucks the ring from the little girl's fingers.

"Thank you," she says in a whisper, slipping it onto her pale, cold finger. It settles perfectly over the white line, the place where it had so recently lived.

The ballerina opens her mouth to reply and Gwen notices that the girl has no tongue—her teeth are black arrowheads, her mouth a foul cavern of peeling gray flesh.

"*Ee uv ooo*," the girl manages. "*Fo eva.*"

Gwen strokes the ballerina's cool cheek with the tip of a finger, then knuckles away a grateful tear from her own eye. "Thank you," she says.

Getting back to her feet, Gwen looks around the room at the other children who have come to welcome her. She grips the knife tightly, excited to have another chance at finding true love, once and forever.

"It's like a do-over," she says quietly to herself, steadying her nerves. "And this time," she says, glancing around at the expectant children, "Robert won't *ever* leave me."

Some of the children nod fervently, others giggle. One of them, she notices, is lying atop another, writhing and moaning. The ghost with the sores on his feet is slumped in a corner, lidless eyes glaring broodingly at the others in the room. The bigger child, the one in the wolf mask and black robe, is repeatedly sticking something into his neck, and bleeding freely. A few of the others appear to be eating something raw, bloody, and wiggling.

Certainly not candy.

Gwen stands tall among them, her eyes on the door. It's so close now.

For a moment, she allows herself to think back to the morning, when she woke up so sad. So alone. She'd seen the emptied bottles on the nightstand that were once filled with booze.

And then there were the *other* bottles.

The smaller ones. The orange ones. The ones once filled with pills. So many pills.

All gone, she thinks in a sing-song voice. *All gone now.*

She hears footsteps on the porch. They're heavy, and slow.

Her wide eyes stare fixedly at the door, and all the children stop their playing and turn to look as well, waiting for their lover to return.

This time there will be no mistake.

Gwen digs the knife into the flesh of her arm, slices upward, from wrist to elbow. The blood runs like a dark stream down her fingers, flowing in long rivulets to the floor.

She ignores the scurrying bodies that fight for it, the aggravated shuffling and slurping taking place beneath her.

Instead, she takes a deep breath, exhales through black lips, and reminds herself that she is a witch. A proud, perfect witch.

A thundering fist strikes the door hard enough to rattle the wood in its frame.

BOOM! BOOM! BOOM!

The violent knocks shake the walls. The whole room—glowing with the deep crimson of the covered lamps and the flickering, climbing orange of the candle flames—waits in anticipation.

He's back, she thinks, knowing it a lie. *He's come back to me…*

Gwen feels herself growing lighter as the blood leaks from her veins, flows freely to the hungry children below. On the porch, the crone hanging on the door begins her cackling laughter, set off by the visitor. Gwen thinks of the bulging, glowing yellow eyes and begins to laugh along with it, cackling loudly and sharply—nearly shrieking—as the door handle rattles. She raises her hands, fingers clawed, her face frozen in a rictus grin of mad amusement—and now she's laughing so hard she can barely breathe, and she cannot shut her wide, tearing eyes bulging in her head, splitting her face open at the edges.

With the final crash of a massive fist, the door slams inward, and her lover is there, right on time.

The children scream in terrible joy as her betrothed enters, ducking into the room, leathery flesh resplendent in the candlelight. Gwen has time to notice the face of the witch hanging on the door, blazing eyes bulbous and leaking, her plastic cheeks puffed out with the efforts of her own plastic grin and hysterical laughter. On the porch, the jack-o'-lantern has split apart, its body melting over the edges of the banister, strings of orange pulp dangling among chunks of pumpkin like greasy hair.

And beyond the porch? There is nothing. No more street, no more houses.

Nothing but swirling, abyssal darkness.

Still laughing in giant, heaving sobs, Gwen drops the knife and goes to him. When their gazes meet her skin dries like parchment left in the desert sun, turning wrinkled and pinched. Her black nails grow long, sharp, and curved. She turns to study her reflection in the window—notices her eyes are now flame-yellow, her raven hair faded to ghost white.

She is the sister of the witch on the door, who is now screaming, and Gwen cackles madly as she steps into her lover's embrace.

As the room dissolves, she knows—knows deep in her dead, blackened heart—that this time things will be different.

This time, no one will be leaving.

IN THE NIGHT, A WHISPER

by Robert Stahl

1

A darkened street on Halloween night. A throng of children follow an adult with a flashlight, their shoes clopping on the sidewalk, all of them giggling, shouting, merry. Costumes flap, rustle, jingle. Flashes of color: gold, white, silver, blue. A skinny skeleton smooths his sleeve. A pint-sized robot steadies an antenna on her head. They carry items to collect their loot: a plastic pumpkin, a shopping bag, a pillowcase. The yellow blob of a flashlight sweeps the lawns glistening with evening dew. All are too occupied to notice the dark figure in the shadows of a hedge. She watches them silently, stealthily before slipping into the group.

2

Her costume is specifically chosen. A scarlet smock pulled from her mother's closet, slightly threadbare and faded. Her dark wiry hair is pulled into a bun to keep it out of her eyes. A waist-length cape flutters on her back. The mask is plastic and cheap, an item she begged for at the drugstore. It conceals the top of her face except her steely blue eyes, which stare out beneath two snaggy horns. Along the mask's bottom, a row of jagged teeth stretches over her own mouth, giving her an infernal, frightening grin. Her sneakers are dusty, the soles as smooth as a cat's belly.

3

She blends in without fanfare, without protest, without the batting even of an eye. Deftly, foxily, cunningly she keeps pace with them on the sidewalk, her feet shuffling with theirs, as silent as a whisper. Soon, it's like she'd always been there. Not all the children know each other. Trick-or-treating is a communal occasion, the more the merrier. Their costumes make it difficult to keep track of everyone, anyway.

4

At every door, the same mantra is heard: "Trick or treat! Smell our feet! Give us something good to eat!"

5

Swooping from door to door, they hunt for confections like flies seeking honey. Their thoughts are of red licorice ribbons, long as their forearms and as supple as rubber bands. Of vibrant hard candies that fizz on their tongues like soda. Of fruity jellies dusted with sparkling sugar crystals. Of warm caramel globs smudging the corners of their mouths. Of fragrant chocolate bars melting on their fingers. Of the satisfying crunch of malt balls. Of sticky brittle clinging like cement to their molars. Of the achy zing of lemon drops on their tastebuds. Of giant sweet lollies that last all day and stain their lips crimson, violet, emerald.

6

Doors swing open. Oohs, ahhhs, gasps. The procession transpires with serpentine precision. Candies drop into bags: thunk, thunk, thunk.

7

"Oh, look at you sweet little things! Happy Halloween to you all! What's this, a pirate? How jolly. With a hook for a hand, no less. I hope you gave that crocodile a good what for! Here, have some toffee and a cinnamon stick. A vampire! Such makeup. Truly frightening. Here you go, here you go. And here! A precious little princess. Three pieces for you dear; shhh, it's our secret. And you, Mr. Doctor. Is the stethoscope your father's? You must tell him to lower my bill. And oh! Lookit this little girl. Is she a witch? Who knows, who knows? Happy Halloween to you, sweetie. And here! A wizard! With a magic wand, to boot. How quaint! And who's this holding up the rear? A cat girl? No, my mistake. A devil, perhaps? My, that's a scary mask, dear. Did you make it yourself? Oh, a quiet one, I see. Didn't your mother tell you it's rude not to answer your elders? And it wouldn't hurt you to smile dear. It's Halloween, after all, my goodness. One piece for you, now off you go, you odd little thing. Next year, try not to take yourself so seriously."

8

In the crowd, she walks next to this child, then that one. Her gaze returns to the boy in the ghost costume. Even without seeing his expression, his eyes tell her everything. He's awkward around others, a little nervous, probably a bit of a loner. Perfect.

9

For the boy in the ghost costume, it's his best night ever. Under the white sheet, a grin crinkles his face, his round cheeks flush in the cool air. His pulse is quick, excited. The plastic bag in his hand, nearly half-full, swells pleasantly. His gaze jumps nimbly from the glowing full moon to the spooky lawn decor, to the remaining doors on the block, to the passing groups of children—so many, so many. He is wondering if his treats will last 'til Christmas when there's a tap on his shoulder.

10

"You like candy?"
          "Oh yes, so much."
     "I know a place that has lots of it. The good stuff. Better than here."
     "Like what?"
     "Like cream eggs and Bon Bons and candy cigarettes and cupcakes as big as your hand."
     "Where?"
     "Just a few streets over. Follow me."
     "Mmm, I don't know."
     "No risk, no reward. What are you, a fraidy cat?"

11

He follows, dreaming of butterscotch clusters and nougat bars. His mouth waters, anticipating the heady rush of sugar in his body. Onward she leads him, around a corner, through an alley, into another neighborhood. When he looks up again, the streets are dark, the houses are ugly, unfamiliar. An owl hoots overhead. Where are his companions, he wonders? Their laughter has died away.

12

"Jump, already," says the girl in the devil costume. She sits on her haunches on the other side of the gully.

He shifts uneasily, gauging the distance—ten feet that seem like a mile. He stares down past the steep drop below where a creek burbles through a rocky bed. It's a good fall if he misses, with nothing to slow his descent except vines, trash, weeds. "You sure it's safe?" he whines over the lump in his throat. "What if I don't make it?"

"You will," she laughs. "If I can do it, so can you."

A running jump, that's all he needs. He takes a few steps back, inhales deeply, the muscles in his young legs coiled like springs.

13

So close, she thinks. He's so close to doing it! She eases forward to watch, trying to keep a straight face. When he misses, the fool—when he falls and he plummets, she will look away. Nor will she gaze down at his young body shattered against the boulders. She's not a monster, after all. Just lonely, just bored, wanting someone to play with. Jump! Jump! *Jump!*

14

Searing light fills the eyeholes in his costume. A hand pulls him back by his scruff. "Bobby!" the adult with the flashlight scolds. "Didn't you hear me calling?" The boy gapes wide-eyed into the light and blinks as if waking from a dream. "What on earth are you doing?"

"Following her," he says, pointing across the chasm at the girl.

Of course, nobody's there.

15

"I hate you," she'd screamed at her mother through the thin bedroom door. Grounded! On Halloween night! If only she hadn't talked back when she'd been asked to take out the trash. But where was the fun in that? By that time in her young life, sarcasm had become a habit, a defense mechanism, a way of existence. Damn it! She simply *had* to go trick-or-treating! Especially when she'd worked so hard on her costume.

So, she'd locked her bedroom door. Turned the radio up loud. Crawled into the smock. Tied on the mask, the cape. While Ritchey Valens sang "Donna," she crept out the window and into the darkness. Within an hour, every door on her street was visited. Her candy bag felt heavy, threating to burst.

16

The officer knelt under a great gnarled tree. He shook his head at the body; such a shame to lose them so young. Her costume reminded him of his own daughter at home, and he grieved silently for her parents. The devil mask soaked in a puddle nearby. Around the girl's neck, dark bruises mottled the flesh.

17

She was heading home, her head held high and a satisfied grin on her face when the old station wagon pulled up beside her. Lost in her thoughts, she barely cared at all—until the car stopped. The door opened. A large man bounded in front of the headlights. In one brutal instant, everything changed. A rough calloused hand clamped over her mouth. Strong hairy arms ensnared her. The stench of his sweat filled her nose. She flailed, kicked, and scratched, but ultimately was forced into the car.

18

She watches the yellow blob of light recede with blue murky eyes. A shudder passes through what's left of her heart. She wrings her hands together, as if to massage away the disappointment. She removes the mask, soaks the smock with her tears. Next year she will try again. Until then she will walk the streets alone, a wraith in the shadows, her only company the moon, the owls, the darkness. Her head drops into her hands, and she huddles under a rotting elm. Above her and all around, the night's shadows creep, gnaw, devour. Her bony shoulders quake with sadness, with shame, with loneliness.

THE HOOPER STREET
HALLOWEEN DECORATION COMMITTEE

by Gemma Amor

"I think the new neighbors are fucking with us," my wife said one morning. She was gazing out the window, chewing on a strand of hair.

"Oh yeah?" Only half-listening, face in my laptop, my brain was working over a particularly-knotty technical paper I had to edit.

"Yeah." She chose not to elaborate.

I sighed. Something was wrong, but Lisa didn't want to venture the information as to *what* exactly was wrong. Rather, she wanted me to drag it out of her. Even though she could see I was working, or trying to. I silently cursed the state of the world for the thousandth time that year, wishing fervently that the stupid goddamn global virus would fuck off so I could go back to the office and *concentrate* for a hot fucking minute, instead of being constantly interrupted.

But I didn't say this out loud.

"Fucking with us how, Lisa?" I dragged my gaze away from my screen. Full-eye contact was the only acceptable way out of this. It was a wrench: I was overdue, a deadline weight pressing down on me. Still, better to nip this mood in the bud now than deal with a full-scale argument later down the line.

Lisa pulled something out of her pocket, handed it to me across the breakfast table. That special kind of summer-end sun spilled in through a window and fell onto her face as she did so, highlighting tired features, worry lines, creases. I thought momentarily how pretty she looked despite this but didn't say anything. I took the piece of paper she offered instead.

My wife went back to chewing her hair.

Unfolding the paper, I saw a note written in bold, child-like capitals. It said:

WELCOME, NEW NEIGHBOR!

YOU ARE CORDIALLY INVITED TO THE HOOPER STREET HALLOWEEN DECORATION PLANNING COMMITTEE

TONIGHT, 7pm, AT NO. 18.

HOPE TO SEE Y'ALL THERE!

A smiling pumpkin had been stamped on the bottom of the note in orange ink.

I rubbed a hand across my face. Our new neighbors were apparently going to be 'that type' of people.

"Halloween planning committee?" I handed the note back. "It's fucking August!"

"I know." Lisa snorted. "I thought we'd be able to avoid all this community crap when we moved here."

Me too, I thought, but for different reasons.

"Well, I *hate* Halloween," my wife continued. "And I particularly hate people talking about Halloween when it's seventy-five degrees outside. I sure as hell won't be joining in any planning."

"I mean..." I chewed on my lip, thinking. "We've been here nearly a month now, and we haven't spoken to anyone much... It might be..."

"I'm not going! Who starts planning Halloween in August? Unless *you* want to go." She lifted an eyebrow at me.

I shuddered. "Fuck no, I've got work to do."

A sharp edge came into her voice. "And I don't?"

I lowered my head. "I'm not getting into this again."

"Of course you're not." Her tone was sour. "You're the breadwinner. Your job takes precedence. Why don't I get back to the laundry and make friends with all the other housewives on the street, is that it?"

I went back to my laptop. "I'm not doing this," I repeated, firmly.

"You don't do *anything* with me. That's the problem!"

I could sense the old, familiar anger bubbling inside her, and cursed the note.

Pulling out my headphones, I slipped them over my ears and went back to work, communicating that her time with me was over.

Lisa stared at me in disbelief for a moment or two as I typed. Then, she pushed back her chair and left the room.

My insides unclenched. I went back to my paper. I really was *very* behind.

At seven thirty-five that evening, as we watched something shitty on TV, our doorbell rang.

Lisa glared at me, then took a long sip of wine without breaking eye contact. "Are you expecting me to get that?"

I heaved myself off the couch. "I would never dream of it."

I opened the door to find our right-side neighbor standing on the porch, smiling. My mind went full tilt, trying to remember her name. *Louisa!* Relief hit me, until I saw what she held in her hand: The invitation to the 'Hooper Street Halloween Decoration Committee.'

My heart sank. "Hi!" I said, brightly. "Louisa, isn't it?"

"Louise," the middle-aged woman with bright pink lipstick corrected. "Jackson." She extended her hand, remembered we weren't supposed to do things like that anymore, then proffered her elbow instead. I bumped mine into hers by way of saying 'hello.'

"It's so nice to finally meet you," I lied, wondering how I was going to explain our snubbing a clearly important invitation. I silently cursed Lisa for leaving me to deal with this shit.

Louise held up the invitation without further ceremony.

"We *did* hope to see y'all at our Halloween decoration planning committee this evening."

She cocked her head to one side, eyes beady and bright.

"Ah," I said, mind still working.

"Y'all did get the invitation, right? Mariah said she put one through your door." She pointed in the vague direction of Mariah's house, across the street. "When y'all didn't show… Naturally, we were *very* disappointed, and then I thought, maybe they're just feeling *shy*, so as your closest neighbor, I thought I'd offer to introduce y'all to everyone else! And here,' she finished, bouncing up and down on her toes expectantly, "I am."

"Oh, jeez," I said, putting on my most beleaguered expression. "I'm sorry, Louise. It's just, well, we haven't had a minute to ourselves since we moved in. And with this virus and all…" I waved a hand, hoping the gesture would explain our antisocial behavior, because I didn't want to reveal the *real* reason.

Louise let out a brittle laugh that reminded me of glass shattering.

"Oh, I understand. Moving is stressful enough without having to entertain your nosey new neighbors. I get it! That's why we thought we'd leave y'all alone at first. But time's ticking on, and Halloween ain't that far off, so…"

"It's August," I said.

She ignored me. "Everything's all set up, and I promise it'll be fun! Frank lit his portable fire pit, all cosy and nice, everything safe and socially distanced. You don't need to worry about any of that virus stuff."

I sighed. "Louise, it's a very kind invitation, and we are *so* grateful you thought of us. But…my wife is not feeling well, and with all the work I'm behind on…we just can't make it tonight. My apologies."

"Oh." Louise let the word linger as her smile froze. Clearly, she was not used to rejection.

"Not even for five minutes?"

I stood my ground. "I'm sorry."

"Oh," Louise said again. She looked devastated.

Then, she rallied. Her eyes narrowed.

"Oh well, never mind," she chirruped, although, obviously, she *did* mind. She minded a whole lot. "These things happen. Maybe we can come over later this week with the minutes from the meeting. How about that? When Lisa's feeling better, of course. Then we can find out what *your* plans are for Halloween, make sure they match up with *our* plans." She turned her smile up to maximum, eyes boring into my face like twin drills.

I began to get the message: Halloween was very, *very* important to the residents of Hooper Street.

"Well…" I was as noncommittal as possible without offending. "Truth told…we don't really go in for all that," I said.

The smile dropped clean off Louise's face. The drilling stare remained. "I'm sorry?"

I felt the blood rush to my cheeks in embarrassment.

"We don't…*do* Halloween. Lisa isn't keen. We're quiet folks. We keep to ourselves."

Louise's expression made me feel as if I'd just run over her pet puppy. My face burned.

"You don't…like Halloween?" Her voice sounded like a small child's.

"It's just not our thing."

My neighbor drew herself up high and tight like a cobra about to strike. "I see."

I tried to salvage the situation. "You're still welcome to come over for a cup of coffee. I'm sure we would both love that. I mean, it's not like we're going anywhere, is it? Ha ha ha!" Gabbling like an idiot, I stopped myself.

"No, that's okay," Louise said, quietly. "You have lots of work to do, and Lisa *isn't feeling well*." She eyed me up and down, then marched away straight-backed as an army major.

"Apologies again!" I called out, wondering why my life was full of angry women.

There was no reply.

I closed the door, letting out a huge sigh.

Great, I thought. *One month in, and we've upset the entire street already.*

But I had no idea how pissed the residents of Hooper Street really were, until a week later.

"**B**abe? *Babe!* Have you *seen?*" Lisa shouted from the bottom of the stairs.

Another day, another interruption, I thought. Such was life working from home.

"*Luke!*" Lisa said.

"*What?*" I bellowed back, annoyed. "I'm *working!*"

"The neighbors!"

"Which ones?" I snapped.

"Right-side neighbors! You gotta come look!"

"Okay, okay, I'm coming, Jesus H, give me a moment!" I levered myself out of my office chair and trudged downstairs.

Lisa waited for me in the hall, beckoning me to come over to the porch window. Her mouth was a thin line of anger. "Look."

I peered through the slim panel of glass.

"See it?"

Lisa's closeness made me shudder. "What am I supposed to be looking f— Oh, wow... What the fuck is *that?*" I laughed.

Because the Jacksons—our *closest* neighbors—had clearly gotten some encouragement at their Halloween Decoration Committee meeting. The result was plain for all to see. Standing in their front yard, bold as brass, towering easily ten, if not twelve feet high, was a giant plastic skeleton. It was enormous, the size of a small tree, and stood with its legs braced wide apart, one arm down at its side, the other raised in a menacing pose, as if to wrestle me. And its head was turned to face our property. The skeleton was, in effect, staring at us.

"Wow," I repeated. "That is…something."

"*Right?* How dare they?"

Confused, I tried to figure out what Lisa was driving at. "I mean, it's tacky, but not worth getting worked up over…"

"Are you out of your fucking gourd?" Lisa erupted, spraying the side of my face with her contempt. "*That* is clearly retaliation for us not going to the stupid meeting!"

I blinked. "What?"

"They may as well have come to the front door and flipped us off!"

"I think you're reading too much into it," I said, putting some distance between us. "They're just Halloween nuts, is all. No one is out to get us."

Even as I said it, I remembered Louise walking stiffly away from our house and down the road, invitation clutched in one well-manicured hand.

"No, the neighbors are pissed at us because we wouldn't go to the stupid fucking meeting, and now they are trolling us with that giant fucking monstrosity!" Lisa was furious. "And it's not even fucking September yet! What are you going to do about this, Luke?"

I frowned. "What can *I* do?"

"I don't know… Something!'

A headache threatened. "You want me to creep out in the middle of the night and dismantle it? Be reasonable. It's just a decoration.'

"It's a declaration of war, that's what it is!"

I could see her eyes doing that strange far-away thing they did sometimes. The veins in her neck were popping too.

"Okay, okay," I said, trying to avoid a meltdown. "I'll go talk to them, but that's the *only* thing I can do. There's no law against putting a giant skeleton in your yard in August. I'll just…casually mention that we noticed it.'

"Now?" she asked.

"When I go to the store."

Lisa stood there clenching and unclenching her fists. I led her to the living room and sat her in front of the TV with a glass of water before heading back upstairs to salvage what I could of my workday.

I timed my visit to the store so I would be out front the same time as Louise, a few hours later. I found her bustling around the feet of the giant skeleton, clearing space for what I could only assume would be *more* Halloween decorations.

"Hey, neighbor!" I said, walking over.

Louise straightened up. "Hey, *neighbor.*" Her cheeks were bright from being outside. "Catching up with all that *important work?*"

"Just heading to the store,' I replied, squinting up at the giant decoration towering above us. "Who's this?"

Louise chuckled. "Ain't he cute? I call him Skeleton Jack."

"He's certainly...something." From where I stood, I could see the damn thing had eyeballs instead of empty eye-sockets. They gave me the heebers.

"They're selling them over at Home Depot." Louise looked at Skeleton Jack as proudly as she might her firstborn son. "Three-hundred bucks! Twelve feet tall, battery-operated, animated LCD eyes, works on a six-hour timer, fully posable arms... Ain't it perfect?"

"Three-hundred dollars?" I scratched my head.

"I know, right? I couldn't resist!"

"LCD eyes?"

"Oh, that's the best part. Keep watching him; you'll see... Give it a moment... Aha!"

Skeleton Jack's round white eyes, which were actually pupil-shaped stickers laid over spherical LCD screens, blinked, then rolled from side to side as if looking one way then the other.

I bit my lip. I didn't think the fucking thing could get any creepier, but the eyes made it a million times worse. I cleared my throat.

"Isn't it a little early? Halloween is a ways off."

Louise's retort was sharp. "Halloween isn't just a date on the calendar, it's a state of mind. And we take it *real* serious around here. The earlier the better. Best start thinking about your own decorations! Oh, wait." Her voice turned poisonous. "Silly me, I forgot. You don't really go in for all that, do you?"

I swallowed. "I'm sorry."

Louise turned without further comment and headed back inside.

I relayed the conversation to my wife over dinner. She seemed in a better mood, so I opened a bottle of red. We shared it while we let our food settle. Times like this, when we weren't going at each other or dancing around unspoken grievances, I could remember why I got married. It was nice, drinking with someone, instead of drinking alone in front of the Xbox.

"I wonder if, instead of a brain, there's just, like, a small pumpkin sitting in her skull," Lisa said, once I'd finished talking. She smirked. "Who the fuck buys a twelve-foot skeleton to put in the yard? In August? She's a Looney Toon."

"I mean, it *is* a good price, I guess." I started to laugh, and Lisa laughed with me. It was such a rare thing for us that it sent a bolt of pure pain right up through the middle of my heart. God, I missed the old Lisa. It made me sad to think about how far we were from the people we'd once been.

"Well," I said, once the laughter died. "I think you were right about it being payback. Kind of bums me out that we're already on the back foot with the neighbors, though. Maybe I should get a three-hundred-dollar skeleton too, to make amends."

"If you do, it'll be instant divorce," Lisa said, and although she meant it as a joke, my good mood dissolved instantly.

Not so long ago, divorce hadn't been a joke.

It had been a very real prospect.

"I'm tired." I put down my wine glass. "I'm going to bed."

Lisa bowed her head. "I didn't mean it, babe."

"I know." I kissed the top of her head. "Goodnight."

She grabbed my hand. "I wish you'd stay down here, with me."

"I can't." I shook my head. "I just can't."

She cried as I went upstairs. Then, I heard her wine glass shatter, as if thrown at the wall.

I didn't sleep.

The next day, Lisa went out. I sank into my work, happy to have the house to myself for once.

It didn't last. Thunderous footsteps came up the stairs as I wrapped up a Zoom call. I bid my colleague a hasty goodbye and disconnected before they heard anything embarrassing.

Lisa burst into my study. "Have you *seen?*" Her hair was wild, eyes wide and round. "It's like a Ray fucking Harryhausen movie out there! How have you not *noticed?*"

With an impending sense of dread, I went over to the study window which overlooked the street and immediately saw what my wife was so upset about.

Skeleton Jack had a friend.

This time, it was our left-side neighbors. They had obviously been to the same Home Depot. Standing tall and menacingly proud on the other side of our property was another giant skeleton, the twin of Skeleton Jack. This one was also positioned so it faced our property, and as an added flourish, one poseable limb had been stretched out, pointing as if to accuse us of some transgression.

As I stared in disbelief, its weird LCD eyes blinked at me.

I felt a tiny chill go down my spine. We *were* being trolled.

Lisa was rigid with anger, her face white and pinched. "It's happening again, isn't it?"

I shook my head. "No. This is just a little fun, that's all—a bit of game playing. Nothing like last time."

Her nostrils flared. "Is there something wrong with me? Is there some reason why this keeps happening to us? Am I…am I *that* fucking unlikeable?"

I swallowed my immediate thought, settled on a more diplomatic response.

"The key is to not let it get to you. Soon enough Halloween will have come and gone and then we'll have to contend with Christmas. But if that's the worst of our problems, we should count ourselves lucky." Memories flashed into my mind: our old house, bathed in the strobing light of a cop car. Me, trying to extinguish a fire someone had set in our trash can. An envelope of dog shit left on the porch. Blood splattered on our drive.

No, a couple of tacky skeletons was nothing like last time.

Or so I thought.

L ater that week, another skeleton appeared on the street.

Two days after that, two more sprouted like terrifyingly tall weeds, just down the road.

As we made our way into September, it became clear that missing out on the Hooper Street Halloween Decoration Committee meeting had been a giant, gold-plated turd of a mistake.

As early October came, I drove home from the store one day and counted no less than thirty-three giant Skeleton Jacks standing to attention on either side of our road. Every single one of them had been positioned to face our house. Due to our position at the end of the cul-de-sac, it made us feel as if we were sitting at the head of a dinner table with all the guests glaring at us because we'd said something wrong.

My wife, scarred by the memories of our last neighborly conflict, spent a lot of time on the front porch, obsessively chewing her hair whilst staring back at the giant skeletons. The other residents of Hooper Street cheerfully ignored her, calling out to each other and popping in and out of each other's yards with a fond level of familiarity.

Lisa's hair chewing soon turned into pulling out individual strands, one by one, until little bald patches appeared on her scalp. Then she moved on to her eyelashes. She ground her teeth at night, and spent so much time tossing, turning, and groaning that I took to sleeping on my study couch. Anxiety was not new to Lisa, but I'd hoped the worst of it was behind us.

It had simply been lurking under the surface, like a sharp stick in muddy waters.

Aweek before Halloween, I woke and found the residents of Hooper Street had leveled up.

Our doorbell rang, so early I'd not had a chance to check outdoors for any new developments. For a blissful moment, I forgot about it entirely, opening the door to find the mailman delivering a parcel.

He grinned. "What'd you do to upset the locals?' He chuckled, poking a thumb behind him.

I looked, and nearly dropped the parcel, swearing and hoping beyond hope that I could prevent Lisa from coming outside today.

All thirty-three skeletons now had their right hands positioned high in the air, middle fingers erected to flip us off. It was breathtaking. Had it been happening to someone else, I would have laughed myself silly.

But it wasn't happening to someone else. It was happening to us.

My wife was going to lose her shit.

"Must have been something *bad*," the mailman said, shaking his head.

He left me standing there, staring.

I couldn't wrap my head around the levels of co-ordinated fuckery playing out. Yesterday, the skeletons had been posed, but not like this. I'd checked the street while emptying the trash not long before going to bed. That meant the neighbors had waited for us to turn out our lights, long past midnight, and repositioned the skeletons collectively so we would see them like this when we woke up.

And all because we'd told them we didn't like Halloween.

I put the parcel down by my front door and went straight over to Louise's. I rang the doorbell, then knocked for good measure.

She opened up after a few moments, looking as perfectly put together as usual, despite the early hour.

"Oh hi, Luke," she said, oozing false civility. "How y'all doing?"

I cut to the chase. "Not good, Louise. Not good. Can we...call a truce? I know we've gotten off on the wrong foot, but honestly, we didn't mean to, and my wife...is really struggling with all...this.'

Louise looked at me, her smile unwavering. "I don't know what you mean. All what?"

"The skeletons. The huge fucking skeletons! Their middle fingers? Come on! This is all a bit hostile, don't you think?"

"I'm sure I don't know what you mean, and I would prefer it if you didn't use that aggressive tone with me." Louise, the picture of injured innocence, began to close the door.

I jammed my foot in the way, desperation setting in. "Look, I get it. You got yourself a community thing going here, and we excluded ourselves from it. But we had good reason. Our last neighbors made life hell for us, and we promised we'd keep our heads down this time. I'm sorry if that made you feel we weren't interested. It's just with Lisa's health...She feels like you're all out to get us. I keep telling her that's ridiculous, but with a whole parade of giant fucking Home Depot skeletons giving us the finger, well...you can see where I'm coming from, right?"

Louise licked her pink painted lips, unmoved. "I told you," she intoned, solemnly. "We take Halloween *real* serious round here. As you're the kind of people who don't... Well... Maybe we don't *want* you to be part of this community. Ever think about that?'

Aghast, I stood there with my mouth open. "What?"

"Have a nice day, Luke," Louise said, kicking my foot.

Yelping, I pulled it back. The door slammed in my face.

Enraged, I banged my fists on it.

"Well, fuck you, lady! And your weird Stepford wives decoration cult!"

There was silence from within.

I wheeled, scowling with frustration, thinking, *That could not have gone worse if I'd tried.*

Only it could, because on turning, I saw the whole street had come out to stand on their porches, some of them dressed, others in their pyjamas. They all stared at me in the same way their stupid-ass giant skeletons did, silent and judgemental.

I felt a cold, hard lump of fear ball up in my throat.

Marching home, I found someone had snuck up onto the porch while my back was turned and stuck a large, homemade banner across the fascia boards.

It read: I LOVE HALLOWEEN. The 'Os' were little skulls.

I ripped the banner down and stamped on it, aware of the eyes still on me. Emboldened by my anger, I then struck a pose and flipped both my middle fingers up at the neighborhood at large, feeling absurd but oddly relieved to return gesture for gesture.

I went inside, locked and bolted the front door, drew all the blinds, and stayed indoors for the next two days, without looking outside once.

And then...

Halloween came.

The night before had been bad. Depressed, stressed, and cooped up together, Lisa and I argued for hours. Things were thrown at each other, and not just unkind words. I felt like our entire identity as married people was wrapped up in hostility, and I was over it. Tired, pissed, raw from the mess our last neighbors had made of our lives, and so behind on work that my boss had been making pointed remarks over email about job security and how lucky I was to be employed, I snapped and used the word 'divorce' again. The result was another uncomfortable night on my study couch listening to Lisa cry, knowing that somehow, for some reason, it was all my fault, but lacking the energy to figure out why.

I slept in the following morning, exhausted from the night's struggles. When I woke, it was to a headache. I decided I needed fresh air, so I crossed my study and pulled back the curtains, only to find the giant head of a Skeleton Jack staring back at me.

I screamed in surprise, then slammed my fist into a nearby wall. The huge decoration had been moved so it was peering *right into my fucking house*, scaring the living, breathing shit out of me.

How had it even gotten there without me hearing anything?

Were the stupid fucking skeletons alive?

Get a grip, Luke, I told myself.

Then it dawned on me—this was part of something bigger.

I stomped over to the next window, ripped open the curtains. Sure enough, another huge-ass skeleton stood there with its face pressed against the glass like a kid staring into a toy store.

Its creepy fucking LCD eyes activated, and blinked.

"That's it," I muttered, dragging on a sweater and some shoes, anger coursing through me. "That's fucking *it!*"

I stormed downstairs, ripping open the front door. When I saw what lay outside, I screeched to a halt.

The residents of Hooper Street had outdone themselves. At some point in the night, unbeknownst to us, they had moved every single one of the giant skeletons so they now crowded tightly around our house. Posed in a variety of ways, some placed flush against our house, heads tilted to peer in through various windows, some around our front door, angled so I had to duck between their outreaching hands, others placed on either side of our car, it became sickeningly obvious from their postures that the neighbors had been listening to our arguments quite closely. One skeleton in particular was hunched forward in a threatening stance, while another held its cheek, as if it had just been slapped.

My hand went to my own cheek, to the bruise flowering there. It wasn't the first time Lisa had hit me, and it probably wouldn't be the last. I felt shame. Our dirty little secret now belonged to the whole of Hooper Street.

But that wasn't all. The Hooper Street Halloween Decoration Committee had not stopped with the skeletons. They had gone to town on our house, smothering it with yards of fake cobwebs, plastic bat garlands, and Halloween banners. Flickering LED candles adorned almost every surface, and on the lawn, over two dozen carved pumpkins had been arranged amongst an assortment of plastic ghosts, zombies, black cats, dismembered latex limbs, black glitter, toadstools, and cutesy red devils.

The pièce de résistance, though, were the two polystyrene grave markers erected right next to the porch steps. It took me a moment to realize someone had spray painted them with two names: 'Lisa' and 'Luke.'

Trembling, I looked up and saw Louise in her yard, smiling. I closed my eyes, thinking, *Damn, Louise.*

Then I heard Lisa howling.

Damn.

My wife erupted from our house with one of my golf clubs clutched in her hand—the heaviest she could find, a lob wedge. She swung it wildly at the closest Skeleton Jack. All human emotion had gone from Lisa's face. Her hair was plastered to her skin, her tits swung freely, her pyjamas slid down her ass and...

"Lisa!" I knew it was futile. I remembered blood spattered on the front drive of our old place. The charges had been dropped, but only because I'd settled out of court for an astronomical amount of money. The debt we were in as a consequence…the number of loans we'd taken out…the credit card bills that came in every day… the blood everywhere…

I felt dizzy.

The skeleton's eyes rolled and blinked as the metal frame holding up the sculpture buckled under Lisa's assault. The decoration then folded at the waist, head between its knees.

My wife snarled and whirled to attack the next.

"Honey!" I said, waving my hands. "Stop! The neighbors are gonna call the cops!"

Louise no longer laughed, hand over her mouth. Other neighbors had come out to watch.

"I don't give a flying monkey dick what they do!" Lisa roared. "The fucking neighbors want to mess with me, then I'll fucking mess with *them*!"

She chopped away at the skeleton with all the fervour of a committed lumberjack. The skeleton's rib cage busted open, its wiry innards spilling out of the hollow plastic spinal column.

"They want to fucking play, do they? Buy a bunch of giant skeletons to mess with my head? Well, how's this for *playtime*?"

She lifted the club high over her head, backed up a few paces, then ran full tilt at the mangled decoration, which somehow still stood. Lisa bulldozed it over then fell on top of it, clubbing the plastic skull to a pulp.

Then, without pause, she went to work on the next.

Louise could take no more. She rolled up her sleeves.

"Hey! *Hey!*"

The lipstick wonder marched over, ready to intervene in the skeleton massacre.

"No, Louise!" I yelled. "You don't know what she's capable of!"

But she found out a few moments later, when my wife wheeled, and, without a moment's hesitation, smashed Louise's head in with the golf club.

I heard an audible, sickening crunch. Louise fell. Lisa, absolutely out of her mind, brought the club down again and again. Brains flew while the horrified citizens of Hooper Street shrieked and scattered like birds.

There would be no settling out of court this time.

No fresh start.

My wife murdered Louise Jackson, and she was going to prison.

I sank to my knees, knowing we were done.

Above us, a gaggle of huge, fake plastic skeletons stood like weird trees, blinking in occasional synchronicity at the death and red mess below.

I hate Halloween.

SOWN

by TJ Cimfel

The pumpkin is a fruit, Kyra thinks. But she isn't sure why it qualifies as such. Something about the seeds? But vegetables have seeds too. They have to so they grow, duh. Is it where the seeds are? Fruits have innies. She's pretty sure, at least.

The wheelbarrow bounces and jolts over the uneven ground behind her. Her father's voice, stretched thin with faux enthusiasm, falls flat against the heat. Something about sticking together. He pretends to want to be here. Actor and audience all in one stoop-shouldered, male pattern of baldness.

Geo sinks a steel toe into a pumpkin that didn't do anything to him. He is a Nazi in the making. Her brother, not the pumpkin. Just look at that shitty haircut, the jackbooted thug.

It's unseasonably hot this close to the end of October. It figures the only redeeming quality of this season—the cardigan—has been rendered pointless on this day. Family day. When there are a hundred other things she can think of that she'd rather be doing. A million. She'd rather be literally dead than be seen out here. Not that there's anyone to see them trudging through this field. This patch? How juvenile. She can't hang out today. She's going to a patch. With her *family*. Kyra wore the cardy anyway.

Geo lets loose another vicious kick, but his next victim shows no resistance, its sun-rotted flesh giving way with ease. Instead of a mighty *thwok*, it is *squelch*, and ectoplasmic innards shoot up in a rain that patters down on Kyra's mother's head, splats her cheek.

Her mother shrieks, then, catching herself, attempts a lackluster rebuke that maybe gets halfway to Geo. He skulks off, bored, and she feigns interest in a nearby row of moldering peppers. Kyra's father makes a half-hearted attempt to keep them close by. But oh well. The family unit spreads like dandelion seeds on the wind. Seeds? Thistles. Seeds. On the outside. She doesn't know. Is the dandelion a vegetable? It must be if they put it in salad.

As Kyra traipses her way across the hay-strewn terrain, something skitters past. Probably the same something that has compromised so much of this patch with its fierce little teeth. It's why she can't leave yet. Her father insists on finding an unblemished pumpkin. But every other one has teeth marks punched into its skin. Or is cracked open like an egg, yolk running rotten on the ground.

Her foot catches on a vine and she nearly trips, can feel her knee try to hyperextend. At least Kyra had the presence of mind that morning to select good footwear. As cute as her sweater is, heather and muted coral and soft, her shoes are the opposite. She has no idea why all running shoes are garishly colored, but they're comfortable and the sole is thick, which is good, considering every once in a while her foot sinks in the earth a little *too* far. Every time it does, she looks down, half-expecting to find she's stepped in gore. Good fruit gone bad. Soup. But the earth underfoot is dry and gray and tangled over with its vast network of squash and gourds, all bulbous-bodied and crooked-nosed.

She's thinking about all these vines—maybe that's how they talk to one another, it's their grid, and when you twist one away until its stem snaps, it goes offline, another lost soul with nothing but static to leave in its wake—when she hears her father call.

She turns around. There's a sea of orange between them. That doesn't make sense. It's only been—checking her phone—twenty minutes? That can't be right. She expected time to move like syrup today, thick and sludgy. The forced banter on the way here had weighed her down like one of those gravity blankets, pinning her to the present, unable to will tomorrow to come, like, ever.

I'm all right, Kyra wonders. She calls out the same. He calls something back, but a crow caws at the same time, and she shrugs and he turns. Geo is back at it again with the kicking. A *thwok* echoes dully in the distance. She doesn't even see her mother. Probably off in the dingy slam-door bathroom, furiously scrubbing her face with water that never heats up, and even if it does, it turns off each time you remove your hand from the faucet.

It occurs to her again that there's nobody else around. This heat must be keeping all the sane people away. She tries to tamp down the dread that fills her midsection whenever she's reminded that climate change is a thing. Who needs scary movies when you've got existential dread?

A ticklish rivulet of sweat slides down the small of her back and carves its way toward her ass. Frustrated, she rips her sweater off, which of course she immediately drops into a cluster of burrs.

She spits out an ugly word and picks the burrs off one by one, but they leave little pieces of themselves behind. Burrlets? Seeds? Burrs are neither fruit nor vegetable, she thinks, and envisions shoving a handful of them down her throat.

Suddenly unsure on her feet, Kyra sways. She swipes the back of her hand across her forehead, closes her eyes, and swallows, then counts to ten. Steadier now, she looks over her shoulder. She doesn't see Geo anywhere. He's probably off terrorizing some chicken.

Her father waves to her. She lifts a hand in return. If he's saying something, she can't hear him. What was it she was just thinking about?

It doesn't matter. But it seems right to leave the sweater. She doesn't even know why she's out here. This whole thing is a farce, it's so hot.

Heat or no, she's sorry, but it's really odd to imagine a spot like this at a time like this wouldn't be overrun by autumn tourists. Feeding the goats and the alpacas, the gentle threat of teeth scraping palm. Eating bag tacos, turning them inside out to lick grease from the foil corners of old Frito packaging. There would be hayrides ridden and tire swings swung. Bunnies held and pigs shooed and cows milked. Geo had fun with that last one, batting at the udder like a speedbag. *What? He doesn't feel a thing. He's too stupid.* Of course, the cow was a she, but Geo wasn't wrong. The dumb thing didn't low or moan or kick. Too bad. Because how nice would it have been to see the muscles in her haunches coil and tighten, all her power transferring from lowered front to rising back like a wave, like electricity, her hooves caving in her brother's smug face.

Do cows have hooves? They don't have seeds. Of this Kyra is sure.

She pauses a moment, confused. As her eyes scan across the sea of orange, brother's flapping cheek and broken smirk still blink in her head, his teeth scattered on the ground like corn.

She frowns to erase her smile. To shake these awful thoughts that seem beamed in from a nearby radio tower. The heat at least has become strangely tranquilizing. Yes, it's sticky and oppressive, but there's something reassuring in its weight.

Kyra smells shit, earthen and heady. Underneath it is the sour tang of rotting meat. Something died out here. But first it crawled under the crosshatched skeins of dead-straw grass, spine shattered from some great blow, its legs jutting out behind it, dragged frozen to some unseen resting place.

There are carcasses all around. Jellied things the color of carrot and beet and cinnamon. Cimarron? Seeds gleam in their stringy innards. Pearls ready to be plucked from guts. Autumn's nacre. Why so many dead?

Kyra stops, wipes the slick from her brow again. She's dizzy. Why are her thoughts squirming? She doesn't even know some of the words she's thinking. It would be best to go back. To find her parents, even Geo. But the thought of walking all that distance is daunting. When she turns, she can't tell where she came from anyway. Viscera shimmers on the horizon like a highway mirage. So many bodies.

There's a wet inhaling sound she mistakes for her own phlegm-ridden trachea. She holds her breath, and the moist vibrations continue.

Things are going wavy in her peripheral vision. Maybe it's the heat, the temperature must be three digits now. She turns her head sap-slow. Can't process what she's seeing.

It sits only a few feet away from her, canted slightly to one side. It's massive, blue-ribbon worthy. Kyra couldn't wrap her arms around it, not even if there were three of her. A matrix of tendrils stretches from its cap in every direction. No tooth or toe has breached its rind. No angry scatter of acne or warts, no sallow indentations, no fontanels. Her father would be overjoyed.

When a great breath creases its sides inward then out, she decides it would be a good time to leave. Her compass, though, is shot, like she got bad water in her ear and now she can't see straight.

Her father is gone. Dad. Daddy. She thinks of her cardigan. She could drape it over her face, shuck the remaining burrs from its sleeves with her teeth and swallow them whole. Somewhere deep inside, she cries out at this incongruity. There are tears on her face, but she cannot feel them. She can barely lift her eyes to behold the grand figure in front of her.

A slit opens across the thing's girth, perpendicular to its ribs. Bone-ivory teardrops dangle from wet threads, strings of loose teeth.

It says *thwok.*

Kyra has decided she is afraid, but the fear is a faraway thing, like her family. She almost can't remember what they look like, where she is, why she's scared when there's so much beauty around her.

Thwok, it says.

Is it coming from inside her head? There are seeds in there, she thinks. But they would rattle like a desiccated gourd. Like a thing in the brush.

Her feet feel pinched, so she kicks off her shoes and socks. Her bare feet sink into warm meat, into fibrous strands. Pulp stew squirts up between the webbing of her toes. It is cool and gelatinous, relief from the scorch of the sun. The rest of her is still so hot though. And so she strips off her pants, followed by her underwear. Peels her sweat-soaked t-shirt off her torso and over her head. Removes her bracelet. Her rings. She does not want to be naked.

The hulking thing is gone. But she can feel its eyeless gaze, can trace its vines into the tall grass. She knows what its breath smells like. Its slit mouth and soft flypaper teeth. It is a miracle it allowed her to see it, but now that she has, she doesn't think she will be allowed to leave.

Thwok.

She does not want to, but she kneels. Lies down in the muck and rolls, flops and flails, opens her legs and her arms. She needs to be covered. To be filled.

Thwok.

It is somewhere very close. When she finds it, she will want to run. But she will not run. Instead, she will reach into its great slit mouth and part it gently. She will insert her fingers and then her fist. She will push her arm all the way inside and probe its warmth. She will know what is happening to her, and it is the knowledge of that knowledge that fills her with dread. For she knows she will rest her head against her shoulder. She will lie her other arm flat against her side, and she will swim. She will enter its cavity with all of herself, and inside, she will wait, as it has been waiting for her. Since the first seed pierced the earth and germinated. Tending its womb and birthing its fruit and dying over and over and over.

She will die over and over again, too. She will scream, but not with her mouth. Her mouth will be filled.

We are all fruit, she thinks, as she slides on her belly into the tall, tall grass.

THE IRON MAIDEN

by Rebecca Rowland

I f it had been a *normal* haunted house, the kind with busted up shutters and a creaky gate, overgrown weeds strangling the entrance and an infamous residential history, then maybe, *maybe* we would have believed Ronnie's story from the get-go. But it wasn't. Just a tidy, unassuming Cape Cod-style home, three bedrooms, one and a half bathrooms (technically, one and a quarter, my dad corrected—though what constituted less than a whole room was lost on me), and an undersized garage that stood a good fifty feet away from the kitchen door. Its back yard was a small but perfect geometric shape with right angled corners of shiny metal fencing. I proposed to the guys that it might, in fact, be a perfect square, and even suggested we bring along a measuring tape to check.

"No, Candy, you fucking tool," snarled Patrick, flicking an ash on the toe of my sneaker. "We ain't moving a sofa into your gramma's house for cripes' sake." He took another drag, holding the filter between his index and thumb like the bad ass guys in movies I'd seen do.

I shoved my fists deep into my sweatshirt pockets. "Yeah, whatever," I said casually, shifting slightly in my seat on the edge of the curb. I nodded over to Ronnie. "Are you sure no one's living there?" It had been Ronnie's idea to break in and take a look around, after all, so we left it to him to do the requisite reconnaissance. "I could've sworn we got candy there last year."

"My mom said the old lady died or went into one of those rest homes," Ronnie said, shrugging. "All I know is, what I saw wasn't a person. It was…" He turned his head to check for eavesdroppers. "It was a woman, but not, like, you know…"—he cleared his throat— "human."

Dave, sitting across from me in the street, burst out laughing. "How'd you know it was a woman, then?" He held his hands in front of his chest, fingers cupped. I threw a small rock at him but that only made him laugh harder.

Ronnie's cheeks were slightly pink, but the sun was particularly hot for the last week of October, so I wasn't certain if Dave's pantomime had been the catalyst. Ronnie wasn't like Patrick or Dave. I'd never seen him ogle a girl—or a boy, for that matter, and though the other two had made half-hearted attempts at flirtation in the past, Ronnie treated me as one of the guys.

"What did she look like?" I asked.

A car careened around the corner, then—something dark and sleek, an old Monte Carlo or Camaro. It blew the stop sign and sailed past us, sending gravel and dust crashing over Dave like a rogue ocean wave. Dave rolled forward, half-crawling along the pavement until he finally collapsed on the lawn next to me, muttering threats against the driver's mother, sister, and possibly the family dog.

Ronnie watched the car disappear down the road, then looked at the ground, his eyes dancing back and forth as if searching an image projected there. "At first, I thought she was wearing a wig, or maybe a Halloween mask," he continued. "Her face was white—I mean, white, like chalk—and her hair was this giant pile of scraggly, red hair. Almost orange." He rubbed the side of his mouth. "I probably wouldn't have noticed her in the window except for that hair. She was standing there, in the big front window, staring out into the street. I damn near ran my bike off the road when I saw her."

"Are you sure she wasn't just the old lady, wearing a wig?" Patrick offered. "It's Halloween tomorrow. Maybe she was trying on a costume."

Dave coughed and spat on the nearby lawn. "Festive gal."

Ronnie laughed suddenly, but it came out like a choking sound. "No, no," he sputtered. "No, it was no costume. I stopped dead, rolled my bike over to the tree belt, and looked again. She stayed standing there, but her eyes didn't move. She kept staring straight ahead, at the street, but then, she saw me."

He looked up at me. I could tell he was doing his best not to start crying in front of Dave and Patrick. I gave Ronnie a small smile and jutted my chin forward, encouraging him to continue.

"She started making this…sound," he said finally. "Like a scream, but not loud. A wailing, like. The whole time, she was staring straight at me. I could hear her, the crying, right through the glass. But that wasn't the worst part." He shook his head. "The worst part was that when she started crying, I could see inside her mouth, and she had these teeth…"

"Oh, for Christ's sake," Dave said loudly. "You're so full of shit. You saw this? Standing in a window two doors down from your own damn house? No fucking way, dude."

"…and then she was just, gone." Ronnie raked a hand through the top of his hair. "Just gone. Poof. In the window and then vanished."

"So, what is it you want to do exactly?" Patrick said, dropping his cigarette on the pavement and covering it with his boot.

"I'm thinking, we check the place out tomorrow night," Ronnie said. "It's not like we have anything better to do."

It was true. At sixteen, we were officially too old for trick-or-treating. Technically, we had been too old at fifteen, what with Patrick sporting a Sam Elliot mustache and at over six feet tall, looming over us like an extra from a Munsters masquerade ball. We'd received more than our share of frowns and head shakes when neighbors found us standing on their front steps, pillowcases open wide in anticipation. One or more of us puffing on a Marlboro certainly didn't help our case.

"You just stood here and told us you were scared shitless watching a ghost scream at you from behind one of the windows in the daytime and now you want to break in and creep around at night?" Patrick asked. "I'm all for doing a bit of ghost-hunting, but we'd better get the lay of the land first." He looked at his watch, a big, meaty number with a bunch of unnecessary accoutrements like a compass and barometric pressure assessment. "Let's go take a look now."

"Now?" I asked. My parents would be expecting me for dinner in a few hours. If I was late, they might ground me for Halloween.

"You got something better to do, Candy cane?" Patrick asked sardonically.

Ronnie offered his hand and pulled me to a standing position. "Come on. We'll just take a quick look around."

I brushed the back of my jeans with my hands. "Yeah, okay," I said. "Cool."

The house was only a few blocks away. As soon as it came into sight, Ronnie nudged my arm. The front of the house was tidy and unassuming. Someone had been keeping the lawn trim—a neighbor overly concerned with a fear of neighborhood blight, most likely. The four of us hurried up the driveway and toward the garage door, keeping our footsteps as light as possible in order to keep from attracting notice from curious neighbors. The grass in the back yard hadn't been mowed in at least a month, and a brown snake of bittersweet crept among the other vines and weeds congregating in the corner of the lot.

Patrick ran his hand along the bottom of the lowest window. "I can climb in through here and then unlock the back door," he said, and before any of us could disagree, wedged his fingers beneath its metal frame and pushed the pane upward. Without being prompted, Dave gave him a boost, and Patrick was inside and shutting the window behind himself in under a minute.

"Is it that easy to break into someone's house?" I asked, silently thankful my bedroom was on an upper floor.

Dave fingered the cigarette he'd stashed behind one ear. "If you play your cards right, maybe you'll find out one of these days." He waggled his eyebrows at me just as the nearby storm door swung inward and Patrick pushed the screen door open and waved us inside.

The interior of the house was tidier than its exterior. There were furnishings: a kitchen table and chairs, a modestly-sized refrigerator and a stove coiled with electric burners, but nothing to indicate that someone was using them. The dish drain was empty, the countertops barren; though a lone hand towel hung perfectly straight from a silver ring, the sink was dry as bone. I wandered wordlessly down a shallow hallway and into the front living room. A blue flowered sofa and chair sat drowsily in the dim light, an empty end table wedged between them. I could see a thick layer of dust on the top of the table.

Suddenly, the ceiling light screamed to life, casting an unnaturally bright glow over everything, but it was extinguished just as quickly. "Dumb ass!" hissed Patrick. "You're gonna draw attention to us."

Dave rolled his eyes. "It's four in the afternoon. No one is going to notice a light going on."

"Shhh," Ronnie cautioned. "You hear it?"

We held our breath, waiting. After a long moment, Patrick opened his mouth to say something more, but as he did, we caught it—a strange sound drifting from a nearby room. It resembled a moan, but a high-pitched one—a crying, but without the jagged changes in pitch. An icy puddle dropped to the pit of my stomach.

"What the…?" Patrick whispered. He edged backward slowly toward the hallway and rested his hand on the knob of the first closed door. As he did, the moan stopped. Patrick, however, continued, slowly turning the knob and pushing the door open. "Bathroom," he reported back. His footsteps echoed along a tiled floor. "Found the source of the sound. Check it out."

We piled into the small space. On one wall was a toilet, its lid covered with an emerald green rug-like cover. Across from it was a simple pedestal sink, an oversized mirror hanging on the wall at eye level. Patrick pointed to the narrow window on the wall that connected them. "The storm window wasn't pushed all the way down, like the kitchen one." I looked at the sill. Sure enough, a crack of light peeked out from under the metal frame. "When the wind blows through, it probably makes a whistling sound. That's what we heard."

"It didn't sound like whistling to me," I offered. "More like… singing. But the same chord on replay or something."

"Well, regardless. Mystery solved," said Patrick.

"That's not what we heard," said Ronnie. "Maybe it was coming from another room."

Sure enough, as if on cue, the high-pitched moan echoed down the hallway, making each of us jump. Now that it was closer, it resembled a circuitous shriek. I glanced nervously at the window, wondering if I would be able to contort my body enough to squeeze through it and escape if necessary. Dave's eyes also fluttered toward the window, and I suspected he was thinking the same.

Patrick pushed past us and back into the hall. "Enough of this bullshit," he mumbled. He disappeared around the corner, and a moment later, the moan ceased, replaced by the sound of another door opening and footsteps pattering away. Then, silence.

Dave looked at me. "Should we follow him?" he asked.

I shrugged and looked at Ronnie. He was staring at the narrow opening below the window.

"Patrick?" Ronnie didn't move his eyes from the window as he called out. "We got the layout. Let's just split and meet up tomorrow, after dinner." He waited a beat, but there was no response.

"Chicken shit probably went home," said Dave.

"Yeah," I agreed, but as we shuffled out into the hallway, I steeled myself for Patrick to jump out from behind a corner.

"We should probably just leave this unlocked," Ronnie said, his hand resting on the back doorknob.

It was then I noticed the other room off the short hallway. Its door was slightly ajar, though the inch of darkness peeking out told me nothing about the room's contents. "Hey, we never looked in here," I said, but Ronnie was already outside, Dave immediately at his heels. I pressed my palm gently against the hallway door. It was surprisingly cold in comparison to the rest of the house, and I pulled my arm quickly away.

As I hurried across the silent kitchen to the waiting exit, I felt a rush of wind at the nape of my neck, like someone had reached out to grab me but missed only by inches. It propelled me into a run, and I was grateful to be outside again, the setting sun warm and blinding as I joined the guys in the overgrown tangle of crabgrass and weeds.

We didn't think anything of it when Patrick didn't show up to school the next day. Ronnie and I never saw much of him normally, anyway; we were both cemented firmly in the honors track while Patrick, on the other hand, was enrolled in an overabundance of weird electives, courses with names like Fitness for Life and Contemporary Issues that weren't compulsory for graduation nor required any sliver of literacy or math skills. Dave attended the nearby vocational school, though none of us were clear on just which trade he was pursuing.

Ronnie and I were slumped together on the city bus headed home when he fished something out of his pocket and held it out to me. "That's Patrick's watch," I said. It appeared even more gargantuan not swaddling our friend's massive forearm. "Where did you—"

"It was wrapped around my handlebars when I passed my bike this morning," he said. "What a goon, creeping around my yard in the middle of the night." Ronnie rolled his eyes. "I'm guessing this is code that he'll meet us at the house at eight o'clock." He turned its face so I could have a better look. The stopwatch function had been turned on, its numbers paused at eight-zero-zero.

I leaned over and hit the signal for the next stop. "What are you telling your parents you're doing?" When we'd started high school, the boys had been granted carte blanche to do whatever they wished, so long as they came home by midnight. My parents adopted the opposite approach, becoming hypervigilant about my activities. I needed a rational sounding plan to be able to go out on a school night, even if it was Halloween.

The bus slowed to a stop. "I think *Ghostbusters* is still playing. *Gremlins*, too," Ronnie said. "Say you're going to the movies."

I hoisted my backpack over my shoulder and walked toward the back exit just as the doors folded open. "Yeah, okay," I agreed. "I'll come by your house at seven?" I hopped down the steps and onto the sidewalk.

"Make sure you wear all black," Ronnie yelled after me.

I turned to wave my acknowledgment just as the doors slammed shut. Despite the dust-caked windows, I could still see Ronnie, but he wasn't looking over at me. He was staring at Patrick's watch, still clutched in his hand.

In the shade of the back yard, it was nearly impossible to see our hands in front of our faces. On the street, hordes of little kids waving their flashlights and glow sticks like semaphores lit up Ronnie's block like it was Times Square, but once we ducked down the driveway and out of the prying eyes of the streetlights, I found myself squinting in order to make out basic shapes. When Dave slid silently beside me and placed a hand over my mouth, I nearly jumped out of my skin.

"Shhhh," he warned. "I think the neighbors are home, so we gotta stay quiet," he whispered. "Pat with you?"

I pushed Dave off me, giving him a hard punch in the upper arm for good measure.

Ronnie's voice sailed over to us from a few yards away. "No," he hissed. "Have you talked to him?"

"*Candy and Ronnie haven't seen him yet,*" Dave whisper-sang, bastardizing the Elton John song lyric we'd heard countless times. The end of his cigarette glowed orange as he sucked in a long drag, casting a faint warm spotlight onto his face for the moment.

"What are you wearing?" I whispered, jutting my chin toward him. "What's with the makeup?" There were black streaks of charcoal at the tops of his cheeks and his blond hair stood straight up on his head, held at gunpoint by a thick black strip of cloth tied along his forehead.

"I'm Rambo," he whispered back. "It's my costume."

"Rambo didn't wear paint on his face," I said.

"Well, maybe if he had, he wouldn't have gotten captured," Dave retorted, playfully curling his hands into fists. "These are the hands that threaten doom, baby!"

"He's probably in the house already," Ronnie interrupted. "Come on."

We huddled together in front of the back door. Dave clicked on a palm-sized flashlight and pointed its small spotlight on the knob. "Go ahead, dude."

Ronnie nodded and opened the door, and before any of us could change our minds, we slipped into the dark kitchen. The air was much colder than I remembered it being the day before, but I reminded myself that it had been daytime and the sun had likely warmed the room. There was an unmistakable smell, however, one that hadn't been there previously—a mélange of old urine, pungent cheese, and something that reminded me of waiting in line at the ice cream truck when I was little, a sweaty assortment of old nickels and dimes pressed excitedly against my palm. I wrinkled my nose.

As if reading my mind, Dave whispered, his voice gaining volume with each syllable, "Holy shit, dude. What stinks?"

"Shhh," warned Ronnie. He waved his hand at something on the other side of the room, but in the nearly complete darkness, it was impossible to determine what. "Shine the light along the wall," he commanded in a low voice. "Start from the left and move it slowly across so we can get our bearings."

Dave sniffed audibly but did as told. Along the top of the silent stove, the bright center of the beam appeared only a few inches wide, its faint halo spilling a foot further in all directions. Dave panned sideways and the light illuminated a toaster covered by a hand-sewn fabric cozy. A bit further, the top of white porcelain sink. Then, the dulled laminate of the speckled Formica countertop. Then, the heavy plastic handle of the refrigerator. Then, the ghastly pale face of Patrick, staring blankly at us from the entranceway to the hall.

Dave jumped and dropped the flashlight, and it hit the linoleum tile with a taunting smack as its light extinguished. I felt Ronnie scramble near my feet, pawing furiously along the floor with his hands. A moment later, there was another cracking sound and the flashlight was alight once more, Ronnie holding onto it with his left hand as he grasped my forearm to pull himself up with his right.

"Pat?" Dave asked hesitantly.

Ronnie held the flashlight in front of us and aimed it in the direction of the hall.

Patrick was gone.

"Oh, so *this* is the game we're playing?" Ronnie kept the light pointed straight. "Well, shit, it *is* Halloween. Let's play some hide and seek." He walked cautiously forward and the wave of dark encroached upon Dave and me from behind.

I took a small step forward and tripped over my own foot but managed to grab Dave's arm and steady myself before falling. "Sorry," I mumbled, taking a deep breath and letting go. Without a word, Dave reached over and felt for my hand. When he found it, he wordlessly entwined his fingers with mine.

The three of us moved methodically to the other side of the kitchen. Ronnie readjusted the flashlight, holding it like a patrol cop on one of those police dramas my parents watched, his fist surrounding the plastic casing as he balanced it just above his shoulder. The stench we'd first encountered in the kitchen seemed to grow more intense the further we ventured. Ronnie did not pause at either of the two doorways in the hallway, but I let my eyes drift to the one with the partially-open door. When we were nearly past, a faint glow of light flickered from beyond the crevice. Dave pulled me forward and I concentrated on trying to remember the layout of the living room.

Once I felt my feet sink into the plush carpet of the front room, Ronnie stopped walking. "Okay, dickhead," he said. "Come out, come out, wherever you are." He panned the beam quickly along the flowered couch, then inched it over the end table and onto the easy chair.

"Wait," I said. "Go back. Shine it on the table again."

Ronnie returned the light to the corner. "Seriously," he said, his voice growing louder. "We can't hang out in this room for long. People on the street might see the light and think it's a burglar. Come on, Pat. Let's just go upstairs together and see—"

"What the hell is that?" I asked, letting go of Dave's hand and placing both of mine on the flashlight. I angled it slightly downward so it centered on the top of the end table again. "Look!"

In the layer of dust on top of the table, there were ten thin lines, stretching from the center of the table to the edge closest to us. Ten fingertips had run along the top of the table since the previous day. Or had been dragged.

Ronnie regained control of the flashlight and quickly shut it off. "Shhhh," he whispered.

From somewhere behind us came the sound. A high-pitched, ravenous shriek—one long, continuous tone echoing from somewhere in the hallway, just a few feet away. A shudder ran through my spine, and I edged further into the dark living room, pressing my back against the nearest wall in a ridiculous attempt to put distance between myself and whatever was making the terrible wail.

The windows in the living room were bare. In stark contrast to the total darkness of the room, the incandescence of the streetlights seemed opulent; we watched transfixed as a few costumed stragglers lugged their bounties of candy past the house's front walk, onto the neighbor's sidewalk, and out of sight. A black Trans Am sped down the road, Bruce Dickinson's operatic vocals screaming from its stereo speakers, the driver gleefully unconcerned about wayward pedestrians. Back in the house, the shriek increased in volume, and I realized with horror that its source was steadily approaching the living room.

"Unlock the front door and run."

Ronnie turned the flashlight back on and frantically waved it toward the sound of Patrick's voice. "*Pat?*" Ronnie cried out. "Pat, where *are* you?"

The light caught a small movement next to the easy chair, and Ronnie steadied the beam in that direction. At first, I had difficulty making sense of what we were seeing. As enormous as he was, Patrick was crouched behind the blue flowered chair, his arms bent forward as if he were crawling. He wore the same t-shirt he'd been wearing the day before, but the collar was visibly soiled with an unknown dark substance. Even in the weak radiance of the flashlight, the skin on his face and neck appeared unsettlingly white.

Patrick's bloodshot eyes focused on Ronnie, unblinking. "Unlock the door," he repeated calmly. "And. Run!" He punctuated his directive by screaming the last word, then opening his mouth in a hideous maw. Where his teeth had once been was a picket fence of broken, yellowed shards. Bloody saliva spilled over his lips and dripped onto the carpet below where we could see, for the first time, that a large puddle of blood and sinew was coagulating as it soaked into the floorboards below.

From somewhere inside Patrick's body rose a sonorous cry. It joined the wail still growing in the darkness of the hallway, generating a collective keening that seemed to turn my legs to cement, rooting my body helplessly in place.

Dave ran to the front door and frantically clawed at the deadbolt until we heard it click free. In one fluid motion, he flung the heavy door open, pushed the screen door forward, and bounded down the steps to the walk. As he did so, the creature that had been making the terrible sound sprang from the hallway and threw herself against the wide window looking out onto the street. From behind, I could see the clumps of matted orange locks slithering down her back. She began to bang her open palms against the glass like a metronome and her shriek grew so loud, I clasped my hands over my ears in primal reflex.

Almost immediately, however, my arm was wrenched down as Ronnie grabbed hold of my wrist and pulled me toward the open door. We ran together down the steps and into the open air, just in time to see Dave continue his run into the street.

A wood-paneled station wagon careened around the corner. Its velocity increased as it sped down the street, passing in front of us just as Dave's foot made contact with the center of the road. The wagon plowed into him, folding his body into an acute angle I'd only seen previously through the scratched plastic of a math class protractor. Dave fruitlessly clawed at the wagon's hood for a split second before being dumped onto the other side of the street in a broken heap.

A muscle car approaching from the other direction, its engine roaring despite its lawful speed, took no notice of the dark mound until after the first dull thump. Then, both cars stopped, the scene on the street hazily frozen like a Polaroid snapshot.

Finally, a harried woman in her late thirties poured from the wagon's driver's side door, screaming incoherently. The shrieking cry from the house went silent, a radio squeal with its cord suddenly yanked from the wall outlet.

Ronnie released my arm and walked, zombie-like, toward the front of the coupe, trying his best not to look at Dave's lifeless legs peeking out from beneath it.

"You were wearing all black!" the driver of the station wagon screamed accusingly at the dented grill of her car. "I didn't see you! You were wearing all black!"

I turned back toward the house. In the window, a woman stood, staring blankly at the crowd growing in the street. Her face was pale, bloodless as a corpse, and her hair shone orange as fire. Patrick stood next to her, staring at the street, his face empty of any trace of affect. I stepped one foot back onto the house's walkway and hugged my arms against my chest. As I did so, the woman turned her eyes toward me. She opened her mouth into a terrible grin, proudly displaying her yellowish-brown teeth of razor-sharp stakes.

From somewhere far away, the wail of an ambulance sounded. And with that, the front door to the house closed, the metallic click of the deadbolt locking in place, a somber echo against the silent October sky.

SPIDERS UNDER MY SKIN

by Larry Hodges

There are spiders under my skin.

Sometimes they just sit there like itchy chicken pox. Other times they wiggle and giggle and bounce about like little kids in suburban backyards where people chat over white picket fences about the weather and politics and the latest fashions, never worrying about spiders under their skin.

Sometimes the spiders bite.

When they do that, I jerk about and slap at them. I have bruises all over from that. Sometimes I can hear the spiders calling out, "Hey, big fella, why are you slapping yourself?" And then they'll laugh and give me a big bite, and I'll slap and it hurts and they'll just giggle more.

I don't like it when they bite.

That's why I started killing myself.

Killing myself is a Halloween tradition. It started when I was trick-or-treating as a kid, filling my bag with Snickers and M&Ms

and candy corn when I got to the bad house. Or maybe it was because of the two candy bars I stole from my brother's bag. He never noticed; probably couldn't see well through the two peepholes in the white sheet that made up his silly ghost costume. Like a junior Arachnologist, I dressed as Spider-Boy. With great access to candy comes great responsibility, and I'd failed the test. I felt bad about stealing his candy, and I was going to give it back. Really, I was.

At the bad-house door, we said, "Trick or Treat!" They smiled and held out a bowl of candy. My brother grabbed one and floated off to the next house, didn't even wait for me. I stuck my hand in, but it was a bowl of spiders, all staring at me with their eight bulging eyes. Black widows with their little red dots, tarantulas, wolf spiders, brown recluse, a few gangly daddy longlegs—they all ran up my arm, shrinking as they did so, and digging under my skin before I could get out a single scream.

I shouldn't have stolen that candy.

At first it was just super-itchy. They didn't start biting until my third day at the institute. I'm immune to their poison, but it hurts like hell—like getting needles jabbed into you from inside. I told the doctors about the itchy spiders and the biting, but they just looked at me funny. I guess they've never had spiders under their skin.

Having grown up with spiders under my skin, they became my family from then on, as I never saw my parents or brother again. When they visited, I wouldn't look up, and they finally stopped visiting. I don't even remember what they look like. And as the years went by, I learned to trick the doctors into thinking I no longer believed I had spiders under my skin. They were so happy that their years of therapy had cured me. I went in as Spider-Boy and came out Spider-Man when they let me leave on my twenty-first birthday, October 31.

Yes, Halloween. That's my birthday.

It wasn't really my birthday, but I was reborn that Halloween night when I was seven and the spiders came. It's been my birthday ever since. I even sneaked out of my room at the institute and changed it on all my medical records, along with a note in the margin that read, *"He no longer believes he has spiders under his skin."*

That's when the suicide tradition began. See, I can live without the spiders, but they can't live without me. It's not a symbiotic relationship; it's parasitic, and I'm the parasitee.

If I want to kill them, all I have to do is off myself.

So, on Halloween on my twenty-first birthday, the night the doctors let me go, while kids trick-or-treated, I stepped in front of a moving car. The driver, having no spiders under her skin, was oblivious to why I had to do this. I bet it ruined her whole Halloween.

Getting hit hurt worse than the migraines I get when spiders bite my brain. I was in the hospital for a long time, but the doctors didn't do anything. It was my little eight-legged friends that put me back together, piece by piece. They were angry at me and kept biting, but I couldn't blame them. If I died, they would lose their home and die.

I promised the doctors I'd be more careful crossing the street next time and assured them there were no spiders under my skin. They let me go, but the spiders…they just giggled and wiggled and bounced about.

I tried again the following Halloween. Kids kept knocking on my door, and I gave out Snickers and M&Ms and the new gummy spiders I'd discovered since no one likes candy corn. I gave out absolutely no real spiders, and some of the kids stole extra candy. Shame on them. Then I got hungry and ate the rest of the candy, and the spiders began biting me. So I ran upstairs and jumped out of my third-floor apartment window, yelling the whole way down.

But the spiders put me back together again. I convinced the doctors I'd been reaching for toilet paper in a tree outside my window, telling them it was probably a kid TPing my house who didn't like Snickers and M&Ms and gummy spiders. Once again, I convinced the doctors I didn't have spiders under my skin, and they let me go.

And so it went, all those Halloweens. In the years that followed, I'd hung myself, been electrocuted, burned, drowned, shot, and so forth, but the spiders just kept putting me back together, and I kept convincing doctors I didn't have spiders under my skin, even though my skin was bubbling with them by that point. After a while, they always let me go. And I kept living, as did the spiders, and the pain from their bites continued.

I deserve it for stealing that candy from my brother so long ago. I can never change that. But I'm not the only one. Every year the kids steal my candy. They'll reach into the basket like they're going to take one and they'll grab a second or a third. Or they'll grab my skinny legs and yank them off.

Yeah, you heard that right. Kids these days.

They deserve spiders under their skin.

Or me.

You see, things have changed. I've always felt like an outcast, but the spiders have invited me into their world. This last time they put me back together, they made me one of them, scuttling about on my four legs. I'm a black widow. I'm the man–spider.

I should have eight legs and eight eyes, but those kids stole my other four legs and six of my eyes. Shame on them. So, I've made plans for this Halloween. This time I'm not going to kill myself. It's a big change for me.

As usual, kids steal extra candy when I'm not looking. It's tough keeping an eye on them with only two eyes. But I'm just waiting. *Waiting. Waiting.*

I almost gave up. There were pirates and princesses and even a Doc Ock—an arch enemy of us spider-people—but that's not what I was looking for. Would I have to wait another year?

And then, there he was. Just like me, so many years ago, dressed as Spider-Boy. He was with a group of other kids, none of them with spiders under their skin, all looking to steal candy and my remaining legs.

Unless I acted first.

"Trick or treat!" they cried, their parents beaming from the sidewalk like wolves who'd soon be howling.

I smiled and held out the basket with Snickers and M&Ms and gummy spiders and absolutely no real spiders, not yet. And they began grabbing. Then Spider-Boy reached in and tried stealing extra candy and maybe one of my remaining legs. But I was too quick. I dropped the candy bowl and leaped at him and ran up his arm, shrinking as I did so. The spiders under my skin climbed out of me and together, we dug under his skin before he could get out a single scream. It was pandemonium—parents screaming, kids screaming, candy everywhere.

Now I'm a spider under *his* skin.

It's nice in here, all spiffy and clean, not gooky and bloody like you'd think. Just me and the other spiders. I made myself a nice silk bed and pillow (don't ask where the silk comes out). When I'm hungry, I nibble him. When I'm annoyed, I take bigger bites with my fangs, and he jerks about and slaps at me like I used to do. Then I giggle and wiggle and bounce against these soft walls, and I'm so happy.

I no longer have spiders under *my* skin.

NOVEMBER EVE

by Bridgett Nelson

hh…Halloween perfume…

A   I inhaled deeply, taking the cool October air into my lungs. The fragrant autumnal breeze had me light-headed with its earthy musk. Walks home from school were notoriously dull, but the gem-toned foliage, cooler temperatures, and bright blue skies of fall made the trek worthwhile.

That aroma, though. This time of year, it filled the valley with its magic and satisfied me in a way that lacked the other eleven months. I'd always heard scent evoked our strongest emotions and memories, and I believed it.

The base note of my favorite fragrance was the smell of endless falling leaves, raked into piles, waiting to be burned. But let's be real—that smell we loved…it was the smell of plants rotting and molding; the smell of decay. Didn't matter. Nothing foiled the pleasant associations the scent summoned, or the nostalgia it caused in the pit of my gut.

The smoke itself was the top note. In any other small American town, leaf-burning was likely illegal, but here, the very act of tossing a burning match into the dry, dead leaves put smiles on residents' faces. The rich, acrid-but-smoky aroma signified the coming of winter, yet, for me, evoked memories of every Halloween I'd experienced.

I strolled down the street happily taking everything in—laughing kids playing in a pile of leaves with a fluffy white American Eskimo puppy; an elderly couple sitting on their rockers, sipping from steaming mugs; some of my classmates walking on the opposite side of the street, wearing thick flannels; a father and daughter on a blue lawn tarp, carving a smiling face onto their bright orange pumpkin. I wished I could live in October year-round. Taking one more cleansing breath of the cool, intoxicating air, I let myself inside.

"Avery, is that you?" Momma yelled from the kitchen as I hung my coat and removed my shoes.

"Yep! I'll be right in!" After dropping my backpack on my bed, I hurried to the kitchen to help Momma prepare dinner.

"Hi, Momma!"

"Hi, there! Did you have a good day?" She was chopping veggies.

"It was fine. The usual." I washed my hands. "What do you need me to do?"

"I thought we'd have some nice omelets for dinner, with some fresh-squeezed orange juice." She grinned. "Something hearty to put meat on our bones. If you could get the eggs and cheese out of the fridge, and then run some oranges through the juicer, that would be great."

"No problem."

"I finished up your costume this afternoon. It turned out nice."

"Momma, that's great! I can't wait to see it."

"I know how much you love Halloween, so I tried to make it extra special."

I kissed her cheek. "Thank you. You're the best!"

Her face flushed in pleasure. "I was happy to do it. You're a good girl, Avery."

After dinner, she showed me her creation. I was stunned. It looked expensive...like something I'd find online at a goth prom store.

"Holy shit!"

"Language, Avery," she scolded, but she couldn't hide the grin that spread across her face. "Try it on. We need to make sure it fits."

Momma was a perfectionist, so I had no doubt it would fit flawlessly. I put on the dress. It featured a full-tiered ruffled skirt in black satin, a steel-boned corset covered in black lace with glossy ebony buttons down the front, and a sorceress chemise, which flowed elegantly around my legs. The dress was off the shoulder, with sleeves that ran form-fitting to the elbow before flaring out, creating a beautiful line that cascaded gently to the cuff at my wrist.

I looked at myself in the full-length mirror on the back of my door. "Momma," I gasped, "it's so beautiful!"

"*You're* beautiful. Here. There's more." She handed me a large box with an orange bow placed on the top.

Speechless, I pulled off the lid. Inside was a lacy obsidian choker, a pair of Victorian boots with a low kitten-heel, and a headdress with black satin flowers in the center, and curved silver horns extending from either side.

"Thank you so much," I said, giving her a hug.

"It's the least I could do." She walked to the door. "I'll leave you to get ready. Just make sure you let me get some pictures before you head off to the party."

"I will. I promise."

"Okay. Have fun."

I couldn't stop smiling.

An hour later, I was ready. I had very pale skin normally, but I'd enhanced it with make-up. My silvery-blonde hair created a lovely contrast against all the dark colors. Smoky eyeshadow made my hazel eyes pop, and the dark plum lipstick, which looked black in certain lighting, left no doubt I was an evil, vampy witch.

Picking up my shawl, I eyed the Halloween memory box sitting on my desk. Removing the lid, I nostalgically ran my fingers across the various items from Halloweens past, then made my way to the living room. Picture-taking commenced, and minutes later, I was zooming across town in Momma's Kia. It was difficult trying to fit my puffy skirt into the tiny car, but I eventually managed.

I parked near Dalton's house and took it all in. Every window shone with spooky red lighting. The front yard was filled with gravestones and zombies pushing through the dirt, glowing jack-o'-lanterns sat on the steps, and cobwebs were strung across the tree limbs and shrubbery. Even from the street, I could hear "Monster Mash" playing inside. Some of my costumed classmates arrived and ventured inside, but I couldn't recognize any of them.

Golly, I loved this time of year.

It would be one hell of a night.

"**A**very! Oh my God, you look incredible!" Josie rushed over to me and gave me a hug. "The most gorgeous witch I've ever seen."

I pulled back and eyed her up and down. "Not looking too shabby yourself, Little Red Riding Hood."

She waved me off. "It's just a costume I picked up at the store. Nothing special. But you…damn. Did your mom make this?"

"She sure did. Amazing, isn't it?"

Josie made me turn around multiple times so she could see my dress from all angles. "It's incredible. Your mom missed her calling."

"Very true." I smiled sadly. Momma worked as a cashier at a local auto repair shop. She worked a nine-to-five job to make sure we had what we needed, although she was very creative and a talented seamstress.

Breaking the somber mood, Josie tugged on my arm. "Come on, let's get you something to drink."

Soon enough, I had a can of beer in my hand and was sitting in the living room with the rest of the guests. While Dalton, our host, regaled us with a boring football game tale, I spent some time checking out who else was there. It was for seniors only, and our class had a grand total of forty-three people.

A quick headcount showed nineteen guests, including Dalton and myself. Better than I expected. This far into the Bible Belt, Halloween was a bad word in many homes around here—an evil holiday full of devil worship and sinister doings.

Which was just silly.

I adored Halloween and all the memories it evoked, and I'm pretty sure that didn't make me Satan's spawn.

Dalton's best friend and fellow athlete, Andrew, was there. Pearl and Opal, best friends since kindergarten because of their names, were smoking by the open front window. Tanner, my on-again/off-again boyfriend, was present…and staring at me. His best friend, Henry, was by his side. And then I noticed a face I wasn't expecting to see.

"Charity?"

Seeing her, an outspoken religious whack-a-doodle, at a Halloween party seemed surreal. In costume, too…an *angel* costume, of course.

She gave a prim smile. "Hello, Avery."

"I'm surprised to see you here tonight."

Charity shrugged. "Just felt the need to come, you know?" I nodded, but had no idea what she was talking about. I took a long swig of my beer and caught her disapproving scowl. "Well, it's nice to see you. I need a refill."

Josie followed me into the kitchen. "Can you believe Charity came? It's like having my mom here looking over my shoulder," she said as she opened the fridge door and pulled two cold cans from within. "All that self-righteous bullshit. Jesus."

Accepting one of the beers, I replied, "Let's be glad it's just her."

At that, Josie shuddered; Charity had an even more annoying twin who loved to tell us we were all going to Hell for one reason or another.

A commotion from the other room signified the activities were getting started. We ventured back in and were soon on a team of four wrapping Henry in toilet paper. The goal was to create the most convincing looking mummy in the least amount of time. We lost.

After that, we played a string of other Halloween-inspired games: Fuck, Marry, Kill; Spin the Plastic Pitchfork (I had to kiss Opal, who tasted like an ash tray); Halloween Charades; Eyeball Beer Pong. We even had a costume contest, which I won. My prize was a large bag of cheap candy.

By that time, it was well after midnight, and some people ventured home. The few of us who remained decided to build a bonfire in the backyard firepit, put on some good music, and make s'mores. The beer had been depleted, so we were forced to drink bottles of the shitty wine that Dalton found in his mother's pantry.

Eh. Whatever. I was feeling *good*.

Pleasantly intoxicated, our bellies full of marshmallows and chocolate, a mellow calm overtook the nine of us who sat around the fire.

"You know, it's after midnight," I said. "This is the time when the veil between the living and spirit world is the thinnest."

Silence.

Then Andrew said, "That's creepy, Avery. Gave me the damn goose bumps."

"Sorry." I giggled. "I just thought it was an interesting fact, is all."

Tanner, a well-known history buff, chimed in. "I bet I know something that would interest all of you."

"What?" I challenged.

"Well, you know my grandmother was born in Wales? She told me about an ancient custom performed every year on All Hallows' Eve. They'd build a huge fire—we're talking massive. They called it *Coel Coeth*." He struggled with the pronunciation. "Every family member would make a mark on a small white stone, identifying it as their own. They'd then toss their stones into the flames, reciting prayers while circling the fire." A weird gleam filled Tanner's eyes. "Here's where it gets creepy. The next morning, at first light, they'd go to the ashes and look for their stones. If someone's stone was missing...it meant they'd die before the next All Hallows' Eve."

"Holy shit, that's bleak," Pearl responded. Opal chuckled nervously.

"My grammy swore up and down it was accurate every single time."

"Hell, yeah, dude. Super cool! Let's do it!" said Dalton. "I'll get some markers. You guys start finding white stones."

"Are you going to?" Josie asked me, as Andrew, followed by Pearl and Opal, began searching the yard.

"I…I don't know."

"If you do, your soul will be in jeopardy," Charity replied, a smirk crossing her pinched, ferret face.

"If Charity thinks it's a bad idea, I'm in." Henry jumped up.

"Yeah, why not? If my grammy could do it, I sure as hell can." Tanner flipped Charity off and joined his friend.

"Well, if everybody else is…" Josie got up.

"Guess I'm in too." I stood and brushed the wrinkles from my dress. "Josie, hey! Hold up. I need to tell you something," I called.

She walked back to me. "This had better be good," she said, her voice full of sass. I leaned close and whispered in her ear. Her eyes shown with confusion.

"Just do it, okay?"

"No prob." She shrugged, then skipped to an empty section of yard to find the perfect rock. I turned to Charity. "What about you?"

"This isn't a game, Avery."

"Of course it is. It's a bunch of high school students drawing on rocks and throwing them into a fire. Not even you can find anything evil in that." I looked at her with my eyebrows raised, attempting to make my point.

"It's the intent behind it that's evil. Not the actions themselves."

I rolled my eyes. "It wasn't too evil for Tanner's grammy, and I've met her. She's sweet as pie."

Hearing our conversation as he returned from the house with a handful of markers, Dalton said, "Either you join in, or you can leave, Charity. And take your 'too good for us' sneers with you. Why'd you even come, anyway?"

Charity's eyes widened, and her mouth formed a perfectly shaped 'o.' She shook her head and made a few unintelligible squeaky sounds. Her skin flushed, as her eyes glistened with tears.

In that moment, I realized something. Charity had a crush on Dalton. And it must have been stronger than her long-held convictions because she began searching for a rock.

After we'd all found suitable stones, Dalton passed out the black markers. I drew a spider web on one side and a spider on the other. Last summer, I'd tried talking my mom into letting me have a pet tarantula, but she'd refused. Her actual response? "I don't want one of those hairy-ass, eight-legged monstrosities in my house."

Fair enough.

Josie had drawn a series of interlocking tiny hearts. Charity drew a cross and the Christian fish symbol; I was about to make a snarky comment just as Pearl screech-laughed while looking at Opal's stone. She'd probably drawn a dick. That would totally track with the Opal I knew.

Dalton added some wood to the fire. The flames burned hotter, brighter, and higher. "Gather 'round, boys and girls. Let's do this!"

Somebody began playing new age music on their phone, which seemed appropriate. Tanner held up his stone. "I'm going to throw my stone in first, while focusing on all my good intentions. We'll take turns, going clockwise, or *deosil,* as my grammy called it, tossing them in, one by one. Then we'll move, *deosil* again, around the fire. You can dance, you can sing, you can spin in circles…whatever. But as you do, send good energies into the universe. Send your wishes out there. Or, you can pray." He gave Charity a curt nod. "Is everybody ready?"

We were.

Giving his stone one final glance and gently rubbing it with his thumb, he tossed it into the blaze. Henry did the same, as did Pearl, Opal, Dalton, Andrew, and Josie. When my turn came, I kissed my stone and carefully dropped it into the licking flames. Charity reluctantly followed suit. We slowly walked around the fire. At first, it was boring. Mundane. But then my body responded to the music, and I felt myself dancing. Unrestrained, unashamed movements. Pearl did as well. Then Josie. Pretty soon, all our bodies were responding to the music. Laughter echoed through the trees. Without a single word spoken, we all gripped the hands of those closest to us and began skipping around the fire—like it was a May pole.

It was surreal.

It was beautiful.

It was life-affirming.

When the music stopped, we were breathless and stone-cold sober, yet…high.

Tanner spoke first. "Now, everyone goes home and straight to bed. Set your alarms. Sunrise is just before eight. Be here by quarter 'til, so we can look for our stones just as the sun peeks above the horizon. Got it?" Each of us nodded solemnly. "All right. Happy All Saints' Day, everyone. See you bright and early…and bring a broom!"

Sometime later, I slid the black Sharpie into my memory box, then I crawled into bed. Sleep pulled me under in seconds.

I didn't even need my alarm. I was already wide awake at seven o' clock. I jumped out of bed, my nerves making themselves known by my gurgling, acidic stomach. Or maybe it was the excessive amounts of alcohol I'd drunk. Either way, I needed to get to the bathroom.

I looked longingly at my gorgeous witchy dress hanging on the back of my door as I did, wishing I could wear it again today. After a scalding-hot shower, I dressed in sweats, a hoodie, old sneakers, and pulled my ratty hair into piggy-tails—a far cry from the way I'd presented myself last night.

Momma was still asleep when I left, so no explanations were needed. Arriving early, I decided to cruise around the neighborhood until the others showed up. "Let Me Bathe in Demonic Light" by The Mountain Goats played on Siri as I stopped at a 7-11 to get some coffee. I needed a java jolt. Ten minutes later, I was back at Dalton's and happy to see my friends' cars. Grabbing my coffee and broom, I made my way to the backyard.

Sirens pierced the early morning silence, damn close based on their sound. Dismissing them, I went to the picnic table where the others were sitting.

My morning greetings received a bunch of half-hearted, hungover grunts in reply. Charity stared brazenly at me but said nothing at all. Her eyes were bloodshot, and she looked as if she hadn't slept.

I sat beside Josie and rested my head on her shoulder. She responded by resting her head on mine. I was comforted.

"Where the hell are Opal and Pearl?" Dalton muttered. "Sunrise is just a few minutes away."

"We've got six minutes. We'll wait a couple more, then get started," Tanner said.

Silence descended. Everyone stared at the table. The exhaustion on my friends' faces aged them dramatically. Two minutes passed. Then three. Still no Pearl and Opal.

"Okay, let's just go ahead," Tanner said.

We gathered around the fire's ashes, holding our brooms. Tanner instructed us to make sure we were in the same positions as last night.

"I don't know why Pearl and Opal aren't here," Henry said. "I texted Pearl earlier, and she said Opal spent the night with her. They were awake and getting ready."

"We'll have to do this without them. Hopefully it doesn't fuck anything up." Tanner glanced toward the street, anxiety etching his features, then back at me with a warm grin. "Right. Use your brooms and sweep away the ashes to uncover our stones. And, hey, good luck, everyone."

Andrew snickered.

We swept. Seconds passed. Tensions grew. Our motions became more frantic, ashes billowing around us and fouling the air. I coughed. Minutes passed and still nothing.

"What the fuck is going on?" Dalton asked, his tone belligerent. "Has anyone even *seen* a stone?" We all shook our heads. "They've gotta be in there somewhere."

Eventually, we admitted defeat. There wasn't a single stone to be found—not one. Henry looked at Tanner. "What does it mean? Where did they go?"

My phone beeped with an incoming text. So did Josie's. Then Tanner's. One by one, all our phones began pinging. Reading the message, my heart sank—Pearl and Opal had been t-boned by a truck on their way to Dalton's house. Neither had survived. The sirens I'd heard earlier must have been emergency personnel convening at the site of their accident.

"Oh my God," Josie said. "Is everyone seeing this? Is it real?"

Henry, sniffling, stared at his phone and wiped tears from his eyes. He'd been smitten with Pearl for as long as I could remember. His sniffles quickly turned to sobs.

Tanner threw his phone to the ground. "Grammy was right. *Goddammit!*" He shouted, running his hands nervously through his hair. "She was awake last night when I got home, so I told her what we'd done. She was horrified, afraid of something like this happening. She said we'd toyed with something bigger than we could comprehend, that the timing—on Samhain—made it even more dire." He looked at his friends. "Grammy said we needed to be prepared to face the consequences—even death." The final word was whispered.

"Are you shittin' me?" Dalton blurted. "We threw rocks in a fire. Big fucking deal!"

"It is a big deal. My grandmother wouldn't exaggerate. Look what happened to Pearl and Opal!" He looked Dalton in the eye. "Now quit acting like a prick, and let's figure out what the hell we need to do."

"Did you just call me a *prick?*" Dalton moved closer, until they were standing face to face.

"I did. You deserved it. This is bad, dude, so just lay off. I'm trying to help us all."

"By scaring us with your bullshit?"

"How do you know it's bullshit?"

"Because stones and fire don't equal death and destruction, and your *grammy* is clearly a damn nutter."

Tanner punched Dalton hard enough to knock him down.

He fell to the ground and didn't move. Dark blood oozed from beneath him.

Andrew ran to Dalton, yelling, "No, no, no...Dalton, you're okay, right?" He rolled him over. A raw, gaping wound showed where his head had struck a large stone. I could see something that looked very much like a brain. Dalton's eyes stared sightlessly at the early morning sky.

Screaming at the top of her lungs, Charity used tiny fists to uselessly pummel Tanner's back. "What did you do? What did you *do*? He's dead, and you're going to Hell, you sick son of a bitch!"

Tanner stood stoically, accepting the blows.

None of it mattered. It was too late for Dalton.

I could only stare at the corpse on the ground. Josie's hand found mine. I gave a hard squeeze.

Andrew fell to his knees, sobbing, and cradled Dalton's body. "I love you. Oh, God, I love you so much, baby. I'll never stop."

I looked at Josie, and she looked at me, tears running from her overly wide eyes. They were a *couple*? We'd had no idea.

Neither had Charity. Her tortured screech was followed by Andrew's pained cry as she stabbed the fire stoker into his back. "You're a liar, Andrew! Dalton wasn't gay! He loved *me*!" Andrew looked from the metal tip jutting from his chest to Charity, who was pulling at her hair as she paced around the yard, and then back to his chest again. His body toppled over.

"What the actual fuck is going on here?" Josie screamed. "I'm calling 911!"

"Don't," Tanner said, his voice flat and hard. He glared at her and shook his head; cowed, she slowly lowered the phone.

Charity had Dalton's ruined head in her lap, rocking back and forth, quietly singing—likely something gospel—to him. Henry's wails echoed throughout the backyard as he grieved his years-long crush. Tanner sat on the ground, knees up, feet flat on the cold grass, arms wrapped around his legs. His mouth moved, but no words emerged. By unspoken agreement, Josie and I remained where we were, not talking, not moving—drawing as little attention to ourselves as possible. Everyone had lost their damn minds, and we didn't feel safe.

"This was your fault, you know," Charity said with quiet malice to Tanner. "If you hadn't pitched that stupid Pagan tradition, we'd all be snug in our beds right now, and my soul wouldn't be tarnished! We're all going to Hell because of you!" Her voice grew louder and more belligerent. "*Eternal* damnation! We're going to rot and suffer because *you* were trying to be cool in front of Avery. Well, I won't have it! My soul will not burn in the fiery pits of He..." Her words choked off, a sudden rush of crimson gore spilling down her face. She lifted her fingers to it, studying the bloody residue as if it was something truly foreign. Her eyes crossed, and her upper body fell backward, Dalton's head still in her lap.

Henry stood behind her, wild-eyed and hyperventilating, one of the stones ringing the firepit clutched inside his hand. "I...I...I'm so sorry," he gasped. "I just...I couldn't listen to her crazy bullshit. Not anymore. Not *now*."

Josie buried her head in my neck. My eyes were glued to the spectacle unfolding before me, morbidly fascinated and unable to look away.

Tanner went to Henry, his hands raised in a defensive posture. "Hey, man. It's okay. Just breathe. It's okay." His hands shook as he gently took the stone from his overwrought friend. As soon as Henry was free of its weight, he ran into Dalton's house, slamming the door behind him. Dropping the stone to the ground, Tanner looked at me, his lips curled into a brave smile. I saw traces of the boy I'd been so hopelessly smitten with throughout my junior year—the confident, smart, witty guy who always had the answers to every trivia question. He looked at our deceased friends, and I saw profound sadness fill his eyes. Then resignation. I knew he felt responsible. "You guys need to go home. I'll handle this."

"Tanner, we can't just leave," I said. "The police will have questions for all of us."

The three of us jumped as a gunshot sounded from inside the house. "Oh God, not again," Tanner said, before running across the yard and through the back door. Seconds later, he was back, the bleak expression on his face telling me everything I needed to know.

Henry was gone.

"I know what to do. Please, both of you, just…go home," Tanner said quietly. "You both left before the ceremony last night, and were never here this morning. Got it?" He turned—head down, shoulders slumped—and walked away.

I didn't require any more persuasion than that. The corpse-filled backyard was the last place I wanted to be. I collected my broom and coffee, drove home, and fell into bed. Shock made me weary. I slept like the dead.

Mom woke me later that afternoon when two cops showed up at our front door.

Tanner had committed suicide. Hanged himself from an oak tree with some rope he'd found in Dalton's garage.

And he'd left a note.

In it, he'd stuck as close to the truth as possible, without naming names. He took the blame for all the deaths.

The cops wanted to hear my version of events, which I reluctantly shared, keeping Tanner's request in mind. I even showed them the bag of candy I'd won in the costume contest, which they merely glanced at without interest.

Later that night, when the house was dark and silent, I dug around in my candy bag, searching. One by one, I pulled the ash-covered stones from the depths of the sugary sweets and placed them side by side in my Halloween memory box.

Seven white stones; two gray ones. I'd whispered to Josie to get anything other than a white stone, which would disqualify us from any potential consequences of the ceremony, even though we'd participated.

I knew enough about Paganism to understand just how effective those ancient rites were. I also realized that by stealing the stones, I was creating chaos. Did I ever! But what a *special* memory.

There was zero chance I'd ever be able to top this Halloween.

I looked in the mirror and smiled.

Momma had come through for me again, mailing the requested gypsy/fortune teller costume for my very first college Halloween party. She'd done an exquisite job, and I couldn't wait to show it off to my friends, including Josie, who was now my dorm mate. She'd left an hour earlier, dressed as an Egyptian priestess, hoping to score some pot from a guy she knew. We were meeting at the sorority house we both intended to pledge next semester.

Grabbing my little satchel, I rode the elevator to the ground floor, exited the building, and turned left toward Greek Row.

I'd almost covered the half-mile to the sorority house when I felt a sharp sting in my neck. I thought it was a bee or wasp, but when I tried to swat it away, I couldn't raise my hand.

Darkness beckoned. I succumbed.

I awoke inside a cage, my hands and feet bound behind me. The room was dark, filled with shadows, and smelled like a slaughterhouse—a coppery, metallic scent permeating the space with its putridity. I gagged.

Pounding on the metal bars as well as I could with my elbows, I yelled, "Is anybody here? Please, help me!" over and over. My brain couldn't seem to think of anything else to say, as the direness of my situation became apparent.

I heard a creak. It sounded like a door opening.

"Hello? Is anybody there? Please, if you can hear me, get help!"

Footsteps seemed to be getting closer, making their way down a set of very squeaky stairs. Nothing about the movements made me feel safe. I could see a shape in the darkness.

"Please, whoever you are, I need help. I've been locked in a cage, and I'm very sick. Call 9-1-1, please."

"Oh, Avery, you always were a hoot."

That voice…

My heartrate tripled. "Charity?" I whispered.

A lantern turned on. "You never were the sharpest tool in the shed, were you?"

The figure stepped into the light. A ghost...?

A warm, tinkling laugh. "I can tell by your expression you think you're seeing something supernatural. It's Amity, you dumb bitch."

In my post-drugged, fear-ridden haze, I'd completely forgotten Charity had an identical twin. This wasn't good. Nope, not even a little.

"I didn't do a thing to Charity. Just let me go, Amity."

Another laugh. "Do you think I went to all this trouble just to let you go? To allow your stink back in the world? Not a chance."

"Josie is expecting me, and if I don't show up, she'll call the cops and—"

Amity cut me off. "This Josie?" She angled the lantern across the room. I saw my friend, her body draped in beautiful silks, her head sitting on the floor beside her. I whimpered.

"Charity told me everything when she got home from the party that night. I know you and Josie were at the ceremony. I know you wrote the whole thing off, just another day in your sinful lives. Nothing to stress or worry about. But it was *my* sister! *My* twin! And now she's burning in Hell because of you and your asshole friends!"

She kicked something at me. It took a minute before I realized it was Josie's head.

"I tried to forgive. I prayed and lit candles and fasted and prayed some more. I even went on a religious retreat to the Holy Lands. Nothing worked. So, you know what I said, Avery? Come on, I bet you can't guess." She let out a madness-filled cackle. "I said, 'Fuck it!' and I decided to kill you. An eye for an eye and all that."

Amity walked toward me, holding some sort of wicked looking axe with a giant curved blade. "It's called a bardiche, and butchers used them hundreds of years ago to lop the heads off oxen."

She smiled wickedly and unlocked the cage.

"This one is for Charity." Amity brought down the blade.

LET THE DARK DO THE REST

by Kealan Patrick Burke

have never been afraid of Halloween. It's a celebration based on artifice, so what is there to fear? Once those masks and costumes come off, and the decorations come down, everything is as it was before, and we abandon mimicking the dead in favor of pretending to live. Or at least I do.

But tonight…

Tonight, it's an hour shy of midnight on October 31ˢᵗ and something is wrong. Because I don't believe in ghouls and specters and grisly things, the only logical conclusion is there's something wrong with *me*.

Simply put, I don't like how the night looks right now. It's odd in ways I can't specify. Different somehow. There's a sense of weight to it, this dark—a heaviness more than the absence of light. It presses back into their frames the frail warm glow of living room lights. It has no voice of its own, but muffles the cries of animals begging and pleading and rutting and dying. This is the hunter's dark, and tonight it feels like it has eaten the world and everyone in it, leaving only me to ponder the loss.

I'm standing here, waiting for the sensation to pass, thereby proving itself an anomaly I can quickly dismiss as errant paranoia. But I can't laugh because my throat is cinched tight against a whimper of alarm, borne of the certainty that past the chain link fence, and just beyond the oblong wedge of light from my kitchen window in which my tremulous shadow is trapped, the dark is watching me. Encroaching.

So go back inside, you say, but Monica doesn't let me smoke inside the house, part of our uneasy truce. She doesn't like me smoking but has quit badgering me about it as long as I keep it outside. I could put out the cigarette, but they've always helped calm my nerves and right now, that's what I need more than anything else. That, and the restoration of logic to remind me that I'm a forty-one-year-old man on Halloween night spooked by absolutely nothing.

I take out my phone, annoyed that my hand is shaking, and send Monica a text. She's working nights at St. Andrew's Medical Center these days, and sometimes I wonder if she took that shift to avoid seeing me.

"You okay, hun?" I text, and I am grateful to see her immediately typing a response.

"Fine," she replies. *"Busy as hell tonight though. Bonfire burns. Pranks gone wrong. Kids choking on candy. It's great.* ☹ *"*

I send back some dismissively cute response and pocket the phone. She's okay, and that's all that matters, which means I can rule her out as the subject of my foreboding.

But…is it just me or has the wedge of light dimmed, my shadow less distinct than before? Perhaps for all my hysteria, it's my vision that really deserves closer inspection.

Time to regroup. I'm being ridiculous, even by my own admittedly-low standards.

The cigarette, burned down to the filter, heats the skin of my fingers, so I take one last dirty drag and flick it into the backyard where the dark is thickest.

The arc of the cigarette is halted in midair and explodes in a firework of sparks. My breath catches. I can't move. There *is* something there and I just hit it with my cigarette. Rooted to the spot with confusion and terror, it is not until I hear a sound like someone with bad knees rising in complaint that I flee inside the house and lock the door.

"I don't have time for this, Kev," Monica says. I know she doesn't, but I don't either. She sounds annoyed, tired, eager to be off the phone, so I make it quick.

"I'm telling you, there's someone out there."

"It's probably one of the neighborhood kids having fun with you."

"This late?"

"It's Halloween night. The later it is, the scarier the prank. Don't you remember being a teenager?"

I do, but fail to see how being a gangly, awkward, friendless introvert has any connection here.

"Turn on the backyard light. That'll scare them off."

"The light's burned out." I say this with an ominous tone, as if some supernatural entity or serial killer is to blame, when in truth, it's been burned out for months and I just never replaced it.

"So, change it," she says, exasperated. She sounds like that a lot lately and I know it's not just the demands of her job.

"That's how dumb characters die in horror movies."

"This isn't a movie, and maybe if you didn't watch so many of them, you'd be better equipped to see how dumb *you're* being right now."

That hurts, but it's also hard to argue. I'm not being myself. You'll have no frame of reference, but on an ordinary day, I'm only mildly unnerved by everything, and to be frank, I don't trust anyone who isn't.

Monica relents. "Sorry. Look, it's chaotic here right now, and I just think you're stressing out over nothing."

Nothing. That's exactly what it is. A roiling, dark, toxic cloud of nothing come to murder me. "You're right. I'll let you go."

"I'll see you when I get home, okay?"

"Okay, love you."

She takes a second too long to respond.

It's after midnight and I'm dying for a smoke, but I'm not going out the side door where that malevolent arthritic darkness waits. No, I'll use the front porch instead, with its nice view of my lawn, badly in need of raking and weeding, and beyond, the mundane suburban ranch houses made macabre by ghoulish decor and lighted pumpkins.

But it's late, and the pumpkins have been extinguished. Even the porchlights are quenched, a signal to stray trick-'r-treaters that the candy dispensary is done for another year. My porchlight works though, and it's turned on so that I can sit in its protective bubble. Everyone has gone to sleep. Why haven't I? How could I? My guts are tied in a knot that would impress a sailor and my brain is full of butterflies. I can be reasonable. The few instances of it are a matter of public record. I don't even believe in ghosts, or evil—outside our own staggering capacity for it—so what about this night has instilled in me a skin-crawling dread of the night? What would a therapist say is the true cause of this idiocy? What element of myself am I imprinting upon the dark?

From my perch on the stoop, I light my cigarette and spew the smoke out into the air. Fear is graduating to irritation. Why am I like this? If it were only the dark, I could forgive my own trespasses, but it's not. Dates, job interviews, confrontation, crowds, any kind of social interaction…I have always been this way. But now here I am with nothing bothering me, and it's bothering me. Every goddamn thing evokes a disproportionately negative response in the scrambled servers of my brain, and it's tiresome.

A lonesome breeze sends dead leaves skittering up the street. Bradbury would love it. I watch them for a moment before I notice the air smells faintly of cotton candy, and there go those alarm bells again. I'm just going to say for the record that if it's an evil clown out there, I'll shit my pants in three different languages. Remember a few years back when clowns just started showing up in random neighborhoods at night? Did anyone ever figure out why? Well, I don't know why, but I didn't like it. Clowns are my undoing. Dogs too. I can't explain the former, but the tiny ellipses of scars on my left wrist from a childhood encounter with a German shephard I mistakenly thought wanted to be petted, is explanation enough for the latter. Consequently, while I can appreciate the cuteness and appeal of dogs from a distance, I prefer to avoid them. Clowns can go fuck themselves, however. They have no appeal. There's no reason for them to exist but they do anyway, because the universe has a cruel sense of humor.

I scan the street for any sign of some Pennywise-looking gimp, but I'm the only one out here. Just me and the quiet houses and the leaves and the dark.

I look to my left and jump at the sound of a metallic shriek. It's not prolonged, not a slow deliberate raking intended to frighten me, rather the quick withdrawal of someone or something that didn't want to be seen. Something whose nails were, until I looked in its direction, resting on the drainpipe that runs down the side of my house.

I rise and start to flick my cigarette away but think better of it, and instead ground it out beneath my heel, then back slowly into the house.

I'm done with cigarettes for the night.

A braver man would already have gotten to the bottom of this, have marched out there with a flashlight and demanded the night explain itself, but a lifetime of being afraid of things has removed that ability. I'll spare you the psychological history lesson on how I came to be this way. It's relevant, and maybe you'd even feel sorry for me, but it wouldn't change your impression of me being a coward, because while I've warred with this description of myself, there currently exists no compelling evidence with which to file a counterclaim.

So, I lock the house up tight, turn on all the lights, and settle down in front of the TV, raising the volume so I can't hear the monsters outside grunting or scratching their nails. *Everybody Loves Raymond* is on, and that'll do fine. I find him easy to like, probably because he's a bit of a browbeaten simp and thus, more like me than I care to admit, though in my case, it's not the wife that's browbeating me, but my own disappointment at how little I've managed to bolster myself against all the uncaring realities of a world that should not need to coddle me.

Here's where I'm supposed to have that delicious epiphany as my pulse accelerates, raw blue blood rushes into my heart and emerges blazing red, and I stand, ripping my shirt open, my face suddenly abrush with designer stubble, and scream about masculinity and how nothing can keep me down because *I am a man, goddammit*, and then, armed with the sharpest knife in the house, I stalk out into the yard and stab the fuck out of the nothing until I'm left with my chest puffed out, one foot propped atop the severed head of my conquered foe. That would be nice, if fundamentally stupid, but it doesn't matter, because if an abrupt infusion of manly manliness didn't happen in my pubescence, it's not going to happen now.

Three episodes into the rerun marathon, and I switch channels. *Halloween III* is on, the one known for not having Michael Myers in it. I watch until a drunk guy's head is forcibly removed by a robot in a suit and decide I can't hack it. I flip the channel and the news is on, and this is the part where they tell me about an escaped lunatic from an asylum who was last seen in *my neighborhood*. But it's just another train derailment in Ohio.

I turn off the TV, second guess myself, and turn it back on. Switch around until I land on a popular comedian whose appeal has always eluded me and pretend to be entertained by his savage thoughts on atheism. I'm not religious despite fear creating that opening in me where a trumped-up deity might find a convenient home, but I'm not atheist either. I'm an abstainer, waiting on someone from either team to pick me like it's grade school tryouts, and just like those awkward days, I expect I'll continue waiting until everyone has gone home and the lights have been shut off.

Scritch-scritch at the window next to the TV and every hair on my body rises to the occasion. I heft the remote as if it's a gun and aim it at the window, thankful I thought to draw the curtains.

Okay, real talk, I think. *I've been told my whole life I'm a disappointment. From Principal Thayle to my parents to my boss at Calico Software, all I ever hear is how short I fell of people's expectations. So, Dear Monster at my window, what is it you think you'll get from me? Why me? Surely there are juicier targets than the weak man who never quite figured himself out and now lives in constant horror that he never will. A horror with which even you with your amorphous presence and scratchy-scratch nails cannot compete.*

I wait a few minutes, but the scratching sound doesn't come again, and I feel somewhat emboldened by its absence, as if my defiant thoughts somehow discouraged it. I imagine the dark floating away down the driveway, offering a consolatory wave. *Sorry, wrong house. My mistake.* The image gives me a chuckle, and I pat the cigarette pack in my pocket, reconsidering my vow to be done for the night. Perhaps that's what's needed here: a good ol' dash of unprecedented rebellion. *Here I am, Eldritch Thing, out here having a smoke despite the history of cancer in my family. Do your worst.* Maybe it'll be therapeutic to simply yell into the face of the nothing that I am not afraid of it because it doesn't exist. Weird logic, but better than hiding in my house like a child.

I decide, yes, I'm going to have a cigarette after all, and pretend it's bravery and not a complete lack of willpower courtesy of my addiction.

I don't go to the front of the house, but the side of it, where that thing first announced itself. Let it show itself. I'm ready.

Feeling stronger than I have all day, all week, all my life—for what is all this if not a reckoning with myself?—I exit the side door and take a long draw of the chilly night air. There really is something unique about October weather, but I wouldn't hang around waiting for me to tell you what it is, because I'm not a fucking poet. All I know is I like the frost it brings to my embittered lungs, even if invariably I expel it on a cough that burns my throat.

The outside looks like the outside always does. There is no inexplicable weight where I thought I saw it before, because it was in my head all along, a boogeyman conjured from the haunted house of my own brain. I light up the cigarette and see something move to my left. Despite my bravado, my head snaps so fast in that direction it sends a bolt of metallic pain up the side of my neck, and I wince, even while trying to track the source of the movement.

It was your lighter, you fucking gummi bear, I realize, the sparks throwing my own shadow against the wall. But no, that's not right. The light is on and while the lighter might cast some impression of me against the house, it wouldn't be that dark or that noticeable.

Cigarette unlit, I pocket the lighter, and peer into the darkness over the backyard fence with an intensity that would have Nietzsche throwing up his hands in disgust.

And perhaps it's still my eyes playing tricks on me, but the dark seems to shift away from my scrutiny, like a dog second guessing its own anger in favor of flight.

"What are you?" I ask, and the vocalization of the thought is confirmation of my own sanity abandoning me. "Show yourself."

Nothing.

Despite every cell of good sense demanding the opposite reaction,

I move to the gate, crunching over the unraked leaves, and undo the small hoop latch. It shrieks as it opens, because I haven't oiled the gate in years, and I have to give it a yank to get it to open. To my left is the deck, the boards warped and worn. To my right, the low fence separating our place from the neighbors, a couple who tried to make friends with us and failed. They have two kids and three dogs who represent a wall of noise every day from dawn to noon, which is when the grandmother arrives to shut them all up. I have no rapport whatsoever with the guy next door—I don't even remember his name—but weirdly enough, I wish he was there now like he is most Friday nights, drinking in the garage with his friends, the door open to let out the marijuana smoke. Maybe I'd finally take him up on his invitation to join them, an invitation he made several times before recognizing me as the kind of person who adds little to any gathering. But the door is shut now, the garage quiet.

There's just me, the fool, out here talking to himself, spooked by nothing.

A light comes on in the house behind mine, which is separated from my property by a high wooden fence in a stern declaration of privacy that speaks volumes about the friendliness of the occupants. One assumes the small narrow window is their bathroom. I see a shape moving behind the frosted glass, but it also backlights the thing standing right in front of me and my breath locks in my throat.

"Oh," I say, and what a fine last word to be remembered by. No "Rosebud" here, folks. Nope. Just "oh", and then the darkness coiled before me unfurls and consumes me. Before I can even think to react, I've been plunged into an icy lake. My lungs freeze, my limbs seize, my heart slows. I'm vaguely aware of being raised off the ground, the cold hard earth falling away as whatever has me hoists me up for inspection or ingestion, maybe both, and I am struck by the saddest thought that if this indeed is the end of me, there may not be a body left behind to mourn. Poor Monica. All that time and hope invested in me only to come home to nothing but unanswered questions.

Slowly, I am turned around so I'm facing the open gate and the side door beyond. I can hear my breath as a tortured rasp, so clearly my organs still work despite the sensation that the dark has crept into me and is squeezing them to test their pliability.

What are you? I think but cannot say.

And to my surprise, there's an answer.

You, says the voice in my head, much like my own, but heavy with grief.

I have more questions but keep them to myself, afraid of the answers. My thoughts halt as the side door of my house opens.

Monica?

No. Too early, assuming time means anything anymore, and besides, her car isn't in the driveway. Still, my heart gives a pathetic lurch of hope.

Until I see who it is.

Me, of course. The me from earlier, lighting up the cigarette and staring at the dark, at me, with marked suspicion. I look pale and tired and weak, and somehow this is upsetting despite it being typical. I suppose it's because I've never been able to see it before because when it comes to honesty, the eyes of lovers are deceptive mirrors. This frail man is the real me and despite all the trauma that brought him here, it's irritating to see it.

The dark shakes me. *Pay attention. You had time enough to mourn yourself.*

The man on the porch shudders, then flicks his cigarette over the fence. It hits me above my right eyebrow and stings. An involuntary grunt escapes me and the man on the porch flinches at the sound.

How can he hear me? I have the illogical desire to beg him for help, to beg myself for help, before he ducks back inside. But then he's gone, the earlier me, the door shut and bolted, leaving me alone with my juror.

The earlier you, it says, mockingly. *Who was that? Who were you earlier? Who were you yesterday, last month, last year, a decade ago? Do you even know? Are you proud enough to claim any of those versions of you?*

I don't know. I do, though.

The you of now, here, in my arms, frightened, raw, ugly, weak and useless, this is you, paralyzed as much by the dark as you've always been in the light. What good are you? What is your worth?

I know myself better than the dark does so I am up to the challenge of justifying my own existence. In theory anyway, because after running my fingers across the spines of all the books that make up the library of my life, I am appalled to find myself illiterate.

"What on earth is that smell?" Monica asks. She looks exhausted but beautiful as always.

I'm hunched before the TV watching *Fright Night 2* and eating cold pizza. I have no idea how long it's been in the fridge, but I'm ravenous and don't much care. Funny though. It's alfredo sauce, spinach, and peppers—Monica's favorite—and I hate all those ingredients, but it tastes delicious right now.

She sniffs at the air. "I don't know. Did you burn something?"

"I don't think so."

"God, it's bad. Can you open a window before you go to bed? Air the place out a bit?"

"Sure. How was work?"

"It was work," she says, and flumps down next to me. "My shoulders are killing me."

"Want a massage?"

She looks at me like I'm a stranger, which, though she doesn't yet realize it, I probably am. Then she sighs. "I'm not in the mood."

"For a massage?"

"For whatever you think your reward will be for giving me one."

"Not what I had in mind."

What I do have in mind is a union of a different kind. The creation of a common bond that will unify us in ways I can't articulate. But I can make the introduction and let the dark do the rest.

"What's with the shades?"

Took me some time to dig these sunglasses out of the closet. I'm not a summer person, never have been, and suspect I'll be even less of one now, but I can't let her see my eyes yet, not until they're finished.

"Migraine. The light was killing me."

She chuckles and sinks down lower on the couch. She'll probably be asleep in minutes, which is when I'll do what needs to be done. "You could have just turned them off."

I look at her and smile. In a moment, I'm going to do that very thing.

She looks curiously at me. "What's gotten into you tonight?"

I reach out a hand that doesn't fit quite right anymore to pat her on the knee. "Nothing."

TWIN FLAMES

by Gwendolyn Kiste

It's three days before Halloween when my twin sister Cate calls me on the phone, the line crackling between us.

"Come home, Lisa," she whispers on the other end. "I miss you."

I haven't heard from her in years, and at first, I barely recognize her voice. A voice that sounds just like my own.

"I can't," I say, pacing back and forth in my studio apartment, running my hands through my hair. "Not right now."

"You have to." A long moment. "You know why."

Without another word, I hang up, already certain what I'll do next. I'll go home exactly like she wants me to. After all these years, I owe it to her.

My girlfriend Roxanne, however, isn't so sure. I tell her at brunch the next day over bottomless mimosas and plates of pumpkin French toast.

"You know we already had plans for Halloween," she says. "We were supposed to go to that rooftop party in the Strip District. I already got our costumes."

Of course, I remember. She's planning to dress up as Morticia, and I'm supposed to be her Gomez. I was even looking forward to it, but now I just shrug and take the last sip of my drink. "I'll only be gone a couple days."

She gapes at me. "You're going without me? I'm not even invited?"

"You can't come home with me," I whisper, and instantly, I know it's the wrong thing to say.

For months, Roxanne's been asking me about myself. Normal questions, harmless questions. Who I've been, where I've come from. I always do my best not to answer her, to pretend I don't hear her or act like it doesn't matter, but that isn't going to work now.

She watches me from across the table, a silent test between us, this moment that will decide everything.

"I'm coming with you," she says, finality churning in her voice.

My throat tightens, and I want to argue, to tell her no, but I already know it won't help. If I leave her here, then she won't be waiting for me when I come back.

It's the night before we leave, only a few hours until Halloween descends, and Roxanne is curled up next to me in bed, her limbs entwined with mine, her body warm and welcoming. But all I can do is turn away from her. I tell myself maybe this won't be so bad. After all, Halloween is my family's favorite time of year. Maybe it will be good to go home again.

I nearly laugh aloud in the dark at that one. Like there's ever anything good about going home.

It's barely sunrise when we're on the road, an overnight bag packed with a couple of toothbrushes and the costumes Roxanne wants us to wear tonight. She always has everything figured out, her life ordered and pristine. Even though she's the same age as me, she's got it together already, her career in advertising on the fast track to the top. Corner office, 401K, the whole nine yards. Meanwhile, I feel perpetually ready to fall apart, my existence barely taped together at the seams.

"You never talk about your sister," Roxanne says, staring out the window at the trees gone bright orange and blood red. "I didn't even know you were a twin."

"There's not much to say." I keep my eyes on the road ahead. "I haven't seen her for a long time."

"What about the rest of your family?"

"They're dead," I say without inflection.

"Everyone?"

"Everyone."

I should have told her all this before, but I wanted to keep my past from her. It seemed better that way. Roxanne and I have been together over a year, but sometimes, it's almost like we're strangers.

The state highway coils through the forest, the leaves golden and crumpled on the trees, the scents of earth and cinnamon rising through the air.

Halloween. The night when the veil between worlds is thinner, more permeable. More dangerous. Anything can slip through the darkness on a day like this.

Roxanne fiddles with the radio. "How long ago did your mother die?"

She's never asked this before. That's because I've never wanted her to.

I hesitate. "A few years."

"Did you go home for the funeral?"

I shake my head. "There wasn't one."

"No funeral?" Her eyes shift to me. "Why not?"

"My mother didn't want it," I say.

My family isn't like everyone else's. I learned that lesson young, and I've never forgotten it.

We cross the county line in the afternoon, and I instantly go numb, the miles rolling past us in slow motion. I'm almost forty, but the moment I'm back here, I'm suddenly the same lost and lonesome kid I used to be. The one who thought she'd never get out. The one who thought this town was a tomb.

I take one last turn, and my old house is waiting on the corner, the once-white siding faded to a sullen gray. Except for tonight, it only adds to the decayed ambiance. The whole place is bedecked for the evening. An army of skeletons crawls across the roof. Pale ghosts hang in the nearby trees. There are votives in the grass and votives in the pumpkins, coffins propped up against the pillars of the front porch, broomsticks arraying every corner. And there are bodies too, the kind that look like they're stuffed with hay, dressed in yellowed shirts and gowns, the centerpiece of the whole ghoulish display.

On Halloween night, this has always been the best house on the street, maybe even the best house anywhere in town.

Roxanne gazes up at the façade, her eyes wide. "It's different than I expected," she says, but I don't bother to ask what she thought my life would look like. Instead, with my head down, I trudge along the walkway, a row of lit jack-o'-lanterns staring up at me with their gap-toothed grins.

My sister opens the front door before I can even knock. "Hi, Lisa," she says.

"Hello, Cate."

We don't say anything else, the two of us simply studying the other's face. Every time I see her, it's like looking into a mirror—dark hair, dark eyes, a tiny cleft in the chin. She's the reason I hate my own reflection. It's a reminder there's another me out there, always eager, always waiting.

At last, I motion to my girlfriend. "This is Roxanne."

"Hello," Roxanne says brightly. "Lisa has told me so much about you."

My sister lets out a laugh, sharp as a dagger. "I doubt that." She turns toward me, one eyebrow raised. "Your costume is on the bed."

Roxanne glances between us. "Your costume?" She thought we were wearing the outfits she brought for us.

"It's an old tradition," I say and edge across the threshold into the house.

Upstairs, my bedroom is the same as I left it—the threadbare daisy curtains on the windows, nothing on the walls. Not that it's my bedroom at all. It was always ours, mine and Cate's. Like it or not, we shared everything.

On the mattress, my sister has laid out my costume, just like she promised. A black dress and black cape with a high collar to match. It's the same style we wore every year since we were little girls in pigtails. Things rarely change in this house, and when they do, it's never for the better.

Next to me, Roxanne unzips the overnight bag and slips into her velvet Morticia dress, trying her best not to let me see the disappointment flashing in her eyes.

Once I'm in my costume, I pull her into me and kiss her. "I'm sorry about not being Gomez this year."

"It's all right," she says and squeezes my hand. "You look great, by the way."

I force a smile. She would say that. Roxanne knows how to make me feel better, to make me feel like I'm someone else entirely. She and I couldn't be more different: I'm a woman with a past, and she's a woman with a future. I tell myself if I can only hold on tight to her, then maybe I can have a future too.

Together, we head back downstairs. Near the basement door, there's a full-size body propped up in the corner, wearing a gingham dress, its dark eyes sunken back in its listless skull.

"That's a funny prop," Roxanne says, giggling, but I just keep walking, never looking too closely at it. I already know I won't like what I see.

As we pass by, the grandfather clock in the living room strikes six. Trick or treat is officially underway. Outside, the street soon overflows with small cliques of children, their faces smeared with grease paint or arrayed in plastic masks, everyone cheering and chortling and jockeying for the biggest fistful of candy.

I stand back on the front porch, watching it all, an outsider in my own life. Autumn always feels like a most fearsome goodbye, another year of your life falling away like the foliage. I grimace at the bodies set around the yard, some of them in wobbly chairs, others splayed out in the grass, everything so realistic most of the children won't even brush up against them.

"It's alive," someone yells at a limp old man in a rocking chair, and a bleached blonde mother only laughs and promises them it's all in good fun.

Fun. That's not quite how I'd describe this house.

Still, I envy these kids a little. My sister and I were never like the others. We never went trick-or-treating.

"You have a more important job to do here," my mother would tell us, and she'd pat our heads, as if we were her obedient puppies. "You're going to help the whole family tonight."

And that's precisely what we learned how to do, even though we never asked for this.

"Why don't we just leave?" I asked Cate when we were still in grade school. "We could run and they'd never find us."

"We can't do that," she told me. "The family needs us."

The day after we turned eighteen, I packed a bag and left her a note, promising I'd return one day. Promising I wouldn't forget her.

Cate doesn't say a word about the past, especially not once the bevy of bodies in the yard are starting to come alive, their forms writhing, their long bony fingers reaching out for anyone who gets too close. She watches with shining eyes, determined to make this another gleeful Halloween.

"So creepy," the little kids squeal, as they take their candy and scurry away.

The old man in the rocking chair lets out a moan that splits the sky, and Cate is at his side, holding him back, seeming to comfort him, all to the delight of the trick-or-treaters.

"Those are really great sound effects." Roxanne looks hard at me. "How does your sister do it?"

"I don't know," I say, and as soon the words tumble from my lips, I hate myself for it, because it's a lie. I've always tried not to lie to Roxanne. That's why I didn't tell her much of anything.

The minutes evaporate around us, the full moon hanging in the sky like a golden schilling. A wave of eager children crowds around the house, and it takes all three of us to distribute candy to them, Cate and me rotating back and forth, the two of us in sync, as though we're the same person. More than once, Roxanne glances up and calls my sister by my name. Cate only smiles back at her, a kind of devilish grin that makes my flesh prickle.

When the group of kids is gone, Roxanne huddles next to me.

"These matching costumes," she says and runs her hand across my collar. "I'm having trouble telling you two apart in the dark."

"It's not the costumes." My heart tightens in my chest. "Everyone always had trouble knowing which of us is which."

Cate and I weren't like ordinary twins. Most of the time, it's easy to distinguish one from the other. It's in the small details—a slightly longer face or closer-set eyes or the way one twin laughs or smiles or scowls. But Cate and I were never like that. We did everything together. We did everything the same. At least until the day I left her behind.

"I've needed your help," she says to me, as Roxanne relights one of the jack-o'-lanterns that went out on the walkway. "It's hard to take care of this place on my own."

"I'm sorry," I say, but we both know I don't mean it.

Cate edges closer to me, cornering me on the porch, her shadow over my face. On the other side of the street, someone laughs, but it feels too far away to matter.

"You know the rules," she whispers. "One of us has to stay here. One of us has to guard the house."

I nod, my body gone numb again. That's not the only rule in our family. There are to be no funerals, no burials. Everyone in town believes all our relatives have been cremated, but Cate and I know better.

Nearby, Roxanne is back on the porch, handing out Snickers bars to a group of pint-size superheroes. She smiles at them and wishes them a happy Halloween. She doesn't suspect what's really happening. No one suspects it. That's why it's the perfect cover.

Tonight, the veil is thin, and the phantoms of the world are more restless than usual. That's the reason Cate wanted me back here. To help her when they come alive—or at least as close to living as they can get. She and I are the gatekeepers, the only family members left, the ones meant to stop the others from going too far, from escaping the confines of our property. From taking the world down to hell with them.

Not that Cate has ever worried about the damnation part.

She gazes around at our family's gnarled remains, a smile blooming on her face. "Aren't they beautiful?"

I shiver. "That's not how I'd describe them."

My sister scoffs. "You were always so ungrateful. You never understood how special we are."

"You mean, how doomed we are?"

"But you're not so doomed, are you? Your life sounds very comfortable." Her eyes are on Roxanne now. "It looks comfortable too."

"Leave her out of this," I say, my jaw set.

After all the trick-or-treaters have hurried home for the evening, Roxanne is cleaning up the candy wrappers and extinguishing the votives in the pumpkins when Cate pulls me into the house. None of the lights are on, and I can barely see her face.

"It's my turn now," she says.

"Then let's go," I whisper. "We can get in the car and drive."

But Cate shakes her head. "You know it doesn't work that way, Lisa."

I back away from her until I'm suddenly pinned against the basement door. Right next to the body that Roxanne giggled at earlier—the one wearing our mother's favorite gingham dress.

All those years ago, I told Cate I'd come back for her. But now, cowering in this house again, the shadows sentient all around me, I realize some promises are meant to be broken.

"I need to leave now," I say, but Cate only smiles, because she knows what comes next.

I try to move away from her, but it's already too late. Our mother's desiccated hands are on me, grasped around my throat, pulling me down into the dark.

In our family, this is our birthright and our curse. To become part of this place. To never leave unless we can find a replacement.

"Don't do this," I wheeze, but my sister stares back at me, impassive as the seasons.

"You left me long ago," she says. "Now I get to return the favor."

Cate and I are the same, so interchangeable nobody might even notice the difference. In fact, she's counting on it. She'll pilfer my life tonight and never look back.

If we're truly the same, will Roxanne even notice that I'm gone? Will Cate kiss her the way I do? Will Roxanne ever for a moment suspect something has shifted, or is it possible she'll like my sister better?

With a guttural scream, I break free of my mother's wicked embrace. Just then, Roxanne steps into the house, the autumn wind stealing in beside her.

"Lisa?" she calls out. "Where are you?"

"Here," my sister and I say at the same time, our mother's rancid breath at our backs.

Her hands clasped in front of her, Roxanne materializes before us, her gaze darting from Cate to me and back again. "What's going on?"

"She's trying to trick you," Cate says, and I can hear her smug smile in the dark. "She's trying to convince you that she's Lisa."

"Please," I whisper. "It's me. You know me."

"Do I?" Roxanne asks, her voice thinner than piano wire. "Do I know you at all?"

This hits me dead center, because she's right. I swallow hard, desperate to say something, *anything* that will make her believe me. It's exactly the opening my sister is waiting for.

"Roxanne," Cate purrs. "Let's get out of here."

I shove my sister away. "Don't listen to her. She's not me."

But back in this place, I'm starting to wonder who is who. For years, I've tried hiding in plain sight, tried hiding who I am, but it did me no good. Instead, I've become no one at all. Even my own girlfriend can't recognize me when I'm standing right in front of her.

I stumble forward, just a step, but there's movement in the doorway behind Roxanne. Something's followed her inside. A whole line of them, their figures lumbering and ancient. I try to turn back, but my mother and sister are waiting behind me. The past is everywhere at once.

"Come on now," Cate says, extending her hand to my girlfriend. "It's time to go."

And as Roxanne walks to us in the dark, still not certain which of us she'll choose, the bodies of my family close in, their hideous faces glinting and grinning in the Halloween moonlight, the scent of fallen leaves filling my lungs until I can no longer breathe.

THE COLLECTING

by Cassandra Daucus

The young ones return home well after dark, clambering through the front door in an arrival punctuated by a blast of cool air and the echoing slam of heavy oak. Mother waits by the table, which has been cleared off in preparation for the sorting.

"My dear hearts. How were the tricks and the treats?" Mother asks, giving each young one a pat on the head as they join her, one at a time pouring out their individual caches to form a great heap on the table. They don't respond beyond shuffling their feet, scruffy black sneakers on the end of spindly legs that jut out from beneath their black mantles. They would appear strange on most days, but tonight they draw no notice. Tonight is the one night of the year when the young ones move about in peace.

Mother hums as she sifts through the pile, just beginning the process of sorting treasure from trash. This is her favorite ritual. It's always a pleasure to see how the young ones have grown in the year since their last visit, and having them to gather and witness makes the occasion special indeed. She was a young one once, so long ago the experience is on the distant horizon. But the annual collecting, she remembers.

One of the things in the pile, a secret so black and so quick she almost misses it, shifts to the edge of the table and tips itself over, landing on the carpet with a quiet thud. The closest young one, moving quickly, stomps on it. The resulting crunch is loud in the quiet room.

Mother tuts and gestures for it to move its foot away. "See what happens?"

The pile shivers. The thing on the floor is flattened but not dead; it squeaks and shudders as she peels it off the carpet and picks out the fibers that stick to its surface. Once it's clean, Mother lays it in her palm and speaks to it.

It whispers of dishes broken in anger, of filling holes in the wall and holes in the heart. Searching the house for bottles of liquor; of late nights lying wide awake with a gun under the pillow, just in case.

Mother shudders. "Who gave you this?" She gazes at the young ones, one after the other, and the one who received it steps forward.

It was from the house at the end of the road, it tells her. It's an old house with a new family, just moved in a few months earlier. Mother hasn't met them yet, but she's seen the toys in the yard and the shiny new car in the driveway. *A woman answered the door; the thing was from her.*

"Thank you," Mother murmurs, and the young one shuffles back to stand among its siblings. She slips the squashed thing into the pocket of her housecoat and returns to sorting.

The large pile soon becomes several smaller piles—dark secrets in one corner, sweet dreams in another, a varied collection of horrible memories in the center, a smaller number of happy memories nearby. Confessions, doubts, revelations, fears and wishes and joys and everything else the young ones had stealthily stolen from the people they encountered over the course of the evening.

Mother has a place for everything.

None of the other things on the table attempt to escape, which is probably smart of them even though they will all end up in the same place eventually.

After a while, the young ones start to get anxious, shifting and moaning under the cover of their hoods and mantles. They only go out once a year, and the excursion expends their energy, so after the excitement wears off, they're tired and hungry and yearning for home. Mother knows how they feel, and she's sympathetic, but she needs to get the ratios right to keep them healthy. It's exacting work, and it takes a while.

She's about to start the feed when a knock comes on the door. The porch light is on, although most people in the neighborhood avoid the house, whether they know why or not. She takes a moment to pick a couple of things out from the fantastic smorgasbord and slips them into the pocket of her housecoat, hushing the young ones when they murmur angrily at their treats being given away.

"It's trick or treat," she whispers, leaning close. "You can take them, or you can leave them. Or both. Okay? Now stay here. You don't want them to see you." They grow quiet, and she skips to the door before the person on the other side has a chance to knock again, or to leave.

She arranges her face into something resembling a smile and tugs open the door. The child on the other side is so small Mother freezes, shocked that such a young one would be allowed out alone so long after sundown. But then the pungent scent of smoke reaches her, and a glowing point at the end of the walk catches her eye, paired with the liquid crystal glow of a phone. She doesn't *love* that this person left their young one alone on her porch, but she supposes it's better than them smoking so close to her door.

"Trick or treat!" the child cries, holding up a paper grocery sack, handles spread wide to hold it open. A crude Jack-o'-lantern of orange and black paper is pasted to the side of the bag; the child is dressed in a blue dress covered in sparkles, with a pointed hat to match. Mother squints and twists her mouth, hoping to give the appearance of a hard think. After a second she holds up a finger.

"Ah ha!" she exclaims. "You're a witch."

The child devolves into giggles. "I'm not! I'm a princess."

"A pretty princess," Mother agrees, and reaches behind her for the bowl of candy that she keeps–just in case. "Do you have a favorite?"

The child stares into the bowl, eyes round and bright like the moon behind them. "Wow!" A wide grin displays gaps between teeth and one just pushing past the gum. "Full-sized!"

"You can have *one*," Mother instructs, and when the child reaches in to grab their favorite, she turns the bowl slightly so their fingers graze. There's a vibration in the air between them, and the child gasps and drops the candy bar back into the bowl.

"What *was* that?" Their voice is quiet and amazed. Mother, on the other hand, is perturbed. She's never had anyone notice before, and neither have any of her young ones. She takes a closer look at the child's face, but it's nothing special. Just another child.

She considers her options for answering its question, but Mother was not built to lie.

"I took a secret." She holds out her palm, and there it is: it's black and twitching, and the child wrinkles their nose at it.

"Yucky."

Mother listens to the thing. The child is correct; it is yucky, and familiar. The details, despite the child-like point of view, are clearly the same as the ones whispered to her earlier by the crushed one in her pocket. She slips this one in next to it, so they don't have to look at it anymore.

"That's a bad secret," Mother whispers, and the child's expression transforms from disgust to abject fear.

Their small voice quivers. "Mommy says not to talk about it or else Daddy will get mad."

Mother tuts. "You didn't tell me anything, did you?"

The child shakes their head, looking slightly reassured. "Are you a witch?"

Mother smiles.

A deep voice calls from the sidewalk. Apparently, Daddy has decided they have visited for long enough.

Mother sets down the bowl and reaches into both pockets. "This is for you." She passes the child a small green thing with a pearlescent glow. It's a memory of fields and fireflies; a beautiful thing to have.

It disappears as soon as it hits the child's palm, and she gasps a second time, eyes brightening.

Mother drops the other one, still flat from its adventure on the floor, into the bag along with the candy bar the child had selected earlier. She presents it along with a warning: "That's for Daddy. Don't touch it."

The child whispers a thank you and hops to the sidewalk, where Daddy stares at his phone and grinds his cigarette butt into the ground with the heel of his shoe. Mother goes back inside and turns off the porch light behind her.

The young ones are where she left them. They haven't touched the table, and although she's not surprised, she is pleased; impatient young ones won't survive long as adults.

"Thank you for waiting. We can feed now."

Their excitement buzzes in her skull, and she selects the first morsel. It's a dream, and as it whispers to her, she can taste the sweetness through the skin of her palm. Unlike the way humans take their meals, she's found that it's better to start with the sweet and light things and then move on to the darker ones to finish. It's also important not to overdo it, which is why she sorts and selects instead of letting them feed themselves. Someday, perhaps, but not yet.

She turns to the first young one in the row. "This is for you."

It reaches out its white-encased hand, and she drops the thing in. One swift move and the hand is under the hood; a soft crunch follows. The young one moans, and the others lean forward, eager for their turn. One by one, she hands them out, and when she reaches the end of the row, she takes one for herself.

This is a memory; it whispers to her of an afternoon spent laying on a large inflated tube, floating down a river. A lazy day, sunny and relaxed, made even sweeter with later recognition that it was also the day when new love blossomed from nothing. The texture is soft. It gives under her teeth and the flavor bursts on the front of her tongue—sunlight and joy, then love and delight. It ends on a wistful note; the memory is fresh but from long ago, and the blossoming love has long since faded. But it's tasty, and it gives Mother what she needs.

The feed is essential, but they don't have to do it this way. Mother could send the young ones off to fend for themselves, tell them to eat whatever they gather and leave it at that. But the collecting is how it was done when she was a young one, and she believes it's important to have a sense of community, so this is how they do it too. Someday they won't be young anymore, and someday her body will give out and they will need to survive on their own. Every year, she grows more confident that they're going to be ready, when it's time. Not yet, but someday.

She goes down the row again, and then again—row after row of secrets and memories and dreams. They eat until the piles are spent, fairy-tale bears preparing for a twelve-month hibernation; all of them sated, high on dreams and full to bursting, sprawled out together on the dining room floor. The young ones cuddle and coo, and Mother holds them there for as long as she can. But eventually, it has to end. It's late, and they need to sleep.

"Time to go home," Mother says, stifling a yawn.

Lying flat on her back, Mother unzips her housecoat and pulls the fabric aside. Her torso, black and skinless, pulses gently of its own accord. As carefully as she can, she wrenches open her ribcage. It's only when she's splayed open that she realizes how empty and cold it is without them. She loves them out, but *heavens*, she loves them in, too.

One by one, the young ones crawl back into their mother, where they will sleep, slowly digesting a year of dreams and wishes until it's time to feed again.

THE PUPPETEER OF SAMHAIN

by Todd Keisling

You kids once asked me why I don't celebrate Halloween, and because you were so young, I told you it's because all the costumes scare me.

But why, *Dad?*

The bane of every parent's existence: *Why?* I couldn't tell you the truth then, so I had to make something up. See, the costumes don't really scare me. It's what's inside that does. And I can see on your faces, even now, that you want to ask those dreaded questions. Why? What's so scary about kids in costumes?

My dear children, I'm not talking about the kids in their costumes. Clowns, goblins, superheroes, and horror movie mascots don't frighten me. I'm talking about something else—something I think you're old enough to hear about now. Something that happened to me in the woods back in '97, when I was a little younger than you are now.

It was the year they canceled trick-or-treating on Halloween night, after what happened on the Fuson farm out in East Bernstadt where that little girl went missing. I was still in middle school then—eighth grade, if we're keeping score—and just old enough to know better, but still young enough to think the universe couldn't touch me.

It's dangerous, that kind of innocence. You can only tempt fate so many times before the universe notices you, and then everything changes after that. The stone you've been hiding under is overturned and all your secrets are laid bare. Hopes, dreams, desires, fears, nightmares—it's all there to be scrutinized with a million-billion eyes. And what you do in that moment will define you for the rest of your life.

It did for me and my best friend, Kenny Rosen.

No, I've never talked about him until tonight for a good reason. I've tried to shield you kids from the world like a good father should. All the bad things out there, all the dangers, they're something you shouldn't have to worry about until you're old enough to understand them. I wanted you to enjoy your childhood because that was taken from me. And now that you're older, I think it's time for you to know why I don't like Halloween, why I've been so strict about your curfew, and why we never go trick-or-treating anywhere outside of town.

I need you to know about the puppeteer.

There are few things I remember fondly about my childhood. This may surprise you, but I didn't have many friends when I was young. I was the weird kid in school who enjoyed being alone with his books and video games. School work came easily enough, and I was bullied for being different. When Kenny's family moved to town, he took some of that heat away from me because he was "the new kid." No one wanted him to sit next to them at school breakfast or lunch, so I guess it was inevitable that we would end up sitting together.

You kids know what it's like to grow up in a small town, how other kids can be to outsiders. Kenny is the reason why I taught you to be kind to people. His first day at school, everyone made fun of him for his looks, his clothes, the way he spoke. He had a cowlick on the back of his head, so his hair was always standing up, and he didn't have a country accent because his family had moved here from Pennsylvania. His clothes were always pressed, clean, and new. Both his parents were doctors, and he was dressed in nice clothes most families in Stauford couldn't afford.

That first day, he approached me with caution, but his demeanor changed when he saw I was wearing a T-shirt with Batman on the front. He sat at the table, stuffed a chicken nugget in his mouth, and asked, "You like comics?"

"Love 'em."

"Me too, but I think Spider-Man could beat Batman in a fight."

We spent the next twenty minutes debating why the other was wrong. It was a fast friendship. That year we begged our parents to let us go trick-or-treating together. I dressed up as Batman, and he dressed up as Spider-Man, of course.

Yeah, laugh it up, kids. I'll be the first to admit we were nerds. Your grandma said it was the first time she could remember me looking so happy, and she's not wrong. Having a friend who *gets* you makes a world of difference when you're growing up, especially in a town like this.

So, my friendship with Kenny is one of those things I remember fondly. We were alike in so many ways, with a mutual love of all the nerdy things that made us outcasts at school. Computers, video games, comics, and movies—you name it, and we probably bonded over it. Kenny's mom picked us up at school every Wednesday to go to Helen's Comic Shop. We went to the movies together, rented video games together, had sleepovers and stayed up late to watch *Are You Afraid of the Dark?* on Nickelodeon. Every Halloween, without fail, we coordinated our costumes and made plans to go trick-or-treating together.

Growing up here, we learned to cling to the things that brought us joy, because the consensus was always working against us. That music we liked was evil. Those video games were too violent. And the comics would rot our brains like candy would rot our teeth. We fought to keep the things we loved because there wasn't much else for us in their absence. And that's how things went for several years, until that one Halloween when we were in eighth grade and word spread through school that trick-or-treating had been canceled.

Me and Kenny were devastated, but more than that, we were angry. Our love for Halloween was the mortar that held us together, the one night of the year we could be more than just ourselves. We weren't about to let the adults ruin our favorite holiday. Especially not over silly fears that whoever killed the Fuson family might still be out there, preying on little kids. It was another urban legend to us, like razor blades in our candy or the crazy old preacher in the woods outside of town.

Looking back, we should've considered how seriously our parents took the news. A father and son had been brutally murdered, and a little girl was missing. A girl about our age. Maybe the perpetrator was collecting kids like the Pied Piper of Hamelin, killing their families while luring children into the dark. It's easy for me to say this now, being a father, but we were just kids ourselves back then, and we were emboldened by our innocence.

My innocence. That's something I lost that night. My best friend was another…

Shhh. Take a moment and listen.

Hear that? That gentle hiss of wind in the trees, those naked limbs scratching the night, all those dead leaves tumbling across the grass—*this* is Halloween to me, kids. It's the mood, the air, the sounds of the night, and that musty smell of browning leaves scattered everywhere. I appreciate you spending the evening with your old man.

How are the s'mores? No, no, you have to hold the marshmallows in the flames a little longer. Wait until they're almost charred black. See? Just like that.

We built a campfire just like this, except we were a bit deeper in the forest. I thought about driving us all out there tonight, but the development where Kenny used to live is long gone. Another casualty of the big fire that broke out in town a couple of years ago.

But this is good, right? Just us and nature. The way our Celtic ancestors intended.

Remember that TV show I mentioned, the one on Nickelodeon? *Are You Afraid of the Dark.* Doesn't surprise me you've never heard of it. I don't think those old shows are streaming anywhere. Anyway, me and Kenny were big fans. The kids on the show—members of the "Midnight Society"—were around our age and social standing, and every Saturday they'd gather in the woods around a campfire to tell each other scary stories. It's stupidly simple, the sort of thing that makes perfect sense on TV, but when Kenny proposed we do the same thing on Halloween night, I thought he was joking.

"They can't just take the holiday away from us," he said. We were huddled together in the school cafeteria during our lunch break. I still remember the meal that day: lukewarm spaghetti and meat sauce. "Just 'cause some stupid kid is missing. She doesn't even live anywhere near us!"

I slurped my food and spoke between bites. "I heard my mom talking about it. They think it was satanists."

"It's always satanists. Chad Meyer's older brother is a satanist, and he said the worst thing they do is make fun of the Jesus freaks."

"Maybe that's all he does. I heard his brother is just a big wuss and all those tattoos are fake. He's always replacing them with new ones."

Kenny tossed the half-eaten crust of his burned garlic bread across the table. It smacked me in the forehead. We both laughed, but Kenny quickly steered the conversation back to the topic at hand. "Seriously, though. We have to do something. Like, a protest."

"Want to go picket outside city hall?" I thought he'd find it as funny as I did, but Kenny didn't laugh. I admit I didn't think he was serious at first.

"No, dipshit. I mean we should have *our* own Halloween, with *our* own rules."

He spent the next ten minutes detailing his plan. We could sneak out after dark and have our own Halloween celebration, just like those kids on TV and countless other shows. The holiday fell on a Friday that year, so I could spend the night at Kenny's place, and our parents would be none the wiser. When he was finished, Kenny leaned back in his seat, satisfied with himself. "I mean, how hard could it be?"

I'd never snuck out before. I was the good kid no one had to worry about. Graduate of the local D.A.R.E. program, member of the middle school academic team, my name on the honor roll every semester—sneaking out wasn't in the script. But this was for Halloween, our favorite time of year, and we were desperate. I mean, it certainly felt that way at the time. Halloween was our special day and worth the risk of being caught. Wasn't it?

Kenny seemed to think so, but to be honest with you kids, I wasn't as keen. This plan was the latest in a long line of escalating mischief on Kenny's part. You remember that book I read to you a few years back, *Something Wicked This Way Comes?* He was Jim Nightshade in this friendship and getting more daring by the day, acting out here and there, often for his parents' attention.

I was at their house enough to notice things weren't great between his mom and dad. Kenny's dad began working more and wasn't around as much, and his mom started hitting the wine a lot more after work. Kenny had changed, too, but I was too afraid to say anything. He began talking back to his mom and dad, copping an attitude with them, and shirking his chores. And it wasn't all aimed at them, either. He became more aggressive when we played games together, to the point I began letting him win. Sometimes he picked on me for no reason, and not in the playful way that friends do. Sometimes his words hurt, and sometimes so did his silence.

So, I said yes, I'd sneak out with him even though I didn't want to. I was afraid to upset him; worse, I was afraid of losing my only friend.

"Cool. Pack a flashlight. Think you can bring something to build a fire?"

"Sure. Got a merit badge in camping last summer."

"Duh, that's why I asked, doofus. My dad's working all weekend, so we just have to wait for Mom to go to bed. Shouldn't take too long, not with the way she drinks."

I expected him to crack a smile, but he didn't, and I remember feeling sad without really understanding why.

You'll have to excuse your old man, kids. I know you've never seen me drink, but there are some stories that can't be told with a sober tongue. A couple of you will understand when you're older.

I'd even offer you some of this whiskey if I didn't think your mom would tan our hides.

Now, where was I?

Friday night. Halloween, 1997. No trick-or-treating anywhere in our county. I heard some of the popular kids were having a party elsewhere in the development, but nerds like us weren't invited to things like that. Instead, Kenny's mom picked us up from school, and we counted down the hours until the evening. Around eight o'clock, just after we'd gorged ourselves on pizza, Kenny's mom poured her first glass of wine. Five glasses and three hours later, Mrs. Rosen excused herself to bed and told us not to stay up too late. And half an hour after that, me and Kenny were racing across his backyard into the night.

We trailed along the tree line, crossing through several backyards and avoiding the lampposts, until we reached an old playground at the edge of his neighborhood. From there, Kenny made a beeline for the forest, and I followed close behind. I don't remember how far or for how long; I just remember the bouncing flashlight beam, the cool night air on my face and the wind's soft hiss in my ears. There was also this utter feeling of isolation, like me and Kenny were the last two kids alive on the planet, two young travelers in the dark on some urgent mission. What can I say? It was exciting, being out there on our own and breaking the rules.

Kenny slowed and trailed the flashlight across a small clearing. "This should do."

Someone had already built a crude firepit in the center, lined it with small stones, and piled kindling upon it. I asked if he'd been out here before.

"Yeah, last summer. Sometimes I come out here when my parents are fighting."

"Sorry, man. You can talk about it if—"

"I don't." He walked to the other side of the clearing. "Can you hurry it up with the fire? I'm freezing my nuts off here."

He wasn't wrong about that. The temperature had dropped several degrees. I went to work starting the fire, but there wasn't much to it, most of the work had already been done.

Kenny paced the clearing, nervous. He walked a few steps, turned back, knelt and picked up something I couldn't see. I figured he was just worried about getting caught, and I didn't want to piss him off by asking, but there was something else nibbling at the back of my mind. Kind of like an itch, a little thing he'd said that didn't fit. *Last summer.*

I struck a match and the kindling roared to life. The clearing was draped in a warm October glow and dancing shadows, framing Kenny's silhouette as he knelt once more. I couldn't see what he was doing, and I was too lost in my thoughts at that point to say anything.

We were inseparable. Rarely did we go anywhere without the other, so to hear that he'd been coming out here was news to me. He hadn't said a word.

I won't lie, kids. I was a little hurt. But more than that, I was angry. We'd made a promise to each other when we were in elementary school that we wouldn't keep secrets. Best friends and all that. And more and more, he'd been keeping things from me. Problems at home were one thing, but this felt more of a betrayal for some reason, a more intimate secret.

"Why didn't you tell me?"

I stood up, intending to confront him about everything, but stopped short when I saw the piles of stones in the clearing. There were five of them, stacked just like this one here, and positioned in an odd design like planets orbiting a star. When Kenny rose to meet me, I saw what he'd been doing: fixing another pile of stones he'd kicked over by mistake. Six cairns in total.

"Tell you what?"

"What is this, Kenny?"

"You gonna chicken out on me now?"

"No." But the truth was that I very much wanted to chicken out. I wanted to call your grandma and scream for her to come and take me home. We didn't have cell phones back then, kids, so believe me when I tell you we were in the wilderness on our own. See my arms? Goose bumps. That's how much this still freaks me out almost thirty years later.

Kenny cracked a smile. "Good, 'cause it's too late anyway."

"Too late for what? Kenny, what's going on? What the heck is this place?"

"*Hell.* What the *hell* is this place. That's the thing about you... You're too much of a chicken shit, always playing by the rules. Always gotta be the Boy Scout."

He wasn't wrong. I was the good kid. I never talked back to my parents, never cursed, and until that night, I'd never broken any rules. Right then, I was a terrified child, afraid of what my friend was saying, afraid of what he'd become, and deep down, I think I was afraid of what he might do to me. Because that's the whole reason we were there. He had *plans* for me.

"I don't understand what's going on, Kenny. Why are you being like this?"

He circled the fire and closed the distance between us. The flames burned tall, but I only felt the cold, and the forest seemed darker now. Thicker and quieter, like we were trapped in a vacuum.

"I made a new friend last summer."

His words hit me like a sucker punch.

"Out here in the woods. It told me I could be popular. That it could make my parents stay together."

Kenny pushed me hard. I stumbled backward, fell over a rotted log. He laughed as he stood over me, blocking the firelight, and in the darkness, I saw a shape lurking at the clearing's edge. Massive, stout, almost as thick as a tree. I thought it might be a black bear, but I'd seen them at the Knoxville Zoo, and this was far too big.

And then it looked at me.

Two bright, blue eyes that pierced the darkness and froze my soul.

Kenny kept talking, but I only half-heard him. I couldn't take my eyes off the thing in the dark. "It said I could have whatever I wanted if I was willing to give up something else. I gave it my first *Spider-Man* comic book, and that wasn't enough. Then I gave it my neighbor's dog. That wasn't enough, either. I gave it so many things."

He looked over his shoulder and nodded. "You can come out. This is what I've brought you tonight, just like you asked. I hope you like it."

A rotting miasma filled my nostrils and twisted my guts. The shape crept closer into the clearing where the dancing firelight fell upon its deformed face. It was animal-like, with fangs and patches of wet fur draped over bone, enshrouded in a blanket of moss and earth. Broken antlers jutted from its skull. When it moved, it did so with careful precision, and it didn't walk so much as glide out of the shadows. This thing was a spirit, a phantom conjured from nature's darkest bowers, and somehow Kenny had managed to make it his pet.

The creature towered over us, hovered a foot off the ground; if it had legs, I didn't see them—not that it mattered. Even if I'd regained my wits and ran, I don't think I'd have gotten very far.

Kenny looked up at his new friend and grinned. "I want what you promised."

A crooked wooden arm extended from beneath its mossy shroud, gnarled and crackling like the kindling in the fire, and flared three sharp claws. It laid its hand upon the top of Kenny's head.

"We promised you nothing, child."

Its voice was desolate, gravelly, dry. The sound of air forced through your lungs when you're sick with a chest cold. That deep crackling noise of all the gunk caught at the back your throat.

Kenny gasped and froze midway through forming words. His mouth hung open in an "o" of surprise, but the clarity was gone from his eyes and his face began to sag. The spirit lifted my friend into the air by his head, its claws sinking deep into Kenny's face, carving it into three ribbons. Blood ran down his face and puddled below his dangling feet.

Kids, I ain't ashamed to tell you I peed myself. Soaked my jeans clean through. I was too scared to move, and I didn't know if this thing would do to me what it'd done to my friend. My mind was racing as fast as my heart, and all I could think about was how much I wanted to go home.

And then Kenny began to speak.

"This one. Weak. Impotent."

His voice was almost mechanical, distorted, like something else was layered over it somehow. Whatever this thing was, it was treating my friend like a puppet, using his vocal cords to speak aloud. His eyes began to glow blue.

"You. Strong. Potent."

And in my head: *"We reward servitude, child. You may have what he wanted."*

"Flesh. Kin."

"Light a fire on this night. Sow the earth and plant your seeds. In return, we will have one sapling."

"Grow. Roots. Crom Crúaich."

Kenny raised a finger, dipped it in his blood. The spirit drifted closer and lowered Kenny's body toward me. Trembling, I closed my eyes and felt the warmth of my friend's touch upon my forehead.

"You belong to us now."

I wish I could tell you what happened after that, but to my relief, I cannot. My memory goes blank there. The next thing I remember is sitting in the swing at the old playground and hearing Kenny's mom shouting my name. I was soaked in cold sweat and shivering in the morning air.

Some years back, when you three were still just babies, I tracked down one of the officers who worked our case and took him out for lunch. Paid him a nice sum to get a look at the case files. There were too many blank spots in my memory, something I attributed to a fog created by trauma, and I needed to know what had happened— because that night had changed something in me.

The file said I was nonverbal for the better part of a month, and when asked if I could write down what happened, all I did was draw pictures. A few of them were in the file—rough sketches of an antlered beast with glowing eyes.

In the meantime, Stauford police combed the forest around Kenny's neighborhood with help from the people in town. They found the clearing, all the piles of stones, and Kenny's blood. There was more than I remembered.

But they never found Kenny's body. The logical conclusion was that whoever had killed that poor girl's family in East Bernstadt had made their way south to Stauford. Two naughty boys decided to defy the curfew and found themselves in the killer's sights. Somehow, one of them escaped, while the other was missing and presumed dead.

Fingers were pointed, of course. Kenny's parents were understandably distraught and frustrated. All that remained of their son was a grisly scene and his friend with a strange blood symbol painted on his forehead. So, I get why they tried to sue my folks. Wrongful death or something like that. Never made it to trial. No evidence, you see.

I spent the rest of that year and part of the next in a facility outside of Lexington undergoing therapy. Detectives came to visit once or twice to see if I'd remembered anything, but what could I tell them? My best friend tried to offer me up as a sacrifice to some dark forest god, and the forest god chose me instead? Even then, I knew that kind of story wouldn't go over well, so I omitted the weird parts. Told them about our Halloween plan and everything up until I lit the campfire. After that, I said we saw someone in the woods, but I couldn't recall what happened next. That seemed to satisfy them. They already had their own monster to pin it on.

We moved out of Stauford later that year, just before I started high school. Good timing, too. That was the year all those students "un-alived" themselves, as you kids like to say these days. I started fresh at a new school here in Landon where no one knew who I was, and something weird happened that I'd never experienced before: Everyone liked me. I was popular for once. Graduated top of the class, valedictorian, and voted prom king alongside your mama. We both went to college in Lexington, exceled in our fields, and got pregnant with triplets a year after graduating.

It's safe to say that Halloween changed my life for the better despite its grim circumstances. I never went trick-or-treating again, never wore another costume, and made it a point to stay inside whenever that holiday rolled around. Your mama was raised to be a good Christian girl, so she had no qualms about it.

But when you kids came along, I wanted you to at least enjoy the holiday. I didn't shy away from showing you the joys of this time of year and season. I wanted you to get the full experience of Halloween, from the costumes to the candy, because I knew we'd end up here eventually. I tried to teach you about the history of the day and why it was important to our ancestors. Remember when you got in trouble at school for correcting your teacher? "It's sau-in, not sam-hain."

I was so proud of you for that. I've always been proud of you kids.

Which is why tonight is difficult for me. There was a time when you were young that I tried to run from the truth, but when I got my hands on the investigation files from that night, I finally understood everything. Hindsight is like that, you know? The symbol that was painted on my forehead was also found not far from the forest clearing. It was carved into a tree—twelve points circling a bunch of lines. Kind of like this. They look like antlers, don't they?

It's the symbol of Crom Crúaich. The reason for our family's prosperity. And like our Celtic ancestors, we must make a sacrifice. The dark god of the forest chose me for my potency, my flesh, and my kin.

No, don't be alarmed, kids. I can see the blue shimmer in the trees. They've assured me this won't hurt— Oh, please don't cry. Please don't make this harder than it already is.

This is why I don't like Halloween, children. It's a time of harvest. I've sowed my seeds, planted a whole orchard, and I owe Crúaich one sapling.

ANY OTHER WEDNESDAY IN A BAR

by Cat Voleur

I am madly in love with the girl at the bar. She is stunning. She looks as though she's been poured into her black and red outfit, which is constructed of leather, silk, and lace. Her dark hair is curled perfectly, and her makeup is immaculate. She oozes confidence even as she sits alone.

She does not remain that way for long.

A man sidles up to the stool beside her and leans over onto the bar, grinning. "Aren't you a little old to be dressing up for Halloween?"

He, too, is confident, to an almost repulsive degree. It is less like he knows women are attracted to him, and more like he believes it doesn't matter. He is a man who has ways of getting what he wants, and it shows.

"We're never too old for Halloween." She smiles, and protruding from her blood red lips are two, long fangs.

The man laughs. "Well then, care to celebrate with me?"

"You don't have a costume. You'd be missing out on all the fun."

"I think the fun is getting to see you."

Their banter is quick. Too quick. He has made a mistake, for which the woman can now judge him. "You can do better than that."

"That was sort of cheesy, huh?"

"Very cheesy."

"Not my best," he admits. "But be honest. You kinda liked it."

Her grin widens. "Maybe. But I still think you can do better."

This is his invitation, his way in.

"All right. Well, how about this? I'll grab us a couple drinks and you can tell me what it is you like so much about this holiday."

"Better." She nods.

"And what drink will my Lady Dracula be having?"

"A *Bloody* Mary, of course."

She purrs the word bloody, so that he cannot miss the pun. Still, his eyebrow quirks in surprise at the order before it registers. He chuckles some when the joke lands and shakes his head. "Ah, because of the blood."

She winks at him.

"If you don't tell me to stop, that's going to be what I get you."

"Why would I want you to stop?"

"A Bloody Mary is really what you want?"

"It's exactly what I want."

He gives her an appraising look, and then nods to himself before flagging down the bartender.

I wonder if *he* is not actually what she wants. She is bold and flirtatious with everyone tonight, and it makes it near impossible to tell. I never can quite get into her head, no matter how hard I try.

Something about the man sparks her interest, though. Perhaps it is that he has not asked her for her name, nor has he offered his.

The idea of a stranger, of anonymity, may be exciting. I understand that…a little.

I don't care for him much personally, however. He is handsome enough, with his strong jawline and his broad shoulders. I'd guess he is late college-age? He looks like the kind of guy you'd see wearing a varsity jacket in a movie—though thankfully he's not wearing one now. That would be too cliche, I think, even for her who loves these little classic nods to horror cinema.

He wins some points for turning back with not one, but two thick, red cocktails. He's almost cute when he scrunches his face up at the first taste.

Almost.

"You don't like it?" she asks.

"No, no. I love it. I love drinking tomato juice instead of beer."

They both laugh at his delivery of such an obvious lie, because he doesn't say it bitterly. She takes another long sip from her straw.

"So. Tell me," he says, "what it is that you like about All Hallows' Eve that makes you, a drop dead gorgeous woman, want to spend her evening dressed so sexily for such an ordinary bar—on a weeknight, no less."

"Well, it's a magical night, isn't it?"

"Is it?"

"The veil between the worlds is thinner. The dead can roam freely."

His smile freezes for just a moment. He can't tell if she's being serious or not, and it's obvious he doesn't know how to proceed. She likes it, but I take it as concrete proof that he is playing her. She is nothing but another conquest to him. I wonder how many of those he has notched onto his bedpost.

It is worth something to me, if not a lot, that he knows to plan his approach with her. Something in him must be aware that he could fail.

She also seems to take note of this, before letting him off the hook, and doing so with grace before he can get frustrated or make a misstep. "I'm kidding."

The look of relief in his eyes is subtle, but undeniable. "I know."

"Do you really want to know the truth?"

"Of course."

"I like the costumes."

This, too, puts him at ease. He wants very much for the conversation to turn to her attire, which must have been what caught his eye in the first place. "The costume certainly seem to agree with you."

"It's more than that," she says. She's giving him a fair chance to converse with her in earnest. I feel myself grow uneasy that perhaps she really does like him. "It's the idea that this one day every year, you can be someone else. Someone new. Whoever you want to be, for just a night."

"And who do you want to be?"

"A vampire," she says, gesturing down to her outfit.

"Are you a vampire every year?"

"No, but it's what I wanted this year."

"What else do you want?"

His tone is suggestive. I am flooded with unwelcome images of him, naked, underneath her. It upsets me to think about.

"Close your eyes."

He does.

My agitation grows as she leans in and whispers, "I want you to feel how real it is."

"How real what is?"

"The magic. My costume. Tonight, I truly am capable of being what would be unimaginable any other day."

"A vampire?"

"Yes." She opens her mouth a bit wider and gently grazes her fangs down his neck. "Do you feel it?"

He could say yes, and he could have her. I begrudgingly respect him more for telling the truth. He opens his eyes, stares at her. "It just feels like any other Wednesday in a bar to me... Perhaps the magic is with you?"

She sits back in her stool. "You don't know me the other three-hundred and sixty-four days of the year. I'm not like this usually."

"What are you like?"

She winces. "I don't want to think about that. Tonight is the one night I don't have to."

"Then perhaps you'll answer something else for me?"

"Perhaps."

He puts his hand on her knee. There is too much familiarity in the gesture for my comfort. The moment of truth is soon approaching. "Is this real leather?" he asks innocently.

"Of course."

"I should have known better than to suggest it wasn't."

I think he should know better than to leave his hand on her leg.

"I only do the most authentic for Halloween," she says. "A true vampire through and through."

"Then maybe you could answer another question for me... something I have always wondered about."

"Yes?"

He leans closer to her as well, his voice dropping low. "What sort of panties does a vampire wear?"

It's all I can do not to cringe at his question, at his phrasing of it.

Part of me is relieved to see him make such a mistake after he had been doing so well at charming the woman. Now he has gone and rushed the end. He's fumbled his goal.

Part of me is afraid, too. I know what comes next.

"Vampires don't need panties," she whispers.

"Is that so?"

"Would you like me to prove it?"

He is all too eager to get some of that Halloween magic thrown his way. The polish of his prior experiences cannot hide the rush in him any longer as he throws money down onto the bar. I wonder how many of his previous partners have come onto him so blatantly. Not many, I'd imagine.

He grabs her hand, and she sets down her nearly empty glass next to his, which has barely been touched. The taste of the drink that had bothered him so now seems entirely forgotten, at the sensation of her skin on his. He pulls her to the door with such urgency.

Timidly, I follow where she is led.

They're a couple blocks away already when she next speaks. "Are you taking me back to your place?"

"It's a far walk," he warns. There is regret in his tone. "I wish I had somewhere closer."

She comes to his rescue. "I have an idea."

"Oh?"

She doesn't answer, she just takes the lead, picking up the pace and dragging him along behind her. They're about seven blocks from the bar in total before she pulls him into a small side-alley that is obviously a dead end.

"Here?" he asks.

He sounds both impressed and incredulous.

"Is there something wrong with that?" she challenges him.

"It's just a little dirty."

"Vampires like it a little dirty."

"What if someone catches us?" He plays it off well, as though he's amused, but there's a real sense of unease beneath the surface of his words.

The night is still early but already dark, and the temperature is plummeting. If he can feel the damp, October chill even through his jacket, he must know the woman before him is freezing too. She has only the thin silk cape to cover her otherwise bare arms.

"What if they do?"

The silk falls away and any doubts seem to fall from his mind, pushed away by the site of her pale shoulders. She glistens in the moonlight, less like a vampire, and more like a goddess. Her cold hands slide under his shirt, and he struggles to shrug off his jacket.

"You are so—"

She strikes while his arms are half pinned by his own clothes, pushing him against the wall with all her force while her veneers puncture his neck. She was a little worried they would not stay in her mouth at such force, but it is surprisingly easy to tear him open. To her surprise, he does not put up half the fight she had expected.

It's clear from the look in his eyes that he doesn't understand. He claws at her arms weakly and tries to push her back.

Her arms shake a little with the effort of keeping him against the wall. Even with every advantage on her side, he is bigger and stronger than her. This does not remain the case for long as his strength leaks out of him in red pulses.

I try not to watch the look of confusion and betrayal in his eyes fading down to nothing. I wish I could turn away so I did not have to see his dying breath.

The woman likes it, though. She stays and watches until the very end, and even though it sickens me, I love her for it.

She is a gorgeous, confident killer, and is everything I wish I could be, but am not.

She'll go to another party soon, and maybe try for one more. The costume looks all the more authentic now, with the blood smeared around her mouth and dripping down to her cleavage.

Maybe they'll find him tonight, but maybe they won't until tomorrow.

Maybe the other patrons of the bar, or the owner, will say he was with a dark-haired woman when he left, and that she was dressed like a vampire. Maybe they'll get close to catching her this time, as they did not last year or the year before that.

To go for a second one tonight is bold, but it is important that my vampire drinks her fill. It's only Halloween for a few more hours, and her powers only last the day.

At midnight, she goes back to being nothing.

Tomorrow, she'll just be me.

NO SUCH THING

by Jacqueline West

We ran out of fairy tales years ago. We've gone through all the folktales I can recall, the old myths, the local lore. Now we're dredging through the stories of my own childhood. They love to hear about things I did—things I did *wrong*—when I was seven or ten years old, just like them. I was an impulsive, drama-prone kid, so there are more than a few. But now even these are getting well-worn, as threadbare as the heels of Simon's socks. The ones I keep meaning to replace.

"Tell a story," says Bee.

I'm lying on the edge of her single bed, balanced between her little body and the dusty dark beneath the mattress. The haze from the old reading lamp covers us like a thin yellow sheet. Simon, across the room in his own bed, rolls toward us. His dark brown eyes turn gold in the light.

"Yeah," he says. "A scary one." It's one week until Halloween, and he's been asking for *a scary one* every night.

"Not *too* scary," says Bee, in a tone of careful compromise.

"Not too scary," I promise, yawning. I think back through all the slumber party classics, the local legends they've heard me unravel a dozen times before. "How about 'The Viper'?"

"You've told that one already," says Simon. "A *new* one."

"Okay." I dig deeper, into places I haven't gone in ages. Places I'm almost surprised are still there. "I'll tell you about 'The Ghost of Forest View Lane.'"

Simon goes still.

Bee makes a tightening squiggle under her blankets.

"You know where Forest View Lane is," I begin. "That hilly road not too far past Gramma and Papa's place, with the big white barn?"

"Yeah," says Simon.

"No," says Bee.

"Well, it's hilly, like I said. Lots of twists and turns. Steep sides in some places, and thick trees all around, right up to the edges of the road. When I was little, there was a car accident on that road. Three high school girls had been driving along, going too fast, and they missed a turn. Two of them were hurt, but they survived. The other one…didn't make it."

I'm careful with the words. Simon and Bee both know about death: They remember Great-Grandpa Fallon's funeral. They understand what happened to Gramma and Papa's elderly collie, Mitch, now buried under the hydrangeas behind their shed. And still, the word feels too hard sometimes. Especially when it's tied to a teenager—a girl only six years older than Simon is now.

"Why didn't she make it?" asks Simon, his eyes wide and steady.

"What I heard was that she'd been thrown from the car," I tell him. "That's why it's so important to always wear your seatbelt." I can't keep myself from tacking on the lesson. I suppose that's what stories are, anyway—a chance to learn from someone else's mistakes.

"After the accident," I go on, "funny things started to happen at that turn in the road. People would see things. Like our old neighbor, Mr. Marek. He's gone now"—*Gone,* another way not to say *dead*—"but he was driving down Forest View Lane one evening, on his way into town, and he noticed a girl standing at the side of the road. She looked cold, he said, so he slowed down and asked if she needed a ride somewhere. She said yes and climbed in. She was shivering, so he turned the heat up, and she thanked him. But then, when they drove up over the hill and Mr. Marek turned to ask where she wanted to be dropped off, the girl was gone."

Bee sucks in a deep breath. She wriggles a little closer to my side.

"Did that really happen?" asks Simon.

"I don't know for sure," I say. "Most people didn't believe him, even though Mr. Marek didn't usually make up stories." I shrug. "I didn't really believe it, either. Until one night, years later, when I was a teenager myself. It was late fall, just like now. I was driving along that road, on my way back home. It was late at night. Past my curfew. I knew I was going to be in *big* trouble with Gramma and Papa when I got home."

Bee gives another wriggle, this time an amused one. Hearing about me getting in trouble is always her favorite.

"So I was driving along that hilly, twisty road, and I was going way too fast. Way over the limit."

Simon, who spends many drives keeping an eye on speed limit signs and warning me when I'm more than five over, gives a solemn nod.

"It was dark," I go on. "It was foggy. And then suddenly, just ahead of my car, I saw someone standing at the edge of the road. She was so close, and I was going so fast, for a second I was afraid I had actually hit her. But I hadn't heard or felt anything. No bumps or thumps. So I slammed on the brakes. Then I backed up, really carefully, and I looked all around, up and down the hill, into the trees on either side of the road. Everywhere. But I didn't see anyone."

"Who was it?" Simon asks. "Standing there?"

"It looked like a girl about my age," I answer. "Sixteen or seventeen, maybe. She had long hair; I remember that. And no coat, even though it was cold. I saw her so clearly, standing right there. But then she just disappeared."

"A ghost," Bee whispers.

"Well, I don't know if it was *really* a ghost at all," I say. "But, because I hit the brakes just then, I probably avoided going around the next curve too fast." I pause, rubbing Bee's shoulder through her blankets. "So, maybe she was there to make sure that what had happened to her didn't happen to me. Or maybe it was just the fog." I smile at them both. "In either case, I drove really, really slowly the rest of the way. I made it home safe. And then I got in *huge* trouble."

Both kids smile back at me.

I squeeze Bee tight, burying my nose in the sweat-and-flowers scent of her tangled hair. Then I swing my legs off her creaking bed and bend over Simon, giving him a kiss on the forehead.

"I love you," I whisper from their doorway.

"Love you, too," says Simon, just like always.

"Leave the nightlight on," says Bee, just like always.

At a quarter past ten, after two loads of laundry and an episode of a cooking competition show, I put myself to bed. I'd like to sleep with a light on myself. For the first several months after the split three years ago, I *did* always leave a light on. Somehow it made me feel less alone. But I'm supposed to think of the electric bill. I'm supposed to remember that leaving the lights on makes you sleep less soundly. I'm supposed to be the grown-up here, and to talk myself out of things I don't need.

I'm curled up in the quilt, nearly asleep, when I hear my bedroom door creak open.

The twitch from relaxed to alert is like a flipped switch. I wait, tripwire-taut, listening for the next sound: small footsteps across the hardwood. A high, worried voice. Maybe the unmistakable gag of a child being sick all over the floor. Someone is sick; someone had a bad dream. Someone needs me.

"Mama?"

It's Bee. Of course.

I slacken slightly, pushing the covers back.

Her silhouette huddles in the doorway, backlit by the glow of the nightlight through her own open door.

"What's wrong, Bee-bee?"

She pulls the door wider. Its stiff hinges squeak.

"I'm scared," she whispers.

And I sigh.

I am an idiot. This is my fault. This is my punishment for telling a "not *too* scary" story.

"Come on," I murmur, hauling myself out of bed.

I take her by the hand and lead her back across the hall into the kids' room. Simon is a motionless lump beneath his covers. At least one of them wasn't traumatized. I hope.

"Climb in, sweetie," I whisper, pulling the covers back and plumping the pillows.

Bee obeys, curling up on one side, making herself as small as possible. I lie down behind her, my body a barricade around hers.

"You're safe," I whisper. "We're right here. You're safe."

"Was that story true?" she whispers back, so soft I'm not sure I heard her.

"Was it true?" I repeat, stalling. "Forest View Lane is real. The accident was real. But what I thought I saw... Probably not."

"But you said you saw it."

"I thought I did. But I know it was probably just the fog. Or maybe moonlight on a tree beside the road. Or I just imagined it because I was thinking about those other stories."

Bee goes silent. But I can tell she's nowhere near asleep. Her body is tense as a pulled knot.

"It's okay," I tell her. "You're fine."

"I'm still scared," she whispers.

"Of what?"

"Of ghosts."

"Bee-bee." I wrap an arm over the huddle of her body. "They're not real. There's no such thing."

Bee goes quiet again. Now she's not only awake; she's thinking. Waiting.

"When people die..." she says at last, and the word in her soft little voice hits me like a stone in the chest. "When people die, or when animals die, their spirits keep on going. Right?"

"Right," I whisper back. Because of course that's what I told her when we said goodbye to Great-Grandpa Fallon, when we put a handful of dandelions she'd picked on Mitch's grave. Even though now the question and the answer feel like a trap. And I've fallen in.

"Those spirits don't just stick around here in the real world, though," I tell her. "Not in a way that we can see." I'm not sure whether I believe or think or just hope this is true. Still, I say it as firmly as I can.

Bee doesn't speak again. She stays silent, coiled around herself, until at last I hear her breathing deepen. Carefully, I roll out of her bed and pad back into the too-dark stillness of my own room.

The next night, I tell a cheerful story, even though Simon objects. "But it's almost *Halloween!*"

I tell about how my childhood friend Ellery and I chased what we thought was a kitten into the woods behind Gramma and Papa's house, and how it turned out to be a skunk instead, and how even though we'd been far enough away when it sprayed that it didn't hurt our eyes too much, we'd still had to sit for hours in an inflatable pool full of hose water and dishwasher soap. Bee finds the idea of a bath in a swimming pool so funny that she giggles until it turns into a coughing fit.

When they've both quieted, burrowed into their late-fall blankets, I kiss them and slip through the door.

I stay up a little too late, half-watching a mindless mystery show, half-texting with my sister. When I haul myself to bed, I fall asleep almost instantly.

But then, just like last night, I hear the click and creak of my door swinging open.

I'm instantly awake. Wide awake. Waiting for whatever's going to come next.

Sometimes, when I get especially lucky, one of the kids will peek in at me and then wordlessly patter back to bed. They're just making sure that I'm still here. I understand. I do it sometimes myself, standing in their doorway, watching their covers softly rise and fall.

But more often, of course, the creak at the door is followed by something else.

I stay still, waiting. But there is no sound.

No sound but the low, soft groan of the door inching wider.

"Bee?" I call out.

She doesn't answer.

That's not like her. It's not like her not to be calling "Mama?" already, or scurrying quickly to my bed. Sometimes, after especially bad dreams, she'll dive straight under my covers. Simon, on the other hand, will occasionally creep into my room without speaking. A few times, I've woken to find him standing right beside my bed, his pale little face staring into mine.

"Simon?" I call now.

But he doesn't answer, either. I hear one more creak from the door as it swings wide open. Wide enough that it thuds softly against the wall.

I shove back the quilt and sit up.

The doorway is empty.

Simon must have headed back to his own room.

To make sure he's all right, I swing my legs out of bed and shuffle into the hall, hunching against the air that feels so cold after the muffling warmth of my blankets.

The children's door is closed. I didn't hear it thud shut, but maybe Simon pulled it extra carefully, embarrassed that he'd gotten scared and come to look for me in the first place.

When I turn the knob and look in, both kids are in bed.

Fast asleep.

Bee's covers are pulled up over her head, just the way she likes them. Simon is a splayed-out lump beneath his quilt. His hair is tangled on the pillow. His eyes are shut. He's breathing deep. When I grasp the edges of his quilt to tuck him in more snugly, he doesn't even stir.

Was it Bee who came to my door? Is she only pretending to be asleep now?

I lift the top of her covers. No. She's out. Her lips are parted. I even catch a tiny buzzing snore.

For a few moments, I stand there between their beds, within the safe gold glow of the nightlight.

Then I force myself to check the rest of the house, because I know I won't sleep unless I do. The front and back doors are locked. The windows are secure. I even make myself turn on all the lights and go down into the basement, in case something is hiding behind the furnace, like in my own worst childhood fears.

But there's nothing there.

I knew there wouldn't be. I know I'm doing these things just to comfort myself, the way I do when I tuck the blankets back over a small, curled-up body and whisper, "It's okay. It's okay."

The next night, I try to be clever and tell the kind of "not too scary" story that will hit every mark: Halloweeny, suspenseful, but with an ending that's just a punchline. One that makes Bee giggle and Simon smile and roll his eyes.

"Tomorrow, tell a scarier one," he says, as I kiss his forehead.

"We'll see," I answer, turning toward Bee's bed.

"*That* ghost was funny," she says softly, when I bend closer. "Not like that other one."

"Remember," I tell her, as I kiss her nose, "they're both just stories."

"They're not just stories," she says. "The other one happened to you. You said it."

I'd like to kick myself.

"Yes, but—I don't know for sure what I saw," I explain again. "Even our memories, even when we're *sure* they're right, they're really a kind of story we make up for ourselves."

"But they can still be real," says Bee, a little frown creasing the skin between her eyebrows.

"They can be. But that one wasn't," I say firmly. "Because ghosts aren't real. Not like that."

Bee doesn't answer. She just stares up at me as I back toward the door, the way she does sometimes when I can tell she's weighing my words, not quite accepting them. That she no longer believes everything I say just because I've said it.

"I love you," I murmur from the doorway.

"Love you, too," Simon mumbles into his pillow.

"I love you, too," says Bee, in a small voice. "Leave the nightlight on."

"Always. I promise."

Then I close the door. I make sure it's firmly shut.

It's the darkest part of the night when my door clicks open.

Even without looking at a clock, I know it's long after midnight, but dawn is still so far off it might as well be imaginary.

Still, that small sound is all it takes. I'm wide awake, lying on my side, staring out into the dimness. I can't see the door from this position. I would have to roll over and sit partway up to catch a glimpse.

I don't move.

It's not because I'm hoping, like I did last night, that whichever one of my children is peeping in at me will just go back to bed.

It's because I know it isn't one of my children.

Just like it wasn't one of my children last night.

I lie still. My lungs freeze in my chest. I take the smallest, thinnest breaths I can manage, and each one burns like frostbite. My eyes are wide open. I barely blink. I don't turn my head toward the door.

I don't *want* to turn my head.

I don't want whoever—whatever—opened my door to know I'm awake.

The hinges creak again. I hear the door swing wider.

Cold. The room is so cold. Like a window has been thrown wide open. Like it's January, not October at all.

There's a step. Something is walking across the hardwood floor, toward my bed.

Still, I don't move. Can't move.

Another soft step.

My heart thuds so hard it makes my chest ache. Like it's pulling the rest of my body inward, collapsing into itself with each pulse.

Another step. And I'm still just lying there.

This is ridiculous, I tell myself. It has to be one of the kids. Of course, it is.

Even though the step is too heavy to be Simon's. Much too heavy to belong to Bee.

But I'm the parent. I'm the grown-up. I need to repeat the line that makes everything all right.

There's no such thing. No such thing.

I didn't see what I thought I saw, all those years ago. There are no spirits drifting through the solid world, kind or unkind, trying to save us, or teach us, or touch us. Or terrify us. No.

No.

My hands clench.

I need to move. I need to call out, "Simon? Bee? Is everything okay?"

That's my job.

I steel myself. I gather all the force that's left inside me, all the frozen breath and blood, and I make myself turn over. I make myself face the doorway and whatever is standing there, looking back.

At the same second, something takes hold of my blankets. Hard and fast, it yanks them away from me, whirling them to the floor.

I bolt up in bed. The air is cold as snow and the color of dust.

No one else is there.

Nothing.

Nothing to prove that I didn't imagine all of this except my door, standing wide open, and the faint light of the moon washing through the curtained windows, and the freezing air, and my heavy blankets lying on the floor beyond the foot of my bed, far out of my reach.

I sit for a while, shivering, not able to move again.

What I saw on Forest View Lane all those years ago had seemed frightening but benevolent. It felt like it was there to teach me something. That I needed to slow down. That I ought to take more care of my one fragile life.

The thing in my doorway tonight doesn't feel the same. Without seeing it, without even a glimpse through a foggy windshield, I can tell it was something different.

Frightening. But not benevolent.

It came to show me something else.

Many of the things I tell my children to believe—stories of fairies, and chocolate-bearing rabbits, and worlds where no one would want to do them harm—will be lies.

And some things I tell them are lies will be true. That the world makes sense. That there's always a good explanation behind any oddity. That there's nothing to be scared of waiting there in the dark, just outside the reach of their nightlight.

I'll know this, and I'll do it anyway.

I'll tell them not to be afraid. I'll tell them everything's all right. I'll tell them to close their eyes and pull up the blankets and go back to sleep. Just like I'm trying to tell myself right now.

Because I'm the grown-up.

And there's nothing else to do.

MASKS

by Brian Keene and Richard Chizmar

"The thing about Covid," Jimmy said, pulling the mask up over his mouth, "is that it makes this shit a lot easier."

Brad and Chris followed his lead, donning their own facemasks. Brad hated wearing the things, and avoided doing so whenever possible, except at school. They were mandatory there, and if he got sent home, his mother would beat his ass. But he had to admit, his mouth and chin were already warmer now that they were covered. It was Halloween night, but the wind blowing in from the Chesapeake Bay made it feel like late January.

"See," Jimmy continued, his voice now slightly muffled, "they got cameras everywhere. In the stores. On traffic lights and telephone poles. In cars. Hell, we're walking around with them in our pockets. Speaking of which, you guys remembered to leave your phones at home, right?"

They both nodded.

"Good. Cops can track that shit. They check if your phone

pinged in the vicinity. Can't do that if you don't have it on you. That facial recognition bullshit don't work if you're wearing a mask. And I see you both remembered not to wear hoodies with logos on them. That's good."

Chris shuffled his feet anxiously. "But won't we stand out, wearing these masks?"

"Stand out? Half the motherfuckers in town are still wearing masks when they go outside. The other half are so used to seeing it, they ain't gonna look twice. And besides, it's Halloween. If anybody is going to attract attention, it'll be the people dressed up in costumes. Not us."

"Joanna's having a costume party later," Brad said, trying to sound casual, as if he hadn't had a crush on her since middle school. "Maybe we can swing by."

Jimmy stared at him with disdain. "You want to learn how to do this, or do you want to go cosplay?"

Brad's shoulders slumped. "I want to learn."

"Okay. Suit up."

Jimmy pulled his hood up over his head. The boys did the same. At fifteen, they were both two years younger than him, so they usually followed his lead.

"When we go inside, spread out and act natural. If there's other people inside the store, you cover them."

"What do you mean?"

Jimmy shoved his hands in the pockets and stalked out of the alley. Brad and Chris hurried along after him.

"You keep watch on them," Jimmy explained. "Intimidate them. If there's more than three people in the store, we'll abort. But if we outnumber them, then just kind of loom over them. Keep them scared. I'll take care of the rest."

Brad's pulse quickened as they crossed the street, heading toward the convenience store on the corner. His lips felt wet beneath the mask, probably because he was breathing so hard. He began to have doubts about this. It had sounded cool when Jimmy suggested it yesterday. And Jimmy knew what he was doing. He always had cash, and he didn't have a job. Brad wanted to have money, too. He wanted to be able to ask Joanna out, and not be some broke-ass loser when he did. But sticking-up a convenience store…? What if someone got hurt? What if they got busted? Sighing, he lowered his head and plodded along. Too late to back out now. Jimmy would tease him mercilessly about it, and Brad knew better than to get on the older boy's bad side.

Chris nudged him with his elbow. "Look at that guy."

Brad glanced up from the cracked, dirty sidewalk and saw a figure across the street, wearing jeans, a red flannel shirt, and a black devil mask. The person stood still as a statue, watching them pass. The mask didn't seem to have holes for the eyes, nose, or mouth, and Brad wondered how they could see or breathe.

Before Brad could comment, they reached the store. Suddenly, he felt short of breath. He resisted the urge to yank off his facemask. He was about to speak up, to tell the others he didn't feel good, when Jimmy reached out and pulled the door open. A bell dinged. They walked inside.

"So anyway," Jimmy said, speaking a little too loudly, "she asked me if I wanted to go see Veer tonight. And I told her fuck no. I'm not into that frat rock shit."

For a moment, Brad was confused, wondering what the older boy was talking about. Then he realized it was just Jimmy trying to seem casual. Brad forced a chuckle, but it sounded like a rasping cough.

Jimmy strolled over to the wall of coolers, selected a bottle of soda, and carried it up to the register. Brad motioned at Chris to fan out. Their eyes met, above their masks. Chris looked as scared as Brad felt. He walked to the rear of the store while Chris shuffled toward a rack filled with lukewarm pizza slices and gnarled hot dogs.

In addition to the guy behind the register, there was one customer in the store—a woman wearing yoga pants and a blue jacket. A blonde ponytail hung down her back, but there was something wrong with her head. Brad frowned as he walked past her. The woman turned toward him. He faltered. She wore a devil mask, just like the person outside. Not a similar one, but *identical*. Recovering, he made a move to slide by her, when Jimmy yelled at the front of the store.

"Give me everything in the register. Nice and easy, motherfucker!"

Brad turned around and whimpered when he saw Jimmy pointing a gun at the cashier. Where had that come from? He hadn't said anything about owning a gun.

"Hurry up," Jimmy ordered.

The cashier nodded frantically, scooping fistfuls of bills out of the register and stuffing them into a plastic bag.

"Brad!" Chris yelled, pointing.

Brad whirled around and stumbled backward, narrowly avoiding a backhanded blow from the devil-masked woman. He fell against a shelf full of dry goods, sending boxes of mac and cheese, oatmeal, and cereal crashing to the floor. He slumped down atop them, gaping up at his attacker. She made no sound. She simply stared down at him through that eyeless mask, her head slightly cocked. Then, she stiffened, as if to lunge.

A gunshot boomed. The woman bent over, clutching her stomach, and then silently crumpled to the floor.

Right before he screamed, Brad noticed there was no blood.

Jimmy shouted something, but Brad couldn't make out what it was over the ringing in his ears.

"Let's go," Jimmy shouted. "Move your asses!"

Moaning, Brad scrambled amidst the wreckage, trying to get to his feet. He glanced at the woman again. She lay still as a toppled mannequin.

"T-there should be b-blood," he stammered.

"Come on," Jimmy ordered.

Clambering to his feet, Brad stumbled down the aisle. Jimmy held the door open with his shoulder, still clutching the gun in one hand. His other fist was clenched around the plastic bag. The cashier gaped at them, wide-eyed and panicked, trembling hands held high above his head. Chris charged through the open doorway, and Brad stumbled after him. Jimmy ran out behind them, and the bell chimed again as the door swished shut.

"This way!" Jimmy pushed past them both and ran down the sidewalk.

As they followed, Brad noticed the figure in the devil mask again—the one wearing red flannel. The person crossed the street, heading toward them. Now that they were closer, he was pretty sure it was a man beneath the mask. The figure didn't run, but he strode with a quick, purposeful, almost menacing gait.

"Back the fuck up," Jimmy yelled, swinging the gun toward the man. "Don't be a fucking hero, bruh!"

The masked-man's step did not falter. He plowed toward them, arms barely swinging.

Jimmy fired the gun again. The shot didn't seem as loud this time. Brad wondered if that was because they were outside, or if his hearing had been impacted by the first one. His ears still rang. The masked man slowed his pace for one step, sort of twisting to the side, and then plodded after them again.

"Fuck this." Jimmy turned and ran.

The boys followed him. He darted left, into a narrow, darkened alleyway between a laundromat and a pawn shop. Their footsteps echoed in the cramped space. Halfway toward the end, they spotted a litter of flattened cardboard boxes spread out on the pavement, indicating a homeless encampment. Sure enough, as they ran by, a bedraggled figure dressed in filthy rags sat up and stared at them.

It, too, was wearing an identical black devil mask.

Chris stumbled at the sight. "What the fuck?"

Brad glanced behind them. The masked man from the street appeared at the mouth of the alleyway, backlit by the streetlights. He stormed toward them with that same purposeful, methodical gait. The homeless person rose fully to their feet and lurched forward with a similar stride.

Chris reached out both arms and shoved his friends. "Go!"

They fled deeper into the shadows, the staccato slap of their sneakers on asphalt reverberating around them. Someone kicked an empty wine bottle, and it shattered against the side of a building. Brad couldn't take it even one second longer. He tore off his mask, gasping for air. His head was spinning.

Emerging from the alley, Jimmy blindly led them across the street and into the park. They ignored the paved walkway and instead sprinted across the open expanse of grass where families picnicked and flew kites and played Frisbee on sunny weekends. Their shadows chased them in the glare of the streetlights.

And then the men in the black devil masks appeared at the mouth of the alleyway and joined in the pursuit. As they crossed the street, a third person wearing an identical mask fell into step beside them.

He was dressed in a suit and tie and expensive loafers with tassels on the front of them. The three men trod into the grassy field without breaking stride.

Deep inside the park, amidst a cluster of softball fields and horseshoe pits, the boys stopped to catch their breath. Jimmy bent over with his hands on his knees, scanning the pockets of shadow behind them.

"I think we lost them," Chris said, dropping to a knee to tie his shoe.

"Shut up!" Jimmy snapped. He cocked his head to the side, listening.

Brad's chest felt like it was going to explode. He could hear the thunder of his heartbeat. If they made it through tonight, he swore he was going to give up chocolate and start riding his bike to school again. He was also going to finally listen to his mother and stop hanging out with Jimmy Perkins. The kid was nothing but trouble.

As if reading Brad's mind, the older boy scowled at him. "Let's go," he said quietly. "And keep up this time or you're getting left behind."

Jimmy took off a jog, Chris right behind him. Brad did his best to stay with them as they crossed a bubbling creek, slipping on a rock and soaking his brand new Adidases, and then made their way up a series of hills where the neighborhood kids sledded every winter.

When they reached the summit of the final hill, they paused to get their bearings. There was a sidewalk running parallel to a curved stretch of road. It was old and cracked and choked with autumn weeds. Across the way was a wide stretch of dark woods, but they could see the glow of distant houselights farther down the street.

"*Now* I think we've lost them," Jimmy said in between heavy breaths.

"You shot her and there was no blood." Chris stared down the hill. "And the second dude ate that bullet like Michael Myers and just kept coming."

"He walked like Michael Myers, too," Brad said without meaning to speak.

Jimmy swung so suddenly in his direction that Brad was certain he was about to get ripped a new one. Instead, Jimmy nodded his head. "I thought the same thing. Michael Myers or Jason Vorhees. Slow and steady."

"And creepy as fuck," Chris added with a shiver.

From their left came the deep rumble of an approaching car. The boys turned to look—and the strobing flash of police lights painted the treetops red and blue mere seconds before the cruiser crept into view.

They immediately dropped to their stomachs and flattened themselves against the hill. Brad closed his eyes and pressed his face into the dead grass, catching a whiff of dog crap as the glare of a spotlight slowly swept over their position. From the open car window, he could hear the urgent chirp of a police radio.

And just like that he had to sneeze.

Carefully lifting his head a few inches, he rubbed his nose with his fingertips until the tickling sensation went away. Relieved, he was about to lower his face to the ground again when he caught a glimpse of the patrol car as it rolled past them. It was a county sheriff's car—green and white. The interior lights were on. The driver wore a black devil mask.

Eyes bulging, Brad held his breath until the car rounded the corner, leaving them in silence once again. Almost immediately, an elbow jabbed him sharply in the ribs, and all the air went out of him with a yelp.

"Shut the fuck up," Jimmy whispered, crawling back to his feet. "Let's get out of here."

As usual, Chris was right behind him. "Shouldn't we—"

Then a hand reached out of the darkness and grabbed his shoulder. Chris screamed and whirled around.

The man in the red flannel shirt, his face hidden beneath the black devil mask, stood right behind him. The other mask-wearing strangers were spread out along his flank, making their way up the grassy hill with that same purposeful gait. There were four of them now.

Chris didn't wait for Jimmy this time. He bolted across the street and thrashed his way into the woods, bare branches slapping at his face and arms. It sounded like he was crying.

Strong fingers suddenly snagged a fistful of Brad's sweatshirt hood and jerked him backward, but before he could faint or scream or piss his jeans, Jimmy's face swam into view. "Follow me!" he shouted, releasing his hold, and then they were running down the road in the same direction the police car had gone.

Arms pumping, chest burning, Brad managed to stay abreast of the older boy. Before tonight, he wouldn't have thought that possible, but stark terror was one hell of a motivator. As they turned the corner, Jimmy risked a glance behind them. The four men in the devil masks had cleared the top of the hill and were walking in a staggered line down the center of the street.

He picked up the pace, and the famous line from his all-time favorite western suddenly surfaced in his brain: *Who are those guys?*

The two boys ran deeper into the night—

Cutting across back yards. Hopping fences. Crawling through drainage pipes. Taking the shortcut between the junkyard and the post office. Ducking behind trees and bushes every time a car's headlights turned night into day. Fleeing from angry dogs and hiding from homeowners on the look-out for late night Halloween pranks.

—until they could run no longer.

Brad went down first, collapsing to the ground as they made their way across the playground by the elementary school. Gasping for breath, he crawled to his knees and vomited the microwave burrito he'd purchased earlier that night from 7-Eleven.

Jimmy plopped down not far from him, stretched out on his back and closed his eyes. His muscular chest heaved and the thick veins in his neck looked like they were either going to rupture or slither away into the grass. After a moment, he sat up and said, "I lost my gun back there somewhere. Correction: My *father's* gun." His voice faltered. "He's going to beat my ass when he finds out."

Using the sleeve of his sweatshirt, Brad wiped a dribble of puke from his chin. "What about Chris?"

Jimmy shrugged. "Probably back at home by now. Don't worry. He won't say a word to anyone."

Before he could stop himself, Brad blurted out what he was thinking. What, in fact, he'd been thinking since the moment Jimmy had grabbed the hood of his sweatshirt back at the park. "Thanks for not going with him. Thanks for…not leaving me behind."

Brad wanted the older boy to pat him on the back and say something cool like, *Hey, man, we're buds. And buds don't leave each other behind.*

But, of course, that didn't happen.

"Chris is a dumbass," Jimmy said with a nasty chuckle. "Even in October, those woods are a fucking swamp. He's probably in the shower right now scrubbing mud-stink off his legs and combing ticks outta his hair."

Brad's shoulders sagged with disappointment. He was surprised to find that he was on the verge of tears. He just wanted to go home and take a shower and climb into bed with his comic books and the original *Halloween* on television. Maybe have a snack, too.

When he looked up, Jimmy was studying him with a narrowed gaze. "You're not gonna say a word to anyone, are you?"

Brad shook his head. "Course not."

"Not even your mom?"

"No way. I wouldn't do that."

"Because we're all in this together, you know." He hocked up a loogie and launched it onto the road. "All three of us."

"I won't tell. I promise." He fidgeted with his thumbs, like he always did when he got nervous. "Especially not after…"

Jimmy's stare hardened. "After *what?*"

"Uh…I just meant…" His thumbs were going a mile a minute. "After you shot those—"

"You didn't see any blood, did you?"

Shaking his head, Brad said, "No, but—"

"No buts. I didn't shoot anyone. I just scared them." He waggled a dirty finger in Brad's face. "You'd do well to remember that." And then he walked away.

Glancing nervously over his shoulder, Brad hurried to catch up. "Where we headed now?"

The older boy surprised him with a grin. "Thought we'd stop by Joanna Mather's party on the way home. Snag a soda and some pizza." His smile widened. "Maybe even some pussy."

Brad walked along in silence, trying desperately to think of a reason—*any* reason—to convince Jimmy that stopping at Joanna's house was a bad idea, but he couldn't come up with anything that sounded even remotely legit. What was he afraid of, anyway? Jimmy knew Brad had a major crush on Joanna. He'd never make a move on her, would he?

If he does, I'll make an anonymous call and tell the police what he did tonight.

And then what, Einstein? You'll go to prison right along with him. Maybe not the same prison, and your sentence will probably be a little shorter, but you'll still be sporting baggy orange overalls with a number on the back.

As they crossed the street into Joanna's neighborhood, Brad took a good look around—and what he saw disturbed him. At first, he wasn't going to say anything, but by the time they reached the end of the block, he couldn't stop himself. "You notice anything weird about tonight?"

Jimmy glanced at him. "You mean other than a bunch of freaks wearing devil masks chasing after us?"

He stopped walking. "Look around." Brad gestured to the empty street and sidewalk and the mostly dark houses. "Where is everyone? Where are all the trick-or-treaters?"

Jimmy spun around in a slow circle, taking it all in. "Maybe they're finished for the night."

"It's not that late," Brad said. "And even earlier tonight, when we were running across town, I didn't see a single kid wearing a costume." He looked around. "I also haven't seen a car drive by in the past ten or fifteen minutes. Maybe longer. And where are all the grown-ups? Usually, they're camped out on porches and driveways with bowls of candy."

"Maybe they all got together to play a prank tonight. Like one of those flash mobs you see on TikTok. Except this time they're all wearing black devil masks and scaring the shit outta people." Even as he said it, Jimmy didn't believe it. Not for one minute. But it was better than admitting the truth.

"*Bradley?* Is that you?" a girl's voice called out from further up the street.

Brad jerked his head around. "Joanna?"

A teenage girl, tall and pretty, her long blonde hair pulled back in a pony-tail, rushed toward them on the sidewalk. She was dressed like a witch. Black bodysuit and tights. A pointy black hat. "Thank God, it's you." She looked and sounded upset. "Oh, hey, Jimmy. I didn't see you."

"What's wrong?" Brad asked, hoping he sounded more confident than he felt.

She answered by grabbing both of the boys' hands and tugging them toward her house.

"What's the—"

"They won't leave," she whined. "They crashed the party and now they won't leave."

Jimmy flashed Brad a grin. "That's not a problem. We'll take care of it, won't we, Bradley?"

The younger boy swallowed and nodded his head.

"I don't know," Joanna said. "Are you sure I shouldn't just call the police?"

"You do that and you'll be grounded all winter." Brad wasn't certain but it felt like she squeezed his hand a little tighter. He couldn't believe his luck.

A moment later, they reached her house—the driveway and both shoulders of the road crammed with cars—and she dragged them up the winding stone pathway to the covered front porch. Letting go of their hands, she opened the door and stepped aside. Brad had just enough time to think, *Wait a minute... If she's having a party, why is the house so quiet and dark?* before two large men in black devil masks sprang out of the foyer, seized Jimmy by the arms, and yanked him inside the house.

Brad took one look at the cunning sneer on Joanna Mather's face and knew that she was one of them. As even more mask-clad attackers shouldered their way out of the doorway, their grasping fingers clawing at his sweatshirt, Brad turned and leapt off the porch, Joanna's angry shrieks echoing behind him. Without looking back, he fled down the street.

And didn't stop until he reached his house more than four blocks away.

Fumbling the key out of his jeans pocket, he hurriedly opened the door, stepped inside, and slammed it behind him. His mother and father—dressed as Bonnie and Clyde this year—were at the Cavanaugh's annual Halloween party in Westlake. They wouldn't be home until after midnight. After locking the door and engaging the deadbolt, Brad turned off the porchlight. Moving to the living room, he carefully eased the curtains aside and peeked out at the street. It was still and empty.

Next, he went into the kitchen and grabbed his cell phone from the island where he'd left it earlier tonight. He pulled up his father's number and hit SEND. Nothing happened. The phone refused to ring. Nothing but dead air. He looked at the tiny row of bars next to the 5G icon. None of them were lit. Instead: NO SERVICE.

He looked up at the flat-screen television affixed to the wall in the breakfast nook. It was on, but there was no volume. A bright red SPECIAL REPORT chyron ran across the bottom of the screen. A well-dressed man and woman sat behind the anchor desk in the studio. They were both wearing black devil masks.

Heart and head numb, making his way across the kitchen in what felt like slow-motion, Brad picked up the remote control from the counter and pressed the MUTE button.

The masks the news anchors wore didn't appear to have holes for their eyes, nose, or mouth, yet Brad could hear them loud and clear. After a while, he slid a chair out from under the table and sat down.

And listened.

Midnight came, then one and two and three. His parents didn't return home.

A few minutes past seven, the rising sun painting the curtains gold and red, Brad got up from the table and went upstairs to bed. He knew he needed his rest for what came next.

DOLL

by Ryan Van Ells

1991

This is the first time I am awake. At least, it is the first I can recall. The man places me on a counter in a studio. I am not alone. A few plastic bats are hanging from the ceiling, and a few jack-o'-lantern stickers in the window. The rest of the apartment is crowded with too much furniture and too little walking room.

The man adjusts me so I am standing straight. He walks back and looks at me with pride. I feel good.

A woman looks at me. There is fear on her face which she tries to hide with disgust, but I can tell.

"Why did you buy that?" she asks. "It's…creepy."

"That's the point." He is still looking at me, grin widening. I think he is proud that I am scaring her.

"You don't even have the space for it." She looks around to verify her point.

He turns and wraps his arms around her. Then he kisses her on the forehead.

"Think of it as an investment in the bigger place we're going to get next year."

This seems to make her happy. She forgets about me.

The man and woman watch a scary movie. I think I will like it here.

1992

The apartment is different this year. Bigger. The furniture is spread out and livable. There are other rooms in the apartment I cannot see. I am placed next to a television on the floor.

There are more decorations this year. The room is filled with an unflinching red light that highlights the mist swirling just above the floor. A plastic skull peeks out from under a ripped cloth sheet. I think it is supposed to be some kind of ghost.

The woman looks just as scared by me this year. It seems like the argument has already happened, though, because there is no discussion of whether I should be here or not.

She stares down at me, discomfort growing in her eyes. She turns to the man.

"It's too much."

"What do you mean?"

"It's too much for a stupid holiday."

"Come on, it's fun! I thought you liked Halloween?"

"No, you liked Halloween. I only pretended to like it." She says this with finality, as if she has revealed a deep, dark secret.

The man only chuckles. He knew all along.

She scoffs. "And when the baby comes you can't have this fucking fog machine in here!"

She storms out, perhaps hoping to make the point her comments couldn't, brushing past the ghost as she goes. Its eyes light up red and it shakes, shouting its prerecorded warnings.

The man gives out candy to trick-'r-treaters.

1994

There are fewer decorations this year—no mist, no bouncing plastic ghost, and no spiders. I am placed in the foyer so the kids can see me when the door opens.

There is something else that screams this year—a baby. The woman holds it as the man puts on his costume. It's the same one as last year.

The woman glances up at me, then looks back at the baby, rocking it.

"I can't believe you brought that thing out again."

"It scared the kids last year."

"Well, it creeps me out."

"That means it's working," he says absentmindedly, adjusting the tie to his Beetlejuice costume.

The baby begins to cry.

Trick-'r-treaters see me, and they don't scream. But they are scared.

1995

I am still in my box.

1997

The man and woman have moved again. I have to be brought upstairs from a basement. I feel damp and stiff, and they have set me in the sunroom but left the door open so the wind comes in.

There are not many decorations around me. Those that are here, I don't recognize. The baby is larger, dressed like a lion with a mane. The man and the woman hurry in and out. They don't have costumes on.

"I don't see why we have to leave a bowl out," says the woman.

"It's for the kids," the man replies.

"The first kid is going to grab all of it and then we're just the family with the empty bowl on the porch. There's no point." The woman is putting on earrings.

"The point is, it's Halloween," the man says under his breath. Only I hear him. He is holding Lion-Baby and bouncing her up and down. She is crying and will not stop. The woman doesn't seem to notice or care. She looks tired.

Lion-Baby looks my direction, sobbing. I smile. She stops crying and, for a moment, looks as though she will start wailing even louder. Then she smiles and giggles and points at me.

The woman stops adjusting her earrings and looks toward us. It's as though she's grown so accustomed to the crying that the absence of it is more startling than the crying itself.

The man follows his daughter's finger to me.

"Do you like the doll?"

She nods and places her index finger in her mouth. She has nothing to say. He bounces her toward me like he is going to throw her at me. She laughs.

The woman rolls her eyes.

"The last thing I need is two Halloween fanatics in this place."

The man and Lion-Baby do not respond. They are too busy playing.

They leave to trick-'r-treat. I scare several kids who look like they will take too much from the bowl and some who I just don't like. When the man, woman, and Lion-Baby return, the bowl is still half full. The man grins at his success.

Lion-Baby brought back a lot of candy she is too young for according to the woman. The man agrees, but likely only because it means more candy for him. I notice he has gained weight.

1999

The man and woman are still in the starter home, I think, not entirely sure where I picked up the phrase. All the decorations I remember are here, even the mist. The room did not seem large last year, but this year, with all the decorations out, it appears bare.

I am in a foyer now, visible from the sunroom to the living room. The main wooden door is propped open with a jack-o'-lantern. The man likes me here because I am his favorite and I scare kids.

The man is on the couch. He is watching a scary movie.

The baby, now larger, runs in. She is wearing a witch costume. A tall pointy black hat tops her painted green face adorned with a plastic nose. It looks cute on her, I decide.

"Hurry up, Daddy! It's time to go trick-'r-treating," she says, bouncing up and down impatiently, her pointed witch hat flopping back and forth.

The man turns off the TV and sets down the bottle he was holding. He smiles at Witch-Toddler.

"We're going trick-'r-treating," he shouts.

"Wait, wait, wait." The woman comes hurrying down the hallway. "Be safe." She kisses Witch-Toddler on the head. She doesn't spare a glance to the man.

"Aren't you coming with us?" Witch-Toddler asks.

"Mommy's handing out candy this year," the man says. He looks at the woman, seemingly seeking approval.

She does not return his gaze.

The man and Witch-Toddler leave.

The woman turns the TV back on and watches more of the scary movie. Then a man comes over, and not for trick-'r-treating.

Some kids arrive, looking for candy. I can see them peering in through the windows, likely wondering why the lit house has no candy bowl outside and seemingly no one inside. They look disappointed. Then they look at me and smile, then they laugh.

I smile back. They scream.

The stranger man left underwear behind in the living room. I hide it under my dress. When he returns to the room, he looks around confused. Soon, he leaves after making a joke about being commando.

The woman looks at me like I was a set of keys she was sure she'd placed elsewhere. Then she shivers, calling herself a fool, and goes to bed.

2003

The man places me on the porch this year. The woman kisses him on the cheek and thanks him.

I wonder how the inside of the house looks. Is the fog machine pumping a swirling, choking mist on the floor? Do plastic spiders still hang from the ceiling? Does the ghost with red eyes light up when the woman walks by? I doubt it.

The man and woman leave together and walk down the walkway with the child—a pumpkin this year—walking between them. The orange bulk of her costume bounces up and down as she goes. They leave a bowl of candy behind on an old rocking chair covered in a blanket (to protect against splinters, the woman said).

A fat teenager dumps the entire bowl into a bag. His greedy pig eyes are so fixated on the candy he never looks up to see me watching.

When my family returns, Little Pumpkin runs inside to count her candy. The woman's eyes are puffy-red. She follows her daughter inside the house, her arms crossed as if protecting herself.

The man sits on a bench on the porch for a while. His black cloak of a costume is thin and offers little protection against the unseasonable cold, but he seems unbothered. Soon, he is out and snoring.

The next morning, he doesn't seem to question how the blanket moved from under the bowl to on top of him.

He does notice a piece of fabric that had loosened from under my dress. He looks at me concerned, like I am breaking, but I am not. And soon he knows that.

He unfurls the male underwear from under me. His face, already sore and tired, somehow drops even more. He heads inside.

2007

I am back in the foyer. There are lots of decorations, more than ever, I think. It makes the living room seem more cramped than the apartment ever was.

The man is dressed as a vampire. He prances around excitedly.

I do not see the woman.

The daughter enters the room. She is not wearing a costume.

"Where's your Halloween spirit?" implores the man. My heart breaks for him. "Don't you want to go trick-'r-treating?"

"I'm too old for that," says Megan. She rolls her eyes and crosses her arms. Typical teenager is another term I don't remember learning, but it seems to fit this moment. "I want to go to Lauren's party."

"You don't even have a costume," the man says.

Megan scoffs in a way that says 'I'm too old for costume parties, too' obviously.

"You used to love Halloween."

Megan rolls her eyes again. "Used to."

She stomps off, using her feet to tell her dad that she's upset, as if her tone hadn't done so already.

The man doesn't go trick-'r-treating. He doesn't hand out candy. He turns out the porch light. He drinks his bottles on his couch. Megan leaves after he falls asleep. There are no trick-'r-treaters this year.

2010

When the man sets me out in the living room, there are tears in his eyes. There are not many other decorations. I recognize the ghost who I haven't seen in several years. Its eyes are dead. I wonder if it will ever haunt again.

"You and me buddy," the man says.

I do not answer.

When Megan goes to leave, he does not look at her, so he doesn't see her little cat ears or her tight black clothes.

"I'll be back by midnight," Cat-Megan says.

The man looks like he is going to say something, but he doesn't. He keeps his head down and grunts.

I don't say anything when she doesn't lock the door behind her.

The man takes a drink from his bottle.

Then he sleeps through the trick-'r-treaters, so they don't see me. I haven't seen kids in years and want to scare them. I am sad.

It is 12:30 a.m.. Megan is not home yet. The man is asleep in the recliner, a half-empty bottle held loosely in his hand, threatening to drop at the slightest motion. His snoring rattles the house. A bowl of candy sits beside the recliner, untouched.

Mr. Sampson does not notice when the door creaks open. He does not notice when the two men in masks not made for Halloween enter. He does not notice when they see him and, after some deliberation, determine he is not likely to wake up. They start to grab things from around the house. He does not notice as Megan stumbles in through the doorway.

Megan falls onto the couch beside her dad. She snores as loudly as he does, so she does not notice as the men in masks see her. She does not notice when they come for her.

The men do not notice me moving, so they are surprised when they die.

I am back in my spot, so I am not a suspect when Megan and the man wake up.

SCATTERGOODS

by Kevin Kangas

The ghosts and zombies and fairies had come out early.

It was only six-thirty on Halloween night, but the neighborhood streets were already pregnant with costumed children and their protective parents.

Ben hadn't intended to get there that early, but the line at Popeye's hadn't been long, traffic had been light and the next thing he knew he was back in his childhood neighborhood for the first time in nearly twelve years.

He pulled his car to the curb and stared across the street at the house he'd called home for the first seventeen years of his life. The new owners must have disliked Halloween, for they had not a single decoration in the windows or on the porch. No pumpkins, no cardboard cutouts, no fake spiderwebs, nothing.

The house hadn't changed much other than a new paint job, though they'd simply repainted it the same banana yellow it had always been. They'd cut down the tree out front he used to climb as a child. He'd always wanted his dad to build a treehouse in it, but his dad had said it wasn't big enough. Ben suspected he just didn't want to do the work, and unlike when he was a kid, he didn't blame him anymore.

It was 1998 and Ben would soon turn thirty, a milestone he'd never really wanted to reach. In his teens, thirty-year olds seemed so old, yet here he was about to *be* that old, and he didn't feel a lick different in his head. Ben had always thought one day you woke up and felt like an adult, but he now had the frightening suspicion that wasn't the case at all. Hell, his dad had been younger than this when he'd had Ben. Had he felt like a child imposter in the body of an adult, terrified that other adults would discover his deception?

He realized he was getting lost in his thoughts, so he focused back on the house. His parents had moved out of it twelve years ago, which probably had contributed more to the death of his childhood than him turning eighteen. He still felt strangely displaced, and it made him melancholy to think he could never walk through that front door again and sit down at the kitchen table for a game of Scrabble with his mom. That he'd never open another Christmas present under the tree in that living room.

He wondered what the current owners would say if he knocked on the door and asked if he could come in and look around for old time's sake. They'd probably call the police or slam the door in his face.

Kids ran by his car, swinging their bags of candy and laughing joyfully, carefree.

A long-forgotten memory surfaced in his mind's eye. He had been eight years old, getting ready to go out for Halloween. He'd just finished watching one of his favorite Halloween cartoons—the

Disney adaptation of *The Legend of Sleepy Hollow*—and had pulled on his store-bought costume. He was pretty sure it was a Ben Cooper Spider-man, but he'd had so many costumes over the years he couldn't be sure.

Because it had been cold out that night, his mother put his shoes in the oven to warm them. When he'd slid them on and went outside, it had been such a peculiar sensation—the cool air on his face and arms had contrasted with the snug warmth of his feet.

Ben got out of his car and locked it, and again thought him being here at all was probably a bad idea. How would an adult man wandering around the neighborhood on Halloween look to parents? It would look like there was a pedophile on the prowl; that's what it would look like. But he was here now, and he had every intention of walking these streets one last Halloween, like he'd done as a child back in the eighties.

They had been *his* streets then—he, Terry, Gerald, and Mark. They'd prowled the neighborhood all of October, young and tough and full of themselves, sweeping through the night streets like little demons on the hunt for souls. On Mischief Night, they'd toilet papered the trees and egged houses. Then, on Halloween, he'd be out with them in costume, clutching the black plastic handle of his pumpkin bucket or gripping the neck of a pillowcase so heavy with candy he couldn't carry it for more than a few houses without stopping to rest his arms.

Even though their jaunt had only lasted a few hours, the night seemed endless, walking the entire circle around Stoney Vista Drive, and sometimes cutting down Severn Road. By the time they had finished they were ready to drop from exhaustion.

Man, you're getting fucking maudlin, Ben thought. His heart ached with the loss of those times.

A young couple with two little ones cast him a curious glance as they walked by, and he tried to nod in a non-pedo kind of way. One of the kids was dressed like a Teenage Mutant Ninja Turtle and the other like someone from *Star Trek: The Next Generation*. Ben realized staring at kids wouldn't help his non-NAMBLA look, but he couldn't help it; he loved Halloween costumes so much.

He wasn't sure which direction he wanted to walk the circle in. As a kid, they'd always started on the uphill section that curved around and then tore steeply down an incline that had been a joy to bike ride with his friends on summer days. Eventually, the road leveled off and brought you back around to this side.

Probably best to do the same route.

He crossed the street and stood on the sidewalk in front of his old house.

The memories came fast then, piercing him with their random mind shows. Playing Kick the Can with the other neighborhood kids. The summer evenings sitting on his porch reading a fantasy book like *The Hobbit* or *A Princess of Mars*. And, of course, the Halloween memories.

For a moment, it was almost like he'd stepped back in time. He had the momentary delusion he could walk up to his front door, open it, and inside he'd find his mom and dad, and a twelve-year old version of himself shoveling peas into his mouth at the dinner table because his parents said he couldn't go trick or treating unless he ate every last one of the miserable mushy pellets.

He shook his head and silently chided himself for being stupid. It was definitely a mistake to come here given how overly nostalgic he could be.

Leaves, brittle and curled dry in death, capered across the sidewalk, ushered along by a light, cold breeze. Ben put his hands in his coat pockets to keep them warm and started walking the sidewalk up the hill the way he and his friends had always done it.

From down the street a ways, he heard the laughter and happy screams of children, and thought, *That's what we sounded like all those years ago.*

He passed house after house that once held kids he'd known. Kevin Densmore used to have a basketball hoop in his driveway, and a bunch of them would play H.O.R.S.E. or maybe a game of three on three. Densmore was a foot taller than everyone else though, so whoever had him on their team always won.

Peter Lily and his little brother lived in a house whose backyard butted against the woods. They used to go out and play army there, or find sticks and pretend they were swords, running through the forest as a barbarian horde straight out of the *Conan* comic books they devoured.

What did I hope to get out of this? Ben wondered as he passed Clint Deaver's house. Clint had a huge backyard with no fence, so they'd played lots of kickball out there with whoever wanted to show up.

Ben picked up his pace. He was accomplishing nothing—unless you counted the festering depression—and decided to take the shortcut past Mago Lara Park that would bring him back around to his car a little faster. This whole thing had been a stupid idea in the first place.

The park had its own memories for him. The rope swing you could take a running leap at then careen out over a shallow stream. You had to grip that thick rope for your life because if you fell, you'd be lucky if you only broke a leg, which is exactly what Terry had done once. They also used to catch crawfish and frogs in the stream, and bring them home to see if their parents would let them keep them as pets. (*They never did.*)

He wasn't going to venture in to relive any of those memories. The parking lot now had bars to block it off at night, which hadn't been there when he was growing up. The lights that had illuminated the black cement path running through the grounds were mostly burned out now, so the whole thing looked uninviting and frankly creepy.

Then Ben saw a kid sitting by himself on the swing set at the edge of the park, rocking back and forth. He was dressed in a black robe and Ben didn't immediately get what kind of costume it was until he saw the Ghostface mask in the boy's hands. The kid looked too young to watch a movie like *Scream*, but Ben remembered how many horror movies he'd watched at his best friend Gerald's house when his parents weren't home.

The kid's head was down, staring at the mask like he was lost in thought, and Ben thought that was no way for a kid to spend Halloween.

His first inclination was to go talk to him and see if he was okay, but how would that look? A grown-ass man walking over to a lone child in a dark playground to talk to him?

Yes, Ben, nothing skeevy about that at all.

Instead of that, he made a deal with himself: He'd walk back to the car—probably would take fifteen minutes—then drive back down this way. If the kid was still here, he'd ask him if he was okay.

He took a detour on the way back into his old buddy Eric's court. He'd spent many days riding his bike into this court. Eric had an in-ground pool, so during the summer a lot of the neighborhood kids would swing by and spend the day playing Marco Polo. For a lot of the guys, half the fun was lying at the pool hoping to catch a glimpse of Eric's mom walking around the house in the see-through nightwear she wore all day long for some reason they couldn't understand but argued about incessantly. Dustin Gorsich even bragged that one day she'd invited him in, and he'd had sex with her, but nobody believed him.

Ben stared at the house for five minutes as the memory assault wavered, and then he circled back.

It took him closer to twenty-five minutes to get back to his car, and somehow, it was nearly nine o'clock. There weren't many trick-or-treaters still out, but Ben saw some kids rushing to cram in a few final houses.

Standing in front of his old house again, he wondered if he'd gotten what he'd come for. If anything, he felt sadder than when he'd arrived. What had he expected? Some great catharsis? A feeling like all the old ghosts in his head would be released, and he could fly across the country and start completely anew?

You're a goddamn idiot.

A group of four adults and five children meandered by, and one of the adults did a double take when he saw Ben. The man was big and meaty like a cartoon chef, but something about him was familiar.

"Holy shit," said the man, which prompted the woman next to him to slap his shoulder. That brought tittering laughter from the children. "Ben? Is that you?"

It came to Ben the moment he heard his name slip out of the man's mouth. "Doug?" he asked. "Doug Curry?"

"Oh my God," said Doug. "What's it been, fifteen years?"

"Something like that," Ben said, feeling awkward because the other three adults were staring at him with polite smiles on their faces. The kids positively vibrated with the need to continue hunting for candy.

"I went to middle school and high school with Ben," said Doug to the other adults.

The one that must have been Doug's wife said, "Nice to meet you," while the other couple nodded and smiled their greeting.

"Hey," said Doug to the rest of them, "you guys go on ahead without me, finish up the full circle…"—he turned to Ben and said— "like we used to, right?"

Ben nodded and smiled, though he couldn't remember ever trick-or-treating with Doug. He couldn't get over how old Doug looked compared to the version he remembered. Doug had been maybe sixteen when he'd last seen him, and now here he was with thinning hair and lines in his face that didn't fit the picture in Ben's head.

Time is a bitch, my man.

Then he had the sudden uncomfortable thought: *Is he thinking the same thing about me?*

The group moved on after saying their goodbyes and left Ben standing there with a virtual stranger he'd known a lifetime ago.

"So, what are you doing back in the neighborhood?" asked Doug, and then he suddenly noticed exactly where they were. "Oh shit, that's your old house, isn't it?"

"Yeah," admitted Ben.

"Wow, blast from the past, huh?" Doug said. "You checking out your old haunt?"

Ben thought about lying, but then figured what did it matter? "I got a job offer on the West Coast. I'm flying out next week. Not sure when I'll ever get back, so figured I'd just come…see it again."

"Sort of say goodbye, huh?" Doug said.

He shrugged. "Remembering some of the great Halloween nights I had here as a kid."

"Right?" said Doug. "I bought my parents' house when they moved down to Florida, so I still live here. It's a great neighborhood, man. Still mostly, you know, good people."

Ben got the impression when he said "good people" that he meant "white people," but he tried to ignore it.

"You married?" asked Doug. "Got any kids?"

"No, and no," said Ben.

"Smart man," said Doug with a laugh. "I got two kids. Been with the wife for nine years. It's a lot of work, but they're pretty great."

Just then, Ben remembered one of the reasons nobody liked Doug much in high school. He was a talker, and always seemed to be waiting for you to stop talking so he could speak, which meant it was impossible to have a real conversation with him. And here he was fifteen years later, not changed a bit other than his physical appearance. It struck Ben as sad.

'Damn man," said Doug. "We should get a beer before you take off for the other coast."

"Yeah, for sure," Ben agreed, but he didn't want to hang out with Doug at all. Besides the one-sided conversation they'd have, they simply didn't have the same interests anymore. Their lives back then had been consumed with going out looking to get drunk and score with some high school girls.

"You got a pen?" Doug asked. "I'll give you my pager number."

Ben pulled his mobile phone from his pocket and saw the surprise on Doug's face. "Damn, you got one of those, huh? My wife's been on me to get one for her."

Ben kept his response short, tired of the conversation, and went through the motions of adding Doug to his contacts, knowing he'd delete it later that night.

"It was good seeing you again," said Doug, and he nodded back. "Don't stay out too late or Scattergoods'll get you." He laughed, but Ben was stunned to suddenly remember something he hadn't thought of in fifteen years. The urban legend passed around by the neighborhood kids about a monster that would come out late at night on Halloween searching for dropped candy, but if it found a kid out that late then it would make do.

Ben remembered one friend telling him about the monster and calling it the Candyman—well before the movie ever came out. Another had named it the Halloween Monster, but mostly it was called Scattergoods, and on occasion they added Mr. before the name.

Any way you looked at it, all the neighborhood kids made sure to be back home well before eleven on Halloween. It was funny how scared of nonsense you could be when you were a kid. Nowadays, the only thing Ben feared was his mortgage payment, and leaving the whole life he had known behind to move two thousand miles away.

"You forgot about him, huh?" said Doug with a superior smile that irritated Ben.

"I guess I did."

"What time did he come out, ten or eleven?" asked Doug.

"Depends on who told the story."

"You remember they said it got Robbie Parcourt, right?"

Wow, Ben hadn't heard that name in a long time. He did vaguely remember it, but it was so hazy it seemed more like a dream. Robbie had lived on the corner and had a big trampoline in his backyard. Ben hadn't played there much or even known Robbie too well, but he remembered one Halloween night he'd woken up to flashing red and blue lights spackling his bedrooms curtains. He'd looked out— had to peer from the edge of his window to get an angle on Robbie's house—and had seen five police cars there.

The next morning, they'd all heard Robbie Parcourt never made it home that Halloween night. Nobody ever saw Robbie again as far as Ben knew.

"Good times," said Doug, and Ben didn't have the faintest idea how that fit into their conversation, but something about that night and Robbie's disappearance crawled on the periphery of his mind, just out of reach.

"Well, I'll see you later," he said to Doug, hoping it would end there.

Doug reached out for a handshake, and Ben didn't want to be rude, so he shook it in cursory fashion. "I'll talk to you soon," he said, stopping mid-turn. "Oh hey, the wife's giving out full-size candy bars to adults, so here ya go. Don't say I never gave you anything."

He guffawed theatrically and handed Ben a giant Almond Joy bar that felt like it was broken in half. Ben took it, said thanks, and then watched as Doug strode off at a good pace to catch up with his family.

Ben looked at the candy bar. He didn't even like Almond Joys. Hell, he was pretty sure *nobody* liked Almond Joys.

He shook his head at wasting an entire night—an entire Halloween at that— reliving stupid childhood memories, and then climbed into his car. As soon as he started it, the warning light came on, dinging three times. His panel read the message TIRE PRESSURE LOW, and a top-down graphic of his car indicated it was his front right tire. His other tires all said 34 psi, but that one had a big red zero next to it.

"Are you kidding me?" he said out loud, and got out to check. Sure enough, the tire was flat. He pushed on it, and it buckled easily. *Damn it, damn it, damn it*, he thought. *I don't need this tonight.*

He could call AAA, but it would probably take them two hours to get someone out. The thought of sitting in his car wallowing in old memories for two hours was positively repugnant to him now. Which meant he was changing his own tire. Shit, he hoped his spare wasn't flat, too. He'd never even looked at it after he'd bought the car.

In his trunk, he spun the wheel that locked the spare-tire cover in place and lifted the whole thing out of the way. Luckily, the spare appeared to be full. He hauled it out and set it in the grass, nodding to a couple who walked by escorting two masked children. He snagged the jack out of the car, jammed it under with some trouble, and cranked the car into the air…

Like a moron, apparently, because he couldn't get the lug nuts off. Every time he tried to unscrew one, the whole tire turned. Obviously, he should have loosened them when the tire was still on the ground, but it had been so long since he'd changed a tire that he'd forgotten.

Stupid, Ben, he thought. The entire night had been one big stupid idea that culminated in this final physical manifestation of just *how* stupid it was.

All in, it took him nearly forty-five minutes to finish changing the tire.

He started his car, and it dinged three times, letting him know his front right tire was low on air, but he pushed the button to ignore it. The spare didn't have the same amount of air in it as a regular tire, so he'd just have to put up with that warning until he could get it fixed.

He pulled a U-turn in the street and drove away from his childhood home for the last time. *So long, thanks for all the fish*, he thought for no particular reason.

He stopped at the end of Mago Lara Road, and that's when he remembered the kid at the park.

No way is he still there, Ben thought. It was almost eleven o'clock. But Ben also knew that if he didn't check, it would bother him for the rest of the night. Best to just look and be sure.

He turned right and cruised down the road until the park was on his left, and damn it, he should have figured it with the way his night had been going; the kid was still there, rocking gently on the swing.

Ben passed the park and used the next street to turn around, pulling to the side of the road. He hadn't wanted the boy to be there. He didn't want to get involved in this at all, and should just drive away. The kid was probably waiting for his parents to pick him up.

But if they didn't pick him up by eleven, are they even coming?

He ran it through the mental paces another time but knew there was no way he could just leave the kid out here. Best case scenario, he would go over to see if he was okay, the kid would tell him to fuck off and mind his own business, and he could be on his way, his moral duty fulfilled, his conscience assuaged.

He got out of the car and tried to look harmless as he approached. The boy saw him coming but didn't alter his slow rocking. He didn't look frightened; he just looked…lonely.

"How's it going?" Ben asked when he got close enough.

"Fine."

"You all right?"

"Yes."

Not too talkative, but he hadn't told Ben to fuck off. He didn't seem to be afraid of Ben, either, but even under the kid's neutral tones he could sense the boy's sadness. Something about it whispered *kindred spirits* to Ben's soul.

"You mind if I sit down for a second?" Ben asked.

The kid shrugged, so Ben sat a couple seats down from him. It was one of those flimsy black rubber seats that gripped your ass, clearly not meant for an adult. It cinched his butt cheeks together so tight it would have been impossible to even squeeze out a fart.

"I'm Ben. I used to live in this neighborhood." When the kid only nodded, he asked, "What's your name?"

"Roddy."

Ben nodded, gave it a second, and then said, "I used to play in this park. You know if there's still a big rope swing over the creek back there?"

"Yeah. I swing on it sometimes."

Ben nodded and smiled. At least it wasn't a one-word answer. "So, what're you doing out here on Halloween night?"

The kid—*Roddy, his name is Roddy*, he reminded himself—turned and stared off down the street toward the end of the road for a moment before he spoke. "My friends wanted to go see a haunted house and I didn't want to. They haven't come back. Or maybe they went a different way."

Ben was thinking about what to say to that when Roddy mumbled something else. "Maybe they're not really my friends at all."

Ben felt for him. He remembered how alienating kids could be to other kids, and how you couldn't really talk to adults about it. *Parents just don't understand indeed.* Words of wisdom from your uncle, the Fresh Prince.

"But you're still waiting for them?" Ben asked.

At that, Roddy dropped his eyes and stopped swinging. "If I walk home by myself, Mr. Scattergoods'll get me."

Ben caught himself starting to smile and stifled it. He didn't want Roddy to think he was laughing at him. "Who told you about Mr. Scattergoods?"

"Kids at school."

Ben nodded and tried to watch Roddy in his peripheral vision; he didn't want the boy to think he was staring at him, either. He wondered what Roddy was thinking, sitting in a park in the middle of the night, afraid to go home because of a monster, yet now talking to some strange adult.

"I have a phone," Ben said. "Did you want to call your parents to come get you?"

Roddy shook his head. "My mom's at work."

"How about your dad?"

A pause that spoke volumes. "No."

Ben wasn't going to make him elaborate. "If you want, I could walk you home. Make sure you get there okay."

Roddy didn't say anything.

"What street do you live on?"

"Stansbury Road," Roddy said.

Ben grimaced. That was way up the on the other side of the neighborhood, all the way around the circle. It was probably a twenty-minute walk. But damned if he could ask the kid if he wanted to get in his car. How would that look? With Ben's luck, Roddy's mom was already frantically looking for him and the cops would pull him over and arrest him for kidnapping.

Ohhhhhh man, thought Ben. *Why do I have to have such an inflated sense of duty?* He certainly hadn't gotten it from his parents.

Not a big deal, he told himself. Twenty minutes there, twenty minutes back. He'd see a few places he hadn't revisited, and what did he have to do tonight anyway?

"Well," Ben said, "what do you think? Want me to walk you to your house?"

The kid stopped rocking on the swing and threw one long look down Mago Lara Road toward where his friends had apparently gone. It was empty, and to Ben, the night felt prematurely desolate, as if it were three in the morning.

"Okay," said Roddy.

"Let's do it," said Ben. He double-clicked his car alarm to set it as Roddy stood up with his sadly-empty candy bag and dropped his Ghostface mask into it.

"Do you like Almond Joy candy bars?" he asked Roddy.

"Yes," he said, so Ben pulled the candy bar from his pocket and held it out for Roddy. The boy opened his bag and Ben dropped it in. At least he wasn't going home completely empty-handed.

Moments later, they were walking up Mago Lara Road. *Nothing strange here, officers, just a child being walked home by an adult he doesn't know.*

They cut across the street onto Stoney Vista Drive, the bottom of the circle that would eventually take them around to Stansbury Road. Ben's friend Mark Hook had lived up there on a connecting road. They used to play a lot of King of the Hill on the slope in front of his house.

Ben looked down at Roddy, who trudged along resolutely. *What do you talk about with little kids?* he wondered. A sudden line from the movie Airplane jumped to mind. "Joey, ever seen a grown man naked?"

"How long have you lived here?" he asked Roddy, breaking the uncomfortable silence.

"Since…forever, I guess," he replied, keeping his eyes on the sidewalk in front of him.

"You like it here? The neighborhood?"

"It's okay."

Aaaaaand right back to the silence. *Can't say I didn't try*, thought Ben. He wanted to pick up the pace, but Roddy's short legs couldn't keep up. *Take note, Karma, of all this bullshit I'm doing. What goes around had better come around.*

They'd started up the hill on the backside of Stoney Vista Drive.

It had always been a bitch to pedal up on his bike, which is why most of the time they'd ride down this direction and go around the other way. His friend Scott had lived on this side in the same kind of split-level house that made up about ninety-nine percent of the houses in the neighborhood.

And since the park, they'd seen not a single soul. No last-minute candy-seekers, no high school kids up to no good, looking for pumpkins to smash or houses to egg.

They passed a house decorated to the max—orange and purple lights still ablaze in the trees and bushes, a trio of full-size skeletons carrying a coffin toward the sidewalk, half a dozen jack-o'-lanterns grinning luminous smiles on the cement porch.

He had just commented, "Cool, huh?" to Roddy, who looked and nodded, and Ben turned back to front and saw it.

It crept along the sidewalk on all fours, and Ben wasn't sure why he thought "it" rather than he—*because it had to be a man, right?*—but its long spindly arms and legs, the way it moved like a spider with slow deliberate probing movements, made him think it wasn't human. It had an irregular patchwork of costumes on its body, none of which fit. A Ben Cooper Batman vinyl costume hugged its upper body so tightly you could tell exactly how emaciated it was, while the bottom had different-colored leggings. It wore a mask of near-featureless white papier-mâché on its face like the ones Ben had seen in vintage Halloween photos. Two rectangles had been carved out for eyeholes, and a baleful golden light glowed dimly behind them.

It seemed to be searching the ground as if it were near-sighted, but he suddenly realized it was smelling, like a dog. Its fingers were long, impossibly so, and tipped with pointy black fingernails.

Suddenly it occurred to him, a relieved laugh stuttering awkwardly from his lips. It was someone from the neighborhood pretending to be Mr. Scattergoods. He must have gotten a kick from scaring kids who looked out their windows.

Then it looked up, sensing them, and a wave of dizziness hit Ben so powerfully he could feel himself wobbling as if he'd stood up too quickly on an empty stomach. A darkness encroached the edges of his vision and, for a second, he thought he was going to black out. He took a deep breath, the cool air in his lungs acting like a splash of water to his face, his mind suddenly clear.

He looked down to find Roddy sitting on his butt on the sidewalk. The boy seemed dazed, gazing up at him, and said, "I think I fell asleep."

All notions of a man in a costume deserted Ben. He knew then, without question, the thing on the sidewalk was Scattergoods, and Ben's memory of the night Robbie Parcourt disappeared came rushing back in a wave.

He'd been playing a game on his Commodore 64 after a successful night of trick or treating, waiting for his parents to yell at him to go to bed since he should have been asleep an hour ago.

Something had caused him to turn and look toward his window. *A sound? A sense?* He wasn't sure, but he had stood up and peered out the window, and seen Robbie in a mummy costume walking home, a full bag of candy smacking his leg with every step.

Robbie must have sensed him too, because he had looked up and their eyes met, and Robbie waved. Ben had held up a hand in return, and then movement behind Robbie caught his eye.

A gangly figure that Ben now knew was Scattergoods had crept toward Robbie like a black widow moving toward a trapped fly. Ben remembered thinking he should open his window and yell something, but instead he'd swooned with vertigo. At the same moment, Robbie and the figure blinked out of existence.

Ben had convinced himself it had been a delusion brought on by too much sugar. When news of Robbie's disappearance had reached him, part of him thought maybe he'd seen Robbie's ghost. At thirteen years of age, he'd even considered it possible that maybe he was psychic like the guy in that *Dead Zone* movie he'd watched over at Gerald's house one night.

Here he was now, a grown man without a doubt in his mind that it hadn't been his imagination tricking him. Scattergoods—whatever *that* was—was real, and it was dangerous, as dangerous as a panther roaming a neighborhood at night.

His legs felt weak from fear, but he knew if he didn't act quickly, both he and Roddy would discover exactly what had happened to Robbie Parcourt seventeen years ago.

He grabbed Roddy's hand and pulled him to his feet. The boy leaned down to pick up his bag, and Ben said, "Leave it." Roddy snatched the Almond Joy and pocketed it, and abandoned the bag. They fled back the direction they'd come. The boy couldn't keep up so, without asking because he didn't care what the kid thought about it, he grabbed him up like a bag of groceries and ran.

He spared the quickest look behind him, careful not to trip and fall, to see whether Scattergoods was chasing them. It was, but the good news was that as spider-like as it appeared, it didn't move with the speed of one. The way it pursued was far more simian, still on all fours but with a shuffling stride.

Ben was confident he could outrun it.

He sprinted, his arms beginning to ache from the weight of the boy, especially with the way he jostled with every pounding step. It had been a long time since Ben had done any serious cardio, and the muscles in his legs started burning much sooner than he'd expected. It didn't help that he wasn't dressed for exercise; Timberland boots were just about the last thing he'd put on his feet to go out for a run.

The adrenaline that fear pumped through his system kept him going, though. They got almost as far as Mago Lara Road before he had to finally stop and rest. He turned to look back. Thankfully, Scattergoods was far in the distance, still making his way toward them with that Mowgli gait, but they had a second.

Ben pulled out his phone to call the police. He had no intention of telling them a monster was chasing them. He'd make something up, some crazed man with a knife, whatever it took to get a squad of cops out there, but it was all a moot point. His phone was dead, just like they would be if Scattergoods got to them.

He checked their pursuer again; it was still more than a block away.

He dragged Roddy up the cement walkway to the house closest to him. Back in the day, he never knew the people who lived in this house, but hopefully they would let them in so they could use the phone. Banging on the plexiglass storm door, he thought better of it, and opened it to pendulum the metal clacker noisily five times. It sounded like a hammer striking a nail.

There was no response.

He whaled on the clacker again and waited as long as he thought he could, but nobody came. Just his luck; probably a Halloween-hater who'd gone to some trunk-or-treat at a church but didn't turn off their porch light.

He grabbed Roddy again, thinking maybe he should sling him over his shoulder to save his weary arms. He glanced back and saw Scattergoods creeping slowly toward them, five houses down. It seemed to be smelling again, as if it couldn't see very well. And maybe it couldn't.

Ben thought the best plan might be to get to his car and drive away. There was no way this thing could follow him twenty miles, right? Something inside of Ben told him Scattergoods couldn't leave this neighborhood, and though he had no real proof of that, he somehow knew it was true.

He jogged this time, not wanting to burn himself out, and knowing Scattergoods was moving slower than that. Even with that belief, he couldn't resist looking back. He had to double-check that Scattergoods couldn't go any faster, that it wasn't right behind him ready to rip into his back with those sharp railroad-spike fingers.

Scattergoods was five houses back and moving with purpose toward them, as if it had their scent.

"I wanna go home," whispered Roddy, his eyes squeezed tight.

"I know," Ben said, and ran because his life depended on it. Fuck the jogging, he wouldn't take another break until he was in his car.

Another block and he turned right on Mago Lara Road. In the distance, his car waited across the street, and if he'd ever seen a more welcome sight, he couldn't think of when. He shifted Roddy so his other arm supported most of the weight, and hauled ass to it.

When they were close, he put Roddy down and dug into his pocket for the keys. He was suddenly sure they wouldn't be there, that he'd lost them somehow, but he felt the cold metal ring attached to the plastic fob and yanked them out.

The fob wouldn't unlock the doors—a fine time for the remote battery to die, so he jammed the key in the lock and unlocked the car that way, pushed Roddy into the passenger seat, and rushed around to his side, dropping in. He looked straight up the road where they had come, and Scattergoods was nowhere in sight yet.

Then Ben had a vision: *Scattergoods rounds the corner, smelling the ground like a hunting dog, then scuttles their direction. Ben starts the car, puts it in drive and revs the engine as Scattergoods crosses the street. Ben depresses the accelerator slowly but firmly, and the car shoots forward and they plow into Scattergoods at a good forty miles an hour. Scattergoods careens off the windshield and over the car, and Ben and Roddy speed away to safety.*

The vision became a reality as Scattergoods rounded the corner, smelling the ground in either direction to see where they'd gone. Then it turned toward them and shambled their way.

Ben turned the car key and nothing happened. The engine didn't even try to turn over. There was nothing but the metallic click of the lock cylinder turning.

He tried again. The metallic click was as ominous to him as the hammer of a gun being cocked. He checked to make sure the car was in park. It was.

Then it all made terrifying sense. "Oh God," he murmured.

"What?" asked Roddy.

He didn't want to tell him. Didn't want the kid any more scared than he already was. But Ben realized he hadn't seen any cars or heard any traffic since they'd first seen Scattergoods. Same for people. Nobody on the streets at all or out in front of their houses. No lights going on or off in any house they passed.

It was as if they'd somehow slipped through a crack in their world to another exact copy, only with all the people gone. The place where Robbie Parcourt had gone all those years ago, to never be heard from again. The only things that existed here were Ben and Roddy, and a monster called Scattergoods.

He was ashamed that for the barest second, he thought to just run. Get away from this thing and leave the boy. Roddy wasn't *his* son, not *his* responsibility. Maybe it would be satiated with just the kid, and somehow Ben would slip back into his own world if he could get far enough away from this neighborhood.

In the days and months to come, Ben would desperately wish he had done just that. But at that moment, seeing the boy look at him desperately with those puppy-dog eyes, he couldn't do it.

He had no idea what to do next. Stay in the car? He had no doubt Scattergoods could get in eventually, so they would only be postponing their death. To the left of them was a wall of houses, most with high fences made of spike-tipped boards. If the gates were locked, they'd essentially be running into a wall.

They could continue running down Mago Lara Road, but Ben wasn't very familiar with those neighborhoods, and they'd eventually exhaust their running space, because the land stopped short as the bay cut in.

Maybe a boat? he wondered, but he dismissed the thought fast. He didn't know how to drive a boat, even if he found one with the keys in it and by some miracle it would start. That left their only real option as a very unappealing one: Get out and run into the darkness of Mago Lara Park, perhaps luck into stumbling onto the path that cut back toward the neighborhood, and then come back across Mago Lara Road farther up.

Scattergoods was only a few houses up, slowing down like it was having a hard time tracking their scent. There would be no better time to run than now.

"Roddy," he said earnestly to the boy. "We have to get out of the car. I need you to run as fast as you ever ran in your life, because I can't carry you."

"Why not?" Roddy asked.

"It's going to be dark in there. If I fall with you in my arms, we could both get hurt bad."

Roddy turned to look back at Scattergoods and didn't seem too enthused about the idea. *That's too bad*, thought Ben.

"We're going right now," he warned him.

The boy turned back and nodded.

Thataboy. "Ready?"

Roddy nodded again, so Ben shoved his door open and stepped out, not bothering to close it. He ran around to the passenger's side and helped Roddy out. Scattergoods had turned their direction, his golden eyes shining like a crocodile's caught in a flashlight beam.

Ben pulled Roddy and they fled into the park. The main path, paved of black asphalt, curved across the playground into the woods, snaking its way to the other side of the grounds. They ran it as fast as they could, but soon approached the wooded section where apparently someone had used the cover of the trees to smash out the path lights.

They had to slow down because it was near pitch black. Only the moon shining through holes in the canopy above gave any light to see by. Somehow, Ben had to find the path he'd ran so many times fifteen years ago. He had to hope it was still there, that it hadn't been grown over and obliterated by nature. And he knew Scattergoods wouldn't slow down, either, because it wasn't hunting them primarily by sight.

Ben stopped as he remembered something. The path he was looking for was just beyond the rope swing he'd played on…

"Roddy," he whispered.

"I wanna go home now," Roddy mumbled. He looked like he was about to break into tears.

"Roddy, do you know where the rope swing is from here?"

Roddy looked both ways, then stared through one wall of trees to where a deserted baseball field sat. "I think so."

"Show me," said Ben, and he let Roddy lead the way.

The kid found it fast; he had to give him that. Ben might have taken them right past it, it was so dark. Ben's eyes were starting to adjust to the darkness though, so once Roddy pointed, he found the clearing with the thick rope hanging from a huge oak tree. The trail he was looking for was down the hill across the stream and to the right, and he knew he had to be careful. The hill they used to swing out over was steep and so dark he couldn't even see a glint of light from the stream below.

Maybe there isn't water there anymore?

"Come on, be careful," he told the boy, and they made their way down the hill. It was uneven and rutted, and halfway down Ben stepped on a rock that slid out from under him. He tried to catch himself with one arm as he went down, but the ground wasn't where he thought it was. He hit hard on his side, found himself rolling full speed down the hill until his hand splashed into cold water that stunk like sewage.

Ben hauled himself to his feet and saw he'd managed to stop himself a bare foot away from the shallow water of the stream. He heard something scrabbling down the hill toward him but couldn't make anything out. For a moment, he couldn't breathe, that childhood fear of the dark swooping over him like a thick woolen blanket, and he was sure that Scattergoods would suddenly open its golden eyes mere inches from his face...

Roddy appeared, his face fearful until he saw Ben. "I thought you left me."

Ben tried to ignore the pain in his arm from where he'd hit the ground. His heart was still racing from the fear-of-the-dark panic attack, but he had no idea how far behind them Scattergoods was.

He grabbed Roddy's hand and pulled him across the stream and ran, hitting bushes and weeds, and suddenly finding the trail, at least what he hoped was the right trail.

An endless five minutes later they came out exactly where he'd hoped, right at Mara Lago Road but further up from his car. If the road hadn't sloped so steeply, he'd have been able to look down the street and see it.

He pulled Roddy's hand, towing him toward Broadview Court. He knew they could cut through there and jump a few fences to shortcut back to his house. He used to do it all the time when he was a kid running late for dinner.

Five houses up, he saw his friend Eddie Ruxton's house, whose yard he'd always cut through. Strangely, it looked like it had the same fence from back then—five feet high, wooden-slatted with a lattice on top.

He cut to it and right to the gate, but it was locked, proving that some things had changed.

"I'm going to lift you over," Ben said. To the kid's credit, he didn't argue.

Roddy wasn't light, especially having to lift him up onto the top edge. He held onto Roddy's hands as far over as he could, then let go. The kid landed with a soft thump.

Ben jumped straight up, boosting himself onto the fence like a gymnast mounting a pommel horse. He swung over and landed clumsily, his momentum almost dumping him on his back in the grass. But he managed to stay upright, grabbing Roddy's hand and pulling him up.

They fled across the yard and around a swing set that had never been there before and repeated the process of getting over the fence. Ben stopped dead in his tracks.

He was in his old backyard. He'd almost landed in the sandbox he used to play in, the one that probably even now contained numerous *Star Wars* toys he'd lost back then. He could see the entire yard the way it used to be when he was growing up, but he flushed the thoughts away because he suddenly had an idea.

He grabbed Roddy's hand and pulled him toward the front gate. The latch was the exact same—lift and push—and they were moving past the trash cans on the side of the house and up the steps to the side door. His plan was to shoulder-pound the door open, but to his surprise it was unlocked.

He pulled Roddy into his old house, which didn't appear to have a single light on, and locked the door behind them. He turned toward the kitchen, letting his eyes adjust to the darkness, and was struck with the strangest feeling. He was in his old house, but it wasn't his anymore. The new owners had remodeled the kitchen so the yellow plastic tiles on the floor had been replaced with hardwood. The kitchen table was completely different, larger and more modern, with six chairs instead of four.

Ben guided Roddy across the kitchen and into the foyer, opening the door to the downstairs. He started down, but Roddy wouldn't budge. The terrified boy stared into the blackness at the bottom of the stairs.

Ben dropped to his knees and looked into Roddy's eyes. "Hey. You have to trust me. This is my old house, and I know a great place to hide. That thing will never find us."

"Please," Roddy whispered. "I wanna go home."

"I'm going to get you there," replied Ben. The boy's gaze was again drawn to the stairs leading into darkness, and Ben touched his cheek gently, so Roddy looked him in the eyes. He put every bit of confidence he didn't feel into his statement. "I'm going to get you home. I promise."

Roddy considered it and appeared to conclude that he had little choice. He nodded, and Ben led him down the stairs into the near absolute black. He didn't blame the boy one bit for his reluctance; the fear was stifling for Ben, and he was a full-grown adult.

Ben paused at the bottom to get his bearings. Shapes resolved as his eyes adjusted. A loveseat and a giant recliner faced the corner of the room where Ben's dad had watched many football games. Ben couldn't quite see it, but he assumed there was a TV there now, though certainly not the big square cabinet one like they'd had back then.

He'd once built a huge fort out of boxes his parents had gotten when they'd bought all the major appliances for the house. He'd crawl through it, hiding in sections, and Ben would have given the world to magically travel back to that time. He'd never been more nostalgic for the past—one where he wasn't being chased by a hungry monster—than at this very moment.

"Come on," he whispered to Roddy, and guided him to the corner underneath the stairs. He felt along the wall and found a latch he hadn't touched in years. He slid it left and opened the miniature door to what his parents had dubbed the "hidey hole." It was a small cubby where his mother had stored various items throughout the years: boxes of old clothes, extra cans of soup and tuna fish, and they'd even had a cat that produced a litter of kittens in the nook one night.

Right now, it was just a black square in the wall, so Ben couldn't tell what the new owners stored inside. He reached out tentatively and recoiled as his fingers touched something fleshy and soft. Plastic, he realized, his heart pounding so hard he could feel the beat in his temples.

He grabbed whatever it was, pulling it out. It was a blow-up raft like you'd use in a pool, but he'd seen no pool in the backyard. He didn't spend time thinking about it, just reached back in to see what else was in the way. Some kind of poles, maybe ski poles, and then the space felt clear enough he could wave his hands around without obstruction.

"Okay, we're going to get in," he whispered to Roddy.

Ben hunched down and crawled into the cubby, pulling Roddy in. There was some resistance, but the kid followed and sat down next to him. Ben reached out and pulled the cubby door mostly closed. The silence loomed. It was like being in a sensory-deprivation tank, Ben thought, and he worried Roddy might start freaking out at any moment, partially driven by the rising panic in the back of his own head.

That panic was shouting that stopping had been a mistake. Ben had thought there'd be no way it could follow their scent over fences, and even if it did, they'd be safe inside this house, but he was wrong. He could sense it now.. Scattergoods was coming, was slithering along the sidewalk in their direction, its face to the ground, following their scent like a hellhound. It wouldn't stop until it found them, and then it would—

From upstairs, glass tinkled as if someone had dropped a champagne flute, but Ben knew it was a window breaking, and the panic almost drove him to scream out loud. Scattergoods was here, had found them just as he'd feared, and a peculiar clarity blossomed in his mind.

He had to lead this thing away from Roddy. They couldn't escape it if he had to keep carrying Roddy around. If Ben could lead Scattergoods far away and lose it, then circle back, maybe they'd have a chance to escape the neighborhood.

And he had no time to debate it. He reached out and found Roddy's shoulder in the darkness, could feel the kid trembling. "Roddy," he whispered. "I'm going to lead it away. You need to stay in here and don't make a sound."

"Don't leave me," Roddy whispered back. The desperate plea sounded like it might crack and morph into crying, but Ben didn't have the time to reassure him.

"I'll be back to get you," he whispered, crawling out of the hole and turning back. He felt around until he got hold of one of Roddy's small hands. "I promised you I'd get you home tonight, Roddy. I'll be back once I've led it away."

Roddy made what sounded like a whimper as more glass tinkled upstairs. Ben gave the boy's hand one last squeeze, then he shut the hidey-hole's door most of the way, because he didn't want to close it completely and make the kid panic.

Ben clambered to his feet and could now make out shapes in the dark. He could see the outline of the washroom entrance, which he knew led to a door that exited to the backyard. He moved as quietly as he could toward the dark opening, remembering how he had hated that room the most. Even with the dangling bulb lights on out here, this room had remained dark.

A single light switch was just inside the door, and as a kid he'd had to reach into the blackness and feel around for it. It had always felt like something in the room would reach back with a moist claw…

Stupid childhood fears, but they all came flooding back as he stood there for a moment he didn't have, couldn't waste. He eased into the room and could tell by the ambient light streaming in through the window that a washer and dryer sat in the same place they had when he was a child. A table had been added to the right, and he could make out the shapes of plastic detergent bottles on it.

He unlocked the door and slipped out into the cement stairwell that led up to the backyard. He hustled around the front of the house just in time to see Scattergoods finish crawling into the now-broken window above the porch bench.

Scattergoods was in the house with Roddy.

"*Hey,*" he screamed with sudden panic, sure that Scattergoods wouldn't come out, that it would search the whole house until it found Roddy cowering in the hidey-hole, and it would reach out and—

Scattergoods' masked face appeared at the hole, those otherworldly eyes gleaming at him . Broken glass on the porch glowed like tiny golden jewels.

"Come on," he yelled at it. "You hungry?"

He started to jog away, looking back, and was simultaneously relieved and horrified that Scattergoods emerged from the window, pulling itself out like some huge, grotesque spider from Hell. It climbed onto the bench below the window, then hopped down and loped after him.

Ben picked up speed, and Scattergoods pursued.

He fled through the neighborhood and up past the elementary school he had gone to for his first five grades. No matter the terror-induced adrenaline surge, the memories battered him. When he was fourteen, he'd jogged this route with his father after his dad had gone on a health kick. They'd come out every morning while it was still dark, the air stinking of the mosquito-killing chemical the county sprayed, and do the entire run before the sun came up. Ben frequently had to stop and walk, a cramp in his gut like someone was knifing him.

No cramps this time, though his legs burned. But the cool air seemed to shrink his lungs so he couldn't take a full breath.

Scattergoods kept pace through his weird gait and didn't seem to tire.

Ben knew he would have to pick up the pace, really pour it on, if he wanted to lose the monster. It didn't matter that he didn't have it in him, that the muscles in his legs burned like his blood was fire. He had one chance to let it all out or that thing would catch and devour him.

He pushed it then, sucking oxygen like a fish plucked from a pond. Legs pumping, he cut left at Broadstream Road and cast a glance back to see Scattergoods cross the grass toward him.

He couldn't tell if it was catching up, and didn't want to think about whether it had just been playing with them, following at its own pace. Now was it finally ready to eat? Would it run him down and—

The fear jolted him with energy. Sweat dripped off him with every pounding footstep. When he glanced back a few seconds later, he saw it was working. Scattergoods was falling behind.

For the first time since he'd started running, he smiled. His plan was sound. He'd keep up this breakneck pace for another five minutes, then he'd veer off and lose Scattergoods for good.

It *did* work.

Scattergoods was blocks behind him and seemed to be tiring, moving slower, so Ben relaxed his headlong pace for a minute before he punched it again. He ran up Windsong Avenue and then almost immediately darted across a dark lawn, jumping the fence into the backyard and hauling ass through yard after yard on a course parallel to Broadstream Road.

The monster would turn onto Windsong and hopefully keep going, having lost track of Ben. At the very least, he figured it would search around for his trail, giving him time to get back to Roddy.

After three backyards, he emerged onto Barrett Road and turned left to get back to Broadstream. A few streets down, he'd use Wilson Road to loop onto Stoney Vista Drive, far up the hill, coming back to his house from the opposite direction.

Approaching his house from this direction reminded Ben of all the times he had walked home from his friend Terry's house after watching a scary movie. Ben wasn't allowed to at his house with how strict his parents were, but Terry's parents were never home so they could watch whatever they wanted, and that always meant some blood-soaked movie with a heaping dose of sex and nudity.

Forget the memories, he told himself. *Grab Roddy and get the fuck out of this neighborhood forever.*

He jogged down the hill and remembered that he'd locked the side door they'd entered from earlier. The front window still had a gaping hole in it, so he could crawl through there if he had to but…

He tried the front door and found it unlocked. He eased through and closed it behind him, then made his way back down to the basement and the hidey-hole where he'd left Roddy.

As he felt his way down the banister, his eyes adapting to the dark, a feeling of dreadful anticipation came over him. *Just paranoia*, he told himself. A justifiable paranoia, but still only that.

"Roddy?" he whispered, and only silence answered him.

He could make out the absolute blackness of the hidey-hole door and realized it was standing wide open now. *Had the kid run off on his own?* Ben wondered, and then felt guilty for the relief that flooded through him at the thought.

Ben got down on his knees and felt around, but the hidey-hole was indeed empty.

Then a noise from his right froze him in place. A slobbery-sucking sound toward the washroom. He held his breath, straining to hear, to understand what it was. Had Roddy moved into that room where he now struggled to hold back a sob? Or was it simply the old sink between the washer and dryer burping from some backed-up gas in the sewer?

Ben crept toward the washroom and there it was again, that wet slosh, and every fiber of his being screamed at him to run. He forced his legs to keep moving until he was standing at the doorway, looking into the dark room, and trying to find the source of the sound.

He was about to whisper Roddy's name when the room was suddenly illuminated in an amber light, and Ben saw what might have been ripped straight from his ten-year-old mind. The thing that would haunt him for years to come. The thing he'd see in nightmares that would jerk him awake, his shirt soaked with sweat, his heart racing as if he'd just finished a marathon. Scattergoods was crouched in the corner like a giant praying mantis. Clutched in its grip was Roddy, the boy's head completely inside of its mouth, a human lollipop, and that disturbing sucking sound again.

Just as the monster closed its eyes again and plunged the room back into black, Ben saw the worst of it. In Roddy's limp fingers was the Almond Joy bar Ben had given him. In that moment, Ben knew why Scattergoods had been following them, how it had found them in the house, and how it had found its way back to Roddy after Ben had eluded it.

The monster opened its eyes and turned its baleful gaze toward Ben as if it had known he was there the entire time, and he felt vertigo again, the ground swelling and shrinking and rolling under his feet. What sounded like someone screaming from the speaker of a drive-in movie turned out to be him, and he fled in abject terror before the monster could move to pursue him.

Arms and legs pushed and for once, memories didn't intrude. Nothing did, just pure running on the terror-fueled adrenaline that coursed through his body. His eyes stung from the salty tears, and he didn't know if they were from the cold night air or whether he was crying, and it didn't matter anyway because he suddenly looked up and found himself jogging on the shoulder of Ritchie Highway, the headlights of oncoming cars stabbing his eyes, and he stopped.

There were people here. Working vehicles. He checked his cell phone; it was on with full bars. He'd escaped the bounds of wherever Scattergoods had taken them.

The plane's cabin was dark, the pilot having turned off the interior lights since it was a late flight and people wanted to sleep.

Ben had punched the button for his reading light even though he wasn't reading. A few others had done the same, but most people appeared to be sleeping, lulled into it by the gentle hiss of the air vents and the mild rumble of the jet's engines as it slid through the clouds at five hundred miles per hour. Ben wished he could have been one of them, but he wasn't sleeping much lately.

Guilt racked him to his core. He couldn't stop imagining what Roddy must have felt in those final moments, believing and trusting that Ben had led it away and would come back to save him, then hearing Scattergoods slink closer and closer, sniffing like an animal until it got to the hidey-hole door, ripping it open, those glowing amber coals casting light in on Roddy. The boy probably had whimpered before it snatched him from the place Ben had told him was safe, before it took him to the washroom to devour him.

Maybe you did it on purpose, some soft voice in his mind whispered to him. *You knew it would come for the kid. You just wanted to save your own ass.*

Ben wanted to argue with the voice, to convince it that he had done all he could to save the boy, but he knew maybe there was some truth there, that maybe there *had* been some relief as he left Roddy behind and ran, no longer burdened by him, only by the task of getting away from Scattergoods.

A thought occurred to him, and he slipped his phone from his pocket and used his code to open the home screen. He removed Doug's phone number from his address book, knowing he'd never go back to his old neighborhood.

Hell, he'd never go back to that state.

He stared out the plane window, at all the twinkling lights in the landscape below. A million sparkling Scattergoods eyes peered up at him.

He pulled the plastic cover down over the window.

AFTERWORD & ACKNOWLEDGMENTS

by Kevin Kangas

Let me tell you how this book came about.

I had written a Halloween story titled "Scattergoods"(full disclosure: Pal Ronald Malfi gave the title to me over beers), but at over eleven thousand words, it was too long to submit to any anthology or magazine. My first thought was to simply put it in a book with some other short stories of mine, and publish that.

The more I thought about it, though, the more I knew this story needed to be in a book with a bunch of other Halloween stories. After much deliberation, I figured I'd invite some of the authors I've met along the years to contribute, as well as some other authors I admire but don't know, and then hold an open call for some more stories, and make my *own* anthology book.

I've been a fanatic of Halloween since I was a little kid, and I've even published a non-fiction book about the holiday. I read as many Halloween books as I can, including anthologies, between September and November 1st, and in my mind, I was trying to build the best anthology ever.

I'm aware some people think it's bad form to publish one's own story in an anthology that they're printing. That doesn't matter to me at all; I've never cared what other people think. My only intention is to create a great Halloween anthology, and anyone who thinks it's not "right" to put my own story into the book I'm completely funding myself at pro-plus rates, well, you're more than welcome to publish your own book and do whatever you'd like with it.

I'd like to thank a few people who were instrumental in making this happen:

First, my pals: Ronald Malfi, who is always my sounding board for ideas. He recommended quite a few of the writers in this book, as well as helped me to select other stories when I was conflicted. He'd also told me ahead of time that he didn't have a story for the book, but then surprised me with one a couple of months later. I also want to thank my other friends, Steve Pattee and Robert Ziegler, who are always the first guinea pigs—I mean, beta readers—for any new story I come up with.

Second, editor Kenneth W. Cain, who gave me excellent advice even before I brought him on as editor. Without him, I'd have floundered quite a bit more than I did, and the product you hold in your hands would not have been nearly as polished as it is. He's an extremely knowledgeable, friendly guy, and anyone putting together an anthology would be smart to hire him.

Third, all the writers out there who are in this as well as all the authors who submitted. Writing is a hard, lonely process that is full of rejections. In many ways, it's comparable to acting, as actors audition hundreds of times for just one yes. The rejections, if you let them, can destroy your spirit and your love of the craft, and I'd encourage anyone writing to not let them do that. Understand that rejection is *always* down to personal preference on someone's part.

It doesn't matter how many editors decided your story wasn't a fit for their book; you just need to find the one editor whose book it *is* a fit for.

And if your story didn't make it into this anthology, it had nothing to do with quality. We took as many stories as we could and had to turn down many others that more than deserved to be in the book. That doesn't mean your story isn't as good or even better than some of these; it simply means my personal preference went a different direction. Don't be discouraged; keep sending it to others, and I hope to someday read it again in one of those anthologies I read every October.

Happy Halloween!

Kevin

ABOUT THE AUTHORS

GEMMA AMOR is a Bram Stoker Award nominated author, voice actor, illustrator and budding screenwriter based in Bristol, in the UK. She has published eleven novels, and is the co-creator of horror-comedy podcast *Calling Darkness*, starring Kate Siegel. Her stories feature many times on hugely popular horror audio fiction anthology shows *The NoSleep Podcast, Shadows at the Door, Creepy,* and more. She has also featured in a number of print anthologies and made numerous podcast appearances to date. The short gothic horror film she co-wrote, *Hidden Mother,* is currently showing in festivals. Gemma illustrates her own works, hand-paints book cover artwork and narrates audiobooks, including *The Possession of Natalie Glasgow* by Hailey Piper.

USA Today and #1 Amazon bestselling author **JEREMY BATES** has published more than twenty novels and novellas. They have sold more than one million copies, been translated into several languages, and been optioned for film and TV by major studios. He has won both an Australian Shadows Award and a Canadian Arthur Ellis Award. Visit jeremybatesbooks.com to receive Black Canyon, winner of The Lou Allin Memorial Award.

INSPIRATION: Halloween is my favorite day of the year. Always has been. So when I was asked to write a short story for this Halloween collection, I said yes without hesitation. I had no idea what I was going to write about, but that was fine. The theme was *Halloween*, and I'm a horror writer, after all. Anyway, the idea for the short story "The Perfect Night to Commit the Perfect Murder" came about easily enough. I started by brainstorming, *What's the scariest thing about Halloween?* And it wasn't long before I thought, *Costumes*. And what's the best way to hide your identity if you're going to partake in a dastardly deed…? Well, I won't spoil anything for you, so please read the story to find out the rest!

Born and raised in Ireland, **KEALAN PATRICK BURKE** is the Bram Stoker Award-winning author of *The Turtle Boy*, *Sour Candy*, and *Kin*. He lives in Ohio with Scooby Doo. Visit him on the web at www.kealanpatrickburke.com.

INSPIRATION: There's no elaborate story behind this one. Much like the main character, I was standing outside my house one cold night having a cigarette when a sound drew my attention to something in the yard, something just beyond the reach of the light. It seemed darker than it should be back there, and the longer I stared, the more I imagined something staring back, something that might know me better than I knew myself. The chill was sufficient enough to send me back inside, where I jotted down the opening lines of this story.

CLAY MCLEOD CHAPMAN writes books, comic books, children's books, and for film/TV. You can find him at www.claymcleodchapman.com.

INSPIRATION: As my sons phase themselves out of their Halloweening, growing too old to go trick or treating anymore, I've personally found myself saddened by the fact that I will no longer be able to live vicariously through them. This story is me dealing with the grief of letting go.

RICHARD CHIZMAR is a *New York Times, USA Today, Wall Street Journal, Washington Post, Amazon,* and *Publishers Weekly* bestselling author.

He is the co-author (with Stephen King) of the bestselling novella, *Gwendy's Button Box* and the founder/publisher of *Cemetery Dance* magazine and the Cemetery Dance Publications book imprint. He has edited more than 35 anthologies and his short fiction has appeared in dozens of publications, including multiple editions of *Ellery Queen's Mystery Magazine* and *The Year's 25 Finest Crime and Mystery Stories.* He has won two World Fantasy awards, four International Horror Guild awards, and the HWA's Board of Trustee's award.

Chizmar's work has been translated into more than fifteen languages throughout the world, and he has appeared at numerous conferences as a writing instructor, guest speaker, panelist, and guest of honor. You can follow Richard Chizmar on Facebook, Twitter, and Instagram. Also check out the Richard Chizmar Fan Page set up by his readers.

INSPIRATION: See Brian Keene's.

TJ CIMFEL is an award-winning screenwriter, author, and creative director based in Chicago. His films include Blumhouse Television's *There's Something Wrong with the Children* (2023), *Intruders* (2015), and Bloody Disgusting's *V/H/S Viral* (2014). He has appeared on Hollywood's Blood List and Young and Hungry List. You can find him online @TeaJaySee on Twitter and @tj_cimfel on Insta.

INSPIRATION: I've been going with my family to the same pumpkin patch in Wisconsin for the past dozen or so Octobers. Every time we go, the weather gets warmer and the patch gets smaller. It's unsettling to see something that was once so majestic, dwindle to a shell of its former self. I figure it's time for the pumpkins to rise up.

Inspired by H. P. Lovecraft, M. R. James, Shirley Jackson, Robert Aickman, and a ton of fan fiction, **CASSANDRA DAUCUS** (she/her) writes soft horror and dark romance. She is intrigued by how the human mind responds to the unknown, and also enjoys a good gross-out. Her story "Teething" appears in *Ooze: Little Bursts of Body Horror*, edited by Ruth Anna Evans, and she has also published drabbles in Trembling With Fear and Hungry Shadow Press's Deadly Drabble Tuesday. Cassandra lives outside of Philadelphia with her family and three cats. She tweets at @CassandraDaucus and her website is https://residualdreaming.com.

INSPIRATION: Like many of my stories, "The Collecting" started with a concept: "trick or treating, but instead of collecting candy they collect memories and dreams." But who are 'they' and why do they do it? Once Mother and her young ones showed up, the theme naturally turned towards motherhood and motherly love, and the rest of the story fell into place.

Raised in the bleak and unforgiving wilderness of Central New Jersey, **PATRICK FLANAGAN** has previously published short fiction with Grand Mal Press, Evil Jester Press, Sam's Dot Publishing and Meerkat Press. His present whereabouts are unknown. If you see anyone resembling his photo in this bookstore please report him to the store manager.

INSPIRATION: When I was a kid trick-or-treating was serious business. There was none of the heavily choreographed and chaperoned events in grade school parking lots or shopping malls, like the ones parents lead their kids through today. You got locked out of the house at 4pm and were told in no uncertain terms to come back by midnight with your plastic jack-o'-lantern filled to the brim with candy – actual candy, not apple slices or bags of microwaved popcorn handed out from "creative" parents living on your block – or else you'd have to sleep in the garage out of shame. Looking back it's perhaps conceivable that I overestimated the importance of the holiday.

PHILIP FRACASSI is the Stoker-nominated author of the novels *A Child Alone with Strangers*, *Gothic*, and *Boys in the Valley*, as well as the award-winning story collections *Behold the Void* and *Beneath a Pale Sky*.

His stories have been published in numerous magazines and anthologies, including *Best Horror of the Year*, *Nightmare Magazine*, *Black Static*, *Southwest Review*, and *Interzone*.

The *New York Times* calls his work "terrifically scary."

Philip lives in Los Angeles and is represented by Copps Literary Services. For more information, visit him on social media or at his website: www.pfracassi.com.

INSPIRATION: My first thought was: What if Halloween never ended? My second thought was: And what if it was the worst day of your life?

BRENNAN FREDRICKS is an Infantry Sergeant in the U.S. Army and an undergraduate student at Grand Canyon University, working towards a Bachelor of Science in Justice Studies degree, with a focus on criminal investigations. His novel, *Oh Come, Oh Come* was published by A15 Publishers in February 2022.

INSPIRATION: "The Wind" was the result of a challenge from a friend of mine to write a Halloween Story. I'm actually more of a mystery than a horror writer, but I do love Halloween, and I do know a bit about fear; and "The Wind" is a story about fear itself. I've learned to overcome fear in my life through my faith, and one of the ways to overcome it is to know and understand its deceitful voice. "The Wind" personifies this voice.

LARRY HINKLE is a copywriter living with his wife and two doggos in Rockville, Maryland. When he's not writing stories that scare people into peeing their pants, he writes ads that scare people into buying adult diapers so they're not caught peeing their pants. He's an active member of the HWA (his work has appeared on the preliminary Stoker ballot twice in the past three years), a graduate of Fright Club and Crystal Lake's Author's Journey program, an HWA mentee, and a survivor of the Borderlands Writers Bootcamp. *The Space Between*, his debut collection from Trepidatio Publishing, will be unleashed on the world in February 2024. Stop by and say hi at writtenbylarry.com.

INSPIRATION: My wife and I don't watch a lot of popular movies, so the year *Despicable Me* came out, we couldn't figure out why so many kids were dressed as little yellow creatures. I thought it could make a cool invasion story, but I couldn't figure out an emotional hook. A few years later, a friend of mine was upset when he realized his daughter would rather go trick-or-treating with her friends than with him, and everything clicked into place.

LARRY HODGES has over 140 short story sales and four SF novels. He's a member of Codexwriters, a graduate of the Odyssey and Taos Toolbox Writers Workshops, and a ping-pong aficionado. As a professional writer, he has 20 books and over 2100 published articles in 180+ different publications. He's also a member of the USA Table Tennis Hall of Fame, and claims to be the best table tennis player in Science Fiction Writers of America, and the best science fiction writer in USA Table Tennis! Visit him at www.larryhodges.com.

INSPIRATION: The story was inspired by another story I'd written about the ghosts of past assassinated presidents haunting the White House, with Lincoln now a soulless spirit that eats live spiders. While writing that story, I wondered what would happen if those spiders got inside someone—and literally stopped working on that story to write this one.

KEVIN KANGAS is a writer/director whose 2002 cult-hit "Hunting Humans" garnered awards and a glowing review from the great Job Bob Briggs who called it "Eerily Prescient" and gave it four out of four stars. His next film, "Fear of Clowns", was picked up by Lionsgate and quickly became a top-ten title for them. All of his films can be watched for free at http://bit.ly/kkftubi

He's also released a novella about vampires called "With Teeth" and a love-letter to Halloween called "Halloween: The Greatest Holiday of All."

INSPIRATION: In my thirties, I once took a trip to my old neighborhood on Halloween night because I thought I'd be moving across the country and might never make it back there again on that night. "Scattergoods" was birthed a few years ago when I noticed that all the kids in my neighborhood seemed to stop coming out at exactly the same time on Halloween night. I thought it might be interesting if there was a reason for that, and I used that old trip to my neighborhood as the entry point. The entire story takes place in a mirror-universe version of my old stomping grounds...

BRIAN KEENE writes novels, comic books, short stories, and nonfiction. He is the author of over fifty books, mostly in the horror, crime, fantasy, and non-fiction genres. They have been translated into over a dozen different languages and have won numerous awards.

His 2003 novel, *The Rising*, is credited (along with Robert Kirkman's *The Walking Dead* comic and Danny Boyle's *28 Days Later* film) with inspiring pop culture's recurrent interest in zombies.

Keene also serves on the Board of Directors for the Scares That Care 501c charity organization.

The father of two sons and the stepfather to one daughter, Keene lives in rural Pennsylvania with his wife, author Mary SanGiovanni.

INSPIRATION: Every author who lived through the Covid-19 pandemic will probably have at least one story come out of it. This is ours. In the midst of social distancing, I remember thinking that Halloween was the one safe holiday group activity, because everyone was masked.

TODD KEISLING is a writer and designer of the horrific and strange. His books include *Scanlines, The Final Reconciliation, The Monochrome Trilogy,* and *Devil's Creek,* a 2020 Bram Stoker Award finalist for Superior Achievement in a Novel. A pair of his earlier works were recipients of the University of Kentucky's Oswald Research & Creativity Prize for Creative Writing (2002 and 2005), and his second novel, *The Liminal Man,* was an Indie Book Award finalist in Horror & Suspense (2013). He lives in Pennsylvania with his family.

INSPIRATION: This story began with two points of origin. The first, a Reddit thread from several years back, about a group of kids whose friend was abducted on Halloween night; the second, my son's 20th birthday, when I found myself pondering what sort of fatherly advice I could impart. Somehow, they both came together with a little occult magic and blood.

GWENDOLYN KISTE is the three-time Bram Stoker Award-winning author of *The Rust Maidens, Reluctant Immortals, Boneset & Feathers,* and *Pretty Marys All in a Row,* among others. Her short fiction and nonfiction have appeared in outlets including Lit Hub, Nightmare, Best American Science Fiction and Fantasy, Vastarien, Tor Nightfire, Titan Books, and The Dark. She's a Lambda Literary Award finalist, and her fiction has also received the This Is Horror award for Novel of the Year as well as nominations for the Premios Kelvin and Ignotus Awards. Originally from Ohio, she now resides on an abandoned horse farm outside of Pittsburgh with her husband, their excitable calico cat, and not nearly enough ghosts. Find her online at gwendolynkiste.com.

INSPIRATION: Like so many horror fans, Halloween is one of my favorite times of the year. I love the foreboding feeling in the air during October, and I wanted to capture a bit of that experience, while also exploring the bonds of family and how they can be just as ominous as the creatures that lurk in the autumnal shadows.

RED LAGOE is the author of *In Excess of Dark*, forthcoming from DarkLit Press. She has authored several horror collections, and her work has appeared in various anthologies and publications. Red is the editor of *Nightmare Sky: Stories of Astronomical Horror,* and the owner of Death Knell Press. When she's not spewing her horror-ridden mind onto the page, she can be found dabbling in the hobby of amateur astronomy. Learn more about Red's work here: www.redlagoe.com

INSPIRATION: As an amateur astronomer who has done a lot of sidewalk astronomy outreach for the public, I've always wanted to bring out the telescope on Halloween night to share views of the moon with trick-or-treaters. Free candy and telescopes would've been an irresistible lure when I was a kid. What could go wrong by taking a peek?

EVANS LIGHT lives in Charlotte, North Carolina, surrounded by thousands of vintage horror paperbacks. He is author of *Screamscapes: Tales of Terror*, the upcoming *I Am Halloween*, and more. Best known for his short stories and novellas, he is also editor of *Doorbells at Dusk* and the *In Darkness, Delight* horror anthology series, and is co-creator of *Bad Apples: Halloween Horrors* and *Dead Roses: Five Dark Tales of Twisted Love*.

RONALD MALFI is the award-winning author of several horror novels and thrillers, including the bestseller *Come with Me*, published by Titan Books in 2021. He is the recipient of two Independent Publisher Book Awards, the Beverly Hills Book Award, the Vincent Preis Horror Award, the Benjamin Franklin Award, and his novel *Floating Staircase* was a finalist for the Bram Stoker Award. He lives with his wife and two daughters in Maryland, and when he's not writing or spending time with his family, he's performing in the rock band VEER. ronaldmalfi.com @RonaldMalfi.

INSPIRATION: …and then I woke up in a cold sweat, thinking, *yes,* thinking, *a thing comes back,* thinking, *back to the place where there's a hollowness left behind, a child-shaped hollowness, and he—it—snaps right back into it, and levels its gaze on the responsible party,* and then I smiled to myself, closed my eyes, and drifted off to sleep…

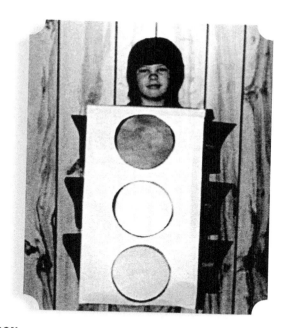

BRIDGETT NELSON is a registered nurse turned horror author. Her debut collection, *A Bouquet of Viscera*, is a two-time Splatterpunk Award finalist, recognized both for the collection itself and its standout story, "Jinx." Her work has appeared in *Counting Bodies Like Sheep, Dead & Bloated, American Cannibal, A Woman Unbecoming*, and several volumes of the *If I Die Before I Wake* series of anthologies.

Bridgett is working on her first original novel and has been contracted by Encyclopocalypse Publications to write a novelization of the cult classic film *Deadgirl*. She is an active member of the Horror Writers Association and the co-chair of HWA: West Virginia. She was a 2022 Michael Knost "Wings" award nominee, and won second place in the '22 Gross-Out contest at KillerCon in Austin, Texas.

INSPIRATION: I was reading Kevin Kangas' *Halloween: The Greatest Holiday of All* and was intrigued by a Pagan ritual mentioned in the book, where families threw stones into a blazing fire on Samhain, when the spirit veils between the worlds were thinnest. If your stone was missing the next morning, Pagan folklore claimed you'd be dead by the following Halloween...

Raised on a healthy diet of creature double features and classic SF TV, **GREGORY L. NORRIS** writes regularly for fiction anthologies and magazines, novels, and the occasional episode for TV and Film. He once worked as a screenwriter on two episodes of Paramount's *Star Trek: Voyager* series and writes the *Gerry Anderson's Into Infinity: The Day After Tomorrow* novels for Anderson Entertainment in the U.K. based upon the classic NBC made-for-TV movie which he watched and loved as a kid. Norris has Honorable Mentioned and Finaled in the Roswell Awards and is a Pushcart nominee. His newest novel, *Desperate Housewolves*, a hilarious soapy paranormal, debuts in September 2023 from the fine folks at Van Velzer Press.

INSPIRATION: I grew up in an enchanted cottage set near a big wood cut through by the new interstate highway. That part of the story is true. So, too, is Peggy, the three-legged dog, a happy beagle that lived summers down the road, and the actual magic trick itself, which was performed by my best friend Jon one brisk October Saturday morning. The rest is all the writer's doing.

FRANK ORETO dwells in the wilds of Pittsburgh, Pennsylvania, writing tales of baby eaters, wereworms, and other things too fierce to mention. His work has haunted such venues as *Pseudopod*, *The Year's Best Hardcore Horror*, and *The Magazine of Fantasy and Science Fiction*. When not writing, Frank puts his creative energies into concocting fantastical meals for his wife, children, and whoever else might drop by.

INSPIRATION: I'm a father of three nearly adult children. Dressing up and trick-or-treating has always been a highlight of our year, but those days are just about done. My own trick-or-treaters will soon disappear. So, I wondered what if everyone's trick or treaters disappeared. And there the horror was waiting for me.

REBECCA ROWLAND is the New England-based author of two dark fiction collections, one novel, a handful of novellas, and too many short stories. She is the curator of seven horror anthologies, including this year's *American Cannibal*. The former acquisitions and anthology editor for Dark Ink Books, Rebecca co-owns and manages Maenad Press, and her speculative fiction, critical essays, and book reviews regularly appear in a variety of online and print venues. Find her at RowlandBooks.com or follow her creepy tomfoolery on Instagram @Rebecca_Rowland_books.

INSPIRATION: I always wanted to write a banshee story; every Celtic myth featuring one seemed to present the creature as relatively innocuous: morbid, but nothing more than a pale-faced deliverer of bad news. Instead, I'd like her reimagined as a device of torture—or at the very least, a harbinger of terror. "The Iron Maiden" was inspired by its namesake's "2 Minutes to Midnight" on the band's *Powerslave* album (released fall 1984). The song is about the anxiety of nuclear war, but it is also about impending doom: perfect for a banshee's song.

Unbeknownst to **ROBERT STAHL**, his body is an empty shell, telepathically controlled by a brain in a jar, which was buried long ago under the floorboard of his home in Dallas. Consequently, his days are filled with the urge to write: stories, letters, articles, whatever. At night he listens to music and when he drifts off to sleep, the brain laughs, a humorless, pitiful sound, as it jiggles alone in the dusty darkness.

INSPIRATION: Got to give credit to my brother-in-law for this one. One Christmas he sent me this *gore*-geous coloring book called *The Beauty of Horror* as a gift, which I use for story inspiration. The girl in the devil costume is based on a drawing in the book. The boy in the ghost costume is probably me when I was a kid. Halloween is my favorite holiday and I still get giddy when it creeps around.

STEVE RASNIC TEM is a past winner of the Bram Stoker, World Fantasy, and British Fantasy Awards. He has published over 500 short stories in his 40+ year career. Some of his best are collected in *Thanatrauma* and *Figures Unseen* from Valancourt Books, and in *The Night Doctor & Other Tales* from Macabre Ink.

INSPIRATION: I've always been fascinated by the way Halloween (or All Saints and All Souls) is observed in other countries/cultures, and especially that tradition of laying out a feast for the dead. "Tutti i Morti" focuses on Italian traditions, but beyond those traditions it is a peek at aging, and how these traditions gain new meaning when seen through the lens of someone who has endured multiple losses and is close to death. Aging and the lives of older people are sometimes seen as unattractive subjects for fantasy/sf/horror. I'm not sure why--most of us are headed in that direction.

RYAN VAN ELLS is a criminal defense lawyer and native Wisconsinite who writes horror fiction with his cat, Lacy. He has a bachelor's in English Literature from the University of Wisconsin and a law degree from the University of Texas. When not lawyering or writing, Ryan's usually replaying the Resident Evil games, reading, and losing at chess. He can be found on Twitter @RyanVanElls.

CAT VOLEUR is the author of *Revenge Arc,* and a full-time horror journalist. You can find her talking about horror movies on Slasher Radio wherever you get your podcasts. She lives with a small army of rescue felines who encourage her to create and consume morbid content. In her free time, you can most likely find her pursuing her passion for fictional languages. Twitter: @Cat_Voleur Website: catvoleur.com.

INSPIRATION: I wrote the story for this anthology, and to express my own love of Halloween. I wanted to incorporate the feeling of carrying holiday magic into adulthood in a way that is both freeing and frightening.

JACQUELINE WEST is a novelist and poet living in Minnesota. Her work has appeared in the recent anthologies *Chromophobia* and *Into the Forest,* as well as in Tales from the Moonlit Path, Strange Horizons, Mirror Dance, and Liminality. Her books for younger readers include the NYT–bestselling dark fantasy series *The Books of Elsewhere,* the YA horror novel *Last Things,* and the award-winning ghost story *Long Lost.* Find her at jacquelinewest.com.

ABOUT THE EDITOR

KENNETH W. CAIN is an author of horror and dark fiction, and a Splatterpunk Award nominated freelance editor. He is also the publisher and editor-in-chief at Crystal Lake: Torrid Waters. Cain is an Active member of the HWA and a Full member of the SFWA. To date, he has had over one hundred short stories and thirteen novels/novellas, as well as a handful each of nonfiction pieces, books for children, and poems released by many great publishers such as Crystal Lake Publishing, JournalStone, and Cemetery Gates Media. He has also edited eight anthologies, with two more coming in 2023. Cain suffers from chronic pain, and as such, likes to keep busy. He lives in Chester County PA with his family and two furbabies, Butterbean and Bodhi. His full publishing history is available on his website at kennethwcain.com.

Printed in Great Britain
by Amazon

28981023R00239